THE
AMERICAN
WAY

Paul Duffé

Special thanks to my good friend Sonya D. for her support and inspiration, Patrick Doran (author of "I'll Try The Possum") for the much needed editing, and Ryan S. for the always appreciated technical assistance.

SEX, DRUGS, CORRUPTION, BLACKMAIL, REVENGE, AND LOVE.

THIS BOOK HAS IT ALL!

PART ONE

INNOCENCE

Chapter 1

Knowing he has a long ten-hour road trip ahead of him, the man pulls his car into a familiar service station to fill up with gas. Looking out across the parking lot while topping off his car's tank, he notices a wooded area behind the station. A sly smile slowly spreads across his lips as he remembers back to a conversation he had in those woods with his best friend Rachel, many years ago…

"Don't throw away the seeds!"
"Why not? They always blow up on me."
"Let me have them, I want to see if they'll grow."
"Why? You don't smoke."
"Yeah, I know, I just want to see what happens."
"But if they grow, then what?"
"I don't know. I guess when they get too big, I'll throw them away."
"What? Are you crazy? Before you do that, give them to me!"
"Why? You don't know about drying and all that stuff."
"Don't worry, I'll take care of it."
"Maybe I should sell them to you… I wonder how much I could make…"
"Hey! Wait a damn minute! They're my seeds!"
"Yeah, but you gave them to me and I'm the one growing the stuff."
"Hmm, I guess that kind of makes us partners then."
"Yeah, whatever. But I should still charge you…"

Every time the man comes to this service station, he remembers that conversation. "Was that really 20 years ago?", he asks himself as

1

he watches the gallons of gas roll by on the pump's display. "Where has the time gone?"

That day long ago had a huge impact on his life for two major reasons: first, it was the first time he took marijuana seeds home to grow. And second, that partnership turned out to be one of the best things to ever happen to him.

The man's name is Devan Ross, and this is his story.

When Devan and his best friend Rachel were teenagers, they would often hang out in the woods behind the station and roll joints. Devan didn't smoke but Rachel and most of their friends did. However, Devan did have a talent, he could roll the perfect joint. The two of them would sit for hours rolling joints to sell to their friends. Sometimes they'd even cut the pot with tobacco or dried leaves. No one ever knew. They figured if people were crazy enough to buy from them, then buyer beware. Besides, they always kept the good stuff –or at least Rachel did.

As Devan looks around, he notices how little the station has changed over the years. Even though the station had changed owners a few times, everything else was pretty much the same, especially the customers, which is one of the reasons he loves filling up there.

Located in one of the wealthier areas of Jacksonville, many of the vehicles sharing the pumps with him are Mercedes, Porsches, BMWs, and various other expensive luxury cars. And at the risk of stereotyping, most of the vehicles that frequent this particular gas station have the same type of owner: either the sorry about your dick Viagra-dependent older man with the young trophy wife/girlfriend or the over-leveraged yuppie trying to maintain an image/lifestyle only made possible by stretching his or her credit to the point of near bankruptcy.

Devan, on the other hand, is in his mid-30's –most people guess late 20's. He could probably pull off younger if it wasn't for a hint of salt in his dark brown hair. He detests shaving, but doesn't care for bushy beards, so he keeps his facial hair trimmed to a uniform stubble. To the casual onlooker, it's obvious he takes pride in his appearance. Daily exercise and a good diet have helped him maintain his natural athletic physique. He's built, but not overly so, just fit enough to look like someone not to piss off. He's happy with how he looks and without being too self-absorbed, he does his best to keep it up. And he drives a brand-new Jaguar XK8 which is what brought him to the station this day.

Devan knows it's a cheap thrill, but he enjoys the attention he commands –especially the looks. On the other side of the pump is Mr. Mercedes. The car may be brand new, but not its owner. The man is in his late 50's or early 60's and stares at Devan with utter contempt. Devan knows what's going through his head –he's seen it many times before from others just like him. The man is thinking, "Lucky bastard! He must have been born into wealth. He probably doesn't even know what hard work is," or "He must be filling up his daddy's car." But with the onset of the gray in Devan's hair, that last one isn't used as much anymore. At least not out loud the way people used to do when he was younger and drove Corvettes and other high-end sports cars. But Devan's all-time favorite is, "He's probably a drug dealer." He loves that one and deliberately sports a goatee to look more the part.

Devan is positive "drug dealer" is what Mr. Mercedes is thinking. So, like many times before when he's finished gassing up the car, he'll be sure to smile and nod at Mr. Limp Dick while making damn sure to cut the trophy wife/girlfriend a mischievous smile and wink as he walks inside to pay. Sure, he could pay at the pump, but where's the fun in that? He'd miss the show!

While pumping gas, Devan again notices the wooded lot behind the gas station. In a way he was relieved to see that it was still there and briefly wondered if the clearing he and Rachel used to hang out in after school was still there, too. Chuckling to himself, Devan shook his head when he remembered some of the after-school activities that took place in those woods.

Thinking of Rachel always makes Devan smile. They've been best friends for over twenty years and if nothing else, their friendship has certainly been entertaining. Probably the main thing keeping their friendship–and partnership–going so long is that they are and always have been just good friends. Right from the start they've had a brother-sister type of relationship. Even their families think of them that way.

Devan and Rachel first met in Junior High School. Rachel and her friend, Stacy, transferred in from a private school. Public school was a shock, to say the least. Stacy had a crush on Devan and before long they started going steady. During that time, Rachel and Devan became good friends and by the end of the school year they knew each other well.

The "pot" thing was mostly Rachel. Devan didn't care much for smoking, since his parents, grandparents, and almost everyone he knew smoked cigarettes. He figured he got enough second-hand smoke to last a lifetime.

Rachel has always been a good balance for Devan. No matter where they go, she draws people to her. It's her personality, possibly one of her best qualities, not to mention the fact that she's fine as hell, too.

The gas pump "clicked," indicating the tank was full, so Devan nods at Mr. Limpy and winks at the Trophy who blushes and looks away before he goes inside to pay. Hearing the Mercedes leave in a hurry, Devan can't help but smile. When he returns to his car he climbs in and drives off. It's a long drive to Gatlinburg, Tennessee from Jacksonville, Florida so he settles in and prepares himself for the trip. Devan was excited about seeing Rachel again. It had been almost a year since they were last together. After accepting her invitation to spend the 4th of July in Gatlinburg a few weeks earlier, he'd been looking forward to the trip. That service station always reminds him of his early years with Rachel, so he lets his mind drift back to pass the time, back to the late 1980's where his story really begins…

Chapter 2

THE LATE 1980'S

Little did Devan know but Rachel transferring to his junior high school would coincide with another important person entering his life...Linda.

Before he and Rachel became friends, Devan, like many 15-year-old's, wanted a job. But he didn't want just any job. No fast food or mall gigs for him. Devan wanted something that paid "the big bucks," something that was cool and would be associated with popularity and, most importantly, would help him get girls. So, he decided to become a male model. He didn't think he was anything special, but when comparing himself with others who were doing it, he figured what the hell; he'd give it a shot.

So, Devan paid his $500, took the required classes, and learned to "walk the walk" –runway work. He also spent a small fortune on a portfolio, but it never amounted to much professionally. He went on a few calls set up by the modeling agency for local department stores and occasionally worked for independent amateur photographers doing studio work, but never anything big. They liked his look, but the local market was just too small and the work too sporadic. Every once in a while, in an attempt to make it appear he hadn't been forgotten and had gotten his $500 worth, the modeling school would call on him and others to perform in seasonal fashion shows at the local malls. It was at one of those cheesy mall shows that Devan met a girl, no, a woman, who would show him a very different world from the one he was used to. For her, this world had become her life ever since she ran away from home three years earlier.

"Devan, you're next. You ready?" asked Dana, the founder and head instructor of Dana Kingston's School of Modeling.

Devan walked up, tugging at the jacket sleeves.

"These clothes are crap. I mean, look at this shit. Can you say Miami Vice?"

"Sorry, baby," Dana said with faked sympathy. Her attention was focused on the model she was helping dress. "These are the clothes the stores choose for us. There's nothing I can do." When she finally looked at Devan she paused and scrunched her face. "You know, in that suit you look like a drug dealer. Scary, but kind of sexy cool, too."

"Thanks," Devan said. "But I doubt a drug dealer would wear this polyester shit, I'm burning up!"

Dana laughed in a squeaky, high-pitched, heavy lady way, then gave him a quick shove. "You're up. Go!"

Runway was the only part of the gig that was the slightest bit rewarding for Devan. First and foremost, he got paid. And second, it offered the opportunity for exposure, which led to reputation, which equaled girls –or at least that was the hope.

Jesus, this is lame, Devan thought to himself as he walked down the runway. Even though it wasn't what he hoped it would be, he was good at it. He had the walk and the look. As he walked, he casually scanned the crowd in a flirty way while searching for people he might know, but only saw the same faces: Mothers looking for something for their children, friends of people in the show, and the store representatives who were there mostly out of obligation.

As Devan approached the end of the runway his eyes were drawn to a beautiful young woman casually leaning against a column. She stood out. She wasn't watching like the others. Instead, she seemed lost in thought. Her beauty attracted him, but her look made him want to know her–know what she was thinking. Devan was hooked. *Finally, a beautiful girl worth getting to know. Maybe this modeling thing is going to pay off after all,* he thought to himself. As he turned to walk back up the runway, he decided he would try to make direct eye contact with her if she was still there on his next trip out.

"I need you to do something," Dana said when Devan returned backstage. "I need an escort for Monica. Joe couldn't make it and you're the only one who can fill the part."

"And what part is that?" Devan asked, knowing he'd probably regret it.

"Put on his tux, but not the shirt."

"What?" Devan asked.

"I need a sexy escort to set off Monica's evening gown and, baby," she looked him up and down, "you've got great abs."

"So now you're pimping me out," Devan said. "Great."

"She's our crown jewel in this show. I'm using you to help her shine. Remember honey, sex sells." Dana looked Devan up and down again. "If I were only 20 years younger."

"From what I hear your age never stopped you before."

Her high-pitched laugh made Devan cringe. Dana handed him a bottle of baby oil. "Rub some of this on, too."

"Great, now I'm beefcake!"

But Devan wasn't as upset as he pretended to be. Bitching about it was more for Dana's benefit. She was right, he was quite fit for a 15-year-old and he knew this would present him with an opportunity to sell himself to the mystery girl. He hurried off to change into the tux attire.

In three minutes, Devan was back, all oiled up with a hot model on his arm. As they "walked the walk" Devan searched the crowd for the young woman and quickly found her. She had moved a little closer and was sitting on the edge of a planter, watching with more interest than the others. This time their eyes met, and they held the gaze. As Devan and Monica approached the end of the runway and made their turn, he looked directly at the girl and winked. Embarrassed, she smiled and glanced down. Now he was feeling good–they'd made a connection. Devan couldn't wait to get back out. For the first time he was actually excited about doing a fashion show.

Backstage, Devan changed into the next outfit and at Dana's direction went back out, but this time the girl was gone. He lingered on the end of the runway a little longer than normal, scanning the crowd, but saw no sign of her. Disappointed, but not devoid of hope, he headed back. His next two trips out were also disappointing. She wasn't there. *Oh well, she's gone,* he thought. *It was fun while it lasted.* Devan put on his best face and reported to Dana for breakdown and cleanup duties.

As usual, Devan and Dana were the last ones left. Dana had to make her customary courtesy rounds, visiting all the stores that were featured in the show, and for a woman her size it usually took some time. Meanwhile, Devan waited by the equipment until she got back. Dana was also his ride home, so he had no choice.

As Devan kneeled to wrap up some power cords, he felt someone walk up behind him and stand there. Knowing it wasn't Dana by the shape of the shadow, he stood up and turned to face the unknown. To his surprise it was the mystery girl. She still wore the embarrassed smile, but there was a strong sense of self-confidence in her demeanor.

"Oh," Devan said. "Hi…I, uh…thought you were someone else."

"Hi. I saw the show and I wanted to tell you I thought you guys were good."

"Thanks," Devan said, smiling sheepishly.

"I couldn't do that. I mean, I'd be too embarrassed. I could never get up in front of so many people, I think I'd just freeze," she said.

"It's not so bad. After a while, you don't even see the people. I just look out past them and focus on something in the distance."

"Don't you worry about tripping or falling?" she asked.

"Actually, I have tripped. One guy fell off the stage last year. It was so funny. He fell right into some woman's lap. It was great."

They both laughed. The awkward ice-breaking stage seemed to be going well.

"Soooo…what brings you to the mall tonight?" Devan asked.

The girl's face suddenly went from soft to serious as if she was reminded of something bad. Devan realized he stumbled into a sensitive area and quickly tried to change gears. "You know, you should be up there instead of me. I mean, you have a good look for this business. You're really pretty."

Her look then became more hurt than hard. On seeing this Devan thought maybe he should just shut up.

"No," she said. "I…I couldn't do this. I mean I wouldn't have the time. I just…no. I couldn't do it. Anyway, you were great. It was nice meeting you. Bye." She turned to leave as quickly as possible.

"Wait! What's your name?" Devan yelled out as she hurried away.

The girl stopped and turned around. "Linda. Linda Cole."

"Devan Ross. Nice meeting you, Linda."

"You, too Devan," she said as she turned again to leave.

"What's the hurry? I mean can you stay and keep me company while I wait for my boss?" Devan asked.

"Oh, well, ah…I have to go," she said. "I'm meeting someone at 8:30 at the other end of the mall."

"You still have 30 minutes. Please? I hate waiting for my boss; you know…sitting here in the middle of the mall. Alone. I'll look like some lonely loser or something. Come on…please stay. The woman can't stop talking. I'll probably be here half the night." Devan was practically begging. "Please?" he asked, this time flirting with her.

"Okay, but only for a few minutes. Then I really have to go."

Sensing that talking about her wasn't a good idea, Devan changed the subject.

"You know what I like to do when I'm sitting here waiting?"

"What?" she asked, raising her eyebrows and looking at him with genuine interest.

"I like watching people, guessing what's going on with them, what they do, what they're thinking, where they've been, that kind of thing." He looked at the crowd still milling around. "Take that older woman in red. Now there's an ultra-reserved church-going woman if I ever saw one, but what if she's here shopping for some sexy lingerie? Like fishnet stockings and six-inch stilettos to surprise her equally reserved husband? Or maybe she's having an affair."

"What? No way!" Linda said, laughing. "Not her. She looks like a grandmother or a school principal."

"It's my imagination, so go with it."

"You're crazy!" Linda said, shaking her head and laughing.

Linda paused and became thoughtful. "Maybe a red teddy, a matching red feather boa, and handcuffs."

"Wow. I can see that. Now you're getting it," Devan said.

"I can see it now, she goes home and gets all dressed up, then in comes hubby, who immediately drops dead from a heart attack when he sees her."

They both laughed.

"But what a way to go," Devan said. They laughed even harder.

They sat in the middle of the mall, ripping on people, losing track of the time until Dana returned.

"Oh, baby, I'm so sorry! You know how I am once I get started, I just can't stop," Dana said. She walked past them to her equipment.

"Oh, God! What time is it?" Linda asked.

"Nine o'clock," Devan said. "Oh, sorry. Your ride."

"Yeah, I better go. I'm sure he's upset from waiting so long."

"Your dad?"

"No. A friend."

"Oh." Devan's disappointment was obvious.

"Just a friend. I kind of work for him."

Devan regained some confidence.

"It was nice meeting you, Devan," she said shyly.

"Can I see you again? I mean, look at all these people we have to pick on. Can I call you?" Devan asked, with a hint of desperation.

For what felt like an eternity Linda remained quiet. He could tell she was thinking about it, but in some other way. It was as if she was evaluating or analyzing him for something.

"How about I call you? she finally said.

As Devan wrote his phone number down, he felt a little foolish. Knowing his desperation showed, it was his turn to smile with embarrassment when he handed his number to her.

"I hope to hear from you soon," Devan said.

"You will. See ya." As Linda walked away, she stopped and looked back, smiling sheepishly. She playfully laughed, and then hurried down the mall.

"She's very pretty," Dana said, walking over to him. "Who was she?"

"Linda Cole," Devan answered still watching Linda walk away.

"Do you know her?"

"No. But I hope to."

"Good luck, baby. Enjoy it while you can. You're only young once."

When Linda walked out of the side exit of the mall, a black Camaro pulled up and she climbed in.

"Any luck?" the driver asked her.

"Maybe," she replied. "I met a guy, but I don't know. He might not be the type." There was obvious doubt in her voice.

"Now, now, Linda, everybody is 'the type' if you make the offer attractive enough. How old is he?"

"15 or 16 I think."

"Perfect. Keep playing him and when you think he's ready, bring him home to meet the family, your real family."

Linda forced a smile and stared out the window. They didn't say another word all the way home.

Chapter 3

Devan's junior high school was made up of three grades, the seventh, eighth and ninth. Ninth graders were, of course, at the top. After living through the hellish previous two years, ninth grade was much more relaxed. It was easy to forget high school was just around the corner and next year meant a new school and a new ladder to climb. Having successfully risen up the junior high ladder, Devan enjoyed a comfortable reputation, one enhanced by his flagrant disregard for school rules and policies. Especially the ones about being on time. He was known far and wide–from faculty to the student body–for pushing absenteeism and tardiness to their absolute limits and beyond. His only saving grace was his grades. He did well despite not attending classes on a regular or timely basis. That kept the faculty at bay and gave his parents some comfort.

"I didn't see you in first period," said Devan's friend Chris, who was decked out in the latest metal fashions.

"Yeah, I was late again. School wouldn't be so bad if it didn't start so damn early. I just don't do mornings," Devan said.

"The world doesn't revolve around you, my friend."

"Well, maybe it should. Hey! I gotta tell you about this girl I met last night after the show."

"Was she hot?" Chris asked.

"Yeah. And kind of mysterious too. I really don't know anything about her," Devan said, thinking back.

"Use them and lose them, I say!" Chris responded casually.

"You would. I don't know why, but she's different. She's interesting, someone I feel like I want to get to know," Devan said, more serious.

"Uh-oh. Mr. Model is going soft."

"Shut up!"

"You know the chicks at our beloved school will be so disappointed to hear you're off the market," Chris sarcastically joked.

"Well, they still have you," Devan said, slapping his back.

"A girl called for you a couple of times today," Devan's mother called out as Devan walked into his house that afternoon. "I told her you were at school. She called once in the morning and again around noon."

"Who was it?" Devan asked.

"She said her name was Linda. I told her you usually got home after three. Who is she? Does she go to your school?" his mother asked.

"No. I don't know. I met her at the mall. She seemed cool," he said, answering her questions in no particular order. "Did she leave a phone number?"

"No. She said she would call back."

A few minutes later the phone rang. It was Linda. They talked briefly and she asked if she could come pick him up. Devan was surprised, but excited that Linda could drive. He would be the first of his friends to know someone with a car. Devan figured this meant she must be at least 16. *An older woman with a car! Sweet! This'll be great,* he thought. He gave Linda his address and directions. After they hung up, Devan took a quick shower and changed. Though this technically wasn't a date, he wasn't going to miss out on any opportunities.

30 minutes later, the black Camaro pulled into the driveway and blew the horn. Linda sat behind the wheel, lost in thought as she looked at Devan's house. She remembered when she and her parents all lived together in a similar looking house in western North Carolina. They seemed so happy at the time, or so she thought. It turned out her parents were anything but happy. Her mother had a problem being faithful and her father was slowly drinking himself into an early grave. Her parents

tried, at first, not to take their problems out on her, but Linda soon began paying a heavy price for being in the wrong place at the wrong time.

When Linda was 10, they finally split up. Unfortunately, it wasn't long before her mother met someone new, Bobby was his name. He seemed nice at first, but Linda soon found Bobby wasn't all that he appeared to be.

The sexual abuse started a few months after Bobby moved in and continued until Linda was 13, when she ran away from home for the last time. Linda tried to tell her mother, but her mother wouldn't hear it. She instead accused Linda of making up stories about Bobby in an attempt to break them up, even insisting that Linda faked her injuries when she came to her mother, bleeding after an encounter with Bobby in their garage.

Linda had run away from home four times in three years after Bobby moved in and every time she was brought back home. Her mother blamed Linda's father for putting things in her head. She knew Linda loved her father and would rather be with him, but his job as a truck driver made that impossible, and his drinking didn't help either.

It was shortly after the garage encounter that Linda ran away for good. Bobby told her nobody would ever believe her. The more people she told, the deeper she dug herself into a hole. He told her she was his and there was nothing she would ever be able to do about it. So, she ran.

As Devan walked to the car, he could tell Linda was miles away in thought, so he approached cautiously, trying not to startle her. This mysterious woman was strangely intoxicating to him; something about her captivated him and drove him to want to better know her. She wasn't like the other shallow or ditzy girls at his school. She seemed real, yet like a puzzle he needed to solve. Devan knew he would have to work hard to gain her trust, confidence, and perhaps even love, but he felt he was ready for the challenge, so he climbed into the car.

"Hi," Devan said. "Nice to, uh…nice to see you again," he managed to get out of his mouth. It wasn't like him to be at a loss for words.

"You, too," Linda said smiling.

"So, is this your car?" he asked.

"It's my friend's."

"The same friend who picked you up at the mall?"

"Yes. The same one," she said. Her beautiful face bore a sly grin.

"I wish I had friends like that," Devan said, checking out the car.

A temporary look of shock, almost horror, came over Linda but she quickly regained her composure. "Do you?" she asked. "Do you really?"

Seeing he was on the verge of making another error, Devan changed the subject. "So where are we going?"

"I thought we'd drive around and hang out. It's still summer. You want to go to the beach?" she asked.

"Sure!" Devan said. Once limited by the range of his bike and favors asked of his parents, now friends with cars and maybe his own car one day would open up his world and give him more freedom and independence.

They talked all the way to the beach, mostly about him, his family, brother, friends, school, and modeling. Linda seemed interested and asked a lot of questions, almost obsessively so, keeping the conversation on or about him. Devan knew the conversation was heavily one-sided, but it made her happy, so he went along with it.

The beach was only 30 minutes away and they arrived in no time.

"That was fast," Devan said. "I can't wait until I can drive. You have so much freedom with a car. When you want, you can get in and go."

"It does have its advantages," Linda said, still holding the steering wheel and looking out the window. "So, now what?" she asked, turning to face him.

"How about we go for a walk on the beach?" Devan suggested. "But I must warn you, I love the beach. I could stay out here all day and night."

"Last summer was the first time I ever saw the ocean," Linda said. "It's beautiful. Yes, let's walk.

They parked in a parking lot by the pier and walked down to the shoreline.

"So last summer was the first time you ever saw the ocean? Wow! I practically grew up here. My family comes all the time during the summer," Devan said, starting conversation as they walked.

Linda remained quiet, looking out over the water, so he pressed a little further. "Where are you from to be so far from a beach?"

"The western part of North Carolina. Mountain country," she said.

"I've never seen the mountains. Are they nice?" he asked.

"It's beautiful there," she said. There was a distant, almost longing in her voice.

Changing the subject Devan said, "Let's walk. The beach is covered with sharks' teeth."

"Sharks' teeth? Where?" she asked.

"In the shells. Look down as we walk." Soon he was finding them and before long Linda was, too. She finally began to relax. Devan could see her outwardly mature shell softening; Linda was starting to look and act like the teenager she was. Though he knew nothing about her except that she was from western North Carolina and only saw the ocean for the first time a year ago, Devan began to feel more comfortable with her. He knew he had a difficult job ahead maneuvering around all the hidden hurdles, but he was hooked.

They walked in silence for several minutes, looking for shark's teeth.

"Do you do this with your parents?" Linda softly asked. "Hunt for shark's teeth I mean?"

"Yeah. My mom's the best. She finds more than anyone." Sensing trouble, Devan changed the subject. "What about sandcastles? Have you ever built one?"

"Sandcastles? Uh…no."

"Well, you can't come to the beach and not build a sandcastle. I'll show you. But I must warn you, we might get a little dirty."

In no time Devan had built a grand sandcastle. Linda helped where she could, but mostly looked on in amazement. Before long, people were stopping, taking pictures, and asking questions. Devan was used to it. He and his family always built impressive castles, sometimes even getting into the local papers. Linda was blown away and having a great time. With her shields temporarily down, she was free to be happy.

They left the castle in the hands of a family vacationing from Maryland and headed back to the parking lot. Devan wiped off as much sand as possible before getting in the car.

"I hope your friend doesn't get upset if I get sand in his car."

"He'll get over it," Linda said with a smile.

They arrived back at Devan's house around eight o'clock that evening.

"Thanks. I had fun," he said.

"Me, too."

There was an awkward silence as each looked down at some imaginary thing on the floor.

"Well, I better go," Devan finally said. "I'm sure they're wondering where I've been."

"I'd better be going, too," Linda said.

"Can we do this again?" Devan asked.

"Yes," she replied. "I'd like that."

There was another awkward silence.

"Okay...then call me," Devan said as he opened the door to get out.

"Devan," Linda called out suddenly and louder than she intended. She put her hand on his. "Thanks, I really did have fun today."

"Me, too," he said, gently squeezing her hand. He stepped out of the car, then leaned back in before closing the door.

"Call me," he said, giving her a quick wink and a smile. He then closed the door and walked up to his house.

When Linda arrived home the man who picked her up at the mall met her in the driveway.

"How'd it go?" the man asked.

Linda avoided his eyes. "Good. But I don't know, Max. He may not be right for us. He's really not the type or profile."

Max put one hand on her shoulder and lifted her chin with the other, forcing her to look at him. "He's 15. He's the type."

"I know, but he's clean. I mean…really clean."

"All the better," Max said. "Maybe the next time you two go out, you should take a few things with you. See if you can't tarnish that squeaky-clean image a little. Maybe even bring him back here," Max suggested, taking Linda by the elbow and leading her inside the house.

Chapter 4

THE LIFE

Linda didn't call again until Friday. When she did, she asked Devan if he wanted to go out and of course he said yes. At six o'clock that evening she pulled into Devan's driveway and blew the horn.

Devan yelled to his mother as he was heading out the front door, "My ride's here, I'm leaving."

"Don't be late!" his mother yelled back from the kitchen.

Devan could barely contain his excitement as he walked toward the Camaro. He had been eagerly anticipating their next encounter. Every day Linda didn't call filled him with disappointment. *What is it about this girl,* he asked himself? *Why was he so interested?* He didn't know. But when Linda called, he knew nothing was going to stop him from seeing her again.

When Devan reached the car, he opened the door and climbed in. He tried to play it cool, but his greeting gave him away.

"Hi, I thought you'd forgotten about me. So how are you? What's going on?" Devan blurted out in one long rambling sentence.

"I'm good," Linda said. She was excited to see him again, too, and was also trying to restrain herself. "It's been a stressful day. I'm having some problems with my boss," she said, trying to hide her more serious concerns.

"Really?" Devan responded with a deeper interest. "I didn't know you had a job."

Come on, Devan, I'm a working girl," Linda kidded. "I make deliveries –kind of a courier. But lately my boss has been acting strange. He's just been…well…different. I don't know. I don't want to talk about it, it's work. So, changing the subject, what do you want to do tonight?"

Devan could tell Linda was more concerned about this problem than she was letting on, but he could also tell she wanted to put it aside for now, so he didn't pursue it.

"I don't know, it's a big town…so many choices," Devan said sarcastically. Being 15, there really weren't many choices at all. Then he remembered the planetarium downtown.

"The planetarium has a laser light show I hear is pretty cool. You want to check it out?"

"Sure," she said and started the car.

As Linda drove toward downtown, they talked and laughed about everything. They were happy; happy to be together again. It was apparent they felt something for each other, even if it was just being comfortable in each other's presence.

When they arrived at the planetarium the show didn't start for an hour, so they decided to take a walk. From the planetarium, a boardwalk extended nearly three-quarters of a mile along the south bank of the St. Johns River. Linda felt a strong bond with Devan and found it easy to lose herself with him. Caught up in the moment, she reached down and took his hand. He didn't resist. They held hands as they walked, still laughing and talking about anything and everything. Before they knew it, the hour passed, and it was time for the show to start.

The planetarium went completely dark. The show was a combination of astronomy, laser lights, popular music, and other special effects. But they didn't care or notice. Holding hands grew into their arms being around each other and then, in that perfect moment, Devan leaned over and kissed her. She kissed him back. Before long they were making out. The show became just a muted background. They were so into each other that nothing else mattered.

The program ended an hour later. When they left the planetarium, they were still holding hands.

"Would you like to come over to my house?" Linda asked. "Do you want to see where I live?"

Devan was excited. He knew this would finally be an opportunity to find out more about her. Up to this point he really didn't know much about Linda, other than vague bits of information.

"I'd love to see where you live," Devan said as he put his arm around her while they walked back to the car.

To Devan's surprise, Linda lived across the river in an older, wealthier part of the city known as Riverside. Fifteen minutes after leaving the planetarium, she turned into a secluded neighborhood. The homes there were mostly large, ranch style houses, built in the 1960's. As they approached a corner house located deep inside the neighborhood, Linda turned the car into the large half-circle driveway. Devan could tell that the house was well maintained, and it looked expensive. He also noticed several other cars in the driveway and assumed other people were home too. But he didn't care. He was excited to finally find out something about her.

After they parked, they walked up a sidewalk that ran next to a long wooden louvered wall leading to a set of large oak doors. Linda opened one door to reveal a stunning, rectangular inner courtyard. In the center of the courtyard was a pool surrounded by a concrete deck. Off the deck was the large L-shaped house on two sides of the courtyard. The walls of the house were all glass. On the other two sides, the front wall, and the opposite end of the courtyard, were wooden louvered walls which offered privacy from the street and the neighbors to the right. *What a great house,* Devan thought. *Like something a movie star might have.*

Linda led Devan across one side of the deck and around a cascading rock waterfall to the front door of the house. The door opened into a large, tiled foyer. To the left of the foyer was a kitchen surrounded on two sides by a low, bar-like countertop. Behind the kitchen was a small extra bedroom. To the right of the foyer was a beautiful dining room/living room combination separated into two rooms by the furniture. Both rooms shared a wall of sliding glass doors opening onto the deck and pool.

Separating the end of the living room from a room in the corner of the "L" was a massive stone fireplace. The next room was a den. Dark wooden paneling made this room different from the lighter atmosphere of the rest of the house. The room not only shared the opposite side of the fireplace, but it also had a corner bar, pool table, four standup video games, a big screen TV, an L-shaped couch, and two leather chairs flanking the fireplace. Devan was in awe.

As they walked into the den Devan noticed two guys maybe a little older than himself smoking and playing pool. They had that distinct "surfer" look. He also saw a young girl watching TV. She might be his age, but something about her made him think she was younger.

"Hi, guys," Linda said. "I'd like you to meet a friend of mine. Devan, this is Lance and Kevin." They shook hands and Lance offered him a beer, which Devan happily took. Linda walked over to the girl.

"Michelle, this is my friend Devan." Michelle was a little shy, but still seemed friendly. She was watching MTV, so they sat down and watched some videos, drank, and talked. None of these people were adults and nobody appeared afraid of getting busted. Devan couldn't believe what he was seeing. *These people are all so cool,* he thought to himself.

After another drink, this time liquor because Kevin liked to show off his bartending expertise, Linda excused herself and Devan by announcing she was continuing their tour. As they walked out of the den, they headed down the longer part of the "L" shape. The sliding glass doors were on the right and two large bedrooms were on the left. The first was Lance and Kevin's and the second was hers. The room off the kitchen was Michelle's and at the very end of the long hallway was the master bedroom. Linda paused at the door to her room and then said, "I have to show you the master bedroom first. You're going to die when you see it!"

These people were all so cool! This is the life he'd always dreamed about! Man, she's lucky, Devan thought as they continued. When they walked through the doors to the master bedroom, Devan's jaw dropped. It was huge and had a modern contemporary style. The poolside of the room was all glass. *This had to be the room of a movie star,* he thought.

"And this is Max's room. He owns the house," Linda said.

Devan was speechless. "Wow! This is nice," he managed to say. "So, are all of you related?" he asked.

"No. Me, Kevin, and Lance work for Max, but Michelle is his niece. She's been living with him for a couple of years since Max's sister disappeared. The sister has a serious drug problem and can't take care of Michelle, so Max took her in. He's been taking care of her ever since."

"That's cool," Devan replied. "So, what does Max do?" Devan asked as he looked around the room, still impressed.

"That's a long story. Let's just say Max is a businessman with a wide range of interests. We don't ask a lot of questions, and, in return, he lets us live here. He pays for everything and takes care of us."

"Fair enough," Devan said, still curious, and becoming even more suspicious. "You're lucky to have someone like that," he added.

"Yeah, I guess. Max does a lot for us. He really helps us out."

Devan could tell Linda was holding back. It was almost as though she was forcing herself to talk politely about Max. But he went along with it and let the subject drop. Frankly, Devan didn't care what Max did. The house was incredible, and Linda was possibly the coolest person he'd ever met. He was happy just being with her. If this is how she wanted it, then so be it. He wasn't going to pry.

As the awe and amazement of the room started to fade, Devan became aware that Linda had walked up behind him. She slowly put her arms around his waist, and they embraced. Then in a low whisper she asked, "Would you like to see my room?"

Devan turned to face her and looked deep into her eyes. "Yes, I would like that."

Linda took his hand and led him back to her room, which was also incredible.

The first thing Devan noticed was the queen-sized bed. The room was decorated in an ultramodern look and in the far corner was another door leading to a walk-in closet and full bath. All the bedrooms, it turned out, had full baths.

"This is a great room, Linda. You really have quite the life." Devan was dying to know, so he finally asked her. "Do you go to school?"

"No, I dropped out a few years ago. I've been working for Max ever since. School just wasn't for me."

"That's cool, I mean you all seem really well taken care of."

"Yeah," Linda said. The peculiar undertone was back as she spoke. "We're a happy group. We try to take care of each other." She then excused herself to the bathroom.

Devan continued checking out her room. When Linda returned, she turned on the radio and sat on the bed. "Why don't you come over here and sit down?" she asked with an inviting smile.

He did. They sat very close. Linda put her hand on his lap, and he slowly leaned into her.

"Would you like to party a little?" she asked as she ran her other hand down his back.

Devan's heart was pounding. He thought he knew what was coming next. "That sounds like fun."

Just when he thought they were going to kiss, Linda surprised him by pulling away and walking off. He thought maybe they had mixed signals. Linda opened a dresser drawer and took out a glass tray and a small stainless-steel vial.

"What kind of party are we going to have?" Devan asked.

Linda smiled mischievously. "A snow party." She rolled the small vial between her fingers.

"A snow party? What's that?" he asked.

"Have you ever done coke, Devan?"

"No."

"Well, you've gotta try it. You'll love it!" she said.

Linda opened the vial and sprinkled some on the tray. She then shaped it into two lines with a razor, one small thin line and another twice the size. She handed Devan a straw and told him to snort it, pointing to the smaller of the lines.

"Snort it?" he questioned.

"Right up your nose," she said.

Okay, Devan thought to himself. *What the hell!* This had been a night of firsts for Devan. Everything was happening so fast. He was with a beautiful girl who he just met a week ago; she drives so he knows somebody with a car; he's in this killer house with these cool people living the life he'd always dreamed about, and now, here she is whipping out a tray of cocaine and asking him to take a snort. He was totally blown away and wasn't about to screw this up. He was going to do it no matter what. Without hesitation Devan snorted the thin line of coke.

It itched and made him cough. Devan instinctively rubbed his nose and blinked his eyes. He wasn't used to this. Then he took a deep breath, forcing it down. His eyes fluttered again for some reason and then he looked at Linda.

"Give it a second," she said. Linda took the straw and snorted the thicker line.

Devan suddenly felt a tingling in his nose and a warm rush across his chest and body. A light-headed, hot burst of energy ran over him. He was buzzing, like a quick alcohol buzz without all the shots. He felt good, and all hyped up.

Linda asked Devan if he wanted another one and he said yes with no hesitation. She made him another small line. This one was a little thinner than the first. Devan quickly snorted it. Linda snorted another one too.

They both sat there for a minute and then Linda said, "Have you ever had sex on cocaine?"

"No. I, I…"

Sensing his hesitation, she asked, "Have you ever had sex?"

"No."

She put her hand on his lap. "Would you like to?"

He didn't have to say a word. She could feel the answer.

Devan definitely wanted to have sex. They looked each other in the eyes and then threw themselves on each other. Within seconds they were ripping their clothes off. They were high on coke, but also high on each other. This was exactly what he'd always wanted. A beautiful girl and the perfect setting. This was going to be it. He was about to lose his virginity and become a man—everything he'd ever dreamt about, all in one night. He was lost in the experience, the passion. He would let it happen—let nature take over. And he did just that.

They were great together. Both wanting the other over. He took her and she took him. Between the sex and coke, they could go all night. As the hours passed, they eventually fell asleep, exhausted.

Around 2:00a.m. Devan awoke when he heard someone at the bedroom door. He was facing away from the door, but he could tell it was opening. Light was filling the room. Devan sensed someone was standing there for a few seconds before the door slowly closed. Then he heard footsteps walk down the hall and into the master bedroom. Max, he thought.

A few minutes later Linda slid out from under his arm. She sat on the edge of the bed and lit a cigarette. Devan could tell something was on her mind but wasn't sure what it was, so he pretended to keep sleeping.

Linda turned toward him and ran her hand through his hair and down his face to his back, then gently shook him awake.

"Devan," she said in a soft voice. "Devan."

He slowly opened his eyes, pretending like he just woke up.

"It's time I took you home. It's pretty late."

"Yeah. Maybe you should." He sat up to look at her.

They got dressed, sort of shy of each other, but happy to be in each other's presence.

What an incredible night. Devan thought. He'd done coke, had sex, and enjoyed them both. It was as intimate as he had ever been with a girl, and he loved it and craved more. He'd become a man, he thought. But he still knew nothing about Linda. Nothing about her background, who she was, her parents, or anything about other friends and family. She remained a mystery. Still, he felt they had made a deep, more personal connection. It wasn't just about the sex. There was something else, something he couldn't quite grasp. He'd never felt this way before. He liked her and he sensed she felt strongly about him as well.

When they left, Devan knew he'd get it from his parents. He hadn't called and was coming home very late. He figured he would be put on some kind of restriction, but he didn't care. It was worth it. For the first time in his life, he felt like an adult. This was a night he would never forget, so he was fine with the consequences.

An awkward but comfortable silence filled the car on their way back to Devan's house. While Linda drove, they held hands and smiled occasionally when catching each other's eye.

When they reached his house Devan turned to Linda.

"I had a good time tonight," he said.

"Me, too."

"When can I see you again?" he asked.

"Soon."

"How soon?"

"Soon enough," she said mischievously.

"I just want you to know–" Devan started.

"No," Linda said cutting him off. "Don't say anything. Let's just see each other again."

Devan leaned over and lightly kissed her on the cheek. "Okay. Call me."

"I will," she said as she forced herself to say goodnight.

Devan watched her drive off, then walked up to the house, unsure of what to expect from his parents.

Chapter 5

To Devan's surprise, he was able to get inside the house undetected. He realized his parents had long since turned in for the night, so he quietly crept up to his room and crawled into bed.

Devan awoke late the next morning. Luckily for him, his parents worked on Saturdays and had already left for their shop across town. His brother was not at home either. Mark was three years younger and an early riser.

Devan lay in his bed for a long time thinking about Linda. He stared at the ceiling in a kind of dream state, not really believing it all happened, but knowing it did. He thought about the saying, "Sex changes people. They lose their innocence," or something like that. Was he different? Had he lost his innocence? Only time would tell. But he knew he wasn't the same person he was the day before. On some level he felt he was more mature, wiser, and more experienced. He could feel it.

Devan got up and tried to get on with the day, but Linda dominated his thoughts. He was hoping the phone would ring at any moment, but it didn't. The day passed without a call. Then the next. No Linda and no calls. Devan was disappointed but he was used to her pattern. The weekend slowly rolled on and before he knew it, it was Monday morning and time for school.

Monday went by with agonizing slowness. Devan couldn't get into school. His mind kept wandering to Linda and their night together. *Where was she? Would they see each other again? Why hadn't she called?*

Finally, the last bell rang out at 3:00p.m. and he was free. As Devan walked out the back exit of the school to meet his bus, he saw her. Linda was casually leaning against a fence, looking as sexy as ever. She wore a short black mini-skirt, heels, tank top and black leather jacket with shades. She was a mix between "Madonna" and "Risky Business." *Damn! She's hot*, Devan thought. He whistled out loud.

"Surprise," Linda said as he walked up with noticeably more enthusiasm than normal. His smile was automatic.

"How was school?" she asked sarcastically.

"It sucked. What are you doing here?"

"I missed you and thought I'd come pick you up and see if you wanted to hang out." She put her arms around him and with force, pulled him to her.

"I can't think of a better way to spend the day," Devan said.

"We need to run a quick errand first. I'm actually working. But after that we have the rest of the day," she said.

"Cool," Devan said, putting his arm around her. "Let's go to work."

When they got in her car Devan saw a small package about the size of a coffee brick wrapped in brown paper and twine.

"Is that it?" he asked.

"Yes. I'd feel a lot better with you there. Some of Max's clients are weird. Really paranoid. With two people, they're less likely to do anything stupid."

Linda's comment alarmed him, but he knew the package was probably drugs. Still, he blew it off. This is it, life in the fast lane. In just a few weeks he'd gone from an honor roll student and model to hanging with suspected drug dealers, snorting coke, and having sex. Oh, the teen years. What fun! Devan threw out all caution and decided to live in the moment.

On the way to Linda's delivery, they talked like two people who were crazy about each other. Linda managed to take off her jacket and asked Devan to put it on. It was a man's jacket, probably Max's, but it fit well, and Devan could tell it was expensive.

"It fits you. You look good," she said. Linda then became more serious. "I need a favor. The people we're going to see make me nervous. I don't know why Max keeps them as clients, but he does. Anyway, when I get out, can you stand by the car and put your hand in your jacket, like you're holding something, like maybe a gun?"

"You're that afraid of these people?" Devan asked.

"Sometimes. I just want them to think I have somebody with me. It's all about perception. They won't try anything. At least I hope not," she added with a forced smile.

Devan knew Linda wasn't bluffing. Her tough shell was cracking.

A few minutes later they pulled up to a modest-looking house. Linda took off her shades and handed them to Devan.

"Put these on, too," she said. "You'll look tougher. Older. From a distance you'll look like someone they won't want to mess with…like my bodyguard or something…" Her voice tapered off.

"Linda," Devan paused, "I'd consider it an honor guarding your body."

She forced another smile and nodded. "Ok, let's do it."

This entire experience was new for Devan. He was still excited to be with her, even though he knew this was serious business. Trying to lighten the mood, Devan winked and smiled at her as he opened her door. She got out and walked up to the house with the package while Devan stood by the car, posing with his hand in his jacket, looking casual but alert.

Linda knocked on the door. There was a screen door so Devan couldn't see who was behind it as it opened. The door opened slowly, and he saw a hand reach out and take the package from her. The door shut and she continued standing there, so he remained in place. A few minutes later, the door opened again, and she was handed a paper bag. Linda took it and returned to the car. They got in and drove off.

"Thanks," Linda said with obvious relief. "You look tough in that jacket and my shades, biker-like. You should keep them."

"Are you crazy?" Devan asked. "Do you know how much this jacket costs? And these shades are Ray Bans!"

Linda shrugged. "Keep them anyway. I might need your help again. Besides, they look better on you," she said, giving him a sly smile.

Feeling that was debatable, he remained silent but was impressed.

Changing the subject, Linda asked, "So what do you want to do now?"

He looked at her and instantly she knew what he wanted.

"Want to go back to my house?" she asked. "Does Devan want to come over and play? Maybe go back to my room for a little while?"

"You know I do," he said looking at her longingly.

They couldn't keep their hands off each other on the drive back. When they arrived at her house, Linda led Devan directly to her bedroom, not even stopping to say hello to the others. They did a few lines of coke and fell into each other.

Time flew when they were together. At 11:00p.m. Devan awoke and got up to use the bathroom. From inside the bathroom, he heard knocking on the bedroom door and Linda inviting whomever it was in. For a second, he thought they were busted, and he was going to get his ass kicked. But the voices were calm. Devan could tell Linda's voice, but he did not recognize the new one. Max, he thought. For better or worse it was time to meet Max. He would have preferred to be dressed for their first introduction, but since his clothes were thrown all around the room, he wrapped a towel around his waist and opened the door.

Sitting on the end of the bed was an older man, maybe in his early forties, and dressed in black. Linda was sitting up, smoking, with a sheet across her chest. Both were calm. Devan knew he had interrupted their conversation when he opened the door and wasn't sure what to expect, so he prepared for the worst. To his surprise, the man stood up and extended his hand.

"You must be Devan; I'm Max. Thank you for helping Linda today. Those particular clients can be difficult sometimes, but hey, they are who they are and I'm certainly not one to judge others." Max stood and extended his hand toward Devan.

"Anytime," Devan said shaking his hand. He was surprised. He thought for sure Max was going to go off on him. He was practically naked. It didn't take a Ph.D. to know what he and Linda had been doing all night. Devan's surprised reaction amused Linda.

"I appreciate what you did and to show my appreciation, let me give you this." Max reached into his pocket and pulled out a $100 bill. "For your trouble."

"You don't have to do that," Devan said, waving him off.

"I insist. Take it." Max shoved the bill into his hand.

Devan was again speechless and completely caught off guard.

"And, I respect everybody's privacy. What goes on in their rooms in my house is their business. I don't mind," Max said, looking down at Devan's towel and then to Linda. "Thanks again," Max repeated as he headed for the door. "I'll leave you two alone. Nice meeting you, Devan. I hope we see you around more often," Max added as he closed the door behind him.

Devan stood there stunned. He couldn't believe how well that went. He thought for sure Max was going to kill him.

Linda sat back and half-smiled. She took a long drag from her cigarette.

"I told you he's cool," Linda said as she exhaled and patted the bed next to her for him to return. "We work for Max. Do him favors. In return he helps us out and lets us live our own lives."

"What was in that package today?" Devan asked, curious if she would tell him the truth.

"What do you think?" Linda asked back.

"Drugs?" Devan answered.

"Cocaine, to be exact," Linda responded, then calmly took another drag from her cigarette before continuing. "Max distributes for one of the biggest suppliers around here. He's a middleman. It's risky, but very profitable. He does well and we don't ask a lot of questions, we just do what we're told to do." She paused and let what she said sink in. "Does that bother you, Devan?"

"No," he answered as he dropped the towel on the floor and climbed back into bed with her. "It's your life and you do what you have to.

Besides, you guys all look like you're doing pretty good to me." Devan motioned toward the room and house. Then becoming thoughtful for a moment, he asked, "But are you safe? You looked worried today."

"Drugs and money make for a paranoid business, and I'll admit, there can be risks, but I think it's worth it," she said.

"Well, it's your life and I'm not one to judge others, either," Devan said, using Max's words. "But are you happy?"

Linda had a blank look on her face. "Yes, I think so." The cigarette filter disintegrated as she crushed the flaming tip in the ashtray on the nightstand.

Devan knew she was troubled and was holding something back.

"What's going on?" he asked.

"Lately, our customers have been pissed off when we deliver. And Max is different. Something's up with him. He's more distant and colder, even picking fights with people in the house. He and Michelle hardly talk anymore. It's strange. I don't know Devan," she said, frustrated. "Everything's changing!"

Devan sensed she was getting agitated, so he stopped pressing and changed the subject by kissing her. They embraced and took each other again. She was opening up; slowly letting him get a glimpse of the inner Linda, her life and her world.

After the last round of lovemaking, they lay under the covers holding each other. Devan knew it gave her comfort. Wrapped in each other's loving embrace, they quickly drifted off to sleep.

Chapter 6

TENSION

It was after 2:00am when Devan returned home to find his parents waiting for him. He had finally pushed their patience too far. They knew he was a young man going through changes and didn't want to be over-domineering, but they also insisted that he respect them and their rules. The second he walked through the door they demanded to know where he had been and why hadn't he called. They were clearly worried.

Devan knew he screwed up. He should have called. He was so lost in the moment, so lost in Linda that nothing else mattered. She was everything to him. His parents were livid. They blamed Linda. His behavior had not been the same since he and Linda started seeing each other and this wasn't missed by his parents. They insisted he end the relationship.

Devan snapped. He told them Linda was none of their concern. He heard himself saying things he'd never said to them before. He was completely out of control. His parents were visibly shaken by his explosive temper; they had never seen him so angry. The argument escalated into a full-fledged shouting match. It finally ended when Devan stormed off to his room and slammed his door shut.

Devan was fuming. Who were they to tell him he could or couldn't see her? Who were they to accuse Linda of being a bad influence? They didn't know her. They didn't know anything about her! All he could see was them interfering with his life, and he was pissed.

A few days passed before Linda called. She picked Devan up after school so they could run an errand and hang out. They cruised the city for a while and eventually ended up back at her house and in her bed. He returned home late again. His parents had had enough.

After another fight broke out, they told him he was on restriction. He was to come home immediately after school, no more "hanging out" and especially no more Linda until he straightened up. The resulting fight was unlike anything they'd ever experienced. In a rage, Devan told them they had no right to ban him from his friends and that they couldn't tell him who he could or couldn't see. Between his language and his total lack of respect, his parents were devastated. They didn't recognize Devan anymore; he'd become a very different person. Devan insisted it was they who had changed, not him. The tension in the house was reaching a breaking point.

Devan filled Linda in on everything when she finally called a few days later. He was still pissed and needed to vent. Who were they to interfere with his life and tell him who he could talk to, who he could see, what he could or couldn't do? She understood, or at least she said she did. So, they agreed the best thing to do was for him to sneak out after his parents went to bed. There was a tree outside his bedroom window; he could climb down undetected. Three houses away at the end of the block, Linda would be waiting, parked under a giant magnolia tree.

This became the routine. Most nights Linda would be waiting to take Devan away and into her world. They'd run their errands and then have the rest of the night together. The drug world never slept. Business was conducted around the clock. First, they took care of Max's business and then took care of their own. It was as if they were addicted to each other. They lived each day for the nights.

As the weeks passed, their rendezvous were becoming more frequent. They had gone from meeting every few nights to nearly every night and it was beginning to wear on Devan. He would meet Linda at midnight and return home around 5:00am. He'd sleep a couple of hours and then go to school. His new routine was starting to show...

Several nights later Lance and Devan were having drinks at the bar in Max's den while they waited for Michelle and Linda to get back from the store.

"You look like shit," Lance said.

"Fuck you," Devan replied and pretended to flip him off.

"No, seriously. You really look, I don't know…bad. What's up?"

Devan sighed. He knew Lance was right.

"All this sneaking around is killing me. I'm on the go from midnight until five. Then I go to school from 7:00a.m. 'til 3:00p.m., sleep about three hours, fake family shit from 6:00p.m. until my parents go to bed, then I'm off again."

"Your parents still giving you a hard time?" Lance asked.

"Now they're bitching about my grades. I can hardly keep my eyes open in class, let alone play the good student. Man, to be honest, I'm getting really tired of the whole thing." Devan took a long drink from his beer. "This school shit just isn't for me. I do some blow before school, off and on in school to stay awake, and then…well…Linda and I practically live off the shit. And even that isn't enough. I still have no energy."

Lance got up from his bar stool. "I think I might have something that can help," he said, walking out of the den.

Lance returned a few minutes later with a bottle full of yellow pills. "Here," he said as he handed them to Devan.

"What's this?" Devan asked.

"Your new best friend. Instant energy," Lance said.

"Like coke?"

"Yes and no. It's speed. You won't get the coke high, but your energy level will spike. Try one."

Devan tossed it in his mouth and washed it down with a swig from his beer. Within an hour he was amped. Speed was indeed his new best friend. But a whole pill was way too much. He got no sleep that night, so he broke the pills in half from that point on.

For the next couple of months Devan couldn't exist without the speed. At that point, his routine was now to sneak out at midnight, run errands, do a hit of speed or coke –sometimes both at once– spend "quality time" with Linda, back home, another hit, go to school, come home, sleep a few hours, spend time with the family, then another hit to start again at midnight.

Ironically, Devan's school attendance improved, but his grades still suffered. He was physically in school, but mentally he was with Linda. Before long, the first quarter was over and report cards were due. And his wasn't good.

Devan had gone from an A/B student to a C/D student and that was unacceptable to his parents, which resulted in more fighting. They knew his poor grades were because of Linda's bad influence, but Devan would have none of it. He wouldn't let them criticize Linda and tear her down. Who the hell were they? They didn't even know her. She was the woman he loved and wanted to be with forever! This pitted them against each other even more.

Each night Devan escaped into Linda's arms. Being with her was such a relief. He went weeks with little or no sleep just so he could be with her. He was coking-up, doing hits of speed, running errands with Linda and also helping Kevin and Lance. He was deep in it. The "darker world" was rapidly becoming his life.

After another major blowout with his parents, Devan felt he'd finally had enough. They didn't understand him, and he was tired of their bullshit. When he escaped with Linda that evening, he told her he was thinking about running away.

"My parents aren't who they used to be. They try to control everything about my life. They don't want me to be happy. I want out," Devan informed Linda.

At this point all Linda had to do was "spring the trap." Devan was hooked. He was right where Max wanted her to get him a few months before. All she had to do was say the word and he was in. But she didn't do it.

"No. They're your family and you need to stay with them," Linda said.

Devan was speechless. That was not the answer he was expecting. He thought at first that she must be kidding.

"Yeah, right!" Devan snapped.

"No," Linda said, almost motherly. "I'm serious."

He saw that she was. This was coming from somewhere deeper. He tried to argue the point but soon realized it was hopeless. Linda held her ground.

Linda loved Devan. She wanted to be with him more than anything – maybe even forever– but she knew she had to keep him from this path. She knew he was better than what that life would bring him. No, she wouldn't spring the trap. Instead, Linda decided to do everything possible to persuade Devan to change his mind. She wanted him to be the guy she first saw on stage that evening in the mall and told him this. She told him as she was watching the fashion show that night that she was thinking about how lucky he was. And after meeting and getting to know him, she envied him for having such a close family and wished that she had his life. She told him he was the lucky one and not to give up on his family. To never take them for granted. She then told him why she was really at the mall that night; she was there recruiting. Looking for the perfect unhappy runaway type to come work for Max. She told him the plan was to hook him with drugs and money, then reel him in. But she didn't count on falling in love. When Linda finished speaking, she had tears in her eyes and had to look away.

Devan wasn't angry. He'd suspected something early on but blew it off, deciding instead to go with it and let fate take over. But he had not counted on falling in love, either.

Even with Linda admitting he was supposed to be just another "pawn" in Max's game, Devan couldn't be mad at her. Seeing her cry, hearing her confession, and pleading for him not to choose her life filled him with pity. For the first time he saw how unhappy she really was.

Devan put his arms around her and held her tight. Linda could no longer hold back her tears, so he held her tighter.

"Thank you for caring so much. I love you more than you'll ever know," Devan whispered softly.

Devan knew deep down he was the lucky one. Lucky to have her and lucky to have his family. He wasn't going to run away. Even though their lives were everything he thought he always wanted, he had a life that Linda and the others did not and would never have.

The months passed quickly and soon it was Thanksgiving. Devan and Linda had been together since the beginning of September. In those short three months, Devan had changed significantly. His grades had tanked, and while he had had many new personal experiences, he also learned that there was a darker side of life. But more concerning was the serious change he observed in Max. At first Max had embraced him, even welcomed him as one of the group, but over the past month his relationship with Max had deteriorated rapidly.

It was well known that Max was shorting his customers by skimming product for himself. To a point this was acceptable and even expected. But Max was getting sloppy and way too greedy. With the product he kept, he would sell some on the side and use the other. Max was quickly becoming his own best and worst customer.

Max's greed also made for dangerous consequences. Customers weighed the packages when they were delivered and knew instantly how much Max was stealing. The angry customers would often take their frustrations out on the couriers, sometimes seriously, to send a message to Max. Kevin and Lance bore the brunt of this since they each worked alone. Linda got a lot of verbal abuse, but Devan being with her gave the illusion of protection and was probably the only thing keeping her from serious physical harm. But none of this had any effect on Max. If anything, his stealing got worse. Since most of Max's customers were dealers themselves, being so blatantly shorted was unacceptable. They made calls to Max's bosses who in turn made calls to Max. On several occasions, it was obvious Max had had a physical encounter, but he wouldn't talk about it. Regardless, Max kept stealing. His attempts to conceal his damage to the customer's products were half-ass and sloppy. Kevin, Lance, Linda, and Devan would often have to try to repair packages in an attempt to hide Max's tampering. In the beginning, the couriers were not supposed to know what was inside a package, only deliver it. But now they were desperately trying to repair Max's damage for their own safety. And if this wasn't bad enough, Max was constantly starting fights with everyone in the house.

One night when Devan left Linda's room, Max ambushed him and slammed him into the sliding glass doors on the opposite wall. Holding Devan by the neck, Max verbally tore into him, calling him "rich boy" and accusing him of thinking he was better than everyone else. Hearing the commotion, Kevin forcibly pulled Max off Devan. Irate, Max spat at them and walked away. It was clear Max was high on something. The frequent violent encounters and Max's erratic behavior had everyone on edge.

Michelle was so terrified of him she slept in Kevin's room, and Lance moved into hers. Kevin and Michelle had a big brother-little sister type of relationship, so she stayed with him for protection. Little did they know but there was more to Michelle's terror than anyone knew at the time.

The tension in the house was becoming unbearable. Nobody knew when Max might go off next. But what could they do? Except for Devan, the rest of them were runaways and part of an illegal business. Nobody could go to the police. They were trapped. There was no other option but to run again. So everyone decided to try and stick it out, hoping Max would come around. They had all spent time on the streets and didn't want to run again. This was the only life they knew; they felt that staying was their only option.

While Devan was out of school over Thanksgiving break, he and Linda met openly. His parents finally lifted his restriction so they could see each other during the day. But Devan continued sneaking out so he could be with Linda in the evenings.

Thanksgiving night, they made their usual arrangement; Linda would pick Devan up under the magnolia tree down the street. Devan waited, but Linda did not show up and he began to worry.

When not with Devan, Linda spent as much time away from the house as possible. She often drove to the beach and would sometimes walk and look for shark's teeth. Other times, she would just drive around or sit in her car listening to the radio. Before picking Devan up, she would go home and freshen up. Having just returned from being out, Linda wanted to stop by the house to clean up before meeting Devan. It was 11:30pm, plenty of time. Having done this so many times before, she had a routine.

As Linda walked toward the front door inside the courtyard, she was stopped dead in her tracks. Through one of the large glass doors, she saw Max throw Michelle over the back of a couch, rip off her panties, and rape her. Linda felt chills running down her spine. She froze. Everything Bobby had done to her flooded her memories. She was scared for Michelle and scared for herself. She felt utterly helpless and threw up in the bushes. Michelle's expression was flat and distant as she stared blankly in her direction with tears streaming down her face. Linda then realized Michelle could see her through the glass but, thankfully, not Max. Michelle silently mouthed "No," and "Go away." Linda snapped-to and ran to her car. For the next hour she drove around in a daze before finally making her way to Devan.

Devan's relief at seeing Linda was short-lived. When he climbed in the car, he immediately knew something was wrong.

"What's happened?" Devan asked.

Linda sat frozen, lost in thought, staring at the steering wheel. She forced herself to answer him.

"I…" she paused for a moment. "I cannot believe what I just saw."

Devan waited in silence.

"I saw Max and Michelle through the window…he was raping her…"

"What! That fucking bastard!" Devan was beside himself.

Linda was quiet and in a state of shock. She suddenly made direct eye contact with Devan. It was so sudden it quieted his rage. She began crying uncontrollably and threw her arms around him, hugging him tight.

Devan tried to comfort her. "We'll take care of Max. He's gone too far this time!"

"No! You don't understand," Linda said in a muffled voice as she sobbed into his shoulder. She sat back and wiped the tears from her eyes. "The same thing happened to me. That's why I ran away. I was Michelle."

Linda told Devan about her parents and Bobby. For the next hour they sat in the car under the magnolia tree on the corner of his block while she told him her terrible secret. When she finished, Devan was consumed with a rage he had never felt before. He would kill Bobby on the spot if given the chance. Same for Max. Max would pay for what he did to Michelle. If he couldn't get Bobby, he sure as hell could get Max.

Devan's emotions swung from one extreme to the other. Deep sorrow and compassion for Linda and Michelle, and then rage for what happened to them. He wanted justice. Payback.

As they sat in silence, Linda's story kept rolling over and over in his mind. The woman he loved and wanted to be with for the rest of his life had been abused by some piece of shit - a piece of shit like Max. Max would pay for what Bobby did to Linda and for what he did to Michelle. Right then and there Devan pledged to himself that Max would never hurt any of them again.

Devan and Linda decided to go back to the house to check on Michelle. They also wanted to protect her and keep her away from Max.

When they arrived, they found Michelle alone. She was in the den watching TV. But she really wasn't watching. Her vacant eyes stared at the screen. She seemed detached and so alone. They could tell she had been crying. Linda and Devan sat down next to her, and they pretended to watch television together. Linda put her arm around Michelle and held her while gently stroking her hair. Michelle began to sob —she was inconsolable. Linda cried silently with her.

Devan felt terrible. He leaned forward and put his head in his hands, aware of his own tears. He couldn't stand what had happened…what was happening; all he had seen and become involved in. This world he wanted so badly to be a part of, these people he admired and wanted to live with, suddenly it all disgusted him. This was not the life he wanted. It was all so sad.

Linda and Michelle went outside and sat by the pool for a long time. The weather was still nice even though it was near the end of November. Devan watched television while the girls talked. He wanted to be with them, but he knew it was better not to interfere. Linda could relate to Michelle in ways Devan could never understand. He knew they needed time together.

Devan was puzzled that Lance and Kevin were not home. Where were they, he wondered? It wasn't unusual for Max to be gone at night, but the guys were usually home by now.

After Linda put Michelle to bed, she and Devan went back to Linda's room to talk. Linda told Devan that Max had been taking advantage of Michelle for several years. It started shortly after Michelle came to live with Max. Michelle couldn't tell anyone because Max threatened to kick them all out if she did. The fact Michelle had been silently suffering from his abuse for so long bother Linda deeply.

"I know where she's coming from. I've been there. I just can't believe I didn't see it!" Linda said as she angrily punched a pillow.

"Don't blame yourself Linda, it's not your fault. This is all Max," Devan hissed, trying to control the anger burning within him.

Devan and Linda discussed the situation until late into the night. They figured Kevin would probably kill Max on the spot when he found out. Max had clearly gone too far. Not only was he jeopardizing everyone's lives with his reckless behavior, but he was also abusing Michelle. It was time for a meeting. Something had to change.

Chapter 7

THE PLAN

Two days after Max's assault on Michelle, everyone met in the den, Michelle included. Max was in Miami, so they had the house to themselves. Linda convinced Michelle she needed to tell the others what Max had been doing to her. They needed to know. They needed to understand what kind of person Max was and that he was not only putting their lives at risk, but he was also sexually abusing his own niece.

"So, that's why that bastard sent us to Daytona that night. He wanted us gone so he could have her!" Kevin said, directing his comment to Lance.

In a fit of rage, Kevin grabbed a fireplace poker and smashed a huge mirror hanging over the fireplace. He then raced around the room, smashing everything and causing everyone to scatter.

Michelle began crying and begged him to stop, but to no avail. Kevin walked up to Devan and with a cold, intense look stared straight into his Devan's eyes. "I'm going to kill that motherfucker," he said. Devan knew the look all too well.

"Kevin, you've got to calm down," Devan said, grasping him by the shoulders. But Kevin wouldn't listen. He was out of control.

"Get the fuck off me, man!" Kevin said and pushed Devan into a set of poolside glass doors.

Devan crashed into the doors so hard he was amazed they didn't break. After recovering from the impact, he ran down the hall after Kevin. He knew Kevin was headed to his car.

"Kevin! Come back," Devan called out. "There's a better way."

Kevin stopped but did not turn to face Devan. "The only thing I want to talk about is killing that motherfucker," Kevin said. When Kevin finally turned to look at Devan he saw a dark and evil grin spread across Devan's face.

"There's a better way to take care of this. A way we can all benefit," Devan said. They went back into the decimated living room and Devan presented his plan.

Devan knew they all had more to lose than he did. After all, he could just go home. But without Max, the others were homeless. A fact Max continuously held over their heads. After listening to Devan's plan, they agreed it was time to act. Knowing there was a lot to do, everyone went right to work.

Devan's plan was to rob Max and set him up with his suppliers. They knew where Max kept the customer coke as well as his own personal stash. They also knew where he hid the cash they collected as well as where Max kept his own personal "emergency" money. They calculated there was $200,000 worth of coke, then found another $100,000 in cash. They split $90,000 five ways and everyone took as much coke as they wanted. Kevin and Lance took the most, knowing they could sell it and make even more money. Linda took more than Devan thought she would. Devan even took a small amount, not to sell but for personal use, enough to last a casual user like him a long time. Michelle only wanted cash. They strategically hid what was left in various places around the house. They even hid some of the remaining cash under Max's mattress. Knowing someone would be paying Max a visit, they hoped what they hid would be found and make Max look like a liar when he told his bosses what they'd done. After setting the scene, everyone hurriedly packed their clothes and any other personal items they wanted to take with them.

The house was oddly quiet as everyone kept to themselves while deciding what part of their lives to take and what to leave behind. Devan was with Linda in her room when the realization began hitting them both. They knew she had to leave and go as far away as possible, which meant they would be separated and maybe never see each other again.

"There has to be some way for you to stay," Devan said out loud.

But he knew there wasn't. Linda was too well-known and could never move her coke safely in this area. Someone would figure it out. They discussed him going with her, but she vetoed it. She told him he would be safer in Jacksonville than any of them. Unknown to Devan, Linda had withheld information or lied to Max when he asked her questions about Devan. Max didn't know Devan's real last name or where he lived or even went to school.

If everything went as planned, Max would soon disappear. His bosses had had enough of him and were on high alert. If he were to be "caught" lying and stealing, well...his bosses would take care of the situation. Completely.

Within a few hours, everyone was ready to leave. The plan was for Lance, Kevin, Michelle, and Linda to relocate with what cash they had and the potential for more by selling their coke. Devan would fade back into his old life in Jacksonville.

Lance had his own car, so it was safe to use. The other vehicles belonged to Max. Linda needed a car of her own, so everyone piled into Lance's car and headed to a "no questions asked" used car lot across town where she bought a well-maintained Firebird.

Linda's plan was to go live with her father in North Carolina. He needed her now. Even though she had run away, she stayed in touch and knew his health was failing. Linda wanted to be with him as long as possible. Devan understood, but it didn't make her leaving any easier.

Lance and Kevin were die-hard surfers and very good. They would take Michelle and go to southern California, sell their coke, and then go on to Mexico. The three of them could live well in Mexico until they all were of legal age. Lance would be 18 in a few months, Kevin in just a little under a year, and Michelle in three years. Lance's long-range goal was to surf professionally.

After Linda purchased a car, Devan rode with her and they all caravanned to a popular restaurant down the street from the car lot and next to Interstate 10 for a late lunch. I-10 was a straight shot to California and a new life for Lance, Kevin, and Michelle.

Over lunch, Devan noticed how alive everyone sounded as they talked excitedly about their futures. It was as if they'd been set free or had just escaped from some horrible prison. But when the waitress brought the check, it hit them all at once that this might be the last time they would see each other. Emotions overflowed. After many farewell hugs in the restaurant parking lot, everyone said their final, tearful goodbyes. Linda and Devan waved as they watched Lance, Kevin, and Michelle drive away. Knowing more pain was still to come, they put their arms around each other and embraced.

Linda wasn't ready to leave, and Devan didn't want her to go so they decided to spend one last night together at the beach. He called his parents. When his father answered, Devan told him he wouldn't be coming home because Linda was moving away for good and that they were spending their last night together. He'd be home the next morning and they could punish him however they wanted. Then he hung up.

Devan and Linda spent the remainder of the day walking on the beach. Linda asked if he would build her a sandcastle, and he did. They valued every minute together, determined not to waste even one precious second. Though they told each other this was only temporary, inwardly they knew it would be their last night together.

When they weren't making love, they held each other, pretending to have all the time in the world. But soon night began giving way to day. Neither could sleep, so they sat on the balcony of the hotel room and watched the sun come up. It was beautiful and the tears started to flow. They had no idea how difficult saying goodbye would be.

At 10:30a.m. Linda pulled up to the magnolia tree on the corner of Devan's block for the last time. Even though his parents were at work, they thought it was only fitting to say their goodbyes under the tree. More tears flowed as they hugged each other. Devan pulled a leaf from the tree and gave it to Linda.

"Here," Devan said, "something to remember me by."

Linda took it and they hugged again. "I love you and I always will."

"Me, too," Devan whispered as he held her tight. "I love you more than you'll ever know."

They kissed one last long kiss and then Linda got into her car and drove off. After watching her drive away, Devan couldn't bring himself to go home. Instead, he walked down to the river a block away and stayed there until evening, depressed and lost in thought.

Devan finally went home at 6:30p.m. and went straight to his parents, expecting the worst. To his surprise, they asked if he'd eaten and offered him dinner. It was obvious he wasn't doing well so they suggested he eat and get some rest; they would talk to him in the morning. They did not punish him, and the entire incident was never discussed.

The next morning Devan's father dropped him off at the main entrance of his school. After entering the building, Devan stood off to one side, observing everything and everybody. He listened to the passing conversations and thought to himself how simple and safe it all seemed.

He heard students talking about girlfriends and boyfriends, who said what about whom, clothes, parties, schoolwork, tests, teachers and what-not. It really was a whole other world, he thought to himself. If only these people knew what he'd seen and experienced. He wondered what Kevin, Lance, Michelle, and Linda were doing at that moment.

Maybe in some ways he was lucky. After all, he had the option of escaping to this world, at least for a while, and playing student without having to worry about the more serious pressures of life.

As Devan stood watching his fellow classmates interact with one another, he decided then and there to keep his past and his experiences to himself. They would be a part of him he'd keep locked away, possibly forever. For now, he would concentrate on being a student and a teenager again.

"The past is the past and the future is now," he said as he pulled himself away and headed off to his first period class.

Unfortunately, Devan's return to school wasn't as smooth as he would have liked. He hadn't done speed or coke in a little over a day. When he awoke that morning, he felt like something was wrong, but blew it off, thinking he was just tired. He wasn't sneaking out anymore so there was no point in doing the drugs, or so he thought. He did take a hit of speed with him just in case he couldn't shake off the fatigue.

A few hours into the school day, Devan noticed his hands were shaking. He thought at first maybe he was coming down with something, but after another hour he was worse. He didn't feel sick in a flu-like way, but it felt like someone was turning up his internal thermostat. His temperature was climbing out of control and his heart was racing. He was visibly trembling –something was very wrong.

Devan forced himself to focus and think. *Could this be withdrawal* he wondered. For the last few months, he'd been dependent on pills and coke; they'd become necessary to get him through the days, nights, school, and practically everything else. He excused himself from class and went to the men's room. Sitting in a stall, he decided to take the hit of speed. By the time his class was over, he felt almost normal. Most of the symptoms were under control, at least for the time being. *Withdrawal! Damn. Something else to have to deal with,* Devan thought to himself. His return to "normal" wasn't going to be as easy as he thought.

Realizing what laid ahead, Devan knew if he quit "cold turkey" the next few days would be hell. But he was determined to get it over with. At least mentally he wasn't addicted, he told himself. However, his body had clearly become physically addicted. Devan knew this was something he was going to have to take on by himself. He had no one to go to for help and he sure didn't want to tell anyone, especially his parents, what was really going on, so he faked an illness.

Convincing his parents he was sick was easy. They thought he was coming down with the flu and kept him home for the whole week. The days were difficult, and he quickly realized he wasn't going to be able to quit cold turkey. To break his dependency, he had to cut the speed into smaller doses and take them twice a day in an attempt to gradually reduce their effects.

It took two weeks before Devan completely rid himself of the drugs, but he finally did it. He was clean. No coke and no speed. He had bottles of speed and a brick of coke —enough to party with for a long time if he wanted. He didn't want to throw them away because he still enjoyed their effects. Still, even though he liked what they did to him, he swore to himself he would never become addicted again; never let anything have that much control over him. He kept both for partying, but he would use them on his terms, not theirs.

Fortunately, it was time for Christmas break, which meant Devan had two weeks off from school. The timing could not have been better. This gave him more time to clean himself up and adjust to his new life. He had a little over $18,000 in cash so he bought some new clothes and a home gym. Physically, he was a wreck. The effects of the last several months had taken both a physical and mental toll on him. So Devan used the break to refocus and finally get some closure.

Only one thing remained. Devan needed to know about Max, especially since he was the only one left in Jacksonville. A chance encounter with Max could be disastrous. Three weeks after everyone had gone their separate ways, Devan called Max's house from a pay phone.

On the third ring the phone was picked up, but nothing was said.

"Hello, Max?" Devan asked.

"This isn't Max. Who's this?"

"I work for Max. Is he there?"

"You're unemployed." Click.

Closure. At least with regard to Max, Devan thought as he smiled and hung up the phone. The rest would take time.

PART TWO

Chapter 8

RACHEL

When Devan returned to school after Christmas break, he was a new person. At least on the outside. He had taken two half-term classes in the fall which meant he had to take two new classes for the spring term.

Standing in the doorway of his second new class of the day, Devan looked around to see if he knew anyone. Immediately, his eyes were drawn to a beautiful girl sitting in the back row staring out the window. Her beauty was intoxicating, surpassing any other girl in the school, but it was her distant look that got his attention. Resting her head on her hands, she sat lost in thought, appearing to be a million miles away. He knew the look well and briefly thought of Linda and the others. *She looks so out of place –like she doesn't belong here,* Devan thought. The girl watched Devan approach as he made his way to the back row. Their eyes met and held for an instant before she looked away.

Devan was as much a mystery to Rachel as she was to him. Having seen him around the school when she first enrolled in the fall, Rachel was aware of Devan's drastic transformation. He had gone from being one of the most popular and well-liked students to barely passing his classes and constantly looking rough and haggard. Like many others, she was curious about what happened to him. Rumors ran wild. Seeing him now, he appeared to be his former self again. But even all cleaned-up and still turning the heads of girls, Rachel noticed a change in him. He seemed distant and more reserved. Older. He was handsome, but not her type. Nonetheless, Rachel was intrigued by the mystery surrounding him.

"Is this seat taken?" Devan asked, pointing to the desk next to Rachel.

"No," she answered as she continued looking out the window.

"What is this class, anyway?" Devan asked, attempting conversation.

"Spanish, I think?" she casually responded still looking away.

"Great. I have enough trouble with English," Devan joked.

She finally looked at him and they both laughed.

"I'm Devan Ross."

"Rachel Winters," she replied.

"Pleased to meet you, Rachel. Good luck!"

"Likewise," Rachel said as she reached over to shake his hand.

Devan and Rachel were alike in many ways. Strangers in a strange new world; Devan with his past and Rachel with hers. But, unlike Devan, Rachel was the casualty of a broken home. Like so many teenagers, her parents were going through a messy divorce and since Rachel was the youngest of three sisters and the only one still living at home, she was caught in the middle. Her parents had equally successful careers, but the cost of the split made money tight and sacrifices had to be made, one of which was Rachel's private school. After being in private schools her whole life, the sudden transition to the public school system was a shock.

However, Rachel lived just a few blocks from Devan, so she was in the same school district. This was fortunate, because as far as public schools go, Jacksonville's southside had some of the best in the county, with many students coming from equally successful upper-class families.

But public school was still an alien world to Rachel, and she missed her friends. She had been in this new school for half a year and was still having a difficult time adjusting. She silently wished she could return to the way things were before the divorce.

Since Rachel and her mother had been allowed to continue living in their home, they found themselves faced with many unexpected expenses. The house was large and older; its upkeep and maintenance were costly. Combined with everyday living expenses and the cost of the divorce, her mother's finances were being stretched to their limit.

In an attempt to try and help, Rachel got a job at a local skating rink. The pay wasn't much, but it did give her money for personal expenses. Her mother also had to work more hours and as a senior administrative official in a local insurance company, it was easy to do. Working late into the evenings, her mother had little, if any, time for Rachel. Rachel understood the situation and was trying to accept it, but she missed her mother, and she especially missed the time they used to spend together.

Devan and Rachel quickly discovered they were kindred spirits and felt comfortable in each other's presence. Neither was trying to impress the other or looking for anything more than friendship. Within minutes of introducing themselves, they were talking as if they'd known each other for years.

While waiting for class to start, Rachel and Devan kidded each other, trying to think of any Spanish words they knew and joked about how they would ever get through the class. Neither of them noticed a girlfriend of Rachel's enter the room and quietly take the empty seat next to Rachel. The girl didn't interrupt but sat and listened in on their conversation. Finally, tired of being ignored, her friend poked Rachel in the side.

"Oh, there you are. Devan, this is my friend Stacy." Rachel and Stacy had transferred together from the same private school for similar reasons.

As the days and weeks passed, Rachel, Devan, and Stacy became good friends. Out of the blue, Rachel informed Devan that Stacy liked him, and soon Stacy and Devan were a couple. Rachel had her sights set on another young man in their school, Tony James. Tony was known as the school's drug dealer and all around "bad boy" and it wasn't long before they hooked up. With a new term, new friends, and a new relationship, Devan finally felt like his life was returning to "normal".

The two couples made for a mixed-matched group. All four of them got along well, but Devan was never that impressed with Tony. Still, for Rachel's sake, he tried not to let it show. The more they all hung out together, the more obvious it became that Devan and Rachel were a lot alike. Stacy was a typical, ditzy junior high "wanna be." She was shallow and superficial –the type of girl Devan usually went out of his way to avoid in the past. But times were different, he was different, so he gave it a chance. Tony was more like Stacy; only out for his own self-gain and not really interested in having more or bettering himself. But not Rachel and Devan. Both were deeper. They could see beyond junior high and wanted more out of life.

At first it seemed that maybe opposites did attract. As different as Stacy and Tony were from Rachel and Devan, their relationships progressed. They all made each other laugh and they had fun when they were together.

Tony supplied the group with pot. Devan didn't have much interest, but Rachel did. Stacy pretended so she wouldn't look bad in front of the others. But Rachel and Tony were the heaviest smokers. Rachel's interest in pot mirrored Devan's in cocaine; she didn't need it, she just enjoyed it. Tony brought coke every now and then, but the quality was so bad Devan usually passed.

Tony liked impressing the girls with his bad boy reputation. His pot and low-grade coke only reinforced his cool rebel image in their eyes. He was an amateur in Devan's opinion, but Devan wasn't about to say anything. Instead, he was content living in the moment.

As the school year progressed into spring, Devan's grades improved significantly. By the end of the third quarter, he was back on the Honor Roll, but the relationships were another story.

Rachel had had a taste of what she thought she wanted –the supposed baddest of the bad boys, and was now underwhelmed. Devan and Stacy's relationship was also waning. The interest, at least on his part, was wearing off. Stacy wasn't his type. Maybe it was still too soon after Linda for a steady relationship. Or perhaps it had something to do with what happened next...

Over the past several weeks it was becoming obvious that Stacy and Tony were flirting a lot more with each other, but Rachel and Devan didn't mind. The two of them got along so well that when all four were together people often thought they were a couple, so they weren't concerned.

After all, they were all good friends, or so they thought. Fortunately, or unfortunately, depending on how one views it, the events of a particular weekend would set in motion a chain of events that would have a profound impact on Devan and Rachel's lives in ways they could never imagine.

One Monday morning, Rachel spied Devan drinking from a water fountain outside his second period class.

"Devan," Rachel called out and hurried over to him.

Devan could tell she was pissed about something but continued drinking and pretended to ignore her. Mornings were bad enough, but Mondays were his least favorite day. Even though it had been three months since committing himself to at least trying to be on time, Monday mornings were still the hardest.

"Devan. We need to talk!" Rachel was standing right next to him.

"What's so urgent? You seem pissed," Devan finally replied.

"I am, damn it! Christine, you know my cousin who lives across the street from Tony, just told me she saw your girlfriend leave Tony's yesterday afternoon around four o' clock."

"So that's where she was," Devan said with little interest.

"And that's not all. Her brother John told her that Tony told him that they fucked!" Rachel said, stomping her foot.

"Really? Tony told John this?" Devan asked, amused.

"Yes! And I believe him! There was some fucking going on this weekend and it sure as hell wasn't with us!"

"Sounds more like it was to us," Devan joked.

"How can you joke? This is serious! What are you going to do about it?" Rachel demanded.

Just then, Stacy walked up, said good morning to them both and started jabbering on about her weekend. Devan raised his hand and cut her off. Devan remained calm, perhaps because he was still waking up. Or, perhaps because now he had an excuse to break off the relationship.

"Stacy, we're through. It's been great, but it's over. I can tolerate a lot of shit, but I draw the line at you screwing other guys. Now if you don't mind, fuck off."

Rachel's jaw dropped. She was stunned –her expression was priceless.

Turning toward Rachel, Devan said, "That's what I'm going to do about it."

Stacy started crying and began babbling an explanation. Devan saw Tony coming up the stairs across from them.

"Now what are you going to do about it?" Devan asked, nodding toward the steps.

Rachel locked eyes on Tony, faked a smile and looked right at Stacy. "Excuse me, bitch. I'll deal with you later." She then pushed past Stacy in Tony's direction to confront him. "Hey! Asshole!" she called out.

After school, Rachel usually walked to Stacy's house and her mother would pick her up later. But given the day's earlier events, this was now out of the question, so she rode the bus with Devan. Since Rachel only lived a few neighborhoods away from Devan, they decided to get off early at a gas station where they could get sodas and talk about the day's events. Behind the station was a clearing in the woods that was a popular hangout spot for kids. Fortunately, at the moment, it was deserted so they sat on an old concrete curb discarded in the woods long ago and talked.

"How did Tony handle your confrontation?" Devan asked.

"Typical," Rachel replied. "He denied it. Then admitted it. He said it was all Stacy's fault."

"Do you believe him?"

"Hell no! It takes two to tango."

"Yeah, Stacy must have given me 10 notes today trying to explain. She blamed Tony for everything."

"They're both full of shit," Rachel said. She then reached into her purse and pulled out a bag of weed. "To be honest, this was the only thing that bastard was good for anyway." She took out some papers and tried to roll a joint. It was a little breezy, which was making it difficult for her. Sticks and seeds also added to the problem.

"Gimme that," Devan said. He put it flat on the ground and then filled and rolled it for her. "Here you go, just like a professional," he said, handing it back to her.

"Maybe you're good for something after all," Rachel kidded. "Man, look at all this crap. I swear I think he keeps the good stuff and gives me the shit." Aggravated, Rachel started picking the sticks and seeds out of the bag and tossing them.

"Don't throw away the seeds!"

"Why not? They always blow up on me."

"Let me have them, I want to see if they'll grow."

"Why? You don't smoke."

"Yeah, I know, I just want to see what happens."

"But if they grow, then what?"

"I don't know, I guess when they get too big, I'll throw them away."

"What? Are you crazy? Before you do that, give them to me!"

"Why? You don't know about drying and all that stuff."

"Don't worry, I'll take care of it."

"Maybe I should sell them to you… Wonder how much I could make…"

"Hey! Wait a damn minute. They're my seeds!"

"Yeah, but you gave them to me and I'm the one growing the stuff."

"Well, I guess that kind of makes us partners then."

"Whatever. I should still charge you," Devan said as they both stood up and started walking down a trail that ran along a creek to the back of their neighborhoods, a short cut home.

It was early March when Rachel gave Devan the seeds. The next day after school, he went out into his backyard looking for a place to plant them. The yard was large, a third of it was dominated by a huge pool off to one side. Around the pool was a wide concrete deck; larger on one end than the other. Bordering the deck was 25 feet of grass on each side. Beyond the grass were a number of overgrown flowerbeds anywhere from 10 to 20 feet deep, depending on where they were in the yard. Most of the beds were filled with giant hibiscus plants growing out of control along with various other trees and bushes. Basically, the pool, deck, and grass were all kept up but everything else was left to grow wild. An eight-foot-high fence bordered the entire backyard, so privacy was not a problem.

Devan was responsible for what yard work was done, so this gave him the perfect opportunity to find and prepare the best locations for the 50 or so seeds Rachel had given him. The plan was to start them in pots and then transplant the young potlings into selected areas in the flowerbeds. It was a little over a week before the first sprouts began breaking ground and Devan couldn't wait to tell Rachel.

Rachel heard the phone ringing but rolled over and tried to ignore it. It continued ringing. Reaching for the other pillow to put over her head, she accidentally knocked it to the floor. Frustrated, she sat up in her bed and looked at the clock; the phone kept ringing. After stretching and rubbing her eyes, she reached for the phone and answered in a sleepy and very irritated voice.

"What?"

"Rachel! They're growing! I've got six of them coming up."

"Devan, I can't believe you called me at eight o'clock in the morning on a Saturday to tell me you're growing pot!"

"Hey!" Devan said, pretending to be hurt. "They're our children. Don't you want to be a part of their lives, to help them grow and mature into solid up-right adults? After all, good parenting is the most important part of a young child's development," he joked.

"Call me back when they're ready to smoke!" As Rachel was leaning over to hang up on him, she suddenly remembered something. "Hey," she yelled, "where are you growing them anyway?"

"In my parents' flowerbeds."

"You're crazy!"

"Best place to hide something is in plain sight."
"You're going to get so busted."
"We'll see..."

The remainder of the school year passed uneventfully and they graduated from junior high. Rachel and Devan would be going to the same high school the following year, but not Stacy. Tony was an unknown. This was Tony's second attempt at ninth grade, and no one knew what Tony was doing or even if he had passed everything.

Even though it had now been months since Devan and Linda parted ways, he still thought about her all the time. Stacy had been a minor distraction, but he knew she was too soon. Though she was clearly at fault for cheating, Devan knew he didn't do as much as he probably should have to make the relationship work.

Rachel and Devan, on the other hand, were a different story. They were practically inseparable. They were destined to be friends, this was apparent from the first day they met. Both cared about the other deeply, but more like a brother and sister. As the summer progressed, their friendship only grew stronger.

Near the middle of summer vacation, Rachel arrived at Devan's house on her bike. Hot and tired from the ride, Rachel made her way to Devan's front door and rang the bell. Even though they were almost always together, they usually hung out at Rachel's house, the skating rink, or at other teenage hangouts like the mall. It had been a while since Rachel had come over to Devan's house.

"It's about time!" Devan said as he opened the door.
"Don't start. It's hot as hell out here and I need AC."
"I don't want you in here stinking up my house," Devan kidded.

"Shut up and move," she said, pushing past him.

As they sat at his kitchen table, Rachel leaned over her glass of ice water.

"So, where are they?" she asked, nearly whispering.

"Who?" Devan replied, whispering back playing stupid.

"You know...them!"

"Oh, outside. Come on, I'll show you."

They went out to his back yard.

"Oh my God! You're crazy! What if you get caught?" Rachel asked as she stood in front of one of Devan's beds, looking at a very healthy "child" of theirs.

"Relax. Nobody knows they're here."

"What do you mean they?" she asked with a puzzled expression.

"They! Them! Look around!" Devan said gesturing toward the yard.

"I don't see anything. Where?" Rachel asked again confused.

"Look!" Devan said pointing out into the yard.

Rachel walked around the backyard looking at all the flowerbeds. After a few minutes of walking, she came back and whispered, "Nobody knows?"

"Nope."

"I can't believe this. You said they were growing but I thought you had a few scraggly looking weeds in a closet or something...I had no idea. Wow...Well, ah... I have to know..."

"What?" Devan asked.

"How does it smoke?" she whispered.

"I don't know. You tell me. Remember, I'm not the smoker."

"Devan, we need to know," Rachel replied, her eyes huge with anticipation.

"Okay. Let's go up to my room. I have a little put away," Devan said.

When they got to Devan's room, he opened his closet door and pulled out a yard bag.

"Devan! Holy shit! I can't believe you! A little? We really need to talk." Rachel was, needless to say, amazed as Devan opened the half-full yard bag and pulled out nearly bursting sandwich-size bags of pot. Some were mostly buds, some mostly leaves, and some were mixed.

"I had to put it in sandwich bags because it stinks!"

"Stinks?" she asked.

"Yeah, when fresh like this, it stinks!"

Rachel was clearly blown away. She began babbling; "How did you…I mean when did you…I mean…" Then, becoming more collected, she said, "Devan, this is pot! A lot of pot! What are we going to do with it?"

"We?" Devan asked with one eyebrow raised.

"Well, I did give you the seeds. Remember?"

"Yeah, yeah, whatever. Here, smoke some and tell me what you think."

"What about your parents?"

"Don't worry. They're out of town for the weekend so it's just you, me, and the kids," Devan said as he jiggled a bag in front of her. "So light up."

"Well then, if I must then I must…"

They went back out into the backyard. Rachel took a deep drag from a joint and suddenly sat frozen. Then she started coughing. Then she took another drag and coughed, and then another. Then she just sat there.

"What? It's no good? Why do you keep coughing?" Devan asked. "Damn! I was hoping we could sell it to some of our friends, but if it's no good…"

"Devan," Rachel paused, blinking her eyes a few times, "this is the best shit I've ever smoked! I'll never have to buy it again! We're going to make a fortune!"

"There you go with that 'we' shit again," Devan joked.

As Rachel discovered, when Devan set his mind to something, he did it in a big way. Growing pot was no exception. By the time Rachel came over that summer, he had every flowerbed in the backyard filled with marijuana plants. They were all growing well and casually intermingled with the existing vegetation. To the inexperienced eye, the beds looked as wildly out of control as normal.

Throughout this growing experience and with some amateur research, Devan discovered that not all the seeds were from the same plant type. The more seeds Rachel gave him and the more he planted, the greater the variety. Some grew tall and scraggly, others were thick and tight, and still others were somewhere in between. Not really knowing if there was a significant difference, he surmised the thicker–tighter types were better, so he separated the plants and devoted different beds to similar varieties. By midsummer he'd harvested a considerable amount of each with relative ease.

The effortlessness of growing pot surprised Devan. Good soil and abundant water seemed more than adequate in meeting the plants' needs. As the weeks passed, all the varieties were doing well. Their abundance and eagerness to grow allowed Devan to harvest large quantities almost at will. With half a yard bag full and more to come, both Devan and Rachel determined it was time to start moving product.

"So, partner, any ideas as to how we're going to sell this?" Devan asked. He chuckled as he repacked the yard bag with the pot-stuffed sandwich bags.

"Yes, I do, actually." Rachel said, smiling back. "I've got the perfect person in mind for the job."

"Someone you trust?" Devan asked.

"We go way back. He's been like an older brother to me for years. Actually, he was my main source before Tony. I'm sure he'd be interested." Rachel took another hit off the joint she was smoking. "Because this really is some good shit," she said, exhaling. "We're going to the beach tomorrow. I'll ask him then."

"Cool. Here," Devan said as he threw her a very full sandwich bag.

"What's this?" Rachel asked.

"A sample. From us to him," Devan said, smiling.

Chapter 9

SALES

"Not bad," Allen said after taking a few hits. "Not bad at all. You say your friend has more and wants to it move fast?"

"Yes. And what do you mean not bad, Allen? This is the best shit I've ever smoked!" Rachel insisted.

"Maybe the best you've ever smoked, but remember, this is my business. Trust me, baby," Allen said as he smiled and winked at Rachel. He rolled the joint between his fingers and took another hit. "It may be difficult, but I think I can help. How much does your friend have?"

"A lot. Almost half a yard bag full."

Allen sat quietly thinking for a few minutes while stroking his chin, then said, "How about I give you one thousand for the whole yard bag?"

"One thousand? Come on! It's got to be worth more than that. I was thinking more in the thousands."

"Whoa! Hold up, girl. It's good, but not that good. It ain't no Gainesville Green. I'm going to have to cut and mix it with other product to move it. At best I was going to use it as a filler."

"Damn! It may not be Gainesville, but I thought it was pretty good," Rachel said, clearly disappointed.

In Jacksonville it was widely believed the best "product" came from the small college town of Gainesville, Florida, about 80 miles southwest of Jacksonville. Gainesville was rumored to be the source of the best "high grade" product as well as other, more potent experimental varieties. Growers there were rumored to be well connected across the state. Allen claimed his "best product" was from Gainesville and often sold those brands at greatly inflated prices.

"Trust me, baby," Allen repeated. "I know what I'm doing. Tell your friend I can take it off his hands, but that's the best I can do." He started the truck and they headed to the beach.

Allen was an old friend of Rachel's. He was three years older, and they'd always been close. Rachel trusted him and valued his expertise in such matters. He was the perfect solution to their problem. And he was the only one she knew who sold pot on such a large scale.

Still, Rachel had her doubts. She'd been around pot for several years and knew good product when she smoked it. She felt obliged to trust what Allen was telling her was true, but her gut told her differently. She and Devan might not have "Gainesville Green", but it was pretty damn good in her opinion.

Devan was disappointed when Rachel told him. However, not really knowing much about the "pot market" he figured $1,000 was better than nothing. After all, it was easy enough to grow.

Over the next several weeks, Devan and Rachel moved product through Allen. Though the money wasn't as good as they first hoped, it was still money.

It became routine for Rachel to take the smaller bags to Allen–a "middle-woman" of sorts. Either Devan would take it to her, or she would come to his house and get it. When she was ready, she'd call Allen to make the delivery. She never told Allen about Devan or what kind of relationship they had; just said he was a friend who had a lot of recently acquired product he wanted to move.

"Why do you put those red stickers on the baggies I bring you?" Rachel asked Allen after a delivery to his house.

"So I can tell your product from others," Allen replied.

"Why?" she asked puzzled.

"So I won't confuse them. I have to mix yours with other shit so I can sell it. You do want me to sell it, don't you?"

"Yeah. I just want you to sell it for more. What are you mixing it with?"

"Better product, of course…whatever it takes to move it. Your stuff is good, but by itself I doubt anyone would buy it," Allen said.

"Allen, I know you're the expert and all, but this is really good stuff. Why can't we make more?"

"Baby, you talk too much. I know what I'm doing," Allen said as he continued putting red stickers on the almost bursting bags Rachel pulled from her backpack.

It was late July and Rachel was at her umpteenth summer party and it was the most boring yet. Little did she know a certain chance encounter was about to set a chain of events in motion that would impact her life for years to come…

Bored and leaning against a wall waiting for a friend to arrive, Rachel heard a familiar voice.

"Hey, girl! What's up?"

Recognizing the voice, Rachel rolled her eyes, weighing in on how to respond. The girl had been practically stalking her all summer in an attempt to befriend her. Cornered and not in a mood to make a scene, Rachel decided to be polite, at least for now.

"Oh, hi, Marianne. I didn't know you were coming to this party," Rachel said, attempting to disguise her complete lack of interest in seeing her again.

"Oh, I've known Kathy for years," Marianne replied with a dismissive gesture.

"Funny. I've never seen you with her," Rachel remarked.

"We go all the way to grammar school. Anyway," Marianne said, feeling uncomfortable and trying to change the subject, "you smoke, don't you?"

"Excuse me?" Rachel asked. She was startled by her directness.

"Weed. You smoke weed, don't you? Because I've got some really good high-grade shit I get from a well-connected guy. You want to try some?"

Curious and wondering why it seemed the geeks always got the best shit, Rachel figured what the hell. Besides, what she and Devan grew was pretty good in her opinion, so she was interested in finding out what someone else thought passed for "high grade."

They left the party and sat in Marianne's car parked in front of the house. Marianne reached under her seat and pulled out a small sandwich bag with a red sticker on it, just like the stickers Allen puts on the bags she delivers to him. Puzzled, Rachel took a hit off Marianne's pipe. There was no doubt in her mind, it was theirs!

"What do you think?" Marianne asked.

"You're right. This is some good shit. I'm curious. What does a bag like this cost?"

"Well since I've known the guy for a while he gives me a deal, $125."

"For this?" Rachel asked shocked and trying to hide her surprise. She was still holding Marianne's almost empty bag. "You know, Marianne, I'd really like to get some of this. What are the chances you could hook me up with your guy? I'd pay top dollar," Rachel offered.

"I'm sure he'd be fine with it. I'll call him and ask."

"Cool, but don't tell him my name. Use a fake one. Just in case," Rachel said with a wink and a smile.

"No problem. I'll be right back," Marianne said and quickly got out of the car to go back inside their friend's house to make the phone call.

After Marianne contacted her "connection" and told him she had a friend willing to pay "top dollar," he agreed to let them come over. Marianne didn't have a driver's license but drove her mother's car anyway. A few minutes later they were on their way.

As Marianne drove, Rachel's anger steadily grew. She knew exactly where they were going. She knew it well. They were going to Allen's.

Twenty minutes later they were at Allen's house. Marianne rang the doorbell.

"Rachel!" Allen gasped, seeing Rachel standing there. Instantly realizing his predicament, he forced a smile and asked them to come in.

"Surprised?" Rachel asked as they entered. "Marianne here has been telling me about some high-grade shit she gets from you. Imagine how surprised I was to find out where it really came from!"

"You two know each other?" Marianne asked, confused.

"Oh, we go way back," Rachel answered, never taking her eyes off him. "Isn't that right, Allen? You've been fucking us -Fucking me!" She was up in his face poking him in the chest. "High-grade? $125? What the fuck Allen?"

"Hey baby, it's just business. Relax. We can work this out. We can renegotiate."

"This partnership is over," Rachel said. She turned to Marianne. "I've changed my mind. Let's go."

"Don't be stupid, Rachel. Without me, you won't move shit!" Allen said as they walked out the door.

"We'll just see about that, Allen." She gave him her best "fuck you" smile and closed the door behind her.

Within days of their "falling out," Rachel and Devan moved product like never before. Inexperienced and a bit reckless, they sold to practically anyone who asked. Fortunately, they somehow managed to avoid getting busted.

By the time school started, Rachel and Devan had a devoted following and a growing reputation. It was the reputation part that eventually caused them to rethink their selling strategy. This became apparent after Rachel had a chance meeting with one of Tony's friends while working at the skating rink one Saturday afternoon.

"Hey girl! What's up?"

Recognizing a familiar voice, Rachel looked up from behind the snack bar. "Will!" She walked around the counter and gave him a hug. "It's been a while."

Rachel asked her coworker, Kelly, to cover for her while she took a break. She and Will sat at a corner table, out of earshot.

"What brings you all the way out here? I didn't think you Arlington boys came this far south," she teased.

"You, baby! You're the reason I'm here."

Rachel blushed. She met Will after she and Tony started dating. They got along well and after the breakup she really missed him.

"And why me?" she asked, flirting back.

Will leaned in closer. "Word has it you and your friend can score some good shit, and...well...to be honest, since Tony got busted for selling, it's hard to come by anything decent."

"Word has it?" Rachel asked, alarmed.

"Yeah, girl. I hear you're the shit! Rumors are flying you've hooked up with some big-time suppliers. So how about it? Can you help out an old friend?" Will asked, pretending to pout.

Taken aback by what he said, Rachel gave it some thought. *Rumors flying? Holy shit!*

"Well? Will asked, noticing her disconnect.

Smiling, Rachel said, "Sure, I think I can help out a friend."

Later that afternoon, Devan came to the rink and they discussed her conversation with Will.

"I know what you mean," Devan said. "A couple days ago, Jimmy, you know, my next-door neighbor, asked me if he could buy some. I was shocked. First, because it was private school Jimmy, and second, how the hell did he know I have pot?"

"Did you ask him?" Rachel asked, concerned.

"Yes. He said someone told him I had good shit and when he told them he lived next door to me, he said people at his school have been after him to get some ever since."

"Damn, Devan! Word spread fast."

"Yeah. Maybe too fast. All it takes is one big mouth and..."

"And we're fucked," Rachel said, finishing his sentence.

"Yeah. Fucked!"

"How much do we have left?" she asked.

"A shit load. I had to cut the big ones back again over the weekend."

Rachel sat quietly tapping her fingers on the table, looking out the front doors.

"We need a plan. A new distribution strategy," Rachel suggested.

"Something that sets up buffers between us and our customers," Devan said.

"Yeah, like the mob has," Rachel added.

"Exactly."

"Good idea. We sell only to select people -people we know and trust. The ones less likely to fuck us," she stressed.

"They can sell to our customers. And that would also make it easier for us to keep an eye on them too," Devan said. "Let's make a list and tomorrow we'll start letting people know this is how it's going to work."

"Some won't be happy," Rachel said.

"Too bad. We'll say our people told us to do it. Who's going to question them? If our reputation has us working with "big time" suppliers, then let's take advantage of the rumors."

"That's what I love about rumors," Rachel said, smiling. "If you control them, they can be very useful."

"Yep. Plant a seed, give it a little fertilizer and it grows all on its own. All we need to do is a little maintenance and upkeep and we can make our reputations into whatever we want."

"Sky's the limit," Rachel said.

"Exactly!" Devan added. "By the end of the school year who knows where we'll be."

"Here's to a new and profitable year. Here's to the tenth grade," Rachel and Devan toasted as they clinked their soda glasses together.

The new strategy worked like a charm. Their "buffer dealers" liked the idea. They got great deals from Devan and Rachel, making it all the more attractive. It took some time, but eventually people understood how the process worked. Devan and Rachel were out, at least on the street level. They still controlled everything, but at a distance. All business was redirected to the dealers who were on the street, willing to take the risks. Since it was widely believed Rachel and Devan answered to higher authorities, authorities made even more impressive by rumors and carefully orchestrated events, no one dared to question their decisions.

Rumor creation and control was probably the most exciting part of the business, and Rachel excelled at it. With her outgoing personality, combined with what was now an endless supply of money, the sky really was the limit. They rented limousines to go to parties and carefully arranged for certain events to occur at particular hangouts, fueling even more rumors. Eventually they created a protective shield of misperception and misinformation. "The real key to making this business work is perception and misperception," Devan always said.

The '80s were the perfect time to sell pot, especially in the high schools. Communities across the country knew drugs were an increasing problem, but most were clueless as to the extent and chose to believe such things didn't happen in their schools or to their children. "Just Say No" was the catch phrase of the day and seemingly the only strategy in combating the problem as far as parents and school officials were concerned. For Devan and Rachel, this couldn't have been further from the truth. Demand was so great they often sold out as fast as they could bring their product to market. "Just Say No" seemed to be falling on deaf ears.

Tenth grade went by with no issues. Rachel kept her rink job –it was a perfect front. Devan pretended to still be modeling even though those days were long over. These "jobs" were important for many reasons, but mostly as a means to explain their income and help "wash it" without arousing suspicion. As the year passed, those explanations became even more necessary as their profits continued to grow.

Devan and Rachel's junior high school was a jumping-off point to three different public high schools. And as word spread, they soon found they had connections across the city's entire Southside, mostly former junior high classmates now looking for reliable suppliers. They also tapped into three of the prominent private schools because many of those students hung out in the same places and circulated in the same party circles as Rachel and Devan. Those connections, combined with Devan and other dealers getting their drivers' licenses that year, gave them an even wider distribution range and expanded their markets. By the end of the school year, Devan and Rachel had connections all the way to the high school at the beaches.

They did have one major setback. Freezing temperatures and heavy frost during mid-January killed all their plants. After selling their stock, the freeze caused a temporary shortage, at least from them. But, by early spring Devan had replanted and they were on their way. By that time demand was so great, Devan was forced to squeeze as many plants as he could onto his parent's property, as well as the property behind their house. A two-acre lot was part of an elderly woman's garden and had become wildly overgrown. She was a shut-in and hadn't been out of her house for as long as Devan could remember. Her yard service barely kept paths cleared through a jungle of plants. It was in that jungle Devan expanded his crop to meet the growing demand, and by the end of the summer they had re-taken a sizeable portion of the pot market, at least at the high school level.

Chapter 10

DRUG WAR

Summer proved to be highly profitable. Devan and Rachel hadn't planned to supply or dominate the entire high school pot market, only to grow and sell as much product as possible to those they trusted. As it turned out, demand was far greater than the supply. Knowing they weren't the only ones attempting to meet the demand, they never believed their little operation would be anything more than a ripple on the huge pot-selling pond. They regarded themselves as small time operators. However, as word spread and demand grew, Rachel and Devan soon found themselves at the center of a vast distribution network that stretched across the city. High school proved to be the perfect market, but a market not without competition.

Eleventh grade was full of surprises. From the first morning back to school after summer break, Rachel and Devan knew their junior year wasn't going to be like their last.

Rachel was chatting with a girlfriend at her school locker when she became aware of someone standing close behind her. A man's hands were suddenly over her eyes. Figuring it was probably Devan playing a joke, she just stood there.

"Surprise! Remember me?" said a familiar voice.

Rachel grabbed the hands and spun around as she threw them off. "Tony! What are you doing here? I thought you were in juvie."

"I'm out and I'm back," Tony said with a cocky smile.

"What do you want?" Rachel asked with disgust.

"Just to say hi and let you know I'm back."

"Great. Happy to hear it. See ya." She started to walk away.

"Wait! I haven't seen you in a long time." He sounded desperate to continue the conversation. "How are you?"

"Are you sure you have the right woman?" Rachel asked, annoyed.

"Funny. Yes, I'm sure."

"Tony. What are you doing here?" Devan asked coldly. He had walked up unseen.

Tony faked excitement at seeing Devan again. "I started school here this morning too."

Completely ignoring Tony, Devan turned to Rachel. "Ready?"

"Let's go," Rachel answered, also ignoring Tony.

"Later Rachel. I hope to see you around," Tony said as they walked off.

"Don't count on it," she replied, not even looking back.

"And nice seeing you again, Devan," Tony added sarcastically.

Devan shot him the bird as they walked away.

"Great, our wannabe dealer is back. I have a feeling he's going to be trouble," Devan said.

Tony was indeed back. He'd been out of juvenile lockup since early summer. Having been released into his grandfather's custody, he was now living just blocks from Devan and Rachel's high school. Since his parents were unable to care for him, mostly because they rotated between jail time themselves, his grandfather was his only option.

Despite the new address, Tony attempted to go back to his old ways. It was all he really knew. Shortly after hitting the streets and talking with some of his old associates, he was surprised to find most were already well connected and not looking for additional business. The more contacts he made, the more frustrated he became.

As the summer passed, Tony could not find buyers, especially at his prices. His old associates were not interested in doing business with him. His market had been taken over and he couldn't believe by whom.

It wasn't because Devan and Rachel dominated the entire market that Tony was having trouble finding business. It was more a result of whom he tried to do business with. Rachel and Devan fell back on who they knew early on when they had few connections. Tony's associates were available, and since he was in jail, the supply naturally found its way to the demand. Tony's people were convenient and more than willing buyers at Rachel and Devan's prices. Not that they were intentionally trying to undercut the market, but since they were their own supplier, they didn't need a drastic markup, allowing them to sell under the market price, which virtually guaranteed constant business and created a loyalty from their dealers. Business for Rachel and Devan was good. But Tony was finding it impossible to compete.

"How can they sell so fucking cheap?" Tony barked at a friend. "Fucking amateurs! If I could find out who their suppliers are I'd cut a better deal and make a killing," he said, outraged.

Desperate to cut Rachel and Devan out and retake his market, Tony spent most of his summer spying on them from afar. He was determined to discover who their suppliers were. But the more investigating he did, the more he was amazed by what he heard.

How could two stuck-up suburbanites have hooked up with such a big-time network? Tony repeatedly asked himself. Believing most of the rumors and gossip he heard, Tony became even more determined to discover their suppliers' identity. He figured if two amateurs could hook up with such people, he would have no problem. But, as the summer passed, Tony had no luck. Frustrated, he decided it was time to try a new strategy. Determined to succeed at all costs, once school started he wasted no time making his move. For the next several weeks Tony came on to Rachel hard, relentlessly calling her at home and passing her notes in school. He was determined to get back into her life, one way or another.

"Good morning," Devan said as Rachel got into his car to go to school.

"Morning," she snapped.

"What's wrong with you?" Devan asked as he pulled out of her driveway.

"Tony. He won't leave me alone! He calls every night multiple times and leaves me notes in my locker. He's even dropping by my work. And last night he came over here! To my house!"

"What does he want?" Devan asked, concerned.

"Me, apparently. He wants me to give him another chance. He says he's really sorry about all that happened between us."

"Interesting." Devan said, thinking about it for a minute. "Do you believe him?"

"Hell, no! Something's weird. He's…well…fake."

"Fake?" Devan asked, confused.

"Yeah, like he's acting or something. I can't quite place it, but he's so desperate that he sounds fake. Not at all like the arrogant son-of- a-bitch I remember."

"Has he asked anything about our business?" Devan asked.

"No. And that's strange, too. I know he knows. His friend, Will, is one of our biggest customers."

"That is strange. What's he up to?" Devan thought out loud. "Oh, before I forget, I won't be able to pick you up tomorrow morning. I have a dental appointment. I'll be late…again," he added with a smile.

"I don't know how you do it. You miss more school than anyone I know," Rachel said, rolling her eyes.

"It's a gift," Devan replied, shrugging his shoulders.

"I'll get Lisa to take me. She just got her license."

"And when are you getting yours?" Devan asked, knowing that was a touchy subject.

"Don't start! You know I suck at parallel parking!" she snapped.

It wasn't long before Tony's true intentions were revealed. Continuing his blatant disregard for attendance policies and now responsible for his own transportation, Devan arrived late to school after his dental appointment. He had to park in the far back parking lot. As he made his way toward the school, he recognized a familiar smell and heard a familiar voice coming from a brown van with its windows open. Standing behind a truck parked next to the van, Devan eavesdropped and soon his suspicions were confirmed.

"It's just a matter of time before we're back together."

"I don't know, Tony. Rachel doesn't seem to like you much."

"Give me time, I'll get her. Shit! Who'd believe she and Devan could control this school's action? Stuck-up, suburbanite rich kids. What the hell do they know about dealing, anyway?" Tony asked, looking at the joint he and his buddy were sharing.

"Word has it they're pretty well hooked up. I wouldn't mess with it, Tony. Prices are good and you have to admit, this is some good shit!" his buddy said as he took a long drag from the joint.

"Screw you, Jack! I'll be damned if I'm buying from them! Screw that! Once I find out who their suppliers are, I'll renegotiate and make a better deal. They'll be out on their assess and coming to me!"

"Tony, I don't know. From what I hear they've got a pretty sweet deal."

"We'll see. I'm sure I can do better. Shit man! I taught them everything they know. You can't school the teacher!"

"Really," Devan said under his breath. "We'll see." He stepped out from behind the truck.

"I wonder what Rachel will have to say about your little plan," Devan said loud enough for them to hear.

Devan turned on his heel and started walking toward the school building. Tony jumped out of the van waving a crowbar. In a fair fight

Devan could take Tony. No problem. But with a weapon, things might have a different outcome.

Facing each other defiantly, both were startled by the bell signaling the end of first period. Students started streaming out of the portable classrooms lining that end of the parking lot. With witnesses all about, Devan smiled at Tony and nodded at the crowbar.

"Maybe next time," Devan said, then continued walking toward the school in pursuit of Rachel.

"Fuck! He's going to tell Rachel everything! How much do you think he heard?" Jack asked in a panic.

"Screw it! It doesn't matter," Tony said, agitated and pacing the parking lot. "I'll find out who they're working with."

After weeks of more spying, Tony was no closer to his answer. Out of desperation, he and a friend approached Rachel and Devan at a party. Seeing them standing with a large group of people, Tony made his way over to them.

"Can we talk business?" Tony asked.

"Sure, Tony," Devan said, ice-cold. "How can we help you?"

"Can we go somewhere more private?"

"No." Devan said. "This will be fine. Our meetings with you will be in public."

"Don't tell me you're scared of me, Devan," Tony said with a cocky smile.

"Of you? No, not at all, Tony. I just don't want to mess up my shirt. I like this shirt. Don't you, Rachel?" Devan asked.

"Oh, yes. It's very nice," she said, smiling back. "One of my favorites."

"Look, I'm proposing a deal. A partnership of sorts. With your suppliers and my customers, we could make a killing!" Tony offered.

"You'd like that, wouldn't you?" Rachel asked.

"Trust me, it would be good for all of us," Tony said, looking at her and then at his friend.

"And how long before you try to cut us out? That was the plan, wasn't it?" Rachel asked, not buying his bullshit.

"Hell hath no fury like a woman scorned," Devan said lightly. "Sorry, Tony, no deal. We're doing fine on our own and our people are happy with the current arrangement. They don't want additional complications."

"Let me talk to them. I'm sure I can change their minds," Tony pleaded.

"Can't do that. Their orders. That's how they want it and trust me, I wouldn't mess around with these people. This isn't junior high, Tony. This is a whole new game," Devan said in a tone signaling they were finished discussing the matter.

"But if there's anything else we can do for you don't hesitate to ask," Rachel added as they walked away.

"Do you think he bought it?" Rachel asked.

"I don't know. He's pretty stubborn. I have a feeling we haven't seen the last of our old friend Tony," Devan said.

A week later, Rachel's friend and coworker, Kelly, was giving her a ride home from work when an old model blue Thunderbird began following them. In the six miles from the skating rink to Rachel's house, the Thunderbird harassed them by flashing its headlights and repeatedly ramming into their back bumper. Terrified and screaming with every hit, Kelly drove on as fast as she dared. Rachel was frightened at first, but her fear gave way to anger. She was sure it was Tony.

Suddenly, the Thunderbird hit them so hard Kelly lost control of the car. Rachel grabbed the wheel and was able to avoid hitting a utility pole by giving it a hard yank; the car skidded to a stop on the side of the road.

The blue Thunderbird blew its horn and sped off. Rachel heard laughter and yelling as it drove away.

"Who was that?" Kelly asked. She was visibly trembling.

"Probably just some stupid kids screwing around. Let's go. It's been a long night," Rachel said, trying to make light of the situation. Rachel called Devan when she got home and told him what happened.

"Do you think it was Tony?" Devan asked.

"I don't know. I couldn't see them. I guess it's possible it was just some stupid kids messing with us," Rachel said, trying to convince herself.

"Maybe, but just in case I think we need to watch our backs, to be on the safe side. Maybe even make a few other changes as well," Devan suggested while trying to check his growing temper.

"Probably a good idea," Rachel agreed.

With everything going on, it became routine for Devan to pick Rachel up from work. He tried to make light of the Thunderbird incident, but he was convinced it was Tony. Ever since their confrontation in the school parking lot, Devan knew Tony was capable of a lot more than he first suspected.

Devan walked up just as Rachel finished cleaning the snack bar.

"Ready?" he asked.

"Oh yes. I'm exhausted. It was a busy night."

"Rachel, why do you keep working? With all the money we're making you don't need this headache."

"I like it. I like the atmosphere, the night life…speaking of which, how was the party?" she asked.

"Boring. I expected more from rich kids," he said, shrugging his shoulders. "Private school…what do they know?" Devan said, trying to provoke a response.

"Hey now, don't knock them. Thanks to them their school is one of our fastest growing new markets. Those 'rich kids' sure love our shit!"

"They pay the most and get the least. Our best customers," Devan joked.

Rachel went to tell her manager, Skip, she was leaving.

"My ride's here. I'm going now," she announced.

"Hold up, I'll walk y'all out," Skip said. "And remember, tomorrow night is the All Night Skate, so rest up." He locked the door behind them.

"I will. Good night," Rachel said

"Night." Devan added as they walked toward his car.

"Are you coming tomorrow night?" Rachel asked.

"No. I've got that thing with Wendy and the beach high school people tomorrow," Devan reminded her.

"She's such a slut. You can do better than that!" Rachel shot back.

"Whoa now. Hold up. You don't hear me criticizing your boyfriends."

"Yes, you do! You do it all the time! Remember Tony, Steve, Joe, Mike, Dave…"

"And you call Wendy a slut?" Devan asked, interrupting her and pretending to be disgusted.

"That's different! That's not, it's not…I'm not," Rachel stuttered, then punched him in his arm as hard as she could.

"Ow! That really hurt! You need to stop working out."

"A girl's gotta know how to defend herself," Rachel joked, waving her fist at him.

"I feel safer already," Devan teased as they got into his car.

"I know she's a little trashy," Devan said, continuing the conversation. "But you must admit, her beach connections bring in a lot of money. Oh, the sacrifices I have to make," he said, acting like it was such a burden.

"Just don't catch anything! That bitch has been around!"

Wendy was, in some ways, a lot like Rachel. She was strong-willed and self-confident. She knew she was "hot" and used it for all she could. But she lacked class. She and Rachel didn't care much for each other, so business with the beaches was mostly left to Devan.

Devan and Wendy met at a party earlier in the year, a one-night stand that turned into an on-again, off-again relationship built mostly on sex. Wendy liked men and Devan accepted that. For Devan, she was a means to an end in more ways than one.

It turned out Wendy was a dealer—one of the biggest at the beach. Just for the hell of it Devan gave her some of their "home grown" to get her opinion and the rest was history. Their occasional one night stands mixed business with pleasure, eventually evolving into a profitable connection for moving product in the beaches market. Devan joked to Rachel that providing his "extra services" was the least he could do since Wendy and her friends were such good customers.

On those rare occasions when all three of them were together, Devan found it humorous. Rachel was so much cooler, smarter, and self-assured. She and Wendy would take shots at each other, mostly because Wendy thought something was going on between them and liked causing trouble. Rachel would cut her down in ways Wendy didn't get or even notice. But Devan did and for him it was always entertaining.

As they pulled away from the rink parking lot, Devan saw the headlights come on from a car parked across the street. He continued watching through the rearview mirror as they drove. He turned down a street and into a neighborhood next to where Rachel worked.

"Where are we going?" she asked, trying to put on her makeup.

"I think someone's following us."

Rachel turned around and looked. "It's the blue Thunderbird from the other night!"

"Let's see if they really are following us," Devan said.

Devan randomly drove through more neighborhoods and soon confirmed it.

After a few minutes Devan grew tired of playing games with their pursuers. "Enough of this shit!" He slammed on the brakes, put the car in reverse, and backed toward the blue Thunderbird at high speed. "Let's see what you've got, asshole!" Devan was enjoying this.

The other car stopped and quickly began reversing out of control, eventually backing into a ditch.

Devan stopped, put the car in drive and squealed the tires as he drove off.

Rachel shot them the bird.

It was no contest. Devan left the Thunderbird in the dust. His '68 Camaro was much more than it appeared. Under its hood was a brand-new Corvette engine, courtesy of a friend and customer.

"This is getting old," Rachel grumbled.

"What a bunch of pussies," Devan said as he watched them disappear in his rearview mirror.

Unfortunately, these encounters were becoming more frequent. If Devan and Rachel weren't being followed, they were being harassed by threatening phone calls, notes in their lockers, etc. Strangers would hang out at the rink staring at Rachel, trying to intimidate her up.

They knew Tony was behind all of it. Having failed at finding out who their suppliers were or partnering with them, he figured he would scare them out of business. At this point, Rachel and Devan had been in business for over a year and were not the least bit intimidated. It had been a lot of fun until Tony came back; they enjoyed tremendous popularity and weren't about to let him push them out. This was their school and their business, and they were determined to keep it that way.

Devan was not as easy a target as Rachel, since he spent most of his free time in the school weight room or the gym not far from his house and was always surrounded by his rather large friends.

Rachel, on the other hand, was more public. Her customer service concession stand job at the rink made it easy for Tony and his goons to play their games. After several weeks of constant harassment, it reached the boiling point for Devan and Rachel during Christmas break.

"Devan, we've been robbed!" Rachel shouted into the phone when he answered.

"Your house?" Devan asked.

"Yes. But not so much robbed more like ransacked, mostly my room," she said.

"You think it was him?"

"Yes. The whole house is a mess, but my room is destroyed. Like they were looking for something. My mom doesn't suspect anything, but she is worried," Rachel said. "I don't like this, Devan. I don't want my mother involved."

"Me either. That asshole has gone too far this time."

"What are we going to do?" she asked.

"We've put up with his shit long enough. Time to get dirty. Do you know where his locker is?" Devan asked.

"Yes...why?"

"Since Tony wants in our business so bad, maybe it's time we let him in."

"I think I know where you're going with this, and I like it," she said.

After the holiday break, with school back in session, Rachel excused herself from her 1st period class and planted a full bag of weed in Tony's locker. Devan slipped an anonymous note under the dean's door, telling him where to look.

Tony was busted and suspended with permanent expulsion pending.

That night Tony called Rachel and told her he thought the three of them should talk. Without admitting to the break-in, Tony told her he thought things had gotten out of hand and wanted to discuss business. Maybe even make a deal that everyone could live with.

"Hell no! Fuck him!" Devan said when Rachel called to tell him about their conversation. Rachel tried to rationalize the situation, explaining that if they didn't do something soon things would probably escalate. Tony might set them up, or maybe something even worse. Like it or not, they were in the middle of a full-fledged drug turf war.

Devan knew the break-in rattled Rachel. She wasn't as concerned about herself as she was for her mother and didn't want things getting more out of hand. Devan knew she was right. The thought of Tony in their business infuriated him, but he knew the risks weren't worth it. Devan agreed to a meeting as long as it was some place public. He would never trust Tony.

Rachel called Tony and told him they were willing to talk. Against Devan's wishes, Rachel agreed to let Tony pick her up at her house. They chose to meet at a restaurant a mile from the skating rink. When Tony picked Rachel up, she noticed he was acting different; like he was up to something.

When they arrived at the restaurant, Rachel and Tony walked to the entrance and Rachel sat down on a bench outside.

"What are you doing?" Tony asked, irritated.

"I'm waiting for Devan."

Tony grabbed her by the wrist. "He can find us inside," he said as he pulled her up from the bench.

"Let go of me, asshole!" Rachel snapped and yanked her arm out of his hand. "Don't start your bullshit with me, Tony. I'm not your girlfriend."

Tony had never been like this to her before. She thought it might be best to just calm down and go inside.

As Rachel followed Tony in, she saw him nod at three rough-looking guys in a booth. He took her by the elbow and pulled her to a high-top table in the bar area.

Rachel quickly realized this meeting was a set-up. She was pissed.

They sat in silence for several minutes.

"Where's Devan? Tony asked. "He's late."

"How would I know? I'm not his mother," Rachel answered.

Tony grabbed her wrist and pulled her to within an inch of his face.

"After tonight, things are going to be very different, so don't fuck with me, bitch!" He pushed her back and let go.

Rachel massaged her wrist. *What is he up to? And where the hell is Devan?* she wondered. Tony supposedly wanted to make a "deal" that would benefit everybody. Devan told her not to go with him, but she insisted she would be okay. She convinced Devan Tony wouldn't hurt her and she'd be safe. Now Rachel doubted her judgment. He'd gotten physical several times since picking her up and she didn't like the looks of those guys in the booth, they were trouble. Maybe this was a bad idea, Rachel thought. She desperately tried to think of a way to warn Devan, but felt helpless. Tony's frustration grew worse as the minutes passed by.

Twenty minutes later, Devan walked in and spotted them in the bar area. He knew something was wrong the moment he saw Rachel's expression.

"Sorry I'm late. I had to take care of some business first," Devan said, knowing his comment would piss-off Tony even more. He sat down next to Rachel.

"This is nice," Devan continued as he looked around with a 'Fuck you, Tony' smile. "Just like old times. But you know, something's missing. Oh, I know what it is, Stacy isn't here."

"Damn!" Rachel said, feeling confident. "I knew I forgot something. Sorry, Tony. Should I go call her?"

Rachel and Devan laughed.

"Enough of this sh–," Tony started, but Devan cut him off.

"So, what do you want, Tony?" Devan asked with little interest.

Ignoring Devan's dismissive tone, Tony settled back into his chair, trying to look cool.

"I want to know who your suppliers are." He kept himself calm and smiled.

"You know we can't tell you that. Their orders, not ours."

"I don't give a shit what they want," Tony said as he grabbed Rachel by her wrist. "You'll tell me now or we'll go outside, and you will tell me there!" He motioned to the guys in the booth. The scraggly looking group of juvenile thugs took up positions behind Tony.

Rachel pulled her arm back, but Tony wouldn't let go.

"You're going to tell me now," Tony said, very satisfied with himself.

Rachel looked at Devan, not so much with fear but with an 'Oh shit we're busted, he's called our bluff' look.

But Devan was calm. Not the least bit intimidated. "Take your hand off her," is all he said as he stared at Tony with ice-cold eyes.

Tony, still self-assured, smiled and let go.

Devan looked at Tony, then at each of his goons, and then over his left shoulder and nodded in the direction of a table across the room. Three large men walked over, taking up positions behind Devan and Rachel.

One was an off-duty police officer, who made it known he was carrying a gun when he put his hands in his pants pockets pulling his jacket open. The other two were Devan's other workout partners from his gym. The four of them regularly worked out together. When Devan told them about a "wannabe dealer" who was harassing him and his friend, they were more than willing to help. They were also all valued clients.

Tony's face froze in panic. His boys backed up, acting like they were not with him. Devan's friends kept their eyes on the thugs. Devan kept his on Tony.

Tony was rattled and nervously looking for an escape.

Rachel sat back and crossed her arms, nice and relaxed, smiling from ear to ear.

"For the final time, the answer is no," Devan said. "And this is the last time we're having this conversation." He paused for effect. "Now go."

Tony remained frozen.

"You deaf? He said go!" Rachel commanded.

Tony and his thugs left so fast they almost knocked the table over. Everyone in the restaurant roared laughing. After Devan introduced Rachel to his workout partners, he bought them all dinner.

Tony disappeared and was never heard from again. Devan and Rachel assumed he dropped out of school since he was on the verge of being expelled anyway. But the rumors and misinformation snowballed at school and the event quickly evolved into some incredible stories. Rachel and Devan never talked about the incident, but if all the people who said they were at the restaurant that night were actually there, the restaurant would have been overflowing with customers. Still, in a strange kind of way, the uncontrolled rumors only worked to further strengthen their hold over the high school pot market. After the "Tony encounter," their fellow students, as well as other business associates across the city, began treating them with even more respect. Fear, it seemed, gave them power, and power gave them control. The Drug War was over.

Chapter 11

DRIVER'S LICENSE

In mid-July, Rachel attempted to get her driver's license for the third time that summer. She had no problem driving; it was the parallel parking that screwed her up. No matter how much she practiced, she failed every time. She hoped the third time would be the charm.

"Rachel Winters," called the DMV examiner.

"You can do it, Rachel. Just do it like we practiced," Devan told her.

"Yeah, I know. Thanks for bringing me. Mom's given up. I think she gets embarrassed when I fail," Rachel said. "I just get so nervous."

Devan walked with her up to the counter and recognized the examiner. He'd seen him at a party a few weeks ago–someone's brother or something.

"Wait!" Devan blurted out. "Excuse me, can I have a word with her real quick? I forgot to tell her something," Devan said.

"Make it quick. Got a lot of people waiting."

They walked over to a corner.

"What are you doing?" Rachel asked. "Now you're making me nervous."

"I think that guy's a customer. I saw him at a party a few weeks ago. He's someone's brother and goes to college here in town. Maybe, if you need to, you can use that."

"What? Bribe him? Yeah, right. And if he says no? Then what? I'll never get my license. Besides, I think I can do this."

Devan wished her luck and gave her a hug.

The test went well until the parallel parking at the end. She lined the car up perfectly and put it in reverse. Unfortunately, she accelerated too quickly and cut the wheel too sharply, causing the car to go crashing over the pole and up onto the curb.

Devan watched from inside the building.

"Shit!" he said out loud. "Guess we'll be back next week."

Rachel just sat there, holding the wheel and looking down. "Damn it!"

"Okay, Miss Winters. Pull the car off the curb and return to the front parking lot. I'm sorry, you fail–"

"Do you smoke?" Rachel asked, cutting him off.

"Excuse me?" the instructor asked.

"Do you smoke pot?" Rachel said, clearly and distinctly.

"Well–uh–I–uh…" he stuttered.

"How about we make a deal?" she said, smiling at him. "I'll hook you up good if you pass me."

"How good?" He was interested.

"Real good," Rachel said still smiling. "Trust me."

"I can't believe you got it! I saw everything! How did you do it?" Devan asked as they left the building.

"I negotiated."

"You bribed him!"

"We made a deal."

As they walked to the car, Devan tossed her the keys. "You drive. You've earned it."

Chapter 12

END OF BUSINESS

The end of Rachel and Devan's senior year marked the end of their business venture. They agreed at the start to close the operation after graduation. They had had huge success, but after summer break, they were going in different directions. Rachel would stay in town and attend the local community college part-time. Devan would leave for the University of Florida in Gainesville. Devan wanted to leave Jacksonville for a long time and college finally gave him that opportunity. It was only an hour and a half away, but it was far enough, another world.

They also decided when they started the business as partners, they would end it as partners. Their customers were disappointed and found it hard to accept. But Rachel and Devan knew it was time to call it quits. It was time to enter the "real world" and they believed a college education would take them to a happily ever-after.

They harvested their last crop at the end of May. By the end of June, the operation was closed for good. Summer was one party after another, mostly given by now former associates and friends to celebrate their graduation and thank them directly for "the business." They reveled in the spotlight and enjoyed a celebrity status of sorts, and for good reason. Being their own suppliers allowed them to be generous over the years, very generous in some cases. They answered to no one. There was no 'profit sharing' with other suppliers, so no need for enormous markups. They sold quality product below market value to carefully monitor and control all aspects of their business. Their generosity created loyalty and protection from their dealers.

Needless to say, their reputations grew, as did their popularity. Image was everything. Some they created. Some was self-generated. Perceived image gave them power and it was the "power" that kept them in control. Not to say they didn't have enemies, but for the most part their enemies were largely outnumbered by friends and associates spread across the city.

Their families were constantly amazed at how well known they were when they were out in public, especially since neither engaged in any extracurricular activities. By the time Devan and Rachel graduated, they were easily the two most popular students in their high school. Their fellow students knew of and respected–even protected–their reputations. The faculty recognized their academic performance and conduct. Both had an air of class, sophistication, and self-confidence. The summer's events were proof positive their high school years were stellar.

As the summer activities were winding down, by mid-August Rachel, Devan, and their friends were either preparing for college or entering the workforce. A few days before Devan left for Gainesville, Rachel insisted on taking him out for one last farewell feast, anywhere he wanted to go.

"Thanks for taking me to dinner," Devan said as they sat down at a table in his favorite restaurant. "You're not such a cheap bitch after all," he mused.

"Ass! I knew you'd pick this place," Rachel said, yawning, pretending to be bored.

"You're the one who said, 'your choice,' remember?" Devan reminded her.

Rachel rolled her eyes.

"Besides, I like the view." Devan said.

The well-established restaurant was on the St. Johns River in downtown Jacksonville. It was frequented by the city's socialites and politicos. Rachel and Devan got a kick out of them looking down their noses and wondering why two teenagers were eating at a table alone on a weeknight without their parents.

"View of what?" Rachel asked. "The river and the jail are all we can see from this crappy table. I should've reserved a table on the other side of the restaurant so we could see the city."

Devan laughed out loud.

"I especially like the view tonight," he said. "Think about it. Here we sit in one of the most expensive restaurants in town…"

"The most expensive," Rachel interrupted.

"And you're going to spend a crap-load of money on me tonight. And where did that money come from?" Devan asked. "Hmmm?" Rachel crossed her arms and stared at him. "From our business venture. Money we made growing and selling pot, to be precise," Devan continued.

A waiter brought them their sodas.

"You've got to love the irony. Here we sit," Devan said, motioning to the table and restaurant, "and there it stands. The Duval County jail. Symbol of punishment for wrongdoers just like us."

"When you put it that way, the view isn't that bad after all," Rachel said. "We did have a great run. Who'd have believed all this started from a few seeds?" Rachel sat back in her chair, looking at the jail across the river quietly reflecting on the past three years.

"Devan," Rachel said, leaning over the table and lowering her voice, "I have over a hundred thousand dollars stashed away around my room. A hundred grand! Can you believe it?"

"Me, too! At least a hundred grand! That should keep us going until we're situated in the 'real world'. How many of our fellow classmates do you know with that kind of advantage?"

Rachel said nothing, knowing none of their classmates were in their position.

"What are your plans now that we've officially graduated into society?" Devan asked. He leaned back and stretched one arm across the top of the empty seat beside him.

Rachel shifted in her chair.

"I'm moving to the beach as soon as I find a place. I've signed up for a few writing classes at the local college and start in a couple of weeks," she said. "Maybe one day I'll write a bestseller and become famous."

"Then I can say I knew you when you were a nobody," Devan joked. "That's a great idea, Rachel. You always wrote the best papers in school, and some great short stories. You've got talent, that's for sure."

"What about you? You got what you wanted; you're going to Gainesville. But do you know what you want to major in?"

"Financial management or accounting, something business-related like that. Mostly I just want to get out of here. I need a change," Devan said.

"That's why I'm going to the beach. It's like a whole different world out there."

Their dinners arrived. They continued talking about their next adventures. Rachel told Devan she thought business was a perfect major for him. The last three years had certainly taught them both a lot about running a business.

"You've got business experience," Rachel said, grinning. "Probably not the kind you'd put on a resume, but valuable in its own right."

They spent the evening reminiscing about the last three years. They ate as though it was their last meal; steaks, loads of side dishes, and multiple desserts. This was their time to privately reflect on and celebrate the end of this chapter of their lives.

As dinner came to an end Rachel finally broached the subject they had been avoiding all night.

"This will be the first time we'll be apart for such a long period of time," she said with a somber tone.

"I know. It'll be weird for sure."

"I'm actually going to miss you! Who will I have to vent to? And who'll protect you from all those skanky sluts you hook up with?" she joked.

"Me? What about you and your loser wannabe-dealer-tough-guy-super jocks you seem so fixated with?"

"Exactly!" Rachel said. "See? We need each other. You can't go."

Devan shrugged. "Come with me."

Rachel was silent for a moment. "I think the beach is as far as I want to go right now." She stared out the window at the now nighttime view. "I'm not ready to play student full-time again. I want to live a little first."

"I've never known you to do anything a little," Devan said. He was smiling at her reflection in the window.

"Oh, please! Without my constant supervision, God only knows what kind of trouble you'll get into," she said.

"Funny," Devan laughed.

"You're right, though," Rachel continued. "Us not being together will be weird.

"We'll visit -both ways. Agreed?" Devan said.

"Agreed."

Rachel presented her glass. "To our past and our future."

"I'll drink to that," Devan said, clinking her glass. "To our future."

PART THREE

PART THREE

Chapter 13

A TIME TO LIVE

Devan was excited about college for more reasons than anyone knew. Not only was he escaping Jacksonville, but he would also be able to finally have a life. The last three years had been good indeed, but it had also been a lot of work. Outwardly, he and Rachel appeared to share the responsibilities of running their enormous distribution network. But behind the scenes, things were very different. For the most part, Devan did the growing, drying, packaging, and storing, as well as helping with the distribution. Everything was prepared at his house since his parents were away for much of the week at their shop, allowing him to maximize his time in the afternoons. Rachel helped as much as possible, but Devan did the majority of the work on the actual "manufacturing end."

Between his parent's yard and the jungle-like lot behind their house, as well as an ever-increasing demand, Devan's days were full. The physical maintenance and upkeep of the crops was also a lot of labor, but the payoff was well worth it. Devan labored in the yard and prepared product in the afternoons. In the evenings, he and Rachel oversaw their operations and made sure everything ran smoothly. Information was critical. Understanding their market and staying informed was a necessity. Both figured the best way to get the information needed was for them to immerse themselves in it. This is where Rachel's gifts came into play. Her high-energy "party girl" personality gave her and Devan that extra edge, both perfectly balancing the other. Rachel brought in the customers and Devan made the deals. Rachel also helped negotiate problems and ease tensions. When necessary, she was a combination saleswoman and goodwill ambassador. She was also image consultant and rumor management coordinator.

They both loved that part of the job. Image creation was never-ending and always exciting. They created, maintained, and managed their images by planting rumors and capitalizing on gossip. Occasionally they even arranged for "special events" to occur at critical times and places. Rachel had a "party girl" image on the outside, but underneath she was a cool sophisticated businesswoman. Devan was perceived more as the no-nonsense businessman. It was widely believed that people who attempted to screw them over were dealt with severely, especially after the "Tony" incident. Planted rumors helped nurture and sustain this perception and established Devan as the muscle behind their operation. It was assumed they were working with other "big time" operators and taking orders from higher up the chain when, in reality, they were playing both ends and the middle.

For the most part, their operation ran smoothly. Never once in their three years did they feel close to getting busted. And over time, they redefined their buffer strategy, further shielding themselves. Though they felt to some extent isolated and safe from legal consequences, it was always in the back of their minds. They weren't overly paranoid, nor did they become complacent. Mostly they remained alert, cautious, and guarded. As fun and rewarding as it was, Devan was relieved to not have to deal with any of it anymore. As far as he was concerned, graduation marked the end of business, and he was happy to move on.

College would be a time to relax, to be stress free. In a way it would be a vacation. Time for him to live! Thinking back, Devan realized that since meeting Linda he'd spent the majority of his teenage life in the "fast lane." From Linda to Rachel and their three years of growing and selling pot, he'd been busy. That's to say nothing of his school responsibilities; doing both was exhausting. Devan knew college would be challenging, but in his mind, it was only college. No more dual lives or secret organizations. It would simply be school and a time for him to enjoy life. And his hundred grand would go far in helping him do just that.

Devan entered college life with zero expectations. He was content to let whatever happen, happen at its own pace. He even stayed in a dorm his first term. By his second term he rented a house within walking or riding distance from the campus. That was mostly for privacy; dorm life really wasn't for him. It also gave Rachel a place to stay when she came to visit.

At first Devan was more or less an unknown and that was exactly how he wanted it. Some of his high school classmates or former customers also made the move to Gainesville, but it was never a problem. After explaining that those days were over, most attempted to strike up some kind of friendship, even inviting him to parties and other functions. Sometimes he went, but mostly Devan tried to avoid the Jacksonville crowd. His and Rachel's years of reputation creation and control helped. To some extent he was feared, so he wasn't hassled when he declined invitations.

Devan's house wasn't anything fancy, but it was nicer than what most students could afford. It was a small two-bedroom, one bathroom cabin on a lake surrounded by a heavily wooded multi-acre lot. Devan loved the illusion of privacy, yet he was still almost in the middle of town. He had some place to escape to, to study, or just hang out. Between kicking back at his house, working out in the campus gym, and going to school, Devan finally had the time he craved for himself. He had a life and was content. Content being by himself and more importantly, content with being an unknown.

Devan wasn't there looking to build off his past reputation and he wasn't one to belong to "cliques," or follow trends, or get involved with shallow, superficial people. If people wanted to get to know him, they could make the effort.

Unfortunately, Devan's past soon caught up with him. Knowing he didn't deal anymore; people were still in awe of his reputation when they did hear about it. Through uncontrolled rumors this time, his reputation spread. Him being regarded as one of "the more notable people" in high school unknowingly fueled those rumors. It was obvious he had money and lived well, and in a college town where budgets are usually tight, he stood out.

Devan drove a Corvette. He had what many regarded as a nice house; dressed well and projected a powerful sense of self-confidence. He did not care how others perceived him. Devan wasn't necessarily trying to keep a low profile; he simply had no desire to pretend to be someone or something he wasn't. In his mind, he was just another student.

However, it wasn't long before Devan found himself surrounded by many new friends. Maybe it was his "I don't care attitude" or maybe it was his not trying to fit in. Whatever it was, it made him infectious. By the end of his second term, Devan was developing a reputation–mostly tied to his past–but many also knew him as just Devan, fellow student.

At the end of his freshman year, Devan stayed in Gainesville and began throwing a few small parties. By the middle of his sophomore year, his parties were legendary. They became the unofficial "must do" events of the season. It was never his intent to buy friends. He just wanted to live it up, so he did. In his mind, a college degree was an investment, and after graduating, he'd get a good job and make a legitimate salary. So why not spend some of what he worked hard for and enjoy it? Live life to the fullest!

Devan went through women like he was changing clothes. He wasn't deceptive or cruel about it. He only hooked up with women like himself– women looking for a good time. He wasn't seeking love, just fun.

Near the end of his sophomore year, almost at the height of his newfound popularity, Devan was introduced to Ray. Ray was an older former UF student and local resident. Devan had seen Ray around the party circuit but was never formally introduced until a Jacksonville friend and former associate brought Ray to Devan's big year-end party.

"Devan! Devan!" called a young man as he pushed his way across the crowded living room in his direction.

Devan pretended not to hear his old friend Clark and tried to slip out onto his back deck overlooking the lake. Much of the party crowd was out there.

Before he could get lost in the crowd, Clark caught up to him. "Devan! This party's kickin'!"

"We've earned it!" Devan yelled over the noise, holding up a beer.

Everyone on the deck and in the house cheered.

"So, what's up, Clark?" Devan asked, looking at the man he brought with him.

"This is Ray. My new best friend," Clark said, smiling from ear to ear. The two men shook hands.

"I'm game. Why is Ray so special to you?" Devan asked.

Ray smiled at Devan, acknowledging Clark's enthusiasm.

"Man, Ray's got some of the best shit I've ever smoked. It's as good or better than the shit you used to sell! I thought you two should meet, you know, being in the same business and all."

"Now Clark," Devan started. He was a little drunk and half-serious at the same time. "You know I'm out of that business, but I'm always honored to meet a fellow businessman. Can I get you guys a drink?"

"I'll get it," Clark quickly offered.

"Beer for me," Devan ordered.

"Same," Ray said. Clark disappeared into the crowd.

"So, you're Jax," Ray said, crossing his arms and leaning back against the deck railing.

Devan was a little surprised at Ray's directness and assumed Clark had been running his mouth. "I guess I am," he said.

"You were a mystery to me for years," Ray said, studying him.

Devan was intrigued. "Was I? How so?"

"Your little operation got my attention down here. From what I heard, you and your people way undersold. That must have cost you guys a small fortune."

"Not hardly. We made out like thieves." Devan didn't sense Ray was trouble, nor did he attempt to deny anything.

Now Ray was intrigued. "Did you indeed?"

Clark returned with their beers and started rambling again. Devan and Ray were curious about each other and silently wished Clark would go away so they could continue their conversation.

Devan recognized Ray from other parties he'd been to throughout the year. He appeared to be a wall fly of sorts. Everyone seemed to know him and now Devan thought he knew why. Ray was a dealer. He operated like he and Rachel used to, mingling with the crowd, and being seen at all the right places. Ray was the front man. "It takes one to know one," Devan thought to himself.

As the party went on, Devan kept a casual eye on Ray, watching him work the crowd. Ray had a different style. Unlike Devan and Rachel, he appeared to prefer keeping a lower profile. Still, it was obvious Ray was a professional–a smooth operator. It was interesting to watch him from an outside vantage point. Ray was a good five to ten years older than most at the party, but no one seemed to notice or care. Ray reminded Devan of a cowboy with some redneck mixed in, yet something about him told Devan Ray was much more than he appeared.

The party began to break as the sun came up. Devan threw a hell of a party–he could afford it. His parents paid his tuition and his grandparents had set up a trust to pay for his living expenses, so he used the money he saved from selling pot to throw lavish parties.

"Another great party," slurred a very drunk Clark, who was being held up by a surprisingly sober Ray.

"I'm having a small cookout for the 4th of July," Devan said to Ray. "Hope you can make it."

"Awww, man! I'm going home for the summer," blathered Clark, who was on the verge of passing out.

"That's too bad, Clark," said Devan, faking disappointment. "You'll be missed." He turned to Ray. "Hope you can come. I'd like to continue our conversation."

"Looking forward to it," Ray said, nodding his acknowledgement.

By the 4th of July, most students had gone home for part or all of the summer, so Devan's next little "get together" was only half the size of his last one. The entire party was outdoors. People swam or canoed in the lake, some played volleyball, horseshoes, and lawn darts. Combined with music, alcohol, and whatever else people brought with them, there was great entertainment to watch. The party began in the afternoon and was stretching into the night when Ray arrived. Devan saw him as he made his way through the crowd.

"You made it. Can I get you a drink?" Devan asked. He was slightly drunk.

"Beer'd be great. Maybe a few if I'm going to catch you."

They made their way to the deck and grabbed a couple of beers from the nearest cooler, then made small talk. Devan sensed Ray wanted to know more about his business in Jacksonville, so he patiently waited for him to bring up the topic.

"So, you never told me how y'all were able to get away with selling so cheap," Ray said.

What took you so long to ask? Devan thought.

"No, I didn't, did I?" Devan said out loud. He made it sound like he wasn't going to say anything.

"Okay," Ray said, "but let me try and guess anyway, so bear with me."

Devan nodded as he put his beer on the deck railing and pulled himself up to sit on it. He waited while Ray collected his thoughts.

"Let's see," Ray said as he sat on the deck railing next to Devan, pretending to think while rubbing his chin. "Either you got some really good deals or," he paused and looked directly at Devan, "you grew it yourselves."

Devan knew Ray was playing him but could also see that he was genuinely interested. *What the hell*, Devan thought. *It's over. Why not tell?* Besides, he figured Ray probably grew it, too. "Bingo," Devan said.

"A or B?" Ray asked.

"B."

"Damn! I knew it. That explains it all," Ray said, slapping his knee as he stood up to throw away his empty beer bottle. "No wonder you were able to sell so cheap. Y'all were your own supplier. And then you just disappeared, what, about a two years ago? It was because you started school, right?"

"You, sir, win another beer," Devan said, reaching into a cooler and tossing it to Ray. "Okay, my turn," Devan said as he settled back against the deck railing. "You're Gainesville, aren't you? And I'm willing to bet you not only own this town, but you're probably well connected across the state…even Jacksonville."

Ray acknowledged with a 'you've got some balls' look. He didn't know what to make of Devan at first. It had been a long time since he'd encountered anyone like him, someone who so obviously didn't fear his presence. Ray's reputation was unsettling to many, but Devan seemed completely at ease. He even appeared to be enjoying their little question and answer session. Ray found it refreshing. *Finally, a real person,* he thought. *Not another ass-kisser or groveling idiot.* Devan wasn't being rude or disrespectful, just direct and honest. Ray was impressed. Though he knew he might eventually have to "explain things" to Devan, at the moment he respected him.

"Well, damn!" Devan said. "I know what we made so I can only guess what you do. High six figures a year?" he asked. He wondered if Ray would be as forthcoming.

"Seven plus."

"No shit? We gave it up too soon," Devan joked.

"Out of curiosity, when and how did you get started?" Ray asked.

"About five years ago. And believe it or not from a handful of seeds my partner gave me." Devan couldn't believe he was telling Ray this. *Must be the alcohol,* he thought.

"That would be about right," Ray said.

"Huh?"

"Well, I started growing," Ray paused, and then said, "shall we say on a large scale about seven years ago. Jacksonville was always one of my biggest markets since it's so close to Gainesville. I only recently began removing or destroying the seeds. Mostly because people like you were growing it themselves and cutting into my business."

"So that explains it," Devan said retrospectively, more to himself than Ray. "I'm really not a smoker. To be honest with you, I wouldn't know good from bad. But my partner and all our clients swore it was some of the best they ever smoked."

"Yep. That's probably because you were growing my shit. My partners and me have been engineering the stuff for years, always trying to make it better. I bet y'all got some of our earlier experimental crops."

"Well, if that's how it really happened then I have to say thanks. You guys make a hell of a product." Devan knew his comment could go two ways and was curious to see Ray's reaction.

Ray looked ahead, frowning, saying nothing. He knew he was keeping Devan in suspense. He folded his arms across his chest and chuckled. "Happy to have been of service." Then he fixed Devan square in his sights. "So tell me, are you really out?"

Devan studied Ray for a second. He was sure he knew why Ray asked the question.

"Yeah," Devan finally said nodding. "We closed up shop after graduating. We're both attempting to make it legitimately now."

"Happy to hear it. For obvious self-serving reasons, of course," Ray added, nodding his head.

"Of course," Devan repeated, waiting for the threat he was sure was coming next.

But it didn't come. Ray surprised Devan instead. "But if you ever want to go back into business, give me a ring. I'm always willing to look into, shall we say, franchised operations," Ray offered.

"Thanks, man. It's good to know if this college thing doesn't work out, I have something to fall back on."

Devan's instinct was spot on. Ray was there to "feel him out" as to what his intentions were in Gainesville. Ray was prepared to explain to Devan that Gainesville was his town and other "entrepreneurs" were not welcome. But it wasn't necessary. Ray believed Devan when he said he was out. He sensed Devan was happy about it as well. And Ray genuinely liked him. Devan reminded Ray of himself at a much earlier time in his career.

Devan spent most of that summer in Gainesville. He took a few summer courses and used them as an excuse for staying. He did not want to go home. He had finally broken away from Jacksonville, made new friends and a new life. But he did miss Rachel and enjoyed her visits. He felt bad for not going to see her as often as she came to see him, but he just couldn't bring himself to go back. Still, he was happy for her. She, too, was living it up and also making a new life for herself at the beach. They tried to stay in touch, but time and distance were causing them to slowly drift apart.

Chapter 14

INFORMAL EDUCATION

Once Ray realized Devan wasn't potential competition, they became fast friends. Ray genuinely liked Devan and it turned out they had many interests in common, particularly working out. As the summer continued, they spent more time together.

Devan respected Ray. Ray was real–much like Devan. Ray was 10 years older and had a great deal more business experience. He was a skilled negotiator and businessman. Devan learned a lot just from hanging out with him. Rachel also took an instant liking to Ray, especially since Ray always hooked her up good when she came to visit.

By Devan's junior year, he and Ray had become good friends. Unlike most of Ray's associates and customers, Devan wasn't a "yes man" and never outwardly appeared to fear him even as he learned more about Ray's "dangerous" reputation. This impressed Ray and continued to earn his respect. Devan also met Ray's partners and they all got along well.

They discussed Ray's business only as much as Ray wanted. Devan understood the unwritten rules and never crossed the line by asking too many questions. Mostly they worked out, hung out, and partied together. They even had the same taste in women. Though Ray was older than the average student, he had no problem finding female company. He was a player. Women were so plentiful he would sometimes share them with Devan.

Ray also owned a large ranch outside of Gainesville and often invited Devan there to go horseback riding and shooting. He had both indoor and outdoor target ranges for archery and a large assortment of rifles and handguns. Devan was no stranger to firearms. His father collected and sold guns, so he felt right at home.

On a hot, sunny afternoon in late July, Ray surprised Devan by asking if he would like to visit one of his production facilities. Devan had long been curious about his operations, but made it a point not to ask, believing he was probably better off not knowing. However, on that day Devan's curiosity got the better of him.

"Well, how about it? Do you want to see one of my farms?" Ray asked.

"I don't know if that's such a good idea, Ray. If you show me, does that mean you'll have to kill me?" Devan asked in typical Devan style.

Ray laughed. "I don't think that'll be necessary. Not if you're blindfolded."

"Blindfolded?" Devan asked.

"Sorry about that. I can't take any chances. Besides, I do like you and really would hate to have to kill you." Ray teased, tilting his rifle at him.

"Thanks," Devan said. His response was sarcastic, but Devan understood and knew it was better this way. Ray's reputation was much more hard-core than he and Rachel's had ever been. From the night they were first introduced and from what he'd gathered on his own, Devan knew Ray was considered "dangerous." It was rumored that Ray had an interesting way of dealing with problems. Many believed the woods around Gainesville concealed the unmarked graves of anyone who tried to cross him.

But knowing all too well how rumors and misinformation can be manipulated, Devan wondered how much was really true. He also knew Ray had checked up on him and wondered how much Ray might know of his carefully created reputation. But, unlike others, Devan never showed fear around Ray. Ray respected this. Devan's reply about being killed was him playing up the rumors.

After 20 minutes, Ray told Devan he could remove the blindfold. At first glance Devan saw what looked like just another farm. Ray parked his truck next to a small house. His two partners came out to greet them. After a round of handshakes and friendly greetings, Ray told them he was taking Devan on a tour and would be back in an hour.

Ray led Devan into a large cornfield behind the house. As they made their way into the heart of the field, a familiar fresh green smell suddenly hit Devan head on. He found himself surrounded by marijuana plants cleverly concealed and growing freely in between the rows of corn. Devan's jaw dropped. Row after row, acres of pot, intermingled in the tall corn.

"Brilliant," Devan thought to himself as they walked. Ray really was "big time," much bigger than he imagined. They made their way to an irrigation pumping station in the middle of the field and climbed up to a metal platform. Devan stood there speechless. The field stretched before him as far as he could see.

"Is all this like what we walked through?" Devan asked.

"Yep," Ray said nodding toward the field. "This field is 500 acres of Gainesville's finest."

"This field?" Devan asked. "You have more?"

Ray smiled.

"Holy shit, Ray! How the hell did you do it?" Devan asked. He was in awe of what he was seeing.

Trusting Devan, Ray leaned back on the platform railing and proceeded to tell his story.

To Devan's surprise, Ray was Ivy-League educated. And like Devan, he wanted to get away from his hometown. His grades got him a full ride to a prestigious northeastern university. Since his parents couldn't help financially, Ray worked part-time at a variety of odd jobs while going to school. It was during this time that he was exposed to the concept of indoor growing or "grow houses." Because of the cold northeastern climate, grow houses were a necessity.

Ray was no stranger to pot. He and his friends partied all through high school and he knew people who grew it around Gainesville. But the indoor concept intrigued him. He got involved with some local growers and it wasn't long before he began supplementing his income by selling their product. Ray learned much from this college work experience.

Grow houses had some advantages over free range. Crops could be grown and harvested faster, and year-round. However, free-range, for those with the time and room, could produce much larger yields. Ray did well for himself while away, both in and out of school.

After graduating, Ray returned home to Gainesville, only to find the family farm on the verge of being seized by the bank. For two generations Ray's family had grown oranges and grapefruit. But after several years of hard freezes–unusual for central Florida–most of their trees were wiped out. They tried growing strawberries and other produce, but soon realized they couldn't compete with the larger commercial growers. Knowing how much Ray wanted to go away for college, his parents never told him they were financially strapped. They didn't want Ray blowing an opportunity at a great education by staying home to help them fight a losing battle.

After returning home and learning of his parents' predicament, Ray came up with an idea. He convinced his father to let him grow one big "cash crop." He told his father just one crop is all it would take to pull them out of the red. It didn't take much convincing; they were about to lose everything anyway. Ray contacted a few of his friends from school and a partnership was born. His buddies came to Gainesville with as many seeds as they could get their hands on. After some strategizing, they decided to plant them deep in the middle of one of his father's cornfields. The plants did well and within months they were ready to be harvested. And Gainesville being a college town offered the perfect ready-made market.

To make a long story short, the property was saved. Ray's father didn't want to make this a permanent way of life, but he did let them grow more crops. Over a short period of time Ray and his partners raised enough money to expand the family farm so it could compete with the larger commercial growers.

Ray, too, was expanding and rapidly becoming a large "commercial grower" in his own right. He even enrolled in chemistry, biology, and horticulture courses at UF. He figured if he was going to grow "product" for a living, then he needed to learn everything he could to grow the best product. Ray found his calling. Farming was in his blood, and he was good at it.

Devan spent nearly all his spare time with Ray, and Ray trusted him. Devan also realized that being Ray's friend came with other unexpected benefits. Devan's friendship with "The Man" earned him a different kind of respect, one based mostly on fear. People, like their mutual friend Clark, helped exaggerate rumors and in time, by association, Devan was regarded in much the same way Ray was. Knowing how rumors and misinformation worked, Devan got a kick out of what he heard about himself. It was an ego trip reminiscent of high school.

By Devan's final year in college, he was closing in on both a formal academic education and an informal one in the art of growing pot. Ray's operations were far more complex than he'd imagined. Ray and his partners had research facilities where they experimented with creating and enhancing the potency of their plants. Using his new education in chemistry, biology, and horticulture, Ray and his partners–both biology majors–applied what they knew to the "R & D" end of the business. The partners engaged in creating new marijuana strands through crossbreeding. They also experimented with growing in different mediums, most notably in hydroponics. Though experimental, the hydroponic lines were in high demand. They offered some of the highest quality marijuana grown. The partners worked constantly to keep improving the new products as well as their farming techniques. By successfully controlling and manipulating light, nutrients, and different growing mediums, they produced more potent crops and brought them to maturity in considerably less time than traditional methods.

It was obvious Ray and his partners dominated the Gainesville market. They really did have the best "shit" and they did not tolerate competition. Ray was a businessman, and he respected the rights of others to do business– as long as it wasn't in his town. Gainesville was his turf and with his money he had considerable influence over local law enforcement, and he didn't hesitate to use that influence to discourage competition.

But before resorting to extremes, Ray would do reconnaissance work and engage in diplomacy before dropping the hammer; similar to what he did the first time he met Devan. Having heard so much about Devan from Clark, Ray was curious and went to Devan's party to feel him out as to his intentions in Gainesville. It was only after their second meeting that Ray determined Devan wasn't a threat.

For those who did not heed Ray's warnings–and he only warned once–and still attempted to encroach on his territory, Ray showed no mercy. After a second "violation" his actions would lay the groundwork for the rumors he was widely known and feared for. Devan liked and respected Ray, but he knew Ray was very capable of doing whatever he felt necessary to protect himself and his business.

Devan learned about the agricultural needs of the plants as well as how to accelerate crop yields with the use of grow-houses. Devan was a natural. Horticulture was his hobby and Ray liked teaching him.

Hanging out with Ray also hardened Devan and made him wiser in the ways of the business. Though they were good friends, Devan never fully participated in Ray's operations. As far as Devan was concerned those days were over and he enjoyed not having the responsibilities or worries associated with that line of work. College was still Devan's first priority and as exciting as Ray's world was, Devan never lost sight of his academic objectives. He believed college would be his key to opening the doors to the "legitimate" world and his eventual success.

Graduation marked the close of another important chapter in Devan's life. He was successful in accomplishing his academic goals and even graduated with honors. Devan was ready to return to Jacksonville and start the "career" he believed awaited him there. But before going home, Devan decided to throw one last party. He thought of the old saying, "It's better to burn out than fade away."

The "big one," as Devan's party came to be known, was a hit on many levels. He had a sizeable amount of money left–at least enough to help him get started back in Jacksonville, so he used what he could and threw one hell of a bash. It was Devan's way of thanking all his friends, new and old. The vacation was as over. It was time to go home.

Chapter 15

THE BEACH

To Devan's disappointment, his best and closest friend did not attend his last big farewell blowout party. For most of Devan's senior year, Rachel had been drifting farther and farther out of his life. At first this didn't concern him too much since Rachel had made a new and equally exciting life for herself living in Jacksonville Beach. But over that last year things were changing, and not for the better.

Ever since Rachel's new boyfriend, Terry, came into her life, Devan felt he was being pushed out. Not necessarily by Rachel, but more by Terry. Devan got the impression Terry didn't like them being such close friends. Terry would get jealous when Rachel went to Gainesville and spent the night. But he was always quick to forgive her when she shared some of Ray's "special gifts" with him. Still, it was obvious Terry was very possessive of Rachel. He was not the type of guy Devan thought Rachel would ever give the time of day to, but Devan wasn't going to interfere. If Rachel liked Terry and was happy, Devan supported her. Her happiness was all that mattered as far as he was concerned. Rachel had always been the one to go looking for "love" and she had a long track record to prove it. As much alike as she and Devan were, when it came to relationships, she was the more serious.

At first, the beach was good for Rachel. She had freedom and a chance to live without the burdens of their business and live she did. Immediately after graduating from high school, she and a girlfriend rented a nice house one block from the beach where Rachel continued to live her "fast lane" life.

Almost as if planned, a new club was opening not far from Rachel's house. Building on her years of "rink" experience and just for the hell of it, Rachel applied for and got the assistant manager position. Rachel loved the work. The club life and energy fit her perfectly. The atmosphere combined with her personality and her many friends–mostly former clients and associates–transformed the club into one of the hottest at the beach. Like Devan, Rachel also benefited from years of reputation creation and control. By the end of Devan's first year in college, Rachel was club manager. She also was attending junior college part-time and was making a serious effort to pursue her interest in writing.

The money Rachel made managing the club, along with her cash from her high school days, allowed her to live far better than her friends. Rachel didn't need any financial assistance, but she enjoyed having a roommate if for no other reason than security. Rachel was also known for throwing some impressive parties, the kind often broken up by the police. It wasn't long before her high-profile job, together with her former high-profile image, made her somewhat of a celebrity at the beach. Rachel was living her dream.

Rachel also enjoyed "playing the game." And why not? She was beautiful and knew how to use her looks. She liked men and wasn't afraid to go after one she found interesting. When she wasn't working, Rachel and her girlfriends either hit the party circuit or club-hopped all over the city. Everywhere she went she knew people. She always found herself surrounded by dozens of friends and enjoyed every minute of it.

Caught up in the moment and not seeing a downside, Rachel believed her future would only get brighter, so she began spending some of her money on herself. Her first big purchase was a new car. Since Rachel loved to play the part of a woman who has it all, she decided it was time to start looking the part–and why not, she could afford it. Rachel bought only the best clothes and accessories. She used her money not only to build the life she wanted, but also to maintain it. Unlike Devan, who sought solace in Gainesville, Rachel thrived on the energy and atmosphere of living in the "fast lane." She knew what she wanted and used her money and image to make it happen.

Rachel's money and popularity were also good for business. The simple fact that she managed the club contributed substantially to its success, which gave her credibility and enormous power. Rachel knew she could make or break the club with little more than a comment, and the club's owners knew it too. Fortunately, they all got along well, and the owners always treated Rachel with the respect she deserved.

Rachel had everything she wanted. Power, wealth, and popularity. For two years this was her life. She rode high atop her self-created wave of success. Men came and went. She wasn't looking for an ever-lasting love, but she took her relationships seriously. Rachel always made a concerted effort to make them work. However, her job and high-profile lifestyle often interfered.

Rachel took her job seriously too and managed like a professional. She didn't take any shit from people and was frequently referred to as "the bitch"–a title she wore with pride. She even had "Bitch" put on her office door under Manager. To some she was perceived as stuck-up or snobbish, but as people talked to her and got to know her, they loved her.

Rachel didn't play to trends or fads. She was unique, original, and beautiful. Unfortunately, her beauty cut both ways. She intimidated some men; many wouldn't attempt to approach her, believing they didn't have a chance. So, she wasn't above making the first move. Her self-confidence was something a man would have to live with…or not.

Rachel and Devan still tried to spend as much time together as possible. For the first two years he was in Gainesville, they were determined to not let distance keep them apart. They interacted in each other's worlds flawlessly, fitting in like it was meant to be. It was also during this time that they rediscovered Gatlinburg, Tennessee. Having vacationed there with her mother several years earlier, Rachel fell in love with the place and wanted Devan to see it.

Since their senior year in high school, they had made it a tradition to drive there the last week in October to get away and relax. They looked forward to the trip each year. The tranquility of the mountains and cool air was a nice change of pace from their high-profile lives in their respective towns. They always rented the same secluded cabin with a beautiful view high in the mountains outside Gatlinburg, Tennessee. People assumed they were a young couple and they found it easier to just go with it.

Even though they went to the mountains for a break, by the second night Devan and Rachel found themselves deep in the action. They might intend to have a quiet night out at a favorite local bar, but within hours they would be laughing and talking between the tables with other customers as if everyone had known each other for years. It was who they were. They made an attractive pair and people wanted to get to know them.

Still, Devan and Rachel valued their time together. Some days they would just sit on the cabin's porch taking in the view, sometimes in silence and other times playing catch-up on the latest events going on in each other's lives. They had a bond–a closeness–that many romantic couples never have. But theirs was more like brother and sister. Their bond was difficult for many to understand, especially Rachel's boyfriends. The ones Devan met pretended to accept it, but it was obvious he made most uneasy. Devan, on the other hand, didn't have this problem. He wasn't interested in lasting relationships or love. He felt there was plenty of time for that later. College was "play time" and play he did.

"I love it here," Rachel said to Devan as he walked out of their cabin while on vacation in Gatlinburg, Tennessee and joined her on the porch. The cabin faced west, and the setting sun only added to the already beautiful fall mountain scenery.

"Yeah, me too," he replied, handing her a cup of hot chocolate before settling into the lounge chair next to her.

"I can never get enough of this view", Rachel said, looking toward the setting sun, holding the warm cup in her hands.

"It's incredible, isn't it?" Devan added.

"I'm going to live here one day; I just know it."

"I don't doubt it," Devan said. "Every time we come up here you say that. It really is the perfect place to write, you know. I mean, it's so quiet and peaceful. All you can hear is the wind in the trees."

Smiling and sipping her hot chocolate, Rachel said, "To sit out here all day and write is my dream. What about you, could you see yourself settling down up here?"

"I don't know," Devan said, thinking about it. "Maybe. But if not, I'll come visit you, often," he added.

"You better," she said, smiling and then looking off into the distance. "You better."

Late in Devan's junior year Terry came into Rachel's life. Terry had become a frequent visitor to Rachel's club and unlike other men, he wasn't intimidated by her personality or self-confidence. That was what attracted him to her. Rachel immediately found Terry refreshing, something different. At last, a guy who wasn't afraid of her and was willing to make decisions and be a man.

In the beginning, their relationship was red hot. They seemed perfect for each other, and Rachel couldn't get enough of him. But early on Rachel discovered Terry was the jealous type. She could tell by the way he acted when he noticed other men looking at her. Terry wouldn't cause problems, but it was obvious he didn't like it. At first it didn't bother her. She was even flattered. Rachel attributed it to a sign of his love for her.

However, unknown to Rachel, Terry had been stalking her for some time. It turned out he knew her from their high school days. Terry didn't go to the same school, but he did hang out in some of the same circles. Since Rachel and Devan's distribution network was so widespread, they worked the party circuit across several counties. It was at one of these parties that Terry first saw Rachel and developed a distant crush. He went to a high school on the other side of town and attempted to work as a third-tier dealer. He was a customer of one of their main dealers and tried to make some extra money for himself by selling. He knew Devan and Rachel's reputations well.

When he and Devan finally met, Terry pretended to accept Devan. Partly out of respect for who Devan used to be, but mostly because Devan often brought gifts, hydro gifts, from Ray. Terry knew they were out of the business, but Rachel told him about Ray and so to some extent Terry respected and even feared Devan.

Terry recognized Rachel at her club months before he approached her. He watched her from afar and checked up on her for weeks. He talked to Rachel's friends and co-workers to find out all he could about her. He even followed her home a few times and to other clubs on her nights off. Terry learned her schedule and who her closest friends were. He even approached the men he saw talking to her and made up things to drive them away. It wasn't until he felt totally confident about his chances that he made his move and Rachel was in heaven. Terry appeared to be the "perfect guy," and why not? He'd had months to practice.

Within a month of Rachel and Terry's meeting, he'd moved into her place at the beach. For Terry, the timing could not have been better. Rachel's roommate had moved out to go live with her boyfriend. It wasn't long after he and Rachel were living together that Terry's true colors began to show. Within weeks, Terry started hassling Rachel about her job, telling her he didn't like it, especially all the men looking at her.

At first, Rachel blew it off. In her mind, that's part of who she was and whom he'd fallen for. She was flattered by his concern but had no idea how serious he was about the matter. As time went on, Terry became more belligerent. His requests for her to quit her job turned into demands, which led to arguments, and eventually fights. Terry started accusing Rachel of wanting to see other men and even cheating on him. Rachel was totally caught off guard and wondered what she'd gotten herself into.

Rachel loved Terry and tried to convince him he was wrong. She genuinely believed everything was a big misunderstanding and that when he realized there was nothing to worry about, he'd change. But that wasn't to be; if anything, Terry only got worse. He began showing up at the club and making scenes. Fortunately, Rachel still had a considerable amount of money, so she decided to quit for a while and spend more time with Terry in an attempt to show him how much she loved him.

Terry also wasn't working. Shortly after moving in, he claimed he injured his back at his construction job and couldn't work. Knowing Rachel had money, Terry began pressuring her to start a business with him. At first, it seemed like a good idea. Believing he knew what he was doing, Rachel fronted Terry money to get started. The idea was for them to make custom T-shirts and sell them at the beach.

It turned out Terry had no idea what he was doing. He was clueless about how to negotiate and/or make deals. Terry paid top dollar to his suppliers for everything. Having a lot of experience in that realm, Rachel offered her help, but Terry refused, insisting everything was under control. Even with the unexpected start-up expenses, the business appeared to do well in the beginning. But after realizing that starting and running a business required a lot of hard work, Terry soon lost interest and within weeks the responsibilities fell on Rachel to keep it going. Since it wasn't the instant success he assumed it would be, Terry convinced Rachel to close up shop in favor of another idea, hot dog stands.

Terry convinced Rachel once more to front the money to buy a few hot dog carts that they could place at key spots along the beach front. This business too showed promise at first, but once again Terry lost interest, claiming it was too hot or that standing all day was bad for his back. He had every excuse.

Rachel enjoyed the work and was good at it. She liked interacting with the public. Since she would set up close to the beach, she often wore bathing suits to work, which attracted a lot of young men who also hit on her. She didn't mind as long as they bought something. Sex sells, she'd say, and she knew how to sell. Her cart outsold Terry's at least ten to one every day, and that infuriated him.

It wasn't long before Terry started insisting on working with Rachel at her stand. He claimed it was because he loved her and wanted to be with her. In reality, he was jealous and couldn't stand all the young men hitting on her. He wanted to be close by so he could keep an eye on her and make it known that she belonged to him. For Rachel, this quickly got old. Terry drove off customers because of his attitude. Again, as a result of his constant pressuring, she was forced to close another business...

Their last big business venture was a bike rental store they opened a few blocks south of what was left of the Jacksonville Beach boardwalk. The average start-up cost for such a business usually ran around $15,000. But with barely more than $20,000 left in her savings, and having closed the other businesses because of Terry's insecurities, Rachel was hesitant to spend any more money. She suggested they slow down, get jobs, and save some money for a while, then try again.

Faced with the possibility of actually having to work, Terry turned on the charm and convinced Rachel the bike rental business was a good idea. He insisted the time was right and if they waited, they'd miss a good opportunity to finally have a successful business. Eager to get something going and wanting to believe him, Rachel agreed to do it.

Rachel still loved Terry, even with his obvious faults. She'd already made big sacrifices in her life to try to make their relationship work. But Rachel, like many women in her position, did not notice herself getting drawn in and dominated by Terry. From an outside perspective, most would say, "How can she be with someone like that? He's a lazy, no good, loser mooch. Doesn't she know he's using her, taking advantage of her?"

But to Rachel it wasn't as obvious. Terry was a charmer. He knew how to manipulate her. Almost from the beginning he'd been pulling Rachel away from her friends and former life in an attempt to isolate her and reduce her friends' influence. Anytime someone would try to enlighten her or criticize him, Terry would drive that person out of her life by telling Rachel that her friends didn't like him and didn't want them together. The more Terry poured it on, the sorrier she felt for him. Terry wasn't combative. Instead, he'd pretend to be hurt and played on Rachel's sympathy. And unfortunately, his strategy worked perfectly.

In time, Terry had driven away almost all of Rachel's close friends, except for Devan. And Terry only tolerated Devan because, at the moment, Terry didn't regard him as a threat. With Devan away at college, his influence was limited, and on those rare occasions when Devan did visit, Terry would turn on his charm and play him, too. Terry knew Rachel liked seeing them get along and as long as he appeared to accept Devan, she wouldn't mind, or maybe even notice he'd driven away all her other friends and was completely dominating her life. Terry also needed Devan since he often brought Rachel "product" Terry would otherwise never be able to obtain on his own.

Within weeks of opening the bike store, Terry's lazy paranoid insecure behavior reared its ugly head once again. Terry cut back on his hours, claiming that standing all day hurt his back. Most days he didn't go into the store at all, and when he did it was either to get money or to check up on Rachel. Once again, she was doing the majority of the work as well as shouldering the responsibilities of the business.

As the months passed, the store was successful, but Terry's jealousy was a daily problem. He began nagging Rachel to close the business so they could do something else together. Terry knew Rachel was too good for him and constantly worried she would be attracted to one of the many male regulars who frequented the store. For Terry, it was a constant challenge to keep Rachel blinded to the alternatives and focused on him. For he knew he had far more to lose than she did. So, by isolating and manipulating her and playing on her sympathy, Terry kept a tight rein on her.

Rachel knew her long hours managing the store angered Terry, but she was determined to make this business work. The money saved from her high school days was almost gone and Rachel believed that this was her last chance to make something of herself. She wasn't going to walk away for his sake, and this caused more tension. Despite Terry doing his best to convince her to close the business, Rachel was finally putting her foot down.

The more Rachel stood her ground, the more irritated Terry would become. Instead of the usual routine of him playing on her sympathy, he got angry and violent. On several occasions Rachel insisted he leave the house. After a few hours to cool down, Terry always came groveling back, knowing he had nowhere to go. He would become the perfect guy–the one she fell for, for a few days, in order to smooth things over because he knew losing Rachel would mean he would be on his own.

Every morning before Rachel left for work, they would have the same argument. It was part of the morning routine. On one particular morning an argument escalated to a point where Rachel experienced Terry's true, nature full force.

Rachel walked into the kitchen and poured a cup of coffee before heading to the store. Terry looked up from the magazine he was reading at the kitchen table. The look in his eyes got her attention.

"What?" she demanded.

"I don't want you wearing that," he said.

"I'm in jeans and a T-shirt, who cares?" she asked flippantly.

"I don't like it. Shirt's too tight."

The hair on the back of her neck stood up at his tone. She avoided looking at him.

"So? Let them look. Sex sells," Rachel said, nonchalant.

"I don't want people staring at you all day."

Coffee splashed from the mug as she slammed it on the counter. She'd had enough.

"I am sick and tired of your bullshit! If you don't want me working, then you go."

"But Baby. You know I can't, my back," Terry said, working the sympathy angle.

"Funny. Your back only seems to give you problems when you're working. You're not hurt. You're just full of shit!" She turned to walk out the door.

Terry grabbed her by the hair and pulled her into him. "What did you say, bitch? I told you to go change." He spun her around and pushed her into the hall toward the bedroom. But Rachel lost her footing and slipped, hitting her nose against the kitchen table on her way to the floor. It bled profusely.

"Shit," Terry said, with a tone suggesting it was a big inconvenience for him. Then, as if a switch had flipped, he realized how much he stood to lose. Terry flung himself to the floor beside her and began apologizing repeatedly.

"Baby. Oh baby...I'm so sorry. I'm so sorry...I...I never meant to hurt you." He stroked her hair, trying to offer comfort. "I'll never, never do it again... I'm so sorry, baby..." It wasn't the first time he'd gotten physical, but he'd not yet made her fear him.

Rachel pushed him away, stood up and walked to a mirror. Blood was dripping through her fingers as she held her nose.

"Oh, God!" she said. "I need to go to the hospital."

They told the emergency room doctor she tripped and fell against a table.

For the next several weeks Terry was the textbook boyfriend. Rachel was encouraged. Though she didn't like how it happened, she believed he had finally changed and that everything would be different between them.

But once Rachel recovered and went back to work, Terry reverted back to his old ways. He finally convinced Rachel to sell the store. She did not recover her original investment and once again found herself on the wrong end of another money-losing venture...and things were about to get worse.

Shortly after the store closed, Rachel learned Terry had a child he "forgot" to tell her about. He had not paid child support in over a year and his ex-girlfriend finally came after him. This is why he never held a job for long.

Each time his ex-girlfriend found out he was working, she tried to garnish his wages. It was only after a confrontation between Terry and his ex at their house that Rachel learned of the situation. Terry convinced Rachel it was all his ex's fault since she "trapped" him by getting pregnant on purpose. He turned on the charm and played the victim, begging Rachel to let him "borrow" some money to pay her off. He swore he'd get a real job and pay her back as soon as possible. Against her better judgment, Rachel gave him the money.

Not long afterwards, Terry wrecked his car and lost his means of transportation. Not having enough money to help him get another car, Rachel lent him hers to supposedly go job hunting. He often returned it with unexplained dents and scratches. Terry had serious road rage and would break whatever was in the car when other drivers made him angry. After only a few weeks of sharing, the car looked bad inside and out.

The same pattern continued into Devan's senior year, eventually costing Rachel thousands of dollars. By the time Devan returned from Gainesville, Rachel had spent all her money. Between the businesses and the money she lent or spent on Terry, Rachel was almost broke. With Terry making it impossible for her to maintain a steady income, Rachel was forced to spend her reserves. Out of desperation and in an attempt to make some fast cash, Rachel agreed to lend Terry the last of her money so he could buy some pot for resale. He claimed he could get a good deal. Unfortunately, they didn't even break even.

Terry knew that every time Devan came to Jacksonville he brought pot for Rachel, and Terry was always waiting. After Devan's last visit, Terry made Rachel give all the pot Devan brought for her to him so he could sell it. In Terry's mind, it was found money and he always kept the profits for himself.

Chapter 16

INTERVENTION

After graduating and returning to Jacksonville, Devan learned that Rachel was broke. Out of necessity, Terry let her work so Rachel could continue to support him. But, not in the clubs. Nothing so high profile. Terry's obsessive jealousy forced Rachel to move from job to job. He was even jealous of her family, and when Rachel suggested going to her mother for help, Terry refused, believing her mother didn't like him and would try to come between them. Devan had been back in Jacksonville for over two weeks and saw Rachel only once to give her Ray's present. He hoped they could hang out more over the summer before he jumped into the workforce come fall. But he got the impression she was avoiding him, and he began to worry.

For the past two years, Rachel had been fading out of Devan's life. She wouldn't even come to his last big farewell party. Devan saw right through what Terry was doing to her. In his opinion, Terry was an angry, insignificant nobody with a huge chip on his shoulder. He surmised Terry only had power in his personal relationships, and he used that power to control and manipulate anyone who got close. It was the only way Terry could feel important, like he was "someone." Terry deliberately targeted strong, independent women. The type one would think least likely to fall into such a situation. Devan finally had had enough. Time for intervention. He was tired of waiting for Rachel to call, so he decided to go to her.

As Devan pulled up to the fast-food restaurant where Rachel worked, he noticed her car. *Was that the same car she bought four years ago,* he wondered. *What the hell? It looked all beat up.* Devan saw her as he walked in the door. Rachel was waiting tables in the back of the restaurant, so he asked the hostess to be seated there. When Devan sat down, Rachel walked to him, overcome with joy.

"What are you doing here?" Rachel asked as they hugged.

"You can't seem to make time for me, so I came to see you."

"Sorry. I've been so busy covering for a girl who's been out for the last two weeks." Rachel was avoiding looking at him.

"I didn't know managers waited tables," Devan said, pointing to her nametag.

"They do when they're short-staffed."

Her appearance alarmed him. She looked older. Tired. Devan came straight to the point. "Okay, Rachel, what's up? Why are you avoiding me?"

"I told you, I've been busy and, well...you know Terry," she said defensively.

Devan paused, collecting himself before tearing into Terry. He started to speak when he noticed a bad bruise on her right wrist. "What the hell is that?" Devan asked. His tone startled her.

Rachel looked at her wrist. "Oh, it's nothing. I whacked my arm, that's all." She attempted to change the subject and grabbed her pad and pen. "What can I get you to eat?"

"You can give me an explanation as to what happened to your wrist. And don't bullshit me, Rachel. You know I can tell when you're lying."

Rachel knew Devan was right. It was pointless to try to deny it. She dropped into the booth across from him and let out a long sigh.

The restaurant wasn't crowded. Devan and an older couple were the only people in her section, so she gave him a quick rundown, mostly about Terry's bad temper. He never beat her, but he had gotten violent, to the point of grabbing and pushing her around. She claimed it wasn't his fault. He just got frustrated by things and had a problem controlling himself. She also told Devan that she was broke and that's why she was working there.

"Leave him. He's done nothing but use you and take advantage of you for the past two years. You're his meal ticket!" Devan was losing his temper. "Come on, Rachel. You're better than this," he said, motioning toward the restaurant. "And you're way too damn good for that piece of shit-"

"Devan!" she cut him off. "It's not like that. I, I..."

"What? You still love him?" Devan asked, shocked.

"Well...yeah...I do. I mean I know he's a good guy, if he'd just change and be who he was when we first met."

Devan did his best to remain calm and compassionate. "Rachel, he can't change. This is who he is. It's about possession and control. You're the only thing he actually he owns."

"No," Rachel snapped. She was angry. "You don't know him like I do. If he was only like the guy he used to be, I know things would be better."

"He was never 'that guy.' He pretended to be to get you. Now that he has you, he doesn't need to pretend anymore. This," Devan said as he took her wrist and held it up, "this is who he really is."

The woman Rachel had been covering for walked over to their table.

"I'm really sorry, Rachel. I called this morning to see who was on the schedule and when they told me you were covering for me, I decided to come in. I'm sorry. I didn't know."

"What are you doing here, Darlene? You still have two days of vacation left."

"We had to cut it short. My husband needed to get back, so I thought I'd see if I could come in and make up some hours. So, how about it? Can I take over for you?" Darlene asked.

"Absolutely! And thanks. I'm going home." Rachel smiled with relief and looked at Devan. Darlene left to get her apron and order pad.

"Thank God! I don't think I could have worked another two days of double shifts," Rachel said, relieved.

"I know you're tired and want to go home, but I'm not finished. We need to talk," Devan said. "I'm worried about you."

"We will. But I've got to get some rest and clear my head first."

"I'm going to hold you to it," Devan said, pointing his finger at her. "I'll walk you out."

Standing next to her car, Rachel searched for her car keys. "Where are my keys?" Rachel looked in her purse and then checked her pockets.

Devan pointed through the driver's side window at the console.

"Shit!" she said, hitting the top of her car. "I was in such a hurry to get to work, I locked my keys in the car. Damn it!"

"Do you have a spare set?" Devan asked.

"At the apartment," Rachel shrugged.

"Apartment?" he asked.

"Would you mind?"

"Of course not. Let's go."

Rachel gave Devan directions to her apartment. After running out of money, she and Terry moved into town and rented a small one bedroom in a not-so-nice area. Rachel sensed Devan's concern for his car as they walked toward her building.

"Relax. The only Corvettes in this complex belong to the dealers. Nobody will mess with it."

"Where's Terry?" Devan asked as they made their way up the stairs to her second-floor apartment.

"Working. He's got a job down the street at some construction site. He's had it since I've been doing double shifts."

"Two weeks. That's got to be some kind of a record," Devan joked.

Walking into the apartment, Rachel heard something coming from the bedroom. They froze and looked at each other. Devan grabbed a baseball bat leaning by the front door and motioned for Rachel to get behind him as they headed down the hall toward the noise. Outside the bedroom door they could hear breathing and a thumping sound, like furniture being knocked around.

Devan kicked the door open and went flying in baseball bat poised to smash whomever was in there. He stopped dead in his tracks, both shocked and amused by what he saw. Terry was fucking some girl in their bed. The banging they'd heard was the headboard against the wall.

Not realizing what had happened or who burst in, Terry jumped out of bed, ran into the bathroom, and shut and locked the door, leaving the girl alone.

"Oh, hell no!" Rachel shouted. "You get your sorry ass out here right now motherfucker!" she commanded.

Oh yeah, this is great, Devan thought. *Rachel's back!* He didn't say a word and sat down on the corner of the bed, smiling. "You might want to go. I think this is going to get messy," Devan said to the panicked girl.

"Who are you people?" the girl asked

"I'm that asshole's fucking girlfriend," Rachel said, pointing to the bathroom door. "Who are you?"

"Oh my God! He didn't tell me he had a girlfriend," the girl blurted out.

"Just how long have you two been fucking?" Rachel demanded.

Scared and reluctant to answer for fear Rachel would kill her, the girl looked at Devan.

Still smiling and holding the bat, Devan was enjoying every minute of this. "Go ahead and answer. Don't worry. I have a bat. I'll protect you," he said.

Rachel cut him a don't-fuck-with-me look. Devan tried hard to stop smiling, but to no avail.

"Uh…about…a week," the girl answered. "Look, I'm really sorry. I didn't know. Please believe me! He didn't say anything about you, I swear!"

"We do," Devan said as he picked up her shoes and handed them to her. "Now get dressed and get out."

She pulled the sheet around her as she jumped out of bed and snatched her shoes from him. Devan frowned. She was good-looking and he'd hoped to see the whole package. It would've helped wash the image of a naked Terry running to the bathroom out of his mind. The girl quickly gathered up the rest of her clothes and ran out.

"Get out here, you cheating piece of shit! Your little piece of ass is gone!" Rachel shouted through the door.

Terry slowly opened the door, now wrapped in a towel while holding up his hands, then said, "But, baby…I can explain."

"I don't want to hear it," Rachel snapped.

"Oh, but I do," Devan said, standing and still holding the bat.

Devan was the same height as Terry, but unlike Terry he worked out almost every day, so he had good reason to be cocky. And he was holding a bat. Truth be told, Devan looked forward to beating the shit out of Terry. It was long overdue.

"Devan," Terry said, shifting his attention to him. "I didn't know you were back. What are you doing here?"

"He brought me home to get my keys, if you must know," Rachel answered. "Now get your shit and get out! This is it, Terry. We're done."

"But, baby, let me explain…" She cut him off.

"I don't want to hear it. Not again," she shouted. "This is the last time you do this to me. Leave your keys on the counter and get out!"

"Again?" Devan asked. "He's done this before?" Devan was trying to provoke Terry. He was itching to fight, and he wanted to keep the intensity of the moment going so Rachel would stay pissed.

"Devan, please stay out of this," she said.

"Yeah, motherfucker. Let's see how tough you are without the bat," Terry said.

Devan smiled and dropped the bat behind him. "Okay. Let's go, Terry."

Called out, Terry wouldn't follow through. Women were the only ones Terry ever got physical with.

"No Devan!" Rachel said. "Get out, Terry." Rachel probably saved Terry's life.

Not one to miss a chance to escape, Terry scooped up his clothes and took off. He wouldn't look at Devan as he passed by. They heard the front door slam shut as the keys hit the counter.

Devan sat down on the edge of the bed without saying a word.

Rachel turned to him, half-smiling and with tears in her eyes. "He's gone. Are you happy now?"

Devan walked over to her so fast it startled her. He gently took her by the shoulders and turned her so she could see herself in the large mirror over her dresser.

"Look at yourself! Look at what you've become. What he's made you." Devan turned her back to him. "This isn't the Rachel I know. This isn't you." Devan motioned to the apartment. "And Rachel," he said, pointing to her nametag, "this sure as hell isn't you. So am I happy? Hell yes! You finally flushed that piece of shit out of your life."

"You've always had such an eloquent way of putting things," Rachel said, wiping her eyes and trying to force a smile.

Devan pulled her into him and held her tightly. "I'm sorry. I'm sorry for being such an ass and I'm sorry Terry is an ass. But I'm your best friend and I'm always going to be honest with you, even if you don't like it."

"I wouldn't want it any other way," Rachel said, melting into him.

It felt good being held but it felt even better knowing she had her best friend back.

Chapter 17

PICKING UP THE PIECES

Over the next few days Devan helped Rachel move to a new, much nicer apartment. It was a small one-bedroom located in a working-class complex. The neighbors seemed like good people and several pitched in to help.

Out of necessity and desperation, Terry also relocated. Somehow, he managed to charm his way back into the good graces of the girl they busted him with.

Free from Terry's domination, Rachel was able to breathe. She reflected on their relationship for the first time without Terry telling her what to think or putting things in her head. Rachel finally could see what Terry had done to her, what she allowed him to do to her. She thought about who she was versus who she had become. For the past year and a half, Terry had taken over nearly every aspect of her life. Other than Devan, she had lost contact with all her friends. Even her relationship with her family had been strained by Terry's paranoia. The life Rachel enjoyed prior to Terry was gone, as was her money. Though they did have some good times at first, when viewing the relationship from her new perspective, Rachel realized the sacrifices were heavy. After two years of being physically and emotionally used and abused, reduced, and taken advantage of, it takes a toll on even the strongest person, and Rachel was no exception.

Perhaps as a result of lingering feelings, or the year-plus of constant brainwashing, letting go proved difficult. From Devan's outside point of view it was cut and dried. Terry was a piece-of-shit loser. Period. But for Rachel it was different. Her relationship with Terry had been a huge investment, and to just let go with nothing to show for it seemed like such a waste on so many levels. But letting go is what she needed to do, so she began taking small steps in that direction.

Devan did what he could to help her. He felt bad, even blamed himself. For the last two years he was so involved in his life in Gainesville he and Rachel rarely saw each other. He was angry with himself for not seeing through Terry sooner.

For the first two years Devan was in college, Rachel visited him regularly. But after getting involved with Terry, Rachel stopped visiting altogether. Devan understood she was in a committed relationship and figured Terry found her going to Gainesville difficult to accept, so it was up to him to come to Jacksonville to see her. When the three of them were together everything seemed fine. Rachel and Terry appeared so taken with each other Devan had no reason to believe that they weren't really happy. To Devan, Terry was the type of guy who always had a plan. He spoke with so much enthusiasm, Devan believed he knew what he was talking about. Devan didn't see through Terry's bullshit because he never had reason to look.

It wasn't until after Rachel quit the club and Devan found out that Terry wasn't working that he became suspicious. And it was when Rachel started her many business ventures, only to close them soon afterwards, that Devan begin asking questions. Over time he pressed further, and the more he learned, the more he didn't like the situation. Devan could see that Rachel was being brainwashed and couldn't imagine what it was like being so completely dominated 24/7 by someone like Terry.

Over time, Devan saw the changes in Rachel. She was no longer the confident, strong-willed woman he once knew. Terry was destroying her self-assurance and identity. Terry was the kind of parasite that latches on to a strong host and little by little drains them until nothing is left. From his perspective, Devan saw Terry for the lazy, sorry loser he was, and in a not-so-subtle way told Rachel how he felt.

Because of his intense dislike for Terry, Rachel and Devan saw even less of each other his senior year in college. When Devan did visit,

Terry usually dominated their conversations. Devan couldn't stand him or what he was doing to Rachel. It drove Devan and Rachel's friendship farther apart and brought Terry and Rachel even closer.

For Terry, Devan was dangerous, so he had to proceed with caution where he was concerned. Terry made good progress in driving Rachel and Devan apart, but he knew he was taking chances. By manipulating her, Terry was able to use Devan's dislike for him to his advantage. He put Devan in the same category as her family, convincing Rachel that no one wanted them together; that they believed he wasn't good enough for her. Terry got Rachel to feel sorry for him and, unfortunately, it worked. The harder Devan was on Terry, the more he unknowingly played into Terry's hands.

It was never Devan's intention to cause trouble between them. He just wanted Rachel to think for herself and stop taking everything Terry said as fact. Devan wanted her to challenge him and push back. After all, she had a lot more to lose than Terry did. Devan would question Rachel when they were alone–which was rare–and got her to think about what Terry was asking her to do. But despite the validity of what Devan said, Terry would use Devan's distrust to prove his point that "everyone" was out to break them up when Rachel did question him. Terry's ability to turn things around was a skill he had mastered.

Devan knew that his friendship with Rachel would be different when he returned to Jacksonville. He knew Terry was a part of her life, and like it or not, Terry was a part Devan would have to accept. Fortunately for Devan and Rachel, Terry's infidelity betrayed him, and the timing could not have been better. Catching Terry literally "in the act" was the sobering dose of reality Rachel needed to finally break away and move on. Not one to miss an opportunity, Devan moved fast to prevent Rachel from slipping back into Terry's constricting grip.

It was still early summer, and Devan had no plans to seek employment until the fall. That gave him the entire summer to hang out with Rachel and support her as she rebuilt her life without Terry. After helping her move and get settled, Devan was quick to get Rachel back out into the social scene. The beaches were officially open for the summer season and he felt this was the perfect place to begin.

Devan believed getting Rachel back into the mainstream was the best medicine, and he was right. Within weeks Rachel renewed old friendships and reclaimed her former self. She thrived in the fast paced, high-energy atmosphere the beaches offered. She was happy. Rachel loved people and needed social interaction. Depriving her of that was like keeping light from a plant. The more he and Rachel partied that summer, the faster her self-confidence was restored.

However, this wasn't the end of Terry. After a short separation, Terry realized his new girlfriend couldn't support him in the manner in which he'd become accustomed. Faced with the prospect of actually having to work and support himself for a change, it wasn't long before he was attempting to worm his way back into Rachel's life.

Showing no regard for his new girlfriend, Terry began calling Rachel. Sometimes he would even show up at Rachel's work to talk and try to work things out. Though living with another woman, Terry begged Rachel to give him another chance. Devan found it humorous and enjoyed pointing out how Terry wasn't going to give up the girlfriend until he was certain of Rachel, further proving what a piece of shit he was. Devan was more determined than ever to make Terry's attempts at reconciliation impossible.

Rachel had to keep her job at the fast-food restaurant for the time being. But without the burden of Terry hanging around, life there was different. She liked working with people and felt freer to interact with the customers and be herself. By the middle of summer, she craved something a little more fast-paced, so she got a job managing a small bar and grill not far from her apartment. It was perfect for her—not too much, but fast-paced enough to keep her satisfied.

Terry was not happy and became desperate. The freer Rachel became, the less chance he had of getting her back. Devan tried to be vigilant, but Terry occasionally slipped by him and got to her in person. Whether through phone calls, visits to Rachel's work, or randomly showing up at her apartment, Terry was a constant annoyance.

Terry believed Rachel's job was preventing them from getting back together so he attempted to get her fired by causing trouble, mostly by being loud and verbally insulting other customers at the bar. This usually continued until Rachel either called Devan and he showed up, or she threatened to call the police. Eventually, because of customer complaints, Rachel was forced to explain the situation to her management. They understood -at least for the time-being.

But Terry would not let up and his visits were becoming more frequent. Rachel was getting concerned that her bosses would eventually have enough and ask her to leave. She and Devan began switching cars so Terry would think Devan was there more often. But that didn't work for long. Stalking her the way he was, Terry figured out what they were doing.

Everything came to a head one night when her new bartender, Rob, walked into her office to report trouble with a customer. Having just been hired, Rob was unfamiliar with the situation and had no idea the customer was Terry and that this happened regularly.

"Excuse me, Rachel, but there's a guy out here making a scene. He's pretty drunk and says he's your boyfriend."

"Damn it!" Rachel said, throwing down her pen. "When will he ever get the message! Sorry, Rob, long story. I've got to call a friend to help take care of this."

"Don't bother, I can handle him," Rob said with a confident grin. "Would you like me to throw him out?"

Rob had just spent the last 10 years in the Navy and looked more like an NFL player. Rachel figured his size and presence alone would be enough to scare Terry off.

"That would be great. But could you just help him find the door... and thanks," she added with a smile.

"No problem."

Terry was spinning an empty bottle on the bar top when Rob walked up.

"Time to leave, sir," Rob said.

"I'm not finished with my drink," Terry said, full of liquid courage.

"You are now," Rob said. He took the bottle and tossed it into the trash can behind the bar. He looked at Terry with an intense, cold stare. "Now you can leave on your own or you can leave with my help, but one way or another, you are leaving."

Terry got the message. As Rob escorted Terry to the door, some customers began to clap and whistle. Everyone was getting tired of Terry's nightly visits.

"Oh, and the lady doesn't want you around here anymore, so don't come back," Rob said as a parting shot, knowing it would piss Terry off.

Terry kept walking and never looked back. He was more jealous and angrier than he'd ever been.

The farther Rachel got from Terry, the more obsessed and out of control Terry became. Terry began calling her house, just to hang up when she answered. He drove by at all hours of the day and night, checking to see if she was home and if anyone was with her. He even vandalized her car several times by slashing the tires in an attempt to keep her from going to work. Terry's obsession was dominating his life.

Rob and Devan teamed up as Rachel's bodyguards. They took turns taking her home after work and staying with her or checking on her throughout the day. Rachel appreciated their assistance and felt safer with them around, especially Rob. Rob even changed his schedule so he could work with Rachel more often and keep an eye on her. Sharing a mutual dislike for Terry, Devan and Rob became fast friends and before long, the three of them were spending most of their spare time together.

Rob was a good guy in Devan's opinion, straight up and honest—not a bullshitter. Rob also respected women, which was obvious by how protective he was of Rachel and his willingness to help. Terry eventually stopped coming to the bar. With Devan or Rob always with her, he had no choice but to cower in the parking lot and spy on Rachel from his car. Actually, his girlfriend's car.

As was typical of his jealous nature, Terry assumed Rob and Rachel were seeing each other. He'd been watching them leave together nightly for some time, which only intensified his jealous rage. Terry was convinced the only way to get Rachel back was to get Rob out of her life.

Devan and Rob had a mutual respect for each other and in their spare time began working out together at a health club not far from the bar.

"It's good to have a partner again," Devan said from the bench press with Rob spotting him. "I won't push it when I'm alone."

"That's smart. You can really mess yourself up if something happened. There's a competitive, ego-thing with guys and weights. I can't tell you how many times I've had to pull weights off guys who pushed too far."

"Competitive thing, maybe," Devan said out loud, not really to anybody. He sensed Rob had something on his mind and seemed unsure how to bring it up, so Devan waited for an opening to help Rob get it out.

They switched positions on the bench but instead of getting into position, Rob sat down and finally opened up.

"So, you and Rachel have been friends since junior high?" Rob asked.

Okay, Devan thought, *we're finally going to have the 'how-can-you-two-just-be-friends' conversation.* Devan was used to it and found it interesting Rob hadn't brought it up sooner, especially since they'd known each other for a while now. Devan figured Rob was probably testing the water in an attempt to see how Devan really felt about Rachel. Devan responded in his usual way.

"Yeah. We've been mutual pains in each other's asses for years," he said. "Seriously though, we've been through a lot of shit together and somehow have managed to stay pretty good friends."

"But," Rob said with hesitation, "how can you two just be good friends? I mean she's, pardon the expression, fine as hell!"

Devan smiled because he knew where the conversation was heading. "I know. To tell you the truth, it's strange. From day one we've been like brother and sister. Nothing more."

"You mean you two never did anything together. Ever?" Rob asked.

"Never. The thought is incestuous in a way. We've talked about it and figured this is just how it's meant to be, the brother or sister we never had."

"Doesn't it cause problems when either of you get involved with someone?" Rob asked.

"We're used to it. We've known each other so long now we're just a part of each other. A package deal," Devan kidded. "The way we see it, if someone can't handle it, well, maybe they're not the right person."

There was a long pause as Rob sat thinking about what Devan just said.

"Rachel tends to have more problems from our friendship than I do," Devan continued. "She gives her relationships 100 percent. If they don't work out, it's not from lack of trying on her end. Case in point, Terry."

"I don't know why she put up with him as long as she did," said Rob.

"Well," Devan said, pausing and looking out the windows in front of them, "maybe I do a little." He looked at Rob. "Rachel is one of those people who still believes in everlasting love. She believes that there's one right person out there for everyone. I don't know if she's right, but I hope so, for her sake anyway. She's a good person and could make the right guy very happy. If she ever finds him, that is."

"And you're not the right guy?" Rob asked

"Nope. Not for that mission. Rachel needs someone like her. Someone who believes in love like she does. That's not me. I'm content with the brother role."

"You don't believe in love?" Rob asked.

"I do. Just not to the depth Rachel does."

They finished their sets and moved over to the curl benches where they took up positions next to each other. Devan could tell Rob was deep in thought and he felt pretty confident he knew what it was about. The three of them had spent a lot of time together over the past several weeks. Devan noticed how much alike Rob and Rachel were and how well they got along. Even when Devan and Rachel talked, their conversations were mostly about Rob and how she looked forward to seeing him every day. Devan was sure Rob felt something for her and figured that was why Rob was probing about their friendship. Sensing Rob's hesitation and not being one to tiptoe around such subjects, Devan pressed on.

"What are your feelings toward Rachel, Rob?"

"What do you mean?" Rob said, caught completely off guard.

"Is she someone you want to have a relationship with?"

"Do you think she'd go for someone like me? I mean, I don't think I'm exactly her type..." Rob said, humbly looking down.

"What? You mean you're not an obsessed, stalking loser who constantly harasses women?" Devan kidded.

Rob laughed and looked away, shaking his head.

"If you want to ask her out, I think you should and see what happens."

"Maybe I will," Rob said, more relaxed and upbeat.

"Good luck. And just remember, we're a package deal, so I hope you know what you're getting into."

"Thanks," Rob said, pretending to be concerned.

Later that afternoon Devan's phone rang. It was Rachel.

"Okay, Devan, tell me what you guys talked about at the gym today— everything, and don't leave anything out."

"Why?" Devan asked. "What's up?"

"Rob asked me out on a date. A real date! What should I do?"

"Wow. That was fast," Devan said.

"What was fast? You did talk!" she insisted.

"Nope. Can't tell. You're on your own on this one."

"Devan! You're an ass! Tell me what you talked about!" she demanded.

"I'm hanging up now, Rachel. Have fun."

With Rob and Rachel acting on their feelings for each other, the next few weeks brought them even closer. Rachel and Rob were together as a couple, and they were happy.

Chapter 18

BOILING POINT

Without Devan, Rachel, or Rob knowing, Terry had been observing Rob and Rachel's relationship grow stronger from a safe, unseen distance. He seethed as he saw them leave the bar every night with their arms around each other. Spotting Rob's truck at her apartment filled him with intense burning rage and jealousy.

After weeks of watching them, Terry's rage reached the boiling point. He couldn't stand it another minute and confronted them as they left the bar. Terry verbally assaulted Rachel, calling her a slut and a whore, and accused her of being unfaithful to him. He was saying anything he could think of to insult her and provoke Rob as well as, hopefully, raise doubts in Rob's mind. His rage and desperation blinded him to Rob's 6'4" body of solid muscle.

Being the gentleman and in defense of Rachel's honor, Rob responded by punching Terry in the face with all his 6'4" might, sending him tumbling through the parking lot. Bleeding and clearly rattled, Terry stumbled to his car and took off.

This was exactly the reaction Terry wanted. He went straight to the police and accused Rob of beating him up and told them he could be found at Rachel's apartment. When the police arrived to arrest Rob for assault, Rachel was furious. She argued with the police officers, telling them it was a lie; Terry was the one who really started the fight and Rob was defending her and himself. But the officers had no choice. Terry was pressing charges and Rob was going to spend the night in jail.

Rachel called Devan to tell him what happened after the police took Rob away. Devan agreed to pick her up and find out what needed to be done about posting Rob's bail. When Rachel hung up the phone, she heard her front door close. She turned to find Terry standing in her apartment.

"What are you doing here?" Rachel demanded. "Get out or I'm calling the police," she said, still holding the phone.

"You don't need to do that," Terry said in a cool, calm tone that made her feel uneasy. "I just want to talk."

"No, Terry. I'm finished talking to you. I'm calling the police." As she started to dial the number Terry leaped on her and pulled the phone away, throwing it across the room. He forced her to the floor and straddled her, holding her face down with one of her arms pulled behind her back.

"Get off me!" Rachel yelled as she struggled to get free. She quickly realized it was pointless. He was too strong.

"See bitch, I can take you anytime I want. You're mine and don't forget that," Terry said as he leaned down and licked her cheek. "Like what I did to your boyfriend?" he asked, gloating.

"Get off me, Terry!" Rachel demanded, but her anger only provoked him further and he slammed her head into the floor, causing her to bite her lip and bleed.

"You're hurting me," she said in a softer, victim-like tone, knowing this is what he wanted to hear.

Terry lifted himself off her just enough to roll her over so she was facing him. He kissed her forcefully. Then he wiped the blood off her lip with his finger and smiled a frightening smile. Putting the finger with blood on it in her face, Terry said, "See? Look what you make me do! Remember, bitch, you're mine, and if I can't have you, no one can." He got up and walked out.

Frightened and upset, Rachel ran to the door, locked it, and nervously waited for Devan.

Devan arrived 15 minutes later. When Rachel opened the door, he knew something was very wrong. As she explained what happened,

Devan became very quiet. When he did this, it was because he was doing everything possible to remain calm. Devan finally spoke.

"It appears we underestimated our friend Terry. He's more dangerous than we thought."

"Should I call the police?"

"You could, but you don't look beat-up enough, so I doubt they'll do much. If anything, they'll probably think you're trying to get him back for what he did to Rob."

"Then what, Devan? I can't take this anymore! The phone calls, him driving by all the time, slashing my tires, this shit with Rob. The threats! I'm sick of it! My customers tell me they see him sitting in the parking lot every night...every night! Watching me! And Rob! What am I supposed to do now? Get a restraining order? Yeah, right! And what good will that do? How will that help? I hold it up and say, stop Terry! This piece of paper says you can't come near me."

"It couldn't hurt," Devan said. "But you're right. It offers little real protection." Devan sat thoughtfully for a moment. "I think it's time we deal with Terry in a way he'll understand."

"Devan, I'm scared. This wasn't the first time he's gotten physical, but it is the first time he didn't apologize. He even seemed to like it. He's dangerous. What if he does it again or something worse?"

"There won't be a next time," Devan said.

She looked at him with raised eyebrows.

"I need to go to Gainesville. I need to see a friend."

"Ray?"

Devan smiled.

"Devan, I don't want him....," she paused, "...you know. I just want him to leave me alone."

"I think we can make that happen," he said.

"What do you have in mind?" she asked.

"Let's go get Rob, I'll explain on the way."

The challenge with Terry's type is that people like him who are overly possessive also believe that those they dominate are their exclusive property. This makes getting rid of one such as them (legally anyway) very difficult. If and when the possessive person does go away, it is generally because something better comes along, like another victim.

Devan knew that getting rid of Terry would require extreme measures, so he headed to Gainesville to seek assistance. Knowing Ray had considerable experience in this area, Devan figured Ray was the perfect man for the job.

Devan's original plan was to borrow a few of Ray's men for a little mission he had in mind. But after Devan presented his plan, Ray couldn't pass up the opportunity to participate himself. Ray liked Rachel and this kind of thing really was his specialty.

A few nights later while Rachel was at work, Devan, Ray, and two of Ray's buddies were waiting in the parking lot. Thirty minutes after Rachel went into the bar and grill, Terry arrived and took up his nightly position backed into a space across the parking lot. Facing the bar, Terry could see through the building's large windows unobstructed. A few minutes after he settled into his spot, Devan walked over and knocked on the driver's side window of Terry's car.

"I think we need to talk," Devan said, looking down at him through the glass.

Terry got out and stood defiantly before Devan.

"What are you doing here?" Devan asked.

"That's none of your fuckin' business."

"Come on, Terry. What's your problem? From what I hear you're living with the girl we caught you banging. You've got someone–your choice by the way. It's time you let go. You can't have them both."

"Fuck you, Devan. Rachel's mine and I'll be damned if I'm going to let another man come between us!"

"But it's okay for you to have another woman?" Devan asked. "Listen to yourself. You don't make any sense." Fighting the urge to just deck him and get it over with, Devan kept talking while Ray and his buddies moved into position. Knowing it was useless to try to reason with such an obsessed idiot, Devan pushed more –he was having fun with it. "You have someone. Why can't Rachel be free to move on, too?"

Terry became agitated and started nervously pacing between the cars. Devan pushed more.

"The way I see it, you can't let go. You fucked up and now that Rachel doesn't want you, you want back in, and she won't have that. What's the real reason you want back with her? Is your new girlfriend making you pull your own weight?"

"Fuck you!" Terry snapped and threw a punch. Devan was expecting it and leaned out of reach, only to counter with a powerful punch to Terry's stomach. Ray and his buddies grabbed Terry, gagged him, put a hood over his head, tied his hands behind his back, tied his legs together, and threw him into the trunk of Ray's car. It all happened so fast Devan got the impression Ray had done this before.

"Not bad, guys. I'm impressed," Devan said, nodding with satisfaction.

"It's all in the timing," Ray replied, smiling and wiping his hands together.

Devan went to get Rachel. She arranged to have the night off but went in as part of the setup.

"Any problems?" Rachel asked as they walked across the parking lot toward Ray's car.

"Not so far."

"I feel bad for lying to Rob. Not a good a way to start a relationship."

"I know. But if you don't want him involved, this is for the best," Devan said.

"I can't tell him about our past; the growing and selling and all that. Not yet anyway. I don't know how he'd take it. He's already paid too high a price for caring about me. Hitting Terry not only got him put in jail, but it also got him fired."

"I still don't understand why he was fired," Devan said, confused.

"I know, but the company has a zero-tolerance fighting policy."

"Even though he was defending you?"

"Unfortunately. Even as manager there was nothing I could do."

"Then maybe it's better this way. With Rob at his new job, it gives us time to take care of this little problem," Devan said, patting the trunk of Ray's car. "Anyway, we'll worry about that later. It's show time!" Devan said as he opened the car door for her.

Rob didn't know all the details of Rachel and Devan's real past, their business or about her "smoking" preferences. With the exception of drinking and cigarettes, Rob was more or less clean-cut and looked down his nose at pot smokers and dealers, believing them to be burnouts and losers. He viewed dealers as the lowest form of criminal and deserving of the harshest punishment. Knowing this, Rachel opted not to tell him everything about their past. She knew it could be a problem one day, but for now, she was content with keeping the truth from him.

Devan also knew how Rob felt about drugs and for Rachel's sake, and at her request, he went along with it. Devan liked Rob and, although they disagreed on this subject, Devan felt he was as good a match for Rachel as she was for him. Devan also knew Rob was more than capable of taking care of the "Terry problem" on his own, but also felt Rob had paid too high a price for getting involved. Devan believed, for Rob's sake, that it was probably better to keep him out of it. Besides, who knew what Terry might say? He was linked to their past after all, and it was their past that Devan was planning on using to get rid of him.

Rachel and Devan rode with Ray in the car he'd "acquired" for this mission, while his two buddies followed in a pickup truck. They drove to a friend of Devan's who lived on the river in the next county. His friend had a pontoon boat and agreed to let them borrow it for the evening.

Ray's buddies pulled Terry out of the trunk and carried him to the boat while Rachel, Devan and Ray loaded the other "props." Once everything was on board, Devan started the motor and took them far out into the middle of the St. Johns River.

In this area, the river was three miles wide. While Devan drove the boat, Ray's buddies wrapped Terry in chicken wire and heavy chains and attached four concrete blocks to him. They were quiet as they worked, occasionally saying things like, "Is it deep enough yet?" "How long will it take for the body to be eaten by the fish and crabs?"

Finally, the boat stopped. Devan pulled off Terry's hood. Terry was scared to death.

"I'm sorry it had to come to this, Terry, but I can't think of any other way to take care of someone like you. If you won't get out of Rachel's life on your own, we'll help you," Devan said in a cold, steely tone of voice. "Dump this trash," he said to Ray's buddies.

Terry pissed himself. They all had to fight the urge to laugh.

Struggling, crying, and attempting to beg for his life through the gag, Terry was in a complete panic.

As they dragged him to the edge of the boat, Rachel said, "Wait a minute boys, maybe this isn't necessary. Maybe he can let me go."

Pretending to fight with her, Devan said, "His type never changes. He's a stalker. He's obsessed! No, sorry. This is the only way to get him out of your life for good."

"Maybe you're right. How deep is it here anyway?" Rachel asked turning to look at Ray.

"I don't know, deep enough. Probably 20 or 30 feet. We're almost in the channel. Ought to be a lot of crabs and fish down there to help get rid of the body."

Terry was hysterical. Struggling, begging, and crying uncontrollably, he was desperately trying to plead for his life.

"Crabs eating you, how horrible. I don't know, maybe we should give him one more chance. Maybe, faced with the alternative…" Rachel said, pointing to the dark black water and leaning over the edge of the boat, "…maybe he can change. Let's ask him," she said, looking at Devan.

"I don't know, Rachel. You know he'll say whatever it takes to save his ass," Devan said, annoyed.

"Yeah, maybe. But I can tell if he's lying. Let's ask. If he is, then we'll send him to the bottom," Rachel said, never breaking eye contact with Terry.

"Okay," Devan said with hesitation. "But if he starts yelling throw him in."

One of Ray's buddies removed the gag and Terry immediately began begging Rachel for his life.

"I'm so sorry! Please forgive me. It's all my fault. I'm sorry for cheating. I can let go. I'll get out of your life forever. I'm sorry! Please don't kill me! Please!" Terry pleaded with genuine desperation. "You'll never see me again!"

Rachel knew above all else, Terry was not only jealous and obsessed, but also selfish and self-absorbed. He never loved her. He liked dominating and controlling her. It was, and always had been, about power. When Rachel kicked him out and refused to let him back in her life, losing to a woman was unacceptable. And now, here he was at her mercy. A woman controlling his fate. And not just any woman, but the one he'd been threatening and harassing for weeks. Terry's groveling and hysterical pleading were well worth it, in Rachel's opinion. Who said revenge isn't fulfilling? She loved every minute of having the power and he knew it.

Rachel fixed Terry in her stare. She gently touched her lip where he made her bleed. Then out of nowhere she slapped Terry hard across the face. "That's for hurting me," she said. Rachel then looked at Devan and said, "I believe him. I think he's got the message."

Devan stepped up and got right in Terry's face. "If I ever find out you've made any kind of contact with Rachel or Rob, you'll find yourself back here and on your way to the bottom of the river. Do I make myself clear?" Devan asked. There was no doubt in anyone's mind that he was serious.

"Yes! Yes!" Terry babbled with obvious relief.

"And Terry," Devan added, "just for the record, I don't believe you, so you better not be fucking with us."

With that, one of Ray's boys put the hood back over Terry's head and threw him down on the deck so they could unwrap the chains and wire. When they returned to the dock, they put him back in the trunk and returned him to his car in the bar parking lot. Wet and stinking of his own piss, Terry jumped into his car and took off.

As Terry sped out of the parking lot, they burst into laughter. They'd been holding back and struggling to stay serious all night, but now they could let it out. Everyone laughed hysterically.

"Thanks, guys–I owe you big. Drinks are on me!" Rachel said as she put one arm around Devan and the other around Ray and then motioned for Ray's guys to follow them into the bar.

Chapter 19

THE REAL WORLD

With Terry gone, the summer ended on a high note. Rachel and Rob had each other and were happy. By fall, they were living together, and their relationship continued to grow stronger.

Devan was looking forward to joining the workforce; it was time for that college education to start paying off. He jumped in with both feet and was encouraged by the job opportunities he found in the local paper. Prospects looked good in the financial services industry. As with other overzealous college graduates, Devan soon realized he wasn't going to just walk in and immediately land the perfect high-paying job. Everywhere he applied he was turned down for "lack of experience" as the reason. Even with a degree, most companies preferred people with years of hands-on experience under their belt. It was frustrating. How was he going to get the experience if he couldn't get hired? There were plenty of other jobs available, but they paid considerably less than he expected. As the weeks passed, it became clear to Devan that finding employment wasn't going to be the cakewalk he first thought it would be.

Devan finally settled for an entry-level financial management position with one of the state's largest banks. His salary was much less than he hoped for, but he believed it was necessary for the experience.

The job was easy and boring; he felt it was beneath him. Devan discovered that the old saying about people only working hard enough not to get fired was very true. Not one to be content with just showing up and putting in the hours, Devan wanted to learn. It wasn't long before he stood out–he was doing more and better work than most of his more senior coworkers.

It wasn't about kissing anyone's ass; Devan simply wasn't a clock milker. He figured if he had to waste his time at this menial job then he was damn sure going to get something out of it. He was amazed at how his coworkers seemed so content with the status quo. They constantly bitched and complained about the work and pay, but no one seemed willing to do anything about it. It was almost as if they were obeying some unwritten rule to just accept their fate and not rock the boat. But not Devan. He wanted out of that cubical prison from the moment he entered it.

Naturally, Devan drew the attention of management and within weeks of being hired, he was given a new position. Though it paid better and was more high profile, at first it was just another menial, paper-pushing job. But he didn't care. It was a step in the right direction as far as he was concerned.

Unfortunately, this small rise up the corporate ladder didn't come without consequences. He became the target of vicious rumors and gossip. Being promoted over other long-term employees caused resentment and gave him his first taste of inner-office politics.

Devan had a lot of experience in this arena. Work reminded him a lot of high school. He and his colleagues were there because they had to be, but this time it was to earn a living. The environments were similar also in that both had the popular people, silly little cliques, and a hierarchy structure. And along with it came the creation of fear, intimidation, resentment, and jealousy. To come so far only to go back, Devan often thought to himself. But he knew how to play this game. He drew on his experience and used it to skillfully maneuver around obstacles and manipulate others, proving himself not only to be efficient and productive with the work, but also at dealing with his coworkers.

Devan's new position had him working directly under the manager of his department. As he continued to prove himself, his manager began delegating more responsibility to him. At first Devan was encouraged, believing this would be an opportunity for him to eventually advance. However, he soon found that all was not as it appeared.

The manager Devan worked for recognized Devan's potential and often encouraged him to share ideas and make suggestions for improving the department's productivity. As Devan settled into his new job, his manager became more dependent on Devan and began giving him more responsibilities. It wasn't long before Devan was shouldering the majority of his manager's work. For the most part Devan didn't mind. After all, this is how one gains experience. But as time went on, Devan noticed his manager was using his ideas and suggestions and not giving him any credit. When Devan approached his manager about the situation, he was told to have patience, give it time, your turn will come–the old pay-your-dues speech. Little did Devan know, but he'd run into what would later prove to be a common theme, and obstacle, throughout his working career: entrenched management.

Devan's manager was one of those who was perfectly content with his job. He didn't want more and wasn't interested in upward mobility. He worked hard to get where he was and believed it was far enough for him.

Realizing he'd reached the limits of his advancement, and with the encouragement of his boss, Devan began applying for other positions within the company, only to be repeatedly denied a transfer. It wasn't until a chance encounter with a secretary from a department he'd been trying to get into that he found out why he wasn't getting anywhere. It turned out Devan's manager was blocking his requests. Now Devan understood. For some time, Devan had been doing the majority of the work while his boss was reaping all the rewards. Not one to be used or taken advantage of, Devan quit. Jobs were plentiful and now he could say he had experience.

Devan began bouncing around the job market, finding the same thing everywhere he went, zombie employees either content with or trapped in their dead end, go–nowhere jobs, and entrenched management. His employers always appeared willing to take him under their wing" but they never allowed him to advance.

To some extent, dead-weight middle management feared people like Devan. He was young and aggressive and not content with the status quo. Devan wanted to make a difference, and in the eyes of the 'dead-weight,' world of middle management, he rocked the boat. Those above him saw him as competition, and as it so often is in the corporate world, self-preservation tends to be the order of the day, especially within the ranks of middle management. Efficient and aggressive people like Devan are often seen by the dead-weight as threats, fearing that their own uselessness will be discovered, and they'll either lose their jobs or actually have to do something to justify their benefit to the company.

Devan equated the more useless members of upper management to leeches, and he made enemies. But he also learned to manipulate and skillfully maneuver among these people, and for a time, he was content with playing the game. Devan's salary did increase, but he remained frustrated by the lack of advancement opportunities. Devan realized if you didn't kiss ass or have connections to powerful corporate officials, one's advancement options were severely limited.

Rachel and Rob were also getting tired of the rat race. They had been working in the "real world" much longer than Devan and were burned out. It was time for change, something radically different. Mostly, they were tired of Jacksonville.

Devan could tell they were burned out with the local scene, especially Rob. Having spent 10 years in the Navy, Rob was used to change. It had been a long time since he'd stayed so long in one place. Rachel was also craving something new. She wasn't ready to leave six years ago with Devan when he went off to college, but now times were different, and she was different. Her world as it was then had long since passed her by.

For Rob, deciding to pack up and hit the road was simple. Unlike Rachel, Rob had no family to leave behind. Rachel would be leaving the only life she ever knew. Still, the decision wasn't difficult to make. She and Rob shared the desire to leave and make a fresh new start someplace else.

Devan could tell Rachel and Rob were serious about leaving and he knew it was useless to try to change their minds. He'd been in their shoes. That's what college was all about for him. But he was concerned by the abruptness of their decision. They both had an impulsive nature and when they wanted a change, they just did it, usually with little thought as to the consequences. Over the years, Devan watched as they switched jobs when tired of the work or moved to different apartments simply for a change of scenery. They claimed it kept their lives interesting. Truth be told, Devan sometimes envied their impulsiveness.

Rachel and Rob always appeared so free and happy together. Even when money was tight, and they were barely getting by, it never affected how they felt about each other. Being together was enough for them. Everything else would work itself out.

The 1990's were a decade of change. The internet was fast becoming the rage and Rachel was drawn into its popular appeal. She was constantly amazed by the stories of "instant financial success" that she heard was all directly attributed to the internet. At first it was a side hobby of sorts for her. But as time went by and her enthusiasm for working was diminishing, she started to look more seriously into online businesses as an alternate way to make a living.

While researching different online possibilities, Rachel learned that a friend of hers had moved to Maine and was supplementing his income running several online businesses. When she told him of their plans to leave Jacksonville, he suggested they come up and he'd show her what he was doing. Rob was all in. If need be, he'd take a job on a fishing boat, do construction, tend bar, or whatever was needed. They now had a destination.

"Maine! What's wrong with you people?" Devan snapped after Rachel called to tell him where they had decided to go. "It's freaking cold up there!" He was blown away by her news.

"Wuss. A little cold weather won't kill you," Rachel said.

"Correction! It kills people every year. Maine? Can't Dan come down here and teach you whatever you need to know and then go back?"

"No! That defeats the purpose. We want out of here!" Rachel said.

"Yeah, but Maine? I can't come visit until summer, late summer at that!" Devan complained.

"You're such a wimp!" Rachel joked.

"Yeah, well I don't have mountain blood in me like you do. I was born and raised in Florida. When it gets under 60 degrees I shut down," Devan said.

"You're pathetic! You know we moved here from Virginia when I was eight. I'm just as spoiled by this weather as you, but I'm still excited."

Rachel heard a long sigh on the other end of the phone.

"So when's the big move?" Devan asked.

"Two weeks. Just enough time for us to quit our jobs and get packed."

"Damn. What's the hurry?"

"You know how it is. We just figured if we were really going to do this, then why wait?" she answered.

Devan did know, and he supported them one hundred percent. Jacksonville was a rapidly growing city, but career-oriented jobs were still hard to come by. People were relocating to the city for a variety of reasons, but companies came because of the relatively cheap labor. Devan knew this from firsthand experience. He'd bounced between major banking institutions, insurance companies, and even a brokerage house. They paid considerably less than their counterparts up north, citing that the lower cost of living did not necessitate the same salary requirements.

Devan understood their desire to get away, and to some extent he wished he could go with them. But he also knew this was something they had to do together. For better or worse, this was their experience.

He'd been moderately successful in carving out a niche for himself within the Jacksonville job market, and figured it was just how it was going to be until he got a lucky break. If nothing else, he was getting a shitload of experience.

"You have to let me take you two out for dinner and drinks one last time before you go," Devan said.

"Great! I want something expensive!" Rachel said.

"I'm thinking more along the lines of Taco Bell," Devan joked.

Two weeks later Devan met Rachel at their apartment so he could pick her up for dinner. Rob was meeting them at the restaurant.

"Damn! This place is almost empty," Devan said when he saw the apartment.

"It's all in that big moving truck out front," Rachel said as she looked for her keys.

"So why is Rob meeting us at the restaurant?"

"He's helping one of his coworkers unload some of the furniture we couldn't take with us. The guy needed a couch and since we had three, we gave him one."

"So Rob's towing his truck behind the moving van and you're driving your car. Fun. How long will it take?" Devan asked.

"About 25 hours. I'm not looking forward to it. I hear the area around New York's a bitch. But Rob said as long as we stay together we'll be okay."

Shaking his head, Devan uttered, "Maine. You people are crazy." He opened the front door and motioned for her to go.

After arriving at a restaurant they frequently visited, they went to their usual table in the bar area.

"So how's work?" Rachel asked. Her cocky grin drove Devan nuts.

"Typical day. Same old lying, backstabbing bullshit."

"Better you than me," she teased.

"Be nice. You should pity me. You're leaving me here in this rat race to fend for myself."

"It's my turn to get out of this town for a while," she said.

"Do you think you'll come back?"

"I don't know. Right now, it's a new beginning that we both need," Rachel said. She averted his eyes by looking down at her drink.

"You're abandoning me, never to return," Devan teased back.

"Oh, please! You've got your job. You hate it but it pays well."

Rachel noticed a woman in a group of other women looking in their direction. This wasn't unusual. They were attractive and made a good-looking couple. But it always amazed Rachel how ballsy some women were when she and Devan were out in public together. She wasn't jealous, but it did piss her off. These women had no idea if she and Devan were a couple or not and yet they still flirted.

Devan saw men looking at Rachel –they always did– but he wasn't bothered. He knew she turned heads and he liked it. Devan thought it was good for her self-esteem and he liked being seen with her.

"Besides," Rachel continued, "you won't leave. You like your life here too much," she said, motioning to the group of women across the room looking at them.

"What do you mean?" he asked with a sly smile.

"You know, Devan, there's more to life than sex."

"Wait! Hold up! Stop! Just because you've found Mr. Right doesn't mean you can start lecturing me on the way I live my life!"

"Okay, okay…slut," she said under her breath and smiled.

"I'm hurt."

Devan turned to look at the woman who'd been watching them and made eye contact with her. "Excuse me, I'll be right back. I need to take care of a little business," he said. He headed to the hallway behind the bar where the bathrooms were located. The woman excused herself and headed in the same direction.

Devan returned with a name and phone number on a cocktail napkin.

"Her name is Cynthia and she's here with friends celebrating a birthday."

"And did she ask who I was or if you were with me or anything?" Rachel asked.

"Nope. Somehow, I don't think she cared," Devan said with a devious grin.

"What about you? Did you ask if she had a boyfriend or was married or anything?" Rachel asked.

"Nope. And I don't really care either."

"Just don't catch anything. You don't know where that's been," Rachel said, pretending to be disgusted.

Rob walked over, kissed Rachel and sat down. "So, what have I missed?" he asked.

"Just Devan picking up a slut. Nothing new," Rachel said as she put her arm around Rob and smiled.

"Really? Where is she?" Rob asked, looking around.

"Over there," Rachel said, pointing in the direction of the group of women. "She's the brunette looking in this direction."

"Not bad, man." Rob said, nodding his approval.

"Don't encourage him," Rachel said, rolling her eyes.

They ate and drank until closing. By the night's end, Devan had a pocket full of napkins.

The next morning Rachel and Rob left for Maine and what they hoped would be a new life together.

Chapter 20

STARTING OVER

After two days of driving, Rob and Rachel arrived in Portland, Maine, where Rachel's friend Dan lived. Maine was beautiful. Rachel had never seen anything like it but there wasn't much time for sightseeing. Having acted impulsively, and in typical Rachel and Rob fashion, they had no idea where they were going to live. Finding a place to call home was their first priority.

Dan was a great help. They stayed with him for the first few days and by week's end, they found a house for rent not far away and quickly settled in. They were not even unpacked before Rob found work at a local construction company.

Rachel threw herself into her new mission. She began working with Dan on a daily basis and was encouraged by everything he taught her. In the midst of her training, Rachel realized she needed a better computer, faster and with more memory –a setup like Dan's. Realizing it would be expensive but believing in the potential income producing possibilities of future online business, she and Rob agreed to use one of her credit cards for the purchase. The computer was a large expense and almost maxed out the card, but both believed it was necessary. They hoped that once Rachel got her online business going, they'd be able to pay it off. But the computer proved only to be the first of many unforeseen expenses that would later come back to haunt them.

Shortly after purchasing the computer, another unexpected expense presented itself. Rob was on his way to work when another motorist ran a red light and crashed into the side of his truck. Neither driver was hurt, but the truck was a total loss, and the insurance company would only give him $2,500, claiming the age and condition of the truck didn't justify more. Now they needed another vehicle.

Believing in their potential income generating abilities, either through Rachel's online endeavors or Rob's work, they took the plunge and bought a brand-new four-wheel drive Dodge Ram pickup. Rachel soon discovered that a new computer alone would not be enough to meet her needs. She needed additional accessories, all sold separately of course, and those additional expenses were put on yet another credit card.

As summer gave way to fall and winter, Rachel and Rob realized they were extremely unprepared for a Maine winter. Both needed complete winter wardrobes, especially Rob since most of his work had him outdoors in all types of weather conditions. Within months of moving to Portland, they racked up a great deal of debt, but neither was concerned. They believed it was necessary to secure a better future. At first, the debt did not appear to be a problem. They were able to make the truck payments and the minimum monthly credit card requirements. But like thousands of other Americans, living so close to the edge was only pushing them closer to the inevitable credit card trap.

As winter set in, their expenses continued to add up. About six months after arriving in Maine, they got an unexpected guest–Rob's brother, Jeff. Out of the blue Jeff called and asked if he could come stay with them until he got back on his feet. He had just left a bad marriage, lost his job, and was basically homeless. Being the generous people they were, Rachel and Rob agreed to let him move in as long as he helped with the expenses. After arriving it was obvious Jeff was also unprepared for Maine winters. Rachel and Rob bought him the necessary clothes he needed, adding even more to their growing debt.

By the end of their first year, Rachel began to worry. The internet businesses weren't making the kind of money she hoped. Dan's sites were mostly adult-oriented and at first she didn't want to go this route, but out of necessity she had to. Still, the money just wasn't there. It was like chasing a pot of gold at the end of a rainbow. Rachel created online adult sites and sold a wide variety of products, but the money hardly justified the time and expense required in keeping the sites going. The "get rich quick" gimmicks and stories associated with the internet just didn't seem to be in the cards for Rachel.

Rob and Jeff were also struggling. Both were working construction, mostly for convenience of transportation, and both were making good money, when they worked. Work was weather dependent, and this particular winter was proving to be one of the worst in recent history. Record snowfall and low temperatures stopped all construction for extended periods of time. The longer the guys went without steady income, the more they were forced to use Rachel's already overloaded credit cards, exceeding authorized limits. Bills began spiraling out of control.

Having maxed out four cards, the interest and penalties kicked in. With insufficient income to cover all cards, plus the truck payment and their living expenses, they were forced to choose between what got paid and what didn't. Most of their accounts were frozen, but the interest and penalties continued to swell their debt. The situation had become serious, and out of desperation, Rachel finally asked Devan and her mother if she and Rob could borrow some money. They agreed to help. Embarrassed, Rachel didn't tell her mom or Devan just how bad the situation really was, so the money they loaned her only helped temporarily.

By the spring, all three were again working more or less steadily. Rachel had abandoned the internet and found a job in Portland. By late spring, they were able to start paying down their debt. But once again, fate intervened to shake things up.

While Rachel and Rob were in Jacksonville for a visit that summer, her sister and brother-in-law claimed to know an acquaintance who ran a landscaping business that generated in excess of a million dollars a year. They told Rachel and Rob that this guy started out as the sole operator and within a couple of years his company had grown so big that he now had multiple crews and still couldn't keep up with demand. Encouraged by his success, Rachel's sister and brother-in-law were willing to front them the money to start such a business, but preferred to remain silent partners and let Rob and Rachel do the work and run the company.

They liked Maine and were finally making progress paying down their debt, but they couldn't pass up the opportunity to own and run their own business. So, by the end of their second summer, Rob, Rachel, and Jeff moved back to Jacksonville. Rachel and Rob believed owning their own business would make it possible to pay off what they owed faster. However, they didn't anticipate the initial growing period and startup costs. The unexpected expenses pushed them back into massive debt again.

Out of pride and embarrassment, Rachel and Rob didn't ask anyone for help this time and quickly found themselves sliding back into the interest and penalties trap. Then, to make matters worse, Jeff decided to leave shortly after they arrived in Jacksonville. With mounting bills, the tension of three adults living together was reaching a breaking point. Rachel and Rob were relieved to have Jeff gone, giving them time to themselves. Jeff still owed them for all they had done for him, but Rachel and Rob decided to let it go, which put even more pressure on them to get things under control.

After a lengthy start-up period, the business began to grow. Rob worked 12+ hours a day, constantly pushing himself to his physical limits. Rachel helped where she could, mostly in sales and bringing in new accounts. But no matter how hard they worked, the money coming in was never enough. Rachel was forced to take on a second job. She and Rob became slaves to their past and present debt. It seemed to them that there was no way out of the vicious cycle.

Finally, Rachel told Devan how bad their debt was. He offered to help where he could but couldn't provide much in the way of financial assistance. While Rachel and Rob were in Maine, Devan's frustration with the lack of advancement opportunities became unbearable. He dropped out of the financial services rat race to take a research and manufacturing position with a local startup. He hoped by getting in on the ground floor he'd be able to grow and advance along with the company. The pay was considerably less than he was used to, but he hoped it would only be temporary.

By his second year, Devan had advanced, but only to a point. By all appearances, the company didn't believe in promoting from within. He continued to prove himself, but he again ran into obstacles. Being a small company and valuing the few experienced employees they had, Devan became trapped. They refused to promote him because he had become too valuable where he was. Instead, they chose to build around him.

Devan was also working 12+ hours a day and pushing himself to his physical and mental limits in an attempt to help the company grow and prosper. But his efforts only succeeded in further trapping him and preventing his advancement. And, to make matters worse, the company was built around a core family structure. Devan soon realized that if you weren't related, your opportunities were limited. He became frustrated… again.

Devan couldn't provide much financial relief to Rachel and Rob so he would call Rob on Fridays and offer to help with his landscaping jobs if Rob was shorthanded. Devan was miserable in his current job and actually looked forward to helping Rob in his free time.

"I'm free tomorrow, so what's the plan?" Devan asked when Rob answered his phone. "I'm offering my services at a very generous rate this week."

"I'll buy you a drink," Rob said.

"Only one?" Devan questioned.

"Okay, two."

"Now we're talking. So, what's on the schedule?" Devan asked.

"We've got the theater in the morning –and I stress morning. You know, that time between dawn and noon, so make sure you're up. Then a few residential jobs. Should be a short day."

"Morning? I need a better union," Devan kidded.

"Hey man, you offered. Besides, we can only do the theater before they open, so we have until 11:00 to get it done. The earlier the better," Rob teased.

"How early is early?" Devan asked with dread in his voice.

"Six…a.m." Rob answered, waiting for Devan to start complaining.

"You're killing me Rob…come pick me up."

"Good thing you're free labor. I'd hate to think how much I'd have to pay to get your lazy ass up every morning," Rob joked.

Devan pretended to bitch, but he didn't mind. His present job had once again lost its initial excitement. With limited opportunities for advancement and positions available, the paranoia, backstabbing, and infighting was worse than he'd ever seen. People were constantly fighting among themselves to keep control of whatever they could in order to have some sense of importance. Devan was able to steer clear and rise above most of the internal bickering. Still, something about this company hooked him early on and he wanted to ride it as far as he could. By staying out of the drama and infighting, Devan was finally promoted to a more prominent position above several longer-term employees. His self-confidence and professional attitude helped to ease tensions and grow the position despite the constant efforts of others farther up the management structure trying to hold him back.

It also helped that Devan, unlike many of his colleagues, could see through management's game. The more preoccupied his disgruntled coworkers were with the infighting and their petty personal issues, the less likely they were to demand from management better pay and promotions. Management encouraged this behavior, fearing the day when the employees would see through the bullshit and realize how much power they really had. The more Devan's coworkers squabbled and bickered with each other, the more they were playing right into management's hands.

Devan knew his rapid advancement had been part of management's game. By being promoted, he took a lot of heat and was the focus of bitter resentment. But Devan knew how to use his personality and experience to turn attitudes to his favor by making allies with key personnel. Knowing he was invaluable to the company and not really having anything to lose, he began using his power and position to benefit himself and his coworkers. Over time, and after some spirited public clashes with management, his colleagues regarded him as somewhat of a "champion of the people."

Devan knew his time was limited. He enjoyed exposing the incompetency of those above him as well as defending the actions of his colleagues when needed. Devan knew he "rocked the boat," but for the time being his superiors had no choice but to put up with him. He was the best at what he did, and he knew it, and so did management. Still, one way or another Devan figured he'd soon be out. He asked himself every day, is this it? Is this the best he could hope for —to always to be a pawn in someone else's game? Devan could not bring himself to accept that his future was to bounce from job to job, always looking for that "lucky break," only to find the same shit everywhere he went. There had to be more to life than this. There had to be a better way. The so called "real world" wasn't what he'd hoped it would be. So far it was proving to be very disappointing.

PART FOUR

Chapter 21

ZONE 23

Rachel and Rob struggled financially to grow their business, but at least it was theirs. They were their own bosses and didn't have to deal with company politics. Devan enjoyed helping them when he could, even with the work being intense manual labor. For Devan the work was real. His efforts were rewarded with genuine gratitude and appreciation, and he felt like he helped make a difference.

Promptly at 6:00am, Rob pulled up to Devan's penthouse apartment on the river. Devan and his brother had moved into the apartment after his brother returned home from college. Together they could afford the rent, but alone it would have been difficult. The apartment was the perfect bachelor pad and ideal for the two of them. Rob laughed out loud as Devan walked out of the building. There was no mistaking that Devan was not a morning person.

"Good morning!" Rob said, full of energy.

"It's a good thing I like you. Somehow, some way, one day you'll owe me big," Devan said as he leaned against the truck door and fell back to sleep.

The theater was Rob's largest commercial client. It was a huge multiplex located off a major road on the city's Southside. It was a recent addition to the area and was still mostly surrounded by forest and swampland. A large mall had also just opened not far away on the same side of the road. The entire area was on the verge of being developed and was expected to grow rapidly over the next decade.

"Wake up Sleeping Beauty," Rob said as he parked the truck and equipment.

"What's the plan?" Devan asked, stretching and trying to wake up.

I'll mow while you blow off the lots. I've also got to cut that front hedge and bag the cuttings. I should be finished by the time you're done. After that, we have to test the sprinkler system. The manager said some heads are broken. I need to get a count so I can get replacements."

"Great. I can hardly wait," Devan said, still stretching.

"Rachel's right. You're pathetic," Rob kidded as he handed him the blower.

"Thanks."

They finished mowing and cleaning the parking lots in no time and began testing the sprinkler system. There were 23 zones spread over multiple acres, so they used their cell phones to communicate. Rob stayed at the control box and activated each section while Devan drove to the different zones and marked the broken heads with orange utility flags. When Rob activated zone 23, the last zone, Devan couldn't find it.

"Are you sure it's on?" Devan asked Rob over the phone.

"Green light's on so it should be running."

"Well, I've been all over the lots and still don't see any sign of it."

"The panel says it's running. Look again."

After driving around the property two more times Devan still couldn't find it.

"I don't see any sign of it, Rob. It's just not here."

"I guess it's possible they never put it in," Rob said. "The box looks like they planned for at least three more zones but they never installed them."

"Great, mystery solved. Look, it's almost eleven so I'm going to pick up the bags of cuttings and start dumping them."

"OK, good. I'll finish resetting the timers and then come help."

Minutes later Devan was dumping lawn cuttings in the woods directly behind the theater. He heard water running and saw mist rising from somewhere deep in the woods. The road running in front of the theater and mall connected two of Jacksonville's more prominent areas of town. But with the exception of these two structures the area was still mostly undeveloped. Curious, Devan pushed his way through the thick undergrowth and stumbled onto a huge field totally surrounded by dense forest and swampland with a large retention pond at one end.

By Florida law, new structures over a certain size are required to incorporate retention ponds into their plans. The theory is that the ponds help drain off and filter excess water, purifying it as it sinks into the ground. A large structure like the theater and adjoining parking lots were required to include a retention pond or ponds into the design.

The theater had two known ponds flanking the property, one at each end. Rob and Devan knew about the two ponds since a majority of the landscaping work required keeping these areas maintained. Each pond and its surrounding area formed a sprinkler zone. As far as Devan and Rob knew, these were the only two ponds on the property.

Devan was surprised to find a third retention pond and even more puzzled by the large clearing off to its right. "Zone 23," he said out loud. "But why is this here," he wondered. He called Rob. "Do you still have 23 on?"

"Yes. Why?" Rob answered.

"I think I found it. There's another retention pond back here, at least twice as big as the others with a large clearing next to it. It looks like it was supposed to be another part of the parking lot or something."

Devan met Rob behind the theater and led him through the woods to the pond and clearing. They were aware that the property had changed ownership several times prior to the theater's construction and figured the plans must have changed, causing this section to never get finished.

"Mystery solved. When John gets back next week, I'll tell him what we found."

"Being manager, you'd think he'd know," Devan said.

"He's only been here a few months. I'll see if he wants us to shut it off permanently. We'll probably have to dig up the pipes and cap them."

"Swell," Devan said. "More work for us."

They finished the theater and moved on to the residential yards. With two people, the work went much faster and by 1:30 they were finished.

Before dropping Devan off, Rob made good on his promise and treated Devan to drinks and lunch at a bar near his apartment. The TV above the bar was on one of the local news channels. Hot and tired from the long morning of physical work, their attention was drawn to a news story about several dozen bales of marijuana washing up on a beach south of St. Augustine. This occurred more frequently than most people knew, but only made the news when it happened in such large quantities.

"I wonder how much was picked up or just disappeared before it was reported?" Devan asked

"Or will disappear," said an older, well-dressed man in his fifties sitting next to them.

"What do you mean?" Rob asked.

"That kind of thing happens all the time," Devan said. "Drug runners dump their loads if they think they're about to get busted. Some even dump at certain places so it will be picked up by others waiting on the beach. I've even heard some people will swim way out in dive gear to make the pickup. Most of the time things go smoothly unless, of course, they have problems like the Coast Guard or bad weather, and are forced to dump it early. Then…well, there you have it," Devan said, pointing to the TV. "It makes the news. I imagine people on the beach take a lot of it for themselves. Finders keepers," he added.

"Even a lot of what the cops get eventually finds its way back on the streets," added the older man. "It just disappears out of evidence one day. The money's too good even for the cops to pass up."

Maybe a little lonely, or just wanting to brag, the older man continued. "I knew a guy 20 years ago who did it. He made thousands on every drop. All he had to do was pick it up off the beach on certain mornings and take it to some designated place. Mexican weed is what we used to call it," the man said.

"I wish I could get a job like that. I'd do it a few times for some quick cash," Rob said.

Devan's jaw nearly hit the bar, but he remained composed. He knew Rob didn't approve of drugs and hated that Rachel smoked pot. When she finally confessed, Rob didn't like it, but accepted it when she told him she only smoked occasionally.

"Yeah, me too," said the older man. "I guess you have to know people in that business. I know my buddy put his two kids through college doing that. I wonder how much they make these days?" the older man said.

Devan wondered why it was called "Mexican weed," especially in Florida. Most of what was smuggled in came from the islands in the Caribbean or South America. Ray referred to this product as "the imports" and its overabundance was one of the reasons Ray and his partners began specializing in a higher quality product.

Devan sat quietly listening while Rob and the older gentleman continued their conversation. He felt relieved after hearing that Rob's attitude toward "pot" seemed to have mellowed. Maybe now, if his and Rachel's pasts were ever exposed, Rob wouldn't take it as badly as Rachel feared.

Later that night Rachel called Devan to vent.

"I'm so pissed," Rachel said when Devan answered the phone.

"Why? What's up?" Devan asked.

"Jay, you know, my supposedly 'reliable hookup' fell through -again! He claims he almost got shot or some bullshit."

"Losing Jay would be such a loss to society," Devan kidded.

"Hey! Since you hardly go to Gainesville these days, he's all I've got."

"So what happened this time?" Devan asked.

"He said the guy he buys from pulled a gun on him; thought his buddy looked like a cop or something. Just because he almost gets shot is no excuse for not getting me my shit!"

"You just can't get good help these days," Devan said. They both laughed.

"It was so much easier when we grew it ourselves. Those were the days. I still run into people who ask if I can get them something. It happens all the time," Rachel said.

"I know what you mean. It happens to me, too."

"I could really use that money now. We're in debt up to our eyes and it never seems to get any better. No matter how much we pay, the interest and penalties keep killing us. We can never get ahead!" Rachel complained.

"I can believe it. That's the scam of credit. They first hook you with the bait, easy credit, then reel you in and trap you the instant you get into trouble. You constantly find yourself struggling just to stay afloat. You're not alone, Rachel. There's a multi-billion-dollar industry built around people just like you. They don't want you getting ahead. They count on you staying trapped and in their debt."

"It's just not right, Devan. I know it's our fault for getting so bad off but if we could just pay what we owe with a fair interest rate it would be so much easier. At this rate we'll never get out of debt."

"Welcome to the real world my friend."

The following afternoon while over visiting his parents, Devan went out into the backyard and walked around the pool. He smiled, remembering his and Rachel's growing days as he looked at the overgrown flowerbeds and the lot behind his parent's house. The old woman who owned it died several years ago and the property was split up and resold. The jungle was gone, and two half-million-dollar homes stood in its place.

"Those were the days," Devan said out loud as he stood on the pool deck, looking around.

The money, the life, and the action, it all seemed so long ago, like another time and world. Devan began wondering if they could do it again. Maybe this time on a smaller scale, something to give them a little extra income for a while.

Devan had long since spent the last of his money and often found himself living from paycheck to paycheck. He made a decent enough income, but he had expensive tastes. Outwardly he appeared to live a privileged life, but it was only an illusion. The money he was making was never enough.

Since becoming bored at his current job, he'd been trying to save money so he could eventually move out of town. Devan was tired of Jacksonville and was convinced a fresh start someplace else was what he needed. Unfortunately, it seemed no matter how hard he tried to save, something always came up.

Maybe growing again is the answer, Devan thought to himself as he looked out over the pool. The market was definitely there. Maybe they could do it again, but where to grow was the question…certainly not at his parent's house. His apartment was also out of the question for obvious reasons. *No,* he thought. *It has to be somewhere else, somewhere not connected to anyone.* Then it hit him: Zone 23! He grabbed his cell phone and immediately called Rachel.

"Can you meet me for a drink later? We need to talk, but I think you'll want to leave Rob at home for this discussion," Devan said excitedly.

"Okay… But why not Rob?" Rachel asked puzzled.

"I'll tell you later."

"I'm intrigued. 9 o'clock at the bar by your place?" she suggested.

"Perfect. See you then."

When they met, Devan told Rachel his idea and she agreed. The clearing behind the theater would be perfect. It wasn't connected to anyone so if it was discovered they'd be less likely to get busted. They were excited and began planning how they'd grow and distribute. Since it was early spring, they would have a three-to-five-month window before anything would be ready to sell, giving them time to plan and set up a distribution network. Rachel figured she'd get back into the club scene, as greater visibility would help re-establish old contacts and bring new ones. Devan would also re-establish connections, but mostly he'd focus on what he knew best –growing and caring for the crops. It was time to use some of that informal education he picked up in Gainesville.

"The way I see it, we only have two real problems, Rob and Ray," Devan said.

Rachel shook her glass, spinning the ice cubes. "I think together we can handle Rob, but Ray," she paused, "that might be more difficult."

"Time I take a trip to Gainesville. A diplomatic mission of sorts," Devan said.

"Do you think Ray will be okay with us going back into business?" Rachel asked, hopeful.

"I'm sure we'll have to make a deal with him, but he'll probably be cool about it," Devan answered. "What about Rob? When should we share this little plan of ours with him?"

"No point in delaying," Rachel said as she grabbed her purse off the seat next to her, then motioned for Devan to get up.

"No point in delaying, indeed. It helps that we're both a little drunk too," Devan said. "Let's go."

Devan and Rachel walked up the sidewalk to her ground floor apartment.

"Last chance to back out. Once we tell him it may open the door to a lot more that'll need explaining," Devan said as they stood outside the apartment door.

"I know, but it may also be the best chance for us to get out of this financial mess and have a better life. For all of us to have a better life," she added.

When they went inside, they found Rob in the living room watching television. Rachel walked over and turned it off.

"Rob, honey, we need to talk. Devan and I have something we need to tell you."

Rob slowly sat up. "There's something going on between you two, isn't there?" he asked angry.

Devan rolled his eyes and dropped down on the couch.

"No! And I can't believe you would think that, Rob!" Rachel said.

Devan cleared his throat. "No, Rob, it's not that. But you probably still won't like what we have to tell you," he said.

"I'm listening," Rob said.

"I'll get right to the point." Devan paused. "Rob," Devan started as he stood up, "Rachel and I were at one time–"

"–In high school!" Rachel interrupted.

"Yes." Devan took a deep breath and continued. "In high school Rachel and I were two of the biggest marijuana dealers in town. We not only sold pot, but we also grew and processed it. And Rob," Devan said, pausing and looking directly at him, "we made a fortune."

"So why do you two feel the need to confess your past to me now?" Rob asked.

"Because we want to use our past to give us all a future," Devan answered. "More to the point, we want to go back into business for a while."

"Long enough to get us out of debt," Rachel quickly added.

"Doing what? Selling drugs?" Rob asked.

"Well..." Rachel started, but then stuttered in her response, startled by the harshness of his voice.

"That's exactly what we want to do," Devan said, unshaken by Rob's anger. "And we need your help."

"Me? You want me involved in this? Why? I don't even like her smoking that shit!" Rob said as he got up and walked across the room.

"Look, Rob, let me put it like this. You're both in debt to the tune of about $60,000 and show no real sign of getting it under control. You bust your asses and despite all your efforts, you barely make a difference in paying down what you owe."

"True," Rob said, "but in time we'll be better off."

"Maybe. But do you really want to keep working at this pace for the next however many years just to reach a zero balance?"

Rob got quiet and sat down in a chair across the room. "So, what are you proposing?" he asked.

"One cash crop. One cash crop is all it'll take to get you two out of debt and give us all some real money for a new start."

"It'll only be for a little while," Rachel added. "Just long enough to get us clear and help Devan save so he can get out of here."

"One crop could pay off all we owe?" Rob asked. He was skeptical.

"Yes," Devan answered. "And then some."

"And what part do I play in this?"

"The clearing behind the theater is the perfect place to grow. Don't tell John you found it. He'll never know. Give us until the end of summer and then you can tell him," Devan said.

"We'll be debt free by the end of September," Rachel said as she walked over to him.

How much can one crop really be worth?" Rob asked Devan.

Devan looked at Rachel and gave her a cunning smile before answering Rob.

"It depends on how much of the clearing we use. Thousands to hundreds of thousands by the time it's all over. Who knows?" Devan said.

"No shit?" Rob was stunned. He wasn't sure he heard Devan right.

"No shit," Devan said, smiling back.

Rob was thoughtful for a moment; he couldn't believe what he was hearing. After what seemed like an eternity of contemplation he responded. "Okay, I'm in," he said.

Devan turned to Rachel. "Well now that that's settled, I guess Ray's next."

"Who's Ray?" Rob asked.

"Oh, Rob," Rachel said and patted him on the shoulder. "We've got a lot more to tell you."

Chapter 22

JAX IS BACK

Devan called Ray the following morning and asked if he could visit. He told Ray he had an idea for some future "business" and wanted to get his opinion. It had been nearly a year since they last saw each other, and Ray was happy to hear from Devan. He agreed and invited Devan down for the weekend, not only to discuss his ideas, but also to meet his son. Since Ray had gotten married about a year and a half ago, Devan began scaling back his weekend visits. He wasn't comfortable in the "third wheel" role. Brandy, Ray's wife, was great and they all got along well. She and Ray had grown up together and were childhood sweethearts. Shortly after Devan returned home from college, Brandy moved back to Gainesville, and they'd been together ever since. She knew his business, but Ray insisted she not be involved for her own sake. Brandy accepted who Ray was as a part of their lives and had learned to live with it.

After Devan arrived and settled in, Ray took him on a tour of the new properties he'd acquired along the hilly southern edge of his ranch. By all appearances, Ray seemed to have mellowed since getting married, but Devan knew that underneath the guise of marital bliss and fatherhood he was still the businessman everyone knew and most feared.

"So, what's on your mind?" Ray asked as they drove down a bumpy dirt road on their tour.

Devan wasted no time getting to the point.

"We want back in," he said as he gazed out the window at the vast expanse of rolling green hills stretching out before them.

Ray stopped the truck on top of the hill they were climbing, giving them a breathtaking, panoramic view of his southern border. Devan couldn't believe this was Florida.

"So, Jax is back," Ray said smiling. "I knew you couldn't stay out forever. You're a natural grower. It's in your blood."

"That depends," Devan said. He paused and looked directly at Ray.

"On what?" Ray asked perplexed.

"You. We don't want to step on your turf this time. Not without your permission, of course," Devan added with a cocky smile.

Ray always liked Devan. He especially admired his genuine lack of fear when around him. Devan's asking permission was a sign of respect and Ray was appreciative. "Welcome back, buddy. It's about fuckin' time!" he said, slapping Devan on the shoulder. "So, how's life in the 'real world' these days?" Ray asked. He cracked himself up.

"Funny, Ray. Fuck you!" Devan said, shaking his head.

"At least you gave it a try. And your timing is perfect. We've been scaling back our operations over the past year to focus only on the high-end products."

"Why?" Devan asked, surprised. "You guys own this market."

"Between my land, my parents' land, and a co-op of other farmers I've organized, we're doing pretty good growing legitimate crops. And now, with the wife and kid, well," Ray paused and motioned to the land around them, "I'm looking to go more legit."

"You?" Devan was stunned and not sure he heard him correctly. "Legitimate?"

"What, I can't give the 'real world' a try?" Ray teased. "But seriously, my partners agree. We've had a good run. Between the three of us we have millions stashed away in accounts around the world. I don't really need this farming shit, but I like it. It's in my blood. Anyway, there's going to be a noticeable shortage in product soon. Being in the right place at the right time could prove to be very profitable for you."

"Wow…," Devan said.

"Who knows? Maybe one day you'll be as big as me. Maybe even bigger," Ray said, enticing Devan with the idea.

"Doubtful. We're looking for one big score. Just enough to get us back on our feet again."

"Just one?" Ray asked. "That's what I said many years ago and look at me now."

"Yeah, look at you now," Devan said. "Going legit! I'll believe that when I see it."

Ray and Devan spent the rest of the day strategizing and planning. Devan told Ray what he had to work with and what he hoped to accomplish. Ray didn't ask for details. He understood the rules better than anyone.

"Sounds like what you need is some good old-fashioned, hardy soil stock. I can help you there," Ray said. Devan wondered what he had in mind.

Devan offered Ray a percentage of their crop in exchange for some seeds, but Ray surprised Devan again. After finishing their tour of the new properties, Ray took Devan to one of his more secluded labs.

Ray parked his truck outside an old, deserted barn overgrown with trees and vines. To the average passerby, it looked as though it might collapse at any minute. After passing through two sets of double doors they entered a large dry air-conditioned room with eight floor-to-ceiling fireproof safes. Ray worked the combination of one and opened it. He pulled out a jar half-filled with seeds and tossed it to Devan.

"Here's a getting-started present from me to you. Good luck, buddy."

Devan caught the jar with both hands.

"Ray, I can't just take this. Let me pay you something–a percentage of sales–something. This could potentially be a lot of money," Devan said, still looking at the jar, mesmerized by its contents.

"Consider it a gift and let's leave it at that. Besides, I've got plenty more." Ray opened both doors of the safe, exposing hundreds of jars filled with seeds. All marked, dated, and labeled. He and his partners had been creating new, better, and hardier breeds over the years.

"Jesus, Ray, that's millions, hundreds of millions, in potential crops! Are all these safes like this one?" Devan asked. He could hardly believe what he was seeing.

"Yep. We call this the nursery. That's why we keep the temperature and humidity constant. These seeds are the best of the best. What you see here is used for breeding and backup stock. There's some good soil-based stock here: potent and hardy. What you're holding is the best of our new and improved cornfield variety. It grows thick and fast. For outdoor natural light, it's the best. It should do very well in the area you have to work with," Ray said. Ray was always confident in his seed stock.

Devan was speechless. He stared at the jar. "Thanks Ray," he finally managed to say. "We owe you big for this."

"No, you don't. But promise to keep in touch more often and let me know how things are going. I'll be your unofficial advisor and consultant," he said. "And if you need help moving product let me know. My Jacksonville people will need a new supplier. I can put in a good word for you if you'd like."

"Thanks Ray. We might just take you up on that," Devan said as he stared into the jar of seeds, imagining the future.

Devan went straight to Rachel and Rob's when he returned to Jacksonville Sunday afternoon and walked into their apartment with his overnight bag slung over his shoulder.

"Well? What did Ray say?" Rachel asked. She had been anxiously waiting to hear how Devan's visit was going all weekend. "Is he okay with us going back into business?"

Devan didn't respond. He put the bag on their coffee table and pulled out four jars filled with seeds.

"Holy shit!" Rachel gasped. "How much does he want for all this?"

"All he wants is for us to stay in touch."

"Free?" Rachel asked. She wasn't sure she completely understood.

Devan said nothing. His smile answered her question.

"Is it...well...good?" Rachel asked.

"The best of the best," Devan answered.

"There's hundreds of thousands, maybe millions of dollars, worth of seeds here," Rachel said, looking at the jars, lost in thought.

Hearing that, Rob perked up with interest. "Millions?" he asked.

The room stayed silent for minutes. The three of them stared at the jars lined up neatly on the coffee table.

"So, when do we plant?" Rob asked.

Chapter 23

THE FIELD

Devan was looking forward to helping Rob at the theater the next weekend. He even took that Friday off so they could get an early start. The manager, John, liked Rob's work and approached him a few weeks earlier to do some re-landscaping around the property. Devan saw that as the perfect opportunity to prepare the lot. Re-landscaping would give them all an excuse for being there several days in a row.

By 6:00a.m. Friday morning Devan and Rob were at the theater. They planned to clear as much of the lot as possible in the early hours before John and his employees arrived. They took the weed-eaters and several dozen orange utility flags with them as they made their way through the dense undergrowth leading to the clearing. Not knowing where the sprinkler heads were prevented them from using the mowers.

Rob and Devan cleared the heavily weeded area by cutting the weeds to their roots. As they uncovered sprinkler heads, each one was marked with a utility flag. The field was approximately 400 feet long by 120 feet wide. It took an hour to clear just a third of it. To save time, they decided to cut the weeds and let them lay where they fell. This would create a mulch and aid in preventing more weeds from growing.

By 9:00, they had the majority of the field cleared so Rob left to begin his routine around the theater. Devan stayed in the field and continued working. He used a flat-headed shovel to clear crater-like areas in the weed debris for the seeds two feet wide and three feet apart in rows extending the entire length of the field. The work was slow. By 11:00am, Rob finished his work. Devan had two-thirds of the field ready for planting. The rest would have to be done the next morning. Before they left, Rob turned on the sprinklers in Zone 23 to see how the irrigation was laid out. As they suspected, only the area around the pond and about a third of the field was irrigated.

"How difficult do you think it'll be to extend the sprinkler system to the rest of the field?" Devan asked.

"Not too bad. We'll rent a trench digger. I think if we extend one line down each side and the middle from the existing system, we can do it. We'll divert water from around the pond to the rest of the field. We can salvage the sprinklers from around the pond too. They'd be perfect for the center section since they're tall and have a long circular spraying area."

Devan could tell Rob was getting more into it now that he had a project. Rob liked to build and create things, so this was perfect for him. After making some quick estimates as to how much PVC piping and how many additional long range sprinkler heads they'd need to extend the system, they headed to a nearby hardware store to get what they needed.

By 5:00am Saturday morning, Devan, Rob and Rachel were all in the field. Rob dug the trenches while Devan unearthed the existing pipes in order to divert water from the pond. He also removed the tall sprinklers and began laying the PVC piping. Rachel cleared areas in the weed mulch for planting.

By 8:30am they had the system diverted and the irrigation in place. In order not to arouse suspicion, Rob went out front to prepare the beds around the theater for the new landscaping John had requested. While Rob worked on the new beds, Devan and Rachel planted the seeds. They planted three seeds two inches under the soil in each crater-like indention. Three seeds should ensure at least one plant per area would grow. By 11:00am, they had half the field planted. The rest would have to wait until the next morning. Rob told John they would be working the entire weekend to prep for the new landscaping. John gave the nod–he was eager for the changes.

They finished planting by 7:30 Sunday morning and tested the system. With a few adjustments, the entire field was being watered. Rob set Zone 23's timer to come on at 3:00am for 45 minutes, five nights a week. At last, they were finished.

Before they left, they stood on the edge of the field, admiring their handiwork.

"Well guys," Devan said, breaking the silence, "nothing we can do now but wait and let nature take over."

"How long before we know what we've got?" Rob asked.

"Seven to ten days, plus or minus," Devan said. "We should know by next weekend."

For Devan and Rachel, the week passed with agonizing slowness. The plants dominated their conversations all week and the waiting was torture. By Saturday, they could hardly contain their excitement.

Rob arrived at Devan's a little before 6:00am and was surprised to find Devan waiting on the front steps of his building. When Devan climbed into the truck he was greeted by a bright-eyed Rachel. Rob, for a change, was quiet and subdued.

"Good morning," Rachel said with noticeable excitement.

"Morning," Devan replied, sharing her enthusiasm.

"So, this is what it takes to get you two up at the butt crack of dawn," Rob said.

"Come on Rob, it's not every day one becomes the proud parent of, hopefully, several thousand children," Devan teased.

"I couldn't sleep at all last night. How many do you think we have?" Rachel asked.

"I have no idea, but even if only a quarter come up, it's still more than we ever had in high school."

"I know! I know! I'm so excited! Hurry, Rob, let's move it," Rachel said as she patted his knee and bounced up and down like an excited little girl.

Rob wasn't as enthused. He listened to the two of them as they rambled on. When they reached the theater, he finally spoke. "Just to remind you two, we still have a lot of work to do after this. It's going to be a busy day."

"You're so serious," Rachel said as she leaned over and put her arm around Rob. "Today could be the beginning of the rest of our lives."

Unlike Rob, Rachel and Devan knew what possibly laid ahead for them all.

They parked the truck deep in the woods at the entrance to an overgrown road they stumbled on the weekend before. They assumed construction crews made it when the property was originally cleared.

When they reached the field, they found its appearance had changed significantly. The thick mat of dried dead weeds was now dark brown and appeared riddled with hundreds of crater-like indentations stretching its entire length.

Devan ran to the nearest row to find all three seeds in the first indentation had broken ground and a real leaf sprouted from each small "potling." As Devan made his way down the length of the field, he was astonished to find nearly all the indentations sprouted three small plants.

"Holy shit!" Devan yelled after reaching the end of the row. "I can't believe it!" He threw up his hands.

"We're going to make a fortune," Rachel said, jumping on Rob and hugging him tightly.

Devan made his way back to them.

"So how much do you think this is worth?" Rob asked. Even he was getting excited.

"I don't know. Depends on how long we let it grow and how many times we harvest. A million, plus or minus," Devan said.

Rob's jaw nearly hit the ground. "A million?"

"Of course, we'll have to thin some out and…," Devan paused and looked up, "we still have the weather to deal with. Even with only a 50 percent yield we should still make a killing"

Fortunately, the weather cooperated during this critical early growth period. Florida was typically dry toward the end of winter and most of spring, which was good for the young potlings. The torrential downpour of a typical Florida summer thunderstorm would devastate such a young crop. With the irrigation system set to mist during the night, the young plants thrived.

At the end of the first month Devan was amazed by the amount of growth in such a short time. Ray was right. These plants were perfect for the area and grew twice as fast as anything he and Rachel had grown before. At this rate Devan figured they could harvest by early summer.

The field proved to be better than they thought in other ways, too. Not only did a dense forest of pine trees and palmetto bushes surround it, but it was also where the debris from the clearings had been burned. The soil was black and covered with charcoal remnants, giving it richness above and beyond what it already had.

As the weeks passed, the plants continued to thrive. By the time the first summer thunderstorms hit, the plants were strong enough to handle them. Devan could have sworn they grew at least six inches in one day after the first heavy downpour.

Chapter 24

THE HARVEST

By early summer it was obvious that they were going to have a lot more "product" than expected. From past experience, Devan assumed a large number of Ray's seeds would not grow, but this time the opposite happened, the field was completely filled with plants.

"Can you believe this? It's only been two months and they're huge!" Devan said.

Every Saturday morning when they visited the field, Devan was continually amazed. He'd never seen such quick growth. Whatever Ray and his buddies had done in the lab was extraordinary. The two-month-old plants looked more like four months plus. Some could be harvested now but they chose to wait. No need to rush. With Ray and his partners not planting this season, the market was quickly drying up. By the time they did bring what they had to market they figured they would make a fortune.

"I've never seen so much pot in one place! What are we going to do with all this?" Rachel asked, completely in awe of what lay before them.

"I thought you said you've done this before," Rob asked, voicing concern.

"Not this much," Rachel said. She looked at Devan. "Even with your people and mine combined, we'll never sell this much. What are we going to do with all this?"

"Relax. I've got it covered," Devan said. He stood up from behind one of the plants he'd been inspecting.

"What do you mean?" Rob asked. "How can we possibly sell all of this? If we cut it all right now it would fill both the truck and trailer - several times!"

"Ray offered to hook us up with some of his people if necessary. And looking at all this, I think it's necessary. When the time's right, I'll give him a call. A few more weeks and the market is ours for the taking," Devan said as he wiped his hands together and looked back at Rob and Rachel with a wicked grin.

As they were leaving, Rachel stopped and snapped off a tightly packed bud cluster from the same plant she accosted every week.

"Damn, woman! You're worse than a swarm of locusts." Devan said. "You pick on that same plant every week!"

Rob stood with his arms crossed and a stern look of disapproval.

"I'm sampling, Rachel said. "Think of it as quality control...you know, product testing. We need to make sure it's as good as we're hoping." It was a half-assed attempt to convince them she was serious.

"Every week?" Rob asked, not buying her bullshit.

"Oh, shut up! I know what I'm doing. Right Devan?

"Yeah...right...quality testing...sure," Devan said. "By the way, how is the quality?"

"Perfecto!"

"See, Rob? What would we do without her expertise?"

The weeks passed and the plants continued to impress. Each time they entered the field the fresh green smell filled the air. The smell was almost overpowering at times. Fortunately, the field was surrounded on three sides by a dense pine forest and a swamp on the other. The pines were helpful in masking the smell. Even from the closest parking lot there was no hint of the pot growing nearby.

They decided to harvest in June. The plan was to divide the field into quarters and harvest one quarter a month through the summer.

This would help stagger the harvesting and allow some plants to mature more. The first yield was a modest mix of buds varying in size. Demand had reached a point where they couldn't wait any longer. People were desperate and looking for whatever they could get their hands on. It was time to get back to business on a full-time basis. It was time to bring the first section to market.

Most of the plants on the edges of the field were bushy and ranged in size from three to six feet tall. Others toward the center were larger. They only cut half of each plant so as not to devastate the entire section. This would allow for a faster recovery and enable them to harvest the section again in a few months.

By 7:30 a.m., they had 20 large yard bags completely filled and stacked in the front corner of the field awaiting pickup. Each bag was heavy and tightly packed with as much "product" as they could get inside.

Rob brought the truck to the field using the abandoned road. They loaded the truck and trailer in minutes and were on their way. They wanted to make sure they were gone before John or any of his employees arrived. Now was definitely not the time to make people suspicious.

They took the bags straight to the house Rachel and Rob recently rented to temporarily store them in their garage.

Devan and Ray had made arrangements with Matt, Ray's main Jacksonville connection. Ray was right. With him and his partners not planting, the market was dry and Matt was desperate to get whatever he could as soon as possible. Fresh cut was fine with him.

After unloading, Devan, Rob and Rachel decided to keep a bag so they could fulfill their obligations to their customers. Devan called Matt to let him know what they had. Matt was ecstatic and agreed to buy it all, sight unseen, for $10,000 a bag. Devan had discussed pricing with Ray, and they agreed $10,000 per bag was acceptable since further processing was still required. He knew Matt would make several times this per bag on the street.

The $190,000 figure impressed Rachel and Rob, but Devan wasn't surprised. Matt knew Ray and Devan knew he was no stranger to moving such large quantities. They agreed to meet later that evening and make the exchange. Devan called Ray to let him know the deal was on and Ray assured him Matt was good for it.

Rob, however, had one stipulation: that Rachel not go. He knew she'd done this before and had lots of experience, but Rob was concerned for her safety and insisted she stay home.

Needless to say, this didn't go over well with Rachel. And while touched by his concern, she still insisted on going. But Rob was adamant and unwilling to give in. Rob loved Rachel and if something happened to her, he'd never be able to live with it.

When their disagreement escalated into a full-blown argument, Devan stepped in and sided with Rob.

"Maybe he's right, Rachel. If something does go wrong at least you won't be involved."

"I don't care! I'm part of this and just as willing to share the risks," she insisted.

"I know, but Rob's right. There is reason to be concerned. We don't know Matt. At this moment he's just a voice on the other end of the phone. How about it?" Devan pleaded. "For Rob's sake please sit this one out."

Reluctantly, Rachel agreed. "But only this time," she said, still angry, but at the same time moved by their concern for her. Rachel knew she was lucky to have two great men in her life. "Just this once," she repeated.

"Agreed," Rob and Devan said in unison.

A few hours later, after reloading the truck and trailer, Rob and Devan were prepared to leave.

"Be careful you two," Rachel said as they walked to the door. "And hurry back. I can't wait to see what $190,000 looks like," she added, trying to hide her growing concern.

Devan and Rob took the bags to a large empty garage complex on the city's Southside where they agreed to meet Matt. When they pulled up to the building, a large metal garage door opened, and two men motioned them in. As they passed under the door it began to close behind them. They continued driving forward and parked next to a van in the center of the empty building.

"Time to rock and roll," Devan said as they got out of the truck and walked back to meet the two men who were approaching them from the now closed door.

The two strangers stopped about 10 feet away and locked on Devan and Rob with a cold hard stare. After a few seconds of awkward silence, one of the strangers stepped forward, shattering his cold frozen expression with a big smile. "I'm Matt. Which one of you is Devan?" he asked as his eyes shifted back and forth between them.

"I am," Devan said, stepping forward and extending his hand.

Matt took his hand and shook it. "Pleased to finally meet you. Our mutual friend talks highly of you."

"And you," Devan said. "This is Rob, one of my partners."

Rob and Matt also shook hands. It was clear Matt was taken aback by Rob's size. Rob looked like the kind of guy not to piss off. Matt introduced his buddy, Nick. Nick was also a big guy, but nothing like Rob. Devan thought to himself that Rob's size made a good first impression even if it was just for show.

Matt took a bag from the trailer and opened it. The smell was heavy. He reached in and pulled out a handful of cuttings.

"Ahhh…fresh and green, just the way I like it. We're going to make a killing with this thanks to Ray starving the market."

Matt told Nick to get the money from the van. Nick returned carrying a medium size duffel bag with a shoulder strap.

"Here you go. Please, by all means, count it. I assure you it's all there," Nick said with sincerity.

Devan was amused. It was obvious Matt and Nick were going to great lengths to make a good impression. Ever since his college days, Devan enjoyed the benefits of being Ray's friend.

Devan took the bag and opened it. There were stacks of twenties, fifties, and hundred-dollar bills. A nice mix. He took out a couple stacks and randomly thumbed through them.

"Ahhh...fresh and green. Just the way I like it," Devan said, smiling at Rob, whose eyes were locked on the money in his hands. "No need to count it. Our mutual friend says you're good for it," Devan said, reinforcing his connection to Ray.

Devan and Rob helped them load the bags into the van. As they loaded the last one, Matt extended his hand. "I hope this is the start of a beautiful friendship," he kidded.

"Same here," Devan said as he waved and climbed into Rob's truck.

Rob and Devan followed them out of the building, and each went their separate ways. After driving a few minutes in total silence, a wave of relief settled over them.

"That wasn't so bad," Devan said, letting out a long sigh before retrieving the bag from the floor. "So, Rob, your first big deal. How does it feel? You're one of the bad guys now."

"Just show me the money again and I'm sure I'll learn to live with it!"

When they returned to the house Devan dumped the money on the coffee table in their living room.

"We're back," Devan said.

"You're damn right we're back. And how!" Rachel said as she picked up a stack of hundreds and thumbed through it. "What do you think, baby?" she asked as she sat on Rob's lap. "This should take care of our debt." Rachel threw the stack of hundreds into the air so they rained down all over the room.

"I knew people did this kind of thing and now I see why. I mean, with this kind of money I'm surprised more people aren't doing it."

"Oh, they will be. It's just a matter of time now," Devan said as he tossed a stack of fifties back into the pile. "It's like the stock market, Rob. We got a hot tip from an insider, Ray, and were able to position ourselves to take advantage of changing market conditions. The field should be extremely profitable for a while."

"You know," Devan continued, more or less thinking out loud, "depending on when we decide to pack it in, after harvesting the other three sections we still may have time to harvest the first section again. Depending on the weather this winter, we may be able to turn the whole thing over one more time before the cold weather takes us out. That is, as long as you don't feel the need to tell John about the field," Devan said, giving Rob a mischievous look.

"What he don't know won't hurt him," Rob replied. He playfully dropped Rachel on the floor so he could run his hands through the pile of money again.

"Then how about we keep growing until the first freeze puts us out of business? After that, we'll walk away with whatever we have. Agreed?"

"Agreed," Rachel said.

"Agreed," Rob said, still mesmerized by the pile of cash.

Devan and Rachel had planned to process and distribute some portion of each harvest through their network. After seeing how easy it would be to work with Matt, they decided it was not necessary. They'd sell what was held back from this first harvest, but after that they'd limit their dealings to only a few close friends and associates. It was much safer staying out of the sales end. Even with built-in buffers and other precautions, they were never 100 percent comfortable. It only took one narc to bring down the entire operation. Devan and Rachel silently hoped that the large pile of money lying before them was a sign of things to come.

"How about you get some of your samples and let me and Devan give our opinions?" Rob asked Rachel out of the blue.

Rachel froze. Devan choked on the Jack and Coke he was drinking.

"Are you serious?" Rachel asked.

"I might as well see what all the fuss is about," Rob said, motioning for her to go get her stash. "You okay Devan?" Rob asked as Devan continued coughing up his drink.

"Fine, fine," Devan whispered, making the thumbs-up sign.

Devan finally recovered. "I never thought I'd see the day."

"What the fuck," Rob said.

Rachel returned with a plastic bag filled with product.

"Samples for testing?" Devan asked with one eyebrow raised.

"It's all about quality," she said and quickly filled her pipe. Rachel wasn't about to pass on an opportunity to smoke with Rob. She'd been dying to get him high ever since he told her how he felt about weed.

Rachel lit the pipe and took the first hit, then passed it to Rob. Without hesitation he also took a big hit and passed it to Devan. Unlike Rob, Devan was no stranger to pot. He'd been a casual user since high school. It had been a long time since he last smoked, but in honor of Rob's first time, he took a hit. Within minutes they were all stoned off their asses.

High and feeling good, they celebrated their first major "deal" throughout the evening. Pot agreed with Rob. His cold military persona was shattered. Throughout the evening they continued cracking each other up, often to the point of tears.

"See baby, this is why people do this shit, it makes you feel good," Rachel said, patting Rob's back.

"Even if it's only temporary, sometimes it's just what the doctor ordered," Devan added before taking another hit.

After several hours of smoking out, they ordered three large pizzas.

"Munchies! An unfortunate side effect," Rachel joked as they devoured the first pizza.

After sobering up they split up the money and discussed their future plans. Devan and Rachel were determined not to make the same mistakes again. This time, things would be very different.

Chapter 25

DOING IT RIGHT

The cash from the pot sale presented the trio with a new and interesting problem: how to spend it. Technically, the money was "dirty"–unwashed. It's not like they could just walk into their friendly neighborhood bank and make a deposit. That amount of cash was sure to attract a lot of attention–a lot of unwanted government attention.

Paying cash for everything wasn't a good idea, either. If a neighbor suddenly goes from driving a piece of shit one day to a brand-new luxury car the next, buys a new house, and starts sporting a Rolex, people talk. The kind of talk that can sometimes attract the attention of the wrong people, i.e., the law. No, going strictly cash with no good explanation as to where it came from was too risky. They were determined to play it safe.

The total yield of the field was expected to produce over a million dollars. By controlling their spending and keeping a low profile, they figured they could wash enough of the cash to significantly raise their standard of living without arousing unwanted attention.

Heeding the lessons learned from their past, they decided to keep their jobs and use them as fronts. They would use cash for basic living expenses. Food, clothing, entertainment, gas –even utility bills and rent– could occasionally be handled with cash or money orders, allowing their "legitimate" salaries to accumulate. The plan was to save as much money as possible, both clean and unclean. Cash, after all, still spends – dirty or not. And having legitimate sources of income would help deflect unwanted attention. They would live well but within limits. By the time the field ran its course, they'd have enough money put away to make a new start doing whatever they wanted. This would be their second chance and they were determined to make the most of it.

For Devan, saving money would be easy, as he had a "regular" job with a good salary and bonus package. For Rachel and Rob, it would be more difficult since they owned their own business.

At first, they agreed Rob and Rachel's company would be the perfect front for laundering large sums of money. The majority of their clients already paid in cash, so it seemed logical to show "growth" with new cash paying clients. A lot of new cash paying clients!

But there was one catch: Rachel's sister and brother-in-law. Technically, they were silent partners, but they were involved in the company's financials. Rachel's sister was an accountant and reviewed the books regularly as a favor. A sudden flood of cash might require some explaining...

An even greater concern of Rachel's was what would happen if they were busted? Rachel worried that her sister and brother-in-law would go down with them. Understandably, she didn't want her family involved. It would be bad enough being related to a convicted dealer, but to be accused of being one could ruin their careers. As long as they were a part of the business, laundering money through it was out of the question as far as Rachel was concerned. They'd have to find another way.

For Devan, the answer was simple. He'd buy them out. It removed her sister and brother-in-law from the picture and made Rob, Rachel, and Devan legal partners. Rob and Rachel liked the idea and helped Devan come up with a buyout price.

Devan offered Rachel's sister and brother-in-law two times their original investment, and they accepted immediately. For them, Devan's offer was a face-saving way out. In their minds, the company wasn't the success they'd hoped for. The reality was that it barely broke even each month. Devan's offer not only got them off the hook, but it also put some money in their pockets. Simply put, it was too good of a deal to pass up.

Partners at last. And more importantly, Rachel, Rob, and Devan had total control of all aspects of the business. First item on the agenda was changing the company's name to D&D Landscaping Inc. "D&D" had a secret meaning known only to them.

The second big change was to cut the number of real clients by 50 percent. After all, the work was backbreaking and uncomfortable, especially during the summer months. They gradually replaced their more "troublesome" clients with new, happy "cash paying" clients who never complained. Their long-term goal was to make 75 percent of their clientele into happy, cash paying customers.

By the end of the month, they'd harvested the second section of the field and made a quarter of a million dollars more. Even with the company and both Devan and Rachel's jobs, they were still only able to "clean" a small portion of it. The money came in faster than they could wash it; a problem they were happy to have.

As the summer passed, D&D Landscaping proved itself the perfect front. By using cash to cover operating expenses, the company began to show a profit. That, plus their regular jobs, and the many new "cash paying" clients they acquired, ended up washing a considerable amount of money.

By Halloween, the entire field had been harvested and the last section was the most profitable. Those plants were huge and very mature, enabling them to command a half-million-dollar sale.

The first two sections were also recovering nicely. New growth was so thick and dense they decided to let the first section continue growing. At the first sign of a hard freeze, they'd harvest everything one last time.

But luck was on their side. That winter turned out to be one of the mildest on record. On Christmas day the three of them went to the beach and enjoyed the 80-degree weather. By January, the first two sections were ready to cut, and the yield was twice the size of the last harvest and so was the money.

Fortunately, the winter passed with little damage to the crops and by spring the plants were bursting with new growth. They were now faced with a decision; what to do? The original plan was to grow until the winter weather put them out of business but, that didn't happen, so they agreed to go another season. The plants appeared willing, so why not?

Once again, they were rolling in money. Even with new growers helping meet demand, prices remained relatively unchanged. It also helped that their product was some of the best on the market. Matt and Nick constantly complimented them on the quality and said that next to Ray and his specialty crops, theirs was the best.

They found that humorous. The only care they gave the plants was watering them. The field was far too large to fertilize. Fortunately, the soil was excellent, and the plants seemed to thrive on neglect. Whatever Ray and his partners had done was obviously working.

As summer arrived, portions of the field were so thick with plants that the rows became invisible. The only explanation they could come up with was that new plants must be growing from seeds that had taken root in the rich, fertile soil. The new additions and the frequent harvesting of the mature plants produced even larger and more profitable yields.

Their plan to maintain a low profile became more and more difficult to stick to as the cash continued to pile up. They had stacks of cash hidden in and around their homes. The desire to spend big burned in all of them. But it was still necessary to exercise restraint. The field had yielded over $2 million in product, but they could only wash about $200,000. It did allow for an increase in their standard of living, but buying a multimillion-dollar home or expensive vehicles was still not in the cards. Not yet anyway. They would have to be content with knowing the money was there if needed.

Even though two million seemed like a lot of money, over time,

Rachel and Devan knew it wasn't. Having already had and spent a hundred grand each, they knew it would take a great deal more to permanently secure their futures. Given this and learning from past experience, they decided to amend their original goal. The new goal was not to make enough money to start over, but to make enough money to never have to worry about money again. If their luck held, they believed the field could make this goal a reality in another year or two. Restraint was more critical now than ever.

With a new goal and tentative timeline, restraint was doable. Yet they still found ways to enjoy themselves. It wasn't long before Devan and Rachel –and now with Rob along– engaged in many of their former social activities. They liked the high-energy fast lane life the money afforded them.

"Man, I love it here. I'd forgotten how beautiful the view is," Devan said as they were being seated at the table he'd requested in his favorite restaurant.

"You've always loved this place," Rachel said. "And this table. I remember the last time we were here; I was complaining about the view."

"My last night before I went off to college. We were pondering our futures. Who'd have ever guessed that eight years later we'd pick up right where we left off?" Devan said.

"This time around we'll do it right," Rachel said as she raised her glass for a toast.

"To doing it right," Devan said.

"To doing it right," Rob joined in as they toasted to their futures.

"Holy shit you guys! Look at these prices," Rob said, looking at the menu. "Now I see how you lost all your money the first time!"

Chapter 26

People say money can't buy love or happiness, but it can buy stability and peace of mind. Knowing one's financial situation is secure and will be for the foreseeable future is a liberating experience. Devan, Rachel, and Rob were finally starting to feel as though they could live for themselves and do what they wanted before they were too old to enjoy it. As Devan often said, life is short so live it up while you can. They had tried to do it legitimately and were unsuccessful. Now, they were doing what they had to do; and they were doing what they knew how to do.

They enjoyed being seen and projecting an image of success. They fed off the envious looks of others and were always playing to the public. It was a familiar world for Devan and Rachel –a world they enjoyed as young adults, but felt they had to abandon. So, after eight hard years they were back. And this time they were tougher, more experienced, and focused on a common goal. Long-term financial security was the objective, and they were determined to make it a reality.

Without having to oversee the sales and distribution end, the three of them had a lot more free time. For Rachel and Rob, it was welcomed. Their relationship was strong, but previous financial concerns and heavy workloads took a toll. Being able to enjoy the money now was just what they needed. Revived and refreshed, they were like kids in a candy store, enjoying their success together. It never failed to impress Devan how perfect they were for each other.

Originally, Rachel planned to re-enter the club scene in order to re- establish distribution connections, but Matt made that unnecessary. Nevertheless, she was ready to return. She craved the energy and atmosphere of club life. She became a local celebrity almost overnight and enjoyed every minute of it. Unlike Terry, Rob supported her all the way. He knew it was who she was and with whom he had fallen in love with.

Rob was also able to devote more time to his favorite hobby –building custom furniture. He bought all the tools and equipment he needed and transformed their garage into his personal workshop. Absorbed by his passion to create, he'd work for hours until Rachel made him call it a night, usually when she returned from the club.

Outwardly, Rachel and Rob seemed like polar opposites, but that wasn't the case. The time they spent apart doing what they loved was the key to making their relationship work. Above all else they respected each other's right to be an individual. When they were together, they were one, a couple, and nothing stood in their way. Being friends with both, Devan witnessed their transformation from separate-to-together each day and admired their mutual respect for one another.

Devan was more the lone wolf type. Some of it was by choice and some out of necessity. Devan was once again living a dual personal life. Rachel and Rob not only had each other, but they were also partners in the business. Devan frequently enjoyed the company of women, but he never allowed himself to get close. The trust the three of them had in each other was the glue that held their partnership together. Bringing another person into the fold wasn't a risk Devan was willing to take. Out of concern for their safety, Devan felt it was better to play the bachelor role, at least until they decided to call it quits. He'd been in love only once in his life and hadn't felt that deeply about another woman since. He believed that one day, when he was free to give himself completely to the right woman with no secrets looming over him, he'd have a relationship like Rachel and Rob's. Meanwhile, Devan was content playing bachelor.

Professionally, the money filled Devan with a powerful sense of self-confidence. He still wasn't fond of his company but having so much money and knowing he could tell his bosses to kiss his ass at any time made working for them tolerable. Furthermore, not getting caught up in the corporate bullshit allowed him to better focus on his work; he honestly liked research and development. It was the people who made him crazy. But none of it mattered now. The job was just a front. He brought home two times his yearly salary from each harvest –tax free. With that kind of money pouring in, spending years attempting to build a "career" just didn't seem worth it.

PART FIVE

Chapter 27

THE HOUSE

By the end of their second summer of growing, the winds of fate began to blow again, this time through the actions of Devan's younger brother Mark. Mark was about to make a decision that would eventually have a huge impact on everyone's future for some time to come.

Mark was one of the fortunate few who caught a lucky break early in his corporate career. About a year after being hired by a local utility, a competitor bought his company in a hostile takeover. At first, Mark worried that "last hired first fired" would apply to him, but the opposite occurred. The competitor company quickly sized up the management structure and cleaned house, eliminating all entrenched obstacles by either encouraging early retirement or through outright termination, effectively clearing all obstacles along Mark's path.

Being young, aggressive, and in the early stages of his corporate climb, Mark had not experienced the frustration associated with dead-weight management. Unlike Devan, Mark saw a future in the disorder created by the takeover. The takeover company appreciated his aggressive style, and being one of the few original employees left and the most familiar with the local market, Mark found himself heading up a large portion of the Jacksonville operation, giving him more authority and a much larger salary.

By the end of that second summer Mark was tired of apartment living and began looking for a house. After several months, he found one he liked a few blocks from the apartment complex. Mark tried to convince Devan that they should buy it together, but Devan wasn't interested in becoming a homeowner. There was something about the word "homeowner" that sounded too permanent for him. After all, D&D Landscaping was originally created to help him save enough money to get out of town and start over some place new. Instead, Devan decided to keep the apartment –he could easily afford it now, plus his salary and bonuses made it believable to his family and friends.

Mark's move also came as a relief to Devan. Like Rachel, Devan didn't want innocent family members caught up in any illegal consequences if he was busted. Mark attributed Devan's success to his job and D&D. These assumptions, along with some carefully created image control, helped Devan maintain his front.

Devan was also proud of Mark. He was a natural born leader and succeeding in a "legitimate" business. Maybe even politician material someday. Mark often kidded about going into politics. Devan believed he would be good at it. Mark was already a successful corporate salesman/ bullshit artist; the perfect prerequisite for politics and another reason Devan thought it best to keep his real occupation a secret. It was safer that way for everyone around him.

By the end of June, Mark had moved out, and with Devan's blessing took most of the furniture with him. Devan had other plans for the apartment. He finally decided it was time to spend some cash on himself. With the property manager's permission, Devan made remodeling the apartment his first major expenditure. Within a matter of weeks, he had the entire place professionally painted, carpeted, and tiled and even bought all new appliances for the kitchen. He refurnished every room to suit his taste. Even though this went against their "low profile" plan, he felt it was safe to do. These kind of purchases were commonly made with cash.

Two months later the apartment had a new, modern sophisticated look– definitely bachelor flavor but with taste, style, and class. Devan was no stranger to a higher standard of living and his apartment reflected it. Mark teased him that he probably could have bought a house with what he spent on the remodeling. Little did Mark know, but he was right.

Mark's house was situated in an older, established neighborhood built around three large lakes that connected to the St. Johns River by a narrow canal. The house wasn't lakefront, but close enough for him. A few months later, Mark's realtor called him, remembering that his brother liked waterfront living. A waterfront home one street over would be going on the market soon. Though it was a fixer-upper, she believed the price was good for the area.

After pestering Devan for a week, Mark finally convinced Devan to go see the house.

Devan arrived at the house 30 minutes early so he could get a look at the place without being bothered. Mark was right, it was a fixer upper. *Nothing a little gasoline and a box of matches can't fix,* Devan thought to himself.

Hidden behind decades of overgrown trees and hedges, the house looked as if it hadn't been lived in for years. As Devan made his way through the jungle, he was surprised to find the house was bigger than he first thought. The back yard even had a beautiful view of a lake.

"For the right price this place might be worth fixing up after all," Devan said out loud.

Devan called Rob and asked him to come take a look. He was interested in Rob's opinion since Rob had years of construction experience. Mark intended for Devan to buy the house to live in, but Devan had other plans.

By the time Devan made his way back to the front, the realtor had arrived and took him inside. The house was built in the late 1930s and looked as though it had seen a lot of abuse over the years, but it had a good layout. All of the rooms looked onto the lake, giving the house a bright, airy appearance, despite its age.

A few minutes into the tour, Rob and Rachel arrived and joined them. "A house? You?" Rachel asked. "I thought you were an apartment person."

"I have ulterior motives," Devan said, winking. He asked the realtor to excuse them for a minute so they could discuss some personal business.

"What do you think?" Devan asked Rob.

"It's old and needs a lot of work, but it's a great house. They don't build them like this anymore."

"How much do you think it would take to bring her back -ballpark?" Devan asked.

"40 or 50 grand. Maybe more, maybe less."

"What are you getting at?" Rachel asked Devan.

"For the right price I was thinking we could buy it, fix it up, and re-sell it at a profit, washing a shitload of money in the process."

"Not a bad idea. Use our cash to fix her up, then re-sell," Rachel said out loud to no one in particular.

"How about it?" Devan asked Rob.

"It'll take some time. Excluding the electrical and roof work, I could do most everything else myself."

"You alone?" Devan asked.

"No, with you and Rachel helping," Rob said, smiling.

"We will?" Rachel questioned skeptically.

"Of course we will. We're partners aren't we? Why not buy it, fix it up, resell it, and split the money –clean money," Devan said.

"How much do you think we'll make?" Rachel asked as she walked around the living room, looking at the water-damaged ceiling.

"It's over 2,000 square feet and located on the water. If done up right, I bet we could get $200,000. Mark's one street over off the lake and he paid $150,000 with similar square footage."

"Why not?" Rachel said, shrugging her shoulders. "How about it? She asked Rob. "Interested in becoming a homeowner?"

"If the price is right, I'm in."

"Asking price is $135,000. Let's offer $100,000 and see what happens. It's only a small part of the field," Devan said with a cunning smile.

They told the realtor they were interested, but were only willing to spend $100,000, naming all the work the house needed. Her client lived in Baltimore and was interested in dumping the property as soon as possible. Without haggling and knowing the house needed a lot of work, the client accepted the offer. A month later, it was theirs.

The house was in good shape structurally. They hired crews to put on a new roof as well as do some of the plumbing and electrical work. The three of them did the interior and exterior cosmetic work, including installing central heat and air conditioning. This was Rob's world. He knew how to make things happen and liked the work. Devan and Rachel helped as much as possible, but they still had their front jobs. They even scaled back the landscaping business again so Rob could spend more time at the house.

As summer gave way to fall, the field continued to thrive. Between the landscaping business, the house, and their jobs, they were busy. Since there was no real hurry to finish the house, they took their time and did it right.

That winter was unseasonably harsh. By Thanksgiving the region experienced its first hard freeze. Luckily, they had paid attention to the weather forecast and made a late-night harvest of the last two sections of the field. It took a couple of trips and truckloads, but they managed to make one of their largest hauls to date. They had so many bags of product they had to store them in the new house.

From late November through February, Jacksonville was repeatedly plunged into freezing temperatures for days at a time. For four days in January, the unthinkable happened: it snowed! Making it the worst winter in Jacksonville's history. It looked like their luck had finally run out.

Fortunately, they had piles of cash and a new real estate investment. By February the house was nearly complete. With no crops to tend to, they had more free time and concentrated on finishing the renovation. By early spring they put the house on the market for $250,000.

Interest was immediate but the price discouraged many. Still, they held firm. After a little more than a month, they got an offer for $235,000 and accepted it, leaving them with over a 100k legitimate profit. *Not bad,* Devan thought. *Maybe there was a future in this...*

Chapter 28

BACK IN BUSINESS

Devan visited Ray a few weeks later and told him about their latest "legal" business venture. Ray was doing well in his non-pot farming role, and like them, he too had been affected by the harsh winter. To Devan's surprise, Ray informed him he would soon be closing the last of their "other" operations for good. For the first time in over 30 years, Ray would be 100 percent legitimate.

Devan knew Ray was downsizing, but to be completely out of the business was unexpected. Ray was like the Central and North Florida "godfather" of growers. *Without him things will be very different,* Devan thought to himself.

"Everything? Even your research facilities and the hydro operations?" Devan asked.

"Yep. We're done," Ray said, slapping Devan on his shoulder. "I'm retiring. Permanently."

"Wow! It's going to be strange not having you around. Everyone knows you're the shit," Devan teased, masking his more serious concerns.

"From what I hear, you're doing very well in the Jacksonville market."

"We were, but the winter wiped us out," Devan said. "All our plants are dead, and I doubt they'll make a comeback. The field was covered with snow and ice for four days"

"You're going to replant, aren't you?" Ray asked.

Devan shrugged. "We have the seeds, but it's getting risky. The whole area is being developed so it's just a matter of time before someone buys the property. Anyway, we had a great two summers thanks to you."

"Anytime, buddy," Ray said, chewing on a straw.

They sat quietly for a few minutes, taking in the view from Ray's front porch and watching his wife push their son on a tire swing in the yard.

"What about specializing? You know, focusing on a smaller, more profitable crop?" Ray suggested, breaking the silence.

"What do you have in mind?" Devan asked. He sensed Ray was leading up to something.

"What about taking over some of our high-end grow house action? I can hook you up with all the equipment and over 30 years of our best R&D efforts." Ray was smiling, but he was serious. "It'd be a shame to just throw it all away," he added.

"It's a thought, but at the moment we have no place to grow."

"Well, the offer's there. Think it over and let me know," Ray said.

On the drive back to Jacksonville, Devan thought about Ray's offer. Growing indoors, grow house crops…but where? Not the apartment… and Rachel and Rob move around too much so that wouldn't work. Then it hit him. Old houses. Fixer-uppers. Combine two profitable ventures and see what happens. When Devan reached Jacksonville, he called Rachel and Rob and invited them over for pizza. Even though he'd just spent a small fortune on new stainless steel kitchen appliances, Devan did not cook.

"I love this apartment," Rachel said, walking over to the wall-to-wall windows overlooking the river. "The view is incredible. I see why you keep it."

"Where else can you live on the river this cheap?" Devan joked.

His $1,600 a month rent may have seemed like a lot to some people, but it was nothing. Property taxes alone on the riverfront could run into the tens of thousands a year. For the money, his apartment on the river was a steal and the remodeling made it even more impressive. And he took advantage of it. When Devan wasn't entertaining female guests, he used it for work and family-related events.

They sat out on the balcony, taking in the view and enjoying the pizza.

"Ray made me an offer. One I think could put us back in business and help us resume our goal of total financial independence," Devan started.

"No more landscaping," Rob said. "I'm done with that shit. It's too damn hot in the summer."

"No landscaping," Devan said. "The field was great but I'm with you. The manual labor and upkeep was a bitch." He sat back and put on his shades. "How do you guys feel about grow houses?" Devan asked.

"Grow houses?" Rachel asked, raising an eyebrow. "Plural…more than one?" she clarified.

"Grow houses?" Rob asked. He'd never heard the term. "Like growing indoors?"

"Indoors in a controlled environment 24/7. No seasons, no weather, and especially no winters or summers," Devan clarified.

"What are you suggesting?" Rachel asked as she settled back into her lounge chair and put on her shades. The sun was setting across the river, casting a beautiful orange glow around them.

"Let me get us some real drinks and then I'll pitch my latest idea." Devan returned with their drinks and settled into a chair across from them.

"So, hear me out. First we officially close the landscaping business."

"I like that idea already," Rob said, toasting with his drink in agreement.

"I thought you would. In its place we buy old houses and do what we did with the lake house," Devan said. "But this time with a twist."

Rachel smiled and put her hand on Rob's leg. "Brace yourself."

"We use them as grow houses while we're fixing them up. Working part time it took us, well mostly you Rob, a little over seven months to bring that house around. That's plenty of time to bring a crop worth at least a hundred grand or more to market. And, if we spread it over a few houses, we'll make that much more. When we're finished growing, we sell it all fixed up and ready to go. Whether we make a real profit or not, we'll still make a fortune. We move on to other houses and do the same."

"Not a bad idea," Rachel said. "Do it long enough to put some real money in our accounts from the home sales while adding to our cash positions. But what about all the growing equipment?"

"Ray has offered to give us everything we'll need. All we have to do is go get it," Devan said, already anticipating the question. "He's even offered to set us up with some of his primo brands…including your personal favorites," Devan added, looking at Rachel.

"I'm in," Rachel said.

Rob spoke up. "One problem, I can't do all this alone. I like the work, but I'm only one person."

"You'll have help," Devan said.

"Who?"

"If we decide to do this, I'll quit my job and work with you full time. The grow houses will require monitoring, not only for the plants but also for security reasons. The more we're visible, the more the houses will look busy, and our presence will discourage people from snooping around. Regardless, we'll still have elaborate security," Devan said.

Rob rubbed his big hands together. "I like the sound of you working for me."

"With you, Rob. Partners, remember?" Devan asked, faking concern.

"We'll see," Rob teased.

"What am I getting myself into?" Devan asked Rachel.

"It's your funeral," she replied, laughing. "You know how he is."

As promised, Ray provided all the equipment and seed stock needed to get started, again, free of charge. Suggesting Devan take over the grow house operations was Ray's way of getting Devan back in the game. He liked Devan and trusted him. He knew offering his high-end products would be too tempting for him to pass up. Thirty-plus years of R&D was a huge investment. Ray's grow house products dominated the high-end market for more than a decade, far surpassing the competition. To throw it all away in favor of retirement was unthinkable.

Suggesting Devan take over these operations was also Ray's way of staying involved. Through Devan, Ray could continue to have a role by offering guidance and advice. He did this out of friendship, but in many ways, Devan reminded Ray of a younger version of himself. Devan was still green in some respects, but he had the same drive and determination to succeed that Ray did. But there was something else; something Ray couldn't quite place. For some reason he was certain Devan was destined for more. *If only I'd had such a generous benefactor when I was just starting out,* Ray thought to himself. Well, Devan did, and Ray looked forward to seeing what Devan would do with the opportunity.

The next few months were busy. At first, they planned to convert D&D Landscaping into a construction business. But after finding out what was involved with becoming a construction company and more importantly, not being licensed contractors, they decided to buy houses individually. This not only enabled them to skirt many licensing requirements, but also enabled them to take advantage of various tax and first-time buyer incentive programs.

The plan was simple. They would buy fixer-uppers in middle to upper-middle class neighborhoods. Mark's area was a wealth of opportunity. Undervalued and 60+ years old, these houses were perfect. Depending on the amount of work each house needed, a one or two crop yield set the timeline for how long they would hold the house before completing the renovation and selling it. Homes with attached garages and large, windowless, inner rooms were preferred, but they could work with just about anything.

The three of them made the perfect partnership. They kept things simple. Professionals would complete major projects like re-roofing, plumbing, or electrical work, but they took care of everything else.

Devan liked working with his hands and caught on fast. It wasn't long before they developed a structured plan for renovating and growing.

First, they took care of the major work requiring professional assistance. By re-using the same crews, a mutual respect and loyalty developed. The impressive cash incentives offered to complete jobs on time also played a major part.

Next, they made the exterior improvements as quickly as possible. If necessary, they would hire additional crews to help with time constraints. Keeping the homes looking well maintained by cleaning up the exterior helped to keep a low profile and better blend the homes into the neighborhoods. They also made it a point to meet the neighbors and inform them of their renovation timeline. They let the neighbors know they were doing the interior work themselves, thus reducing any suspicion caused by the frequent trips to the houses during the renovation period.

Upon completion of the major projects and exterior work, security was next. First, they installed burglar bars and steel doors. The bars were placed on the inside so as not to draw attention and put only on windows that lent themselves to a break-in. Those two additions alone made the homes virtually impenetrable, but they still connected an alarm system to every window and door. But unlike other systems, theirs wasn't set up to call a security company or the police. It was meant to be a deterrent. They even installed motion sensitive lights outside in select areas. The idea, of course, was to keep uninvited guests away and, more importantly, out of the house.

Preparing the growing areas was next. That sometimes meant building false rooms or installing temporary walls. Re-configuring the layouts as well as covering any windows in the growing areas with plywood or blackout curtains was almost always necessary.

Next, they set up the growing equipment. Grow houses require a large amount of electricity due to the lighting systems needed to accelerate growth on a 24/7 basis. Additional ventilation was also necessary and also used a large amount of electricity. Having so many plants in a concentrated area produced a strong aroma, making it necessary to pump fresh air into and out of the growing rooms using a temporary ventilation system. The contaminated air was filtered before leaving the house, usually through the chimney.

The different growing mediums also had special power requirements. For the hydro crops, pumps kept the nutrient rich solutions flowing regularly. They used the existing climate control system to keep temperatures and humidity constant.

So much energy being consumed in an empty house was bound to attract attention. Therefore, it was necessary to bypass the meter, allowing it to register only enough usage to appear normal. Older homes gave them an advantage since the main power line usually entered either through the attic or garage, providing easy access and allowing them to divert the electricity before it reached the meter.

Along with the equipment, Devan's knowledge of chemistry and his college experience growing in this type of setting paid off. Within days of planting, a whole new generation of premier brands broke ground.

"Jax is back," declared Devan as he and Rachel examined multiple rows of young potlings in their first grow house. Ray had provided them with the best of the best and they knew this time things were going to be very different.

By mid-year, only months after planting, their first homes produced impressive yields. When they brought their first crop to market, Matt was beside himself. After Ray informed Matt of his retirement, Matt feared losing Ray would force him to seek other, less reputable suppliers. Matt and Ray went back many years and Ray's superior brands were the backbone of his business. With Devan, Rachel, and Rob taking over, Matt was more than willing to negotiate very favorable terms. He wasn't privy to the details of Ray and Devan's deal, but he knew this was how Ray wanted it and for that single reason, Matt was happy with the new arrangement.

Devan, Rachel, and Rob were also pleased. Grow houses were much easier to deal with than free-range crops. The yields were considerably smaller than those of the field, but being high-end product meant the money was just as good, if not better.

By the end of the first year, they had three grow houses producing at full capacity and four more projects under way. Houses with attached garages were now a necessity, especially for rotating established plants between properties. Since starting their new business ventures, sales from both increased. The future was indeed looking bright.

Chapter 29

D&D RENOVATIONS IS BORN

With the success of their home renovation/grow house business, Devan and Rob found it necessary to get their contractor's licenses. "Might as well do it right if we're going to do this thing," they often said. Being properly licensed also helped clear other previously unforeseen hurdles.

Having officially closed the landscaping business, D&D Landscaping was now D&D Renovations, Inc. Since the new business consisted of buying, remodeling, and reselling houses, they had to meet an endless series of licensing and other small business requirements. In other words, it was necessary to deal with the incompetent, redundant, and often corrupt city government bureaucracy. Having grown up in Jacksonville, Devan knew the system for what it really was: Jacksonville was for sale at any price.

Jacksonville's growth and development was a touchy subject for Devan. Having been raised in a more affluent family, he knew about the behind-the-scenes dealings of the city government. Much of Jacksonville's recent growth explosion was the result of a select few business groups, city officials, wealthy land-owning families, quick cash developers, and a prominent religious organization all working together, forming a partnership of sorts, to profit at the expense of the locals.

On the surface, these entities would never be perceived as like-minded enough to be partners. However, in order to ensure their survival and retain control over the city's future, they found it necessary to create a kind of second secret city government. Jacksonville was exploding with growth. In time, the individual influence of these groups over city affairs would have otherwise been diluted or replaced by the constant inflow of people, money, and business, unless something was done to prevent this from occurring. United behind the common goal of retaining power and profiting at all costs, this partnership became the real power behind the local scenes.

Publicly, these groups constantly proclaimed their love for the city and their determination to control growth under the guise of protecting its citizens and local businesses. Behind closed doors, however, things were very different. Working together, these "pillars of the community" controlled every aspect of city government, allowing them to exercise their power at will. With nothing to stand in their way, they freely sold the city out from under its citizens while augmenting their already considerable fortunes.

The city government openly bent over backwards, offering incentives for companies to relocate to Jacksonville, giving away valuable land, condemning private property, and offering tax exemptions. It also broke, or completely rewrote, local laws to line the pockets of the exempt few. They hid behind public declarations of how growth would benefit Jacksonville by attracting businesses and jobs.

The reality was totally different. With so many out to benefit themselves, the city's growth was left unchecked. Over a 10-year span, Jacksonville saw cheap, poorly constructed housing developments ("affordable housing" to be politically correct) built all around the city with no regard to planning, making the existing highway system a congested mess. Blinded by quick money and controlled by a powerful few, city officials recklessly granted permission to build anywhere, doing nothing to control or limit development. It disgusted Devan on a personal level seeing entire forests of 100-plus year-old trees and protected wildlife areas wiped out by the city's greed. Strip malls and carbon copy neighborhoods sprung up everywhere. The city was indeed for sale to anyone willing to put up the money, pay the price, and play the political game. It was the reality of Jacksonville's politics and had been for decades. Anyone not willing to play the game didn't last long.

Devan knew the system well and being who he was he knew he was powerless to make any changes. So why try? If the city was so hell-bent on taking this path and construction was fast becoming big money, why not join the club? Construction really was the perfect front for their grow house operations. But, unlike the cheap crap constructed in the suburbs, they specialized in renovating older homes, and took pride in the quality of their work. And most importantly, again drawing from past experience, they knew the best place to hide something was always in plain sight. So, after jumping through all the necessary bureaucratic hoops and several thousand dollars later, D&D Renovations Inc. was born, all licensed and legal. To celebrate, the three of them went to dinner at their favorite restaurant.

"I love this town! There's nothing money can't buy," Devan said as they drank to the future of D&D Renovations Inc.

A benefit of being licensed contractors was attending a yearly conference hosted by the city and some of the area's largest developers. Outwardly, these conferences were designed to show the public that the city was actually doing something to control and coordinate growth. Inwardly, however, they were used as an opportunity to network and vie for potential business. By getting a "heads-up" on future projects, deals and contacts were often made.

The networking was what attracted Devan, Rob, and Rachel. Having met many people in the industry since entering the renovation business, they used these conferences to socialize and further enhance their cover. A typical meeting format consisted of an hour of boring speeches about how important it was to control the city's growth, followed by an hour (or more) of networking among guests. Rob and Devan rubbed elbows with their peers, often getting tips on where equipment and supplies could be bought at good prices. For them the time flew. For Rachel, these meetings went on forever.

"I hate these things," said Rachel as they walked out of Conference Room B in a prominent hotel downtown. "It's the same boring people every time."

"I know, but it's good to be seen and mingle. And the extra cover doesn't hurt either," Devan added.

"You know, between the three grow houses plus the other four legit rehabs, we've become a fairly large operation. Most of these guys only do a few projects at a time. We've got seven. We're becoming big time, baby!" Rob said, putting his arm around Rachel. "Besides, you know you liked being the hottest woman in there."

"Uh...I was the only woman in there," she said, hugging him back.

"Nightcap anyone?" Devan asked, pointing toward the bar. "I'm buying."

"I'm too tired to drink. It's been a long day," Rachel said.

"And tomorrow we start gutting that monster house in your parents' neighborhood —our biggest project yet," Rob added.

"Couldn't pass up that basement. It's the perfect place to grow," Devan said, smiling.

"We'll be growing in one of the most upscale neighborhoods in the city," Rachel reminded them.

"Rain check then?" Devan asked.

"Rain check," they said in unison.

A beautiful blonde walked by, making direct eye contact with Devan on her way to the bar. Like every other man in the lobby, Devan and Rob's heads turned. They followed her with their eyes.

"Damn!" Rob said.

"I haven't seen anything like that since Las Vegas," Devan mumbled. "Maybe I'll have that drink after all," Devan said out loud to no one in particular.

"Yeah, it's not that late," Rob said as they started walking toward the bar.

"I don't think so, Mister." Rachel pulled Rob by his arm.

"But..."

"But nothing," she said cutting him off. "You've got all you can handle right here."

Smiling and putting his arms around her, Rob said, "I was just thinking of Devan. Someone needs to make sure he doesn't get into trouble."

"Him? Please! Good night, Devan. Have fun."

"But Baby!"

Rachel rolled her eyes and pulled Rob toward the exit. Rob looked back at Devan, pretending to be afraid.

"Sorry man, maybe next time," Devan said, waving to them on his way to the bar.

Devan walked in casually, looking for the woman in the dimly lit room, but didn't see her, so he had a seat at the bar and ordered a drink. Sensing someone behind him, he turned to find the blonde woman standing there.

"Is this seat taken?" she asked, and pointed to the empty chair next to him.

"No," Devan answered, undressing her with his eyes. She was even more attractive than he originally thought. She wore a short, silk cocktail dress with a plunging neckline revealing ample cleavage. Two thin straps that he could barely see under her cascading hair held up her dress. The dress flattered her body and showed off her long legs, accentuated by stilettos.

As she sat down, he offered to buy her a drink, which she politely declined.

"What brings you here tonight?" Devan asked.

"Business," she said with an inviting look from her crystal blue eyes.

"Are you staying in the hotel?" he asked.

"I have a room on the eighth floor. Would you like to see it?" she asked as she raked her long fingernails lightly down his arm.

"I don't think my wife would like that," Devan said.

"Well, she doesn't have to know, now does she?" the blonde said with a flirtatious smile.

Devan's only real weakness (if one could call it that) was a beautiful woman. He wasn't one for relationships or long-term commitments. He liked variety. He especially liked aggressive women who weren't afraid to go after what they wanted. Mixed signals, game playing, and flirty women not willing to follow through were of no interest to him. He liked their company and he liked sex. Making the "wife" comment was his way of clarifying his intentions and not mixing signals.

"I guess she doesn't, does she?" he asked.

Moments later they were in her room. She was a beautiful, refreshing sight. Far better than any of the women he'd been with in some time. With her heels, she was almost as tall as he was. Standing in the center of the room several feet from him, she slowly slid one hand under her hair and lowered a strap. She smiled at him, playing the seduction game. She lowered the other strap and let the dress fall to the floor, exposing her flawless naked body. She then walked over to Devan and removed his coat.

"You're not really married, are you?" she asked, taking it off and tossing it into a chair.

"No." Devan replied as she began to unbutton his shirt. She removed the shirt, revealing his tightly muscled torso, then smiled as she knelt to unzip his pants.

"Good, because I don't think she'd like what I'm going to do to you," she said as she pulled his cock from his pants and went down on him. Surprised by how fast she moved, Devan had no complaints. As the night went on, they took each other repeatedly, using the other for all they could. Around 2:30am, she got up and started dressing. A tired and worn-out Devan sat up in the bed.

"Where are you going?" he asked.

"Home. It's late," she answered.

"Isn't this your room?"

"Yes. For business."

Devan was confused. "Business?" he asked. "What kind of business?"

She looked at him, not sure if he was serious. "Business." She cocked her head to one side and looked at him.

"You mean...me? Us...this?" he asked motioning between himself and her.

"What? You thought this was a freebee?" she asked.

"Well...," he paused. "Yeah."

"What? This kind of thing happens to you all the time?" she asked, acting offended.

"Well, actually..."

"I bet it does," she said, running her eyes over his body and raising an eyebrow. She dropped into a chair across the room and started laughing.

Devan also laughed while rubbing his face with both hands, then stretched. "I guess we had mixed signals after all, didn't we?"

"I knew it was too good to be true," she said.

"How much do I owe you?" Devan asked.

She was surprised by the question and his willingness to pay. "$500, but...given the miscommunication..."

"How about I give you a thousand if you come back over here and have breakfast with me in the morning," Devan said with a mischievous smile.

"Are you serious?" she asked, completely out of character.

"Why not? This is a first for me," he said. "What's your name?"

She undressed as she made her way back to the bed.

"Candy Prescott," she said, extending her hand.

"Devan Ross." He took it and pulled her to him. "Nice to meet you, Candy," he said, and they took each other again.

By breakfast they were two completely different people. They talked and laughed as if they'd known each other for years. Little did they know but this was the beginning of a mutual friendship and lucrative business arrangement. Candy was an entrepreneur herself and her business was just getting started.

Chapter 30

LIVING

The next several years were extremely profitable for D&D Renovations, Inc. The houses–in both capacities–continued to make big money. It was also during these years that the three of them enjoyed their prosperity on a much grander scale.

The "clean" money made from the sales of the houses offered a credible explanation for their wealth. They could finally spend it. And spend it they did.

Rob and Rachel at last committed to buying a house in one of the most popular and rapidly growing parts of Jacksonville, Mandarin. Though they still had nomadic tendencies, the home became a jumping off point. Surrounded by 10 acres of forest and located on a deep creek leading to the river, it was perfect–and Rob could finally have a dog. They had the illusion of being in the country even though it was one of the fastest growing parts of the city. There was an old barn on the property that Rob converted into a workshop. Between his workshop and dog, Rob was content. But Rachel wasn't as easy to please. She had fallen in love with the exterior of the house and the property, but the inside needed work. After a year of remodeling and redecorating, Rachel finally had it the way she wanted.

Like Devan and Rob, Rachel was also busy working for D&D. She'd taken over much of the office and bookkeeping duties during the past several years as well as continued to manage one of the city's hottest nightclubs. Her experience with the business end of club management made her the natural choice for the job. Devan's experience in the business world also came in handy and he often assisted Rachel when needed, but for now, his services were needed by their many projects–especially the grow houses.

Between working part-time for D&D during the day and managing her club at night, Rachel was always busy, but she didn't mind, she liked the work. When Devan asked her why she chose to keep working for other people, she said it was because she liked the nightclub atmosphere. The music and energy was like a drug to her. She'd even become a local celebrity to some extent, again.

Rachel wasn't a trendy carbon copy of the latest fad. She was unique. Her style was an equal mix of class, sophistication, and self-confidence. Her physical presence matched by a keen intellect made for a formidable combination. As in years before, Rachel was the club, and her management knew it. It was no coincidence their business had remained number one among Jacksonville's nightclubs every year since she took over. In many ways it was a part of her, and she loved being in the spotlight.

It was also obvious from their lifestyles why Devan and Rachel could never be together; they were too much alike–too high energy. At first, they would have likely lived fast and furious, but eventually they would have burned each other out. Rob was the perfect balance for Rachel. He was perfectly content working alone in his shop for hours at a time, and equally comfortable living it up out on the town. His calm, laid-back demeanor contrasted with Rachel's, but it worked. It created a balance that successfully held them together over the years.

Rob and Rachel made it a point to spend as much time together as possible, often satisfying their "nomadic urges" by traveling. Rachel was in love with the mountains of Tennessee as well as Colorado and California. Rob didn't have a preference. He just liked to travel. Occasionally, the three of them would take trips together. Devan liked Las Vegas, but those trips were rare. With so many grow houses in operation, it wasn't good to be away for long.

Being able to live their success openly brought other changes as well. They began going out and being seen in expensive restaurants, bars and other clubs. Rachel liked to keep an eye on the competition. As their success grew, so did their tastes. Cars, trucks, furniture, home entertainment centers–if they wanted it, they bought it. Some things were bought with legitimate money and some with cash. D&D was a demanding business, but they spread their projects out so as not to feel overloaded. They were in control, and everything was on their time. No need to stress.

Devan revived Ray's premium brands and used the grow houses as his own personal R&D facility. He continued much of Ray's research and, like Rob, lost himself in his work for hours at a time. He kept busy experimenting with different crossbreeding techniques and took trips to Canada and the Pacific Northwest to bring back new varieties. The work and trips were well worth it. He created impressive new breeds, surpassing Ray's best, taking quality to a whole new level.

Having enjoyed such positive results, Devan figured that more education on the subject couldn't hurt and decided to go back to school once again. It was also his way of staying grounded. Between the business and his high-energy lifestyle, having a committed relationship like Rachel and Rob's was out of the question, at least for the time being. Going back to school brought some semblance of order to his life.

Only one local college offered courses in horticulture, so Devan enrolled and became a student again. But this time he had a specific goal.

Having been away from college for years, he'd forgotten what campus life was like. Jacksonville was no Gainesville, but the campus energy was still there. Devan always liked school. He enjoyed learning new things and enhancing his personal knowledge. Along with horticulture courses, he took classes in other subjects that interested him, most notably, archeology. It was his way of relaxing and indulging himself.

For whatever reason, archeology had fascinated Devan since he was a boy. He was always interested in dinosaurs, mummies, ancient civilizations, and the histories of each. After touring the ruins of ancient cities in Mexico on a family trip when he was 10, Devan was hooked. He took it upon himself to learn all he could about Central and South American civilizations long before he took actual courses. As a hobby, Devan collected artifacts and books, too. Since becoming financially independent, he was able to pursue his interest on a grand scale.

After four consecutive terms, Devan had taken all the available courses at the local university. But he wasn't finished. Knowing Gainesville had one of the best archeology programs in the country, he applied in order to pursue his love for all things ancient.

Even though the Gainesville program was difficult to get into, his past history with the university and superb GPA made getting accepted no problem. Devan was eager to go back but he knew this time it would have to be different. He was a successful businessman now and had higher priorities in Jacksonville. Devan would have to play student from afar and commute to Gainesville two times a week for classes, attending on a part-time basis. Between D&D and school, he was busy, but he liked it.

As part of the program, the university arranged summer-long research expeditions to sites in Central and South America. They were still expensive–even at a student discount–and selective.

The expeditions were well known nationally and the subject of numerous TV documentaries. Having followed the university's work for years, this was Devan's real reason for wanting to get into the program. He knew the university was sponsoring a summer long expedition to Peru to retrieve some mummies for preservation, as well as, begin mapping the ruins of an ancient city recently discovered by a crew building a road. Having the time and the money, Devan couldn't pass up the opportunity. Knowing how much he wanted to go, Rachel and Rob agreed to handle the business while he was away. Little did anyone know, but this trip was about to add a whole new chapter to their growing experience.

"That? You've got to be kidding," Devan said to Miguel, the Peruvian official responsible for the expedition. "That's the plant that causes all the trouble? That's where cocaine comes from?" he asked. Miguel nodded. "I expected something more impressive…it's so…ordinary," Devan said, rubbing a leaf between his fingers. "How do they get the coke from this?"

"Methods for refining cocaine go back thousands of years to the Mayan civilizations," Miguel explained. "They used it for quick energy. The process has changed over the years, but the end result is basically the same."

Miguel enjoyed pointing out to tourists how common the coca plants were and how unlikely it was that they would ever be controlled.

"Your government thinks sending money will get rid of all these plants," Miguel continued.

"Does it?" Devan asked.

"Look around. What do you think?" Miguel said.

Devan examined the rolling hills replete with plant life–mostly coca– and laughed out loud. "Nice to see American tax dollars making a difference." What a joke. Eradicating coca plants would be like launching a war on crabgrass. It's impossible.

"So where does the money go?" Devan asked.

"Every time your government gives money to fight the war on drugs a politician gets a nice car, boat, or another house in Europe. Very little goes to destroying any plants. Besides, on the other side are the local growers who also bribe the politicians. Money is always being thrown at them from one side or the other. Being in politics pays off down here if you're willing to play the game."

"What if you're not willing to play the game?" Devan asked.

"One way or another, everyone plays the game," Miguel answered.

As the weeks passed, Devan's interest alternated between the expedition and the local foliage, especially the coca plants. He befriended

Miguel and over the weeks, picked his brain as to how cocaine was produced. As Devan suspected, Miguel wasn't just a government employee, but also the cousin of a prominent drug lord and he had expert, first-hand knowledge of the local growing industry. Like when he first met Ray, Devan thought to himself, *it takes a grower to know a grower.*

Devan returned to Jacksonville late summer with three-dozen coca plant seeds and planted them immediately in the grow house closest to his apartment. They grew quickly. It was a whole new game and with a limited amount of experimental stock, Devan decided to go slow and play it safe. Seven months later he harvested what he thought would be enough to make a small amount of cocaine for testing.

Between Miguel's input and what he learned from the internet; Devan produced his first sample batch. He'd guessed right about the amount. Heeding the internet's advice, he found ways to compress the leaves and stems more efficiently, allowing him to better process what he'd harvested. However, the end result hardly seemed worth the effort. It had taken a considerable amount of each plant to produce only a couple of ounces. But it was pure so that should account for something, he thought to himself as he took the small jar of coke and went home for the night.

Since Devan started processing the cocaine, the temptation and anticipation had been steadily mounting. Would he try it? Should he try it? Devan sat on his balcony, looking at the small jar filled with finished product. What the hell, he finally decided. *There's only one way to really test it,* Devan thought as he opened the lid. Being pure and having been decades since doing any coke, he cut it and then did a very small amount.

"I hate that!" Devan said out loud. He never did like the initial sensation. It didn't take long before he started feeling the effects. *Just like old times,* Devan thought as the feelings flowed through him. But something was missing. Even through the effects of the coke he could sense it. As Devan sat on his balcony staring out over the dark moonlit waters of the river, he let himself drift back to his first coke experience. He remembered everything like it was yesterday, and he remembered her. For the first time in years, Devan let himself drift back to those early years and back to Linda.

As the effects of the coke began wearing off, Devan forced himself to return to the present.

"We can't go back," Devan said as he slowly screwed the lid on the small glass jar. "Those days are gone forever."

Matt tested the coke a few days later and was blown away by its purity. "Where did you get this? Never mind. I don't want to know. But if you can get more, I want it." To Devan's surprise, Matt paid him a small fortune for the entire sample. It seemed they had a new product after all.

For the next year, coke production was stepped up, but because of the processing requirements it was only a small part of the business; Devan thought of it more as a side hobby. A very profitable side hobby with huge market demand. His return to school was once again indirectly responsible for the birth of a new product and marked another turning point for their business. With the addition of the coca plants, business continued to grow and all three performed their roles well in all capacities. The past several years had brought about many new changes. The money and freedom to spend it was liberating. They were finally able to live their lives in the open and on a scale of their choosing.

After leaving his corporate job to work with Rob and Rachel, Devan let his hair grow out and made it known he'd never again shave on a daily basis. His rugged image together with his tireless devotion to exercise and taking care of his body only heightened his sex appeal.

Rachel also improved with age. Always dressed in the latest fashions, her natural beauty and shapely body turned heads wherever she went.

She was probably the only nightclub manager whose customers imitated her style. Men wanted her and women wanted to be her.

Rob went from crew cut to totally bald and unlike many, it worked for him. Combined with his physique, Rob was the definition of "badass." He was really a nice person when one got to know him, but first impressions were intimidating. Rob knew he made people nervous and often used it to his advantage.

Together, Rob and Rachel were an impressive pair and when the three of them were together, they were formidable. They were confident, secure, and comfortable in almost any situation. Whether club-hopping in town, traveling across the country, or going to some big social event, they always looked the part and usually became the center of attention. Rachel and Devan thrived in that environment. They had finally arrived and were determined to enjoy it for as long as they could.

Chapter 31

HIDING IN PLAIN SIGHT

Four years into the grow house operations another chance opportunity presented itself. As a favor to one of Rachel's club regulars, who happened to be a prominent local artist, Rachel agreed to attend an invitation-only showing of his work at a prestigious Jacksonville art museum. With Rob passing on this one, Rachel convinced Devan he had to go with her. Art shows and the crowds that came with them were not Rob's thing.

Devan walked toward the gallery with Rachel on his arm. Seeing the crowd that was gathering, he rolled his eyes.

"How could Rob sit this one out?" Devan asked.

"Be nice. We'll make an appearance, mingle for a few minutes, then sneak out. Sound good?" Rachel suggested

"Absolutely," he said, opening the door.

The lobby and reception area were filled with many of the city's elite. In one corner, a beautiful young woman, looking noticeably out of place, played a white baby grand piano. With the exception of a few children, Devan and Rachel were the youngest people there.

Heads turned and watched Rachel and Devan as they walked in, but they pretended not to notice. Rachel, in a form-fitting black strapless dress, raven hair flowing down her shoulders, and Devan in a dark suit, long hair slicked back, were an impressive sight.

They greeted their host, made the customary rounds, and headed straight to the bar. Two quick drinks later and taking a third as a traveler,

Rachel and Devan set out to explore the rest of the museum. Neither were really "art people" and between the constant classical piano and mind-numbing conversations, it was too much even for them to bear. They needed to get away.

Wandering aimlessly around the modern art section of the museum, lost and not really looking for a way back, Rachel stopped and sat down on a nearby bench to remove one of her shoes.

"You okay?" Devan asked.

"Yeah…just tired. I've been on my feet all day," Rachel said, rubbing her foot.

"Me, too," Devan said and joined her on the bench. Her head was cocked sideways as she stared at something intently.

"What are you looking at?" Devan asked.

"What the hell is that?" Rachel pointed to a small painting. He followed her gaze. "It looks like a red smear on a white piece of paper," she said.

"I don't know," Devan said. He reached into his coat pocket and pulled out his reading glasses. They were the latest style, but Rachel laughed every time he put them on.

"You look like a yuppie in those glasses," she teased.

"My eyes aren't what they used to be," Devan said and leaned in to read the caption under the picture. "It says it's an original Roxanne."

"Give me a tube of red lipstick and white paper and I'll give you an original Rachel."

"For only $2,500 this can be yo…"

He stopped mid-sentence and turned to Rachel, who must have been reading his mind. "Are you thinking what I'm thinking?" Devan asked.

"That it's time to go into the art business?" Rachel suggested with a cunning smile.

"Exactly!" he said.

For the last four years D&D Renovations was proving to be very lucrative, but they could launder only a small percentage of what was being generated from the grow houses. The renovation business was doing well, but piles of cash were accumulating. Each house project had a three to six- month hold time, slowing down their sales cycle. The amount of cash generated from the grow houses was staggering. They literally had piles of money stashed around their homes. For some time, they'd not had much luck finding additional ways to wash it, but the exhibition experience gave them the perfect solution: open their own gallery.

The simplicity of the gallery idea was a stroke of genius. Art is worth whatever one is willing to pay for it. From priceless to worthless, a few dollars to millions, the possibilities were endless. Aside from historical significance, art and art appreciation were subjective and a matter of individual taste. Who's to say a white canvas with a red smear isn't worth $2,500? To someone it would be. They'd make sure of that.

Rachel and Devan found an empty two-story building in the upscale community of San Marco for rent. The building was located on the corner of busy San Marco Boulevard and a small cross street. Several buildings along that stretch of San Marco were empty because of inadequate parking, which was perfect for them. Though they weren't necessarily looking to attract much walk-in business, they liked the area and felt it further legitimized their front. Who would put a major money laundering operation right in the middle of an upscale community? The best place to hide something was in plain sight.

The building had been vacant for a couple of years. The lack of sufficient parking made it inconvenient for customers, therefore difficult to rent. Devan contacted the owner to see if he would be interested in selling, he was, and they quickly cut a deal.

The existing layout of the building suited them well. The first floor was divided into two sections. The front section, the smaller of the two, faced San Marco Boulevard and was all windows with a set of double doors in the corner. The windows continued down the cross street and ended where the front section stopped. Behind it was a larger, windowless section perfect for storage. There were two doors at the back of the building, a large metal roll-down and a regular metal door. Inside, another door connected the front and back sections and a beautiful, sweeping staircase led to the second floor. With a little work, the first floor would make a perfect showroom.

At the top of the stairs was a large reception area lit by an impressive diamond-shaped skylight. Bordering the reception area were three good-sized offices and a narrow hallway leading to bathrooms, a utility closet, and a small kitchen. It was perfect: downstairs for the gallery, upstairs for D&D's main offices. D&D was currently located in Devan's apartment and Rachel and Rob's third bedroom. Having a real office would allow them to have a central base of operations under one roof.

It was also important for other reasons. As an incorporated company, D&D Inc. was its own entity. With an address, it was no longer just a paper front. It now had a physical presence and a significant dollar value. Along with the renovations business, they had acquired several commercial rental properties; legitimate income-producing investments that were becoming a larger share of the business. But nothing came close to the grow houses in terms of income-generating potential. The grow houses were and would remain the priority.

Within a few months, the building was completely transformed. With a much-needed face-lift as well as being one of the few occupied buildings on this section of the boulevard, the property stood out. Along the top of the building and facing San Marco Boulevard, three-foot high letters proudly displayed "D&D Renovations, Inc." "The Gallery Of San Marco" was painted on the first story windows in gold and black professional text.

The building's original hardwood floors in the gallery were stripped and refinished to such perfection no one wanted to walk on them. The walls were painted a bright white and illuminated with expensive custom lighting. They spared no expense giving it the look of the high-end gallery it was designed to be.

The staircase was refinished and carpeted down the center. The elegant curve of the stairs along the back wall added a touch of class to the gallery and blended in well with its new modern look.

The upstairs lobby was transformed into a comfortable sitting room furnished with two brown leather sofas, a pair of matching leather chairs, and a reception desk. Adorning the walls were works of art they'd collected over the years.

Like the lobby, the three offices were decorated to reflect each partner's unique tastes. They even added additional windows in two of the offices for better lighting. It was an expensive renovation, but they didn't care. They were proud of their accomplishments and wanted the building to make a statement. Hiding in plain sight was all the more exciting because of who they were and what they did. They were living large, projecting an image of success, and flaunting their accomplishments right under the noses of the city's elite and loving every minute of it.

The gallery setup was simple and brilliant. To create a gallery look, they randomly displayed works on the walls. They also fashioned free standing display units where more art was purposefully hung with precise lighting to showcase the artists. Most of their inventory was acquired online from art dealers in the U.S. and other countries or from other, less credible sources. Devan had bought sketches and paintings in South America from street artists; acquisitions from area flea markets, antique stores, and local college galleries provided a substantial collection of inventory for props. By mixing real works from reputable artists with unknowns, they had an impressive collection of eclectic works. They often rotated displays, giving the appearance of constant turnover for the benefit of the occasional window shopper.

The idea was to launder large amounts of cash through the sale of overly inflated art. With prices from a few thousand to $50,000 and higher, they were washing sizable sums within a short period of time. They would even sell the same paintings over again with different names. With the help of creative bookkeeping, bogus inventory records, and anonymous sales to fictional international clientele, the gallery showed a profit–at least on paper. And they paid their taxes. On the surface, the business appeared to be a legitimate enterprise and they were determined to keep it that way.

"I detest paying taxes," Rachel complained one day as she and Devan worked to doctor the books. "The government is stealing all our hard-earned profits."

"Now, Rachel, remember it's our duty as honorable citizens to pay our taxes. Remember what the money's used for," Devan said. She tossed him a blank look. "To fight the war on drugs! I'm all for the government helping to eliminate our competition," Devan added.

"By all means then we must do our part," Rachel said, returning his smile. "For the children of course," she added.

"Absolutely!" he replied.

They both knew this was a crock. For one, the war on drugs was a joke. Most of the money ended up in the pockets of corrupt government officials who used the war as a front for their "own" causes. And that was just in the U.S. Not all of its "allies" in the war have second homes in Europe and new luxury cars. Second, and the most irritating of all, was that every time politicians wanted something they'd claim it was "for the children." The hypocrisy of politics and the political arena repulsed them. When compared with politicians, Rachel and Devan couldn't help feeling morally superior, even though technically they were supposed to be the "bad" guys.

In the months following the building's renovation and gallery opening, they had many visitors, but as expected, no real sales. With walk-in business never being the goal, they were not disappointed. Rachel and Devan actually preferred it that way.

Fortunately, the gallery didn't require much attention. Most of the time they kept the front doors locked, preferring instead to handle sales in their own unique way, with creative bookkeeping. Drawing from past experience and their more innovative talents, Devan and Rachel found laundering on such a blatant scale not only exciting, but also extremely rewarding. As the months passed, their laundering skills only continued to improve.

Then one day the unthinkable happened. The gallery made a legitimate sale. It was 11a.m. on a beautiful autumn morning when Devan was meeting Rachel to help finish some paperwork before joining Rob on a new project. Together he and Rachel were an impressive financial team. Though much of their work centered on finding ways to wash dirty money, they showed considerable skill when dealing with their legitimate interest. Living so much closer, Devan usually arrived before Rachel, so he left the front doors unlocked and went to up to his office to get started.

"I told you it was a Duffey," said a lady's voice. Hearing this, Devan looked up from his desk at the video monitor showing the gallery showroom. He saw two middle-aged women walking around the showroom.

"Damn! Customers. I knew I should've locked that door," Devan said to himself. "Might as well play the part." He trotted down the stairs to greet them, figuring they would leave as soon as they heard the prices.

"Good morning, ladies. Can I help you?" Devan got a kick out of playing the salesman.

"Oh, thank heavens. I've been trying to come in for a week but you're never open," one of the women said.

"I apologize. Most of our sales are international. After opening, we realized the city wasn't quite ready for such a business, so we decided to use the store as a base for our global clientele. We're typically by appointment only."

"Don't give up on us just yet, young man. We may be a small city, but we have a few deep pockets in this town," the woman joked.

"Feel free to look around, ladies, and if you have any questions let me know."

"I do," said the other woman. "Is that painting in the window by Edgar Duffey, the painter from Scotland?"

Devan was surprised the woman knew Edgar. "Yes. Are you familiar with his work?" Devan asked.

"Oh, yes. My husband and I saw some of his paintings in New York last year and before that in Paris. I regretted not buying anything at the time, but I won't make that mistake again. How much is it?"

Impressed by the woman's knowledge of the painter, but liking the piece himself, Devan threw out what he thought was a ridiculous price, so she would lose interest.

"We're asking $5,000. It's truly one of a kind," Devan answered.

"Sold!" she said and reached in her purse for her checkbook.

"Hilda!" said the other woman. "What will Donald say?"

"He spends at least that much on suits. I let Mr. Duffey get away from me once. I'm not going to let it happen again. Do you have any more of his work?" the woman asked.

Completely stunned, Devan was speechless, but managed to keep his composure.

"Do you have any more?" she repeated.

"Well, actually, I do," Devan replied. "Wait right here and I'll bring down the one from our storeroom."

Upstairs in the lobby Devan looked at the other painting of Edgar's hanging on the wall. "Sorry, Eddie my friend, but a sale's a sale."

Devan had met Eddie several years before through a friend and former co-worker. Having been a fan ever since, he followed his career over the years and was disappointed it hadn't taken off like he hoped it would. Specializing in contemporary abstracts of nude women, Edgar's work impressed Devan and over the years he bought three of his paintings. Two were at the gallery and one hung in his apartment. Occasionally he rotated them as part of the gallery's displays.

This could be Eddie's lucky day, Devan thought to himself as he presented the second painting to the lady.

"I'll take it!" she said without even asking the price.

Mrs. Hilda Donald Weatherton, III was one of the wealthiest women in the city and believed by most to be the pinnacle of Jacksonville's upper-class. Her social functions and society events were known far and wide.

"Thank you so much," she said as Devan helped load the paintings into her car.

"Here's my card. If there's anything else I can do for you, please call," Devan offered.

The women drove off as Rachel pulled into the parking lot.

"Who was that?" Rachel asked, walking up to Devan still standing in the lot.

"That was Mrs. Hilda Donald Weatherton the Third, one of the wealthiest women in the city."

"Did she buy anything?" Rachel asked.

"Oh, yeah."

She looked at Devan in disbelief.

"Both Duffey's."

"Damn! I wanted the one in the showroom. How much?"

"$5,000."

"No shit?"

"Apiece."

"No shit!"

By the week's end, the gallery had been flooded with requests for appointments, many asking for more Duffeys. With such a huge demand, Devan called Edgar's representatives and had as many paintings as possible shipped to the gallery. By the end of the following week, they sold seven more, along with several other works, bringing in $50,000 of legitimate money. Mrs. Weatherton was 100 percent responsible. It appeared the city's social elite had taken an interest in their little business in a big way.

PART SIX

Chapter 32

ONE LAST PROJECT

The businesses under the D&D Renovations umbrella continued thriving through the years. Out of necessity, Devan and Rachel devoted more time to the gallery. To keep it fully stocked with inventory, Devan made frequent trips outside the country. They continued to selectively mix both known and unknown artists as well as works by local artists and students. Their willingness to support local talent was viewed as a positive example of community outreach and often led to feature articles about The Gallery of San Marco in the local papers.

Rachel finally had to dedicate herself full time to overseeing the administrative needs of the business with Devan. Rob had several crews working for him and with the exception of the administrative responsibilities, he ran the "legitimate" side of the renovations business on his own. Between the gallery, renovations business, commercial rental properties, and the production, distribution, and D&D of both grow house products, they stayed busy.

By the gallery's third anniversary, the time had finally come to begin scaling back and eventually phase out the grow house operations. The unanimous decision was bittersweet. For six years the grow houses had served them loyally and provided the means to finally beat the very system that once appeared destined to dominate their lives forever. Like Ray, they reached a point where living in the legitimate world was again possible thanks to the "sins" of their past–a past they would remain forever grateful to. But before they closed operations completely, one last project remained. After that, they would be out of both "illegal" businesses forever.

"So, you're finally throwing in the towel," Ray said as he and Devan sat on his front porch, enjoying the country air.

"I prefer to call it passing the torch," Devan said. "I feel better knowing it'll stay in the family."

"Clay owes you big. My nephew has no idea how far you've brought quality since taking over from me," Ray said.

"His continuing our work is thanks enough. Like you said many years ago, it would be a shame to just throw away all that R&D," Devan said.

"A shame indeed," Ray repeated. "So, what's your timeline?"

"One year. I've got one last big project to do before we're completely out."

"Totally legitimate?" Ray asked with one eyebrow raised.

"Totally legitimate."

"Back to the real world...again?"

Devan nodded.

Ray always envied Devan's high-profile life. Though their business was one of secrecy, Devan refused to live in the shadows. He and Rachel were social people and liked to be seen. It always impressed Ray how effortlessly Devan managed to live on the edge of both worlds. He had what Ray always wanted but it wasn't meant to be. Because of the way he conducted business, Ray was forced to live almost underground. But not Devan. He refused to live that way. Instead, Devan chose to live out in the open, in public, right under the noses of the very people who were out to get them all.

The club project was one of the more ambitious and probably the most significant turning point in their lives. By the time the club idea was born, Devan, Rachel, and Rob were well on their way to legitimacy.

Marijuana operations and coke production had been scaled way back. Devan wanted to keep some of each going through the club acquisition in case they needed any "extra leverage" during negotiations. Then they would close both operations for good and be 100% legitimate.

The construction division was also doing well. Rob and his crews had been turning real profits for over three years. For some time, they'd been branching out and taking on bigger projects. Rob had 50 employees and at any given time five large commercial projects in process.

With Devan and Rob's encouragement, Rachel began to pursue her writing ambitions. She published a few short stories and enrolled in writing classes part-time at a local college. Her dream of becoming a professional writer was still very much alive.

Between the businesses administrative and gallery responsibilities, Devan and Rachel had their hands full. Since the gallery had become trendy with the city's elite, the last three years were busy ones. They moved the art almost as fast as it came in. Between the laundering and the legitimate sales, the gallery was a serious moneymaker. They'd amassed a considerable fortune over the years (reported and unreported), making the real world more inviting than in years past.

Unfortunately, it was in the so-called legitimate world of business that they encountered more hypocrisy, corruption, illegal business practices, and outright betrayal than they ever believed possible. The level of corruption astounded them, spreading from the lowest to the highest pillars of the community. Real estate and Jacksonville politics, they discovered, proved to be the biggest racket in town, far greater than their drug trade could ever hope to be. But unlike the seedy drug underworld, illegal business practices and corrupt city officials operated in plain sight, right under the noses of the authorities and the public they claimed to represent and serve. There was no honor. No respect. Unlike the drug world, a person's word or handshake meant nothing. They had no idea what lay before them.

For some time, Devan had his sights on a local bank building in the San Marco area. The three of them thought the two-story building, with its huge open foyer, would make a great upscale club, something of Las Vegas caliber, and something Jacksonville sorely lacked. The area and building were perfect. The bank had gone out of business and the building sat vacant for over a year before Devan made his move.

The property was owned by A-1 Holdings, a local commercial real estate company. At first, everything appeared to be going well. Devan even had his architects create several possible designs for the club with the work designated for D&D Renovations.

But negotiations abruptly halted during the final stages of the deal. A-1 began a deliberate stalling campaign. Even though good-faith contracts had been signed and agreements reached, A-1 continued being uncooperative. Eventually, they stopped taking D&D's calls altogether. No one could figure out what had happened.

Finally, they'd had enough. Using their many new legitimate business connections, they began making inquiries. Due mostly to the gallery's successes, they had established many connections throughout the city's legal and financial circles. By using these contacts, it wasn't long before their friend and attorney, Ari, discovered what had happened.

It appeared a large and influential church heard about the deal and decided it wanted to acquire the property. This particular church already had enormous private and commercial holdings throughout the city and using its considerable clout pressured A-1 to stall the deal.

When Devan's real estate firm discovered the church's involvement, they further complicated matters by pulling out and abandoning him. Realizing D&D had grounds for legal action, Devan began the search for a law firm specializing in such matters to file suit. Not a single attorney would step up. Everyone feared the consequences of taking on the church. Ari, through friendship, was the only one willing to stand by them, and at great personal risk to his own practice.

On many occasions D&D tried to reach out to church representatives in an effort to negotiate a compromise, but were repeatedly blown off.

Then Ari began to feel their pressure. Those same church representatives "encouraged" Ari's clients to seek different representation in an attempt to get him to abandon Devan. But Ari was a lot like Devan and Rachel–stubborn and hardheaded–he did not like to be pushed around. Ari was a fighter.

The deal continued to stall for weeks until finally A-1 announced the deal was officially off and they were selling to the church. Ari called Devan at the gallery offices and told him the news. Devan was furious. They had signed contracts, the deal was pending, there was no way this was legal, Devan insisted.

Ari agreed and recommended suing, but bluntly told him he didn't think much would come from it. The church had its hands in everything and controlled or could exert considerable influence over many city officials, judges, financial institutions, real estate firms, and lawyers. Lots of lawyers. They could make or break local politicians in accordance with their will. The church owned the law and constantly bent it to meet its needs. D&D wouldn't be the first to get screwed. The list was long and full of disgruntled people who'd been burned by the church and other corrupt city politicians –even other churches!

"Devan, if you want my honest advice, I think you should give up. We tried. Chalk it up to you win some and you lose some. I don't know what else we can do," Ari said. His genuine disappointment was evident as they discussed the matter on the phone.

"Ari, you've known me a long time, and you know I'm not one to give up without a fight," Devan said, not liking Ari's advice.

"Well, my friend, I'm afraid you may be in over your head on this one. I don't think we'll be able to get much help from anyone, not legally anyway. They own the law in this town."

"I want you to go ahead with whatever legal procedures you can do on your end. It's our turn to stall them for a change. They'll see I'm not one to just roll over and give in," Devan said. "But mostly I need you to buy us some time to do a little digging." Devan paused, looking at a picture on his desk of himself, Rachel, and Rob standing on the southern rim of the Grand Canyon. "If they want to play dirty, I can do that. You provide the smoke and I'll see what kind of fires I can light." Devan was cool and calm.

"Okay, but be careful. They may hide behind the law and word of God, but you know I've had experience with these people. They can make your life very difficult," Ari said.

Without hesitation, Devan immediately made another call, this one to an old friend and current associate. He dialed the number and by the second ring a soft, sexy voice answered.

"Hey, it's Devan. I have a little problem I think you may be able to help me with. Can we get together later?"

"Business or pleasure?" she asked. "I hope it's the latter."

"I'm afraid it's business. How about we do dinner at our favorite restaurant?"

"8 o'clock?"

"See you then."

After placing the phone on the receiver, Devan sat back in his chair and thought about Jacksonville. It was a city on the grow. For years city leaders promoted growth and development with the benefits concentrated in the hands of a select few. Still, the city was proving attractive to people and businesses across the country. Each year more and more people were relocating to Jacksonville than ever before. Even large companies found the city attractive, some for strategic reasons and others for the comfortable and more favorable climate. This growth, combined with the city recently being awarded an NFL expansion team, catapulted Jacksonville into the business and commerce spotlight.

Yes, Devan thought to himself, a lot of people were profiting and none more so than the church and its web of corrupt accomplices. Through questionable business practices, they benefited from an incredible real estate boom going on throughout the city. Devan thought to himself how successful he, Rachel, and Rob had been over the past eight years. But their success was nothing compared with the kind of money being made in the local real estate market. They were small-time, not even a drop in the bucket by comparison, and they each had several million dollars to their names –legitimate and not so legitimate!

From the sidelines Devan watched as land was claimed under the guise of "imminent domain" in order to build another strip mall or condemn and tear down buildings, making way for some new project advertised to "benefit everyone." In the end, it cost taxpayers millions, and many lost their homes, businesses, and livelihood in the name of progress. There was little to no resistance, seeing as how the church and city government dominated all areas of legal recourse. These were just a few examples that kept rolling through his mind.

Devan thought how different the city might have been if not for all of the corruption and behind closed-door dealings; Jacksonville was proving it could be just as dirty and corrupt as the country's largest cities. And sitting atop this mass of corruption was one very prominent church. That set Jacksonville apart from other cities and presented a unique problem; how to deal with a church? It had its hands in everything and its alliances with other powerful political figures and local families gave the church a loud voice in any business deal it wanted to be involved in.

So, what to do? Devan thought to himself. He thought back to his theory of perception and misperception. Had anyone ever really challenged the church and its allies? One was sure to lose if he or she tried to do it by the law. But, what about on a personal level? What about real "dirty business," below-the-belt stuff? *What the hell,* Devan thought. He was a drug dealer, the lowest of the low, the bottom rung on the ladder of illegal businesses. Why not fight dirty? Real dirty. It was time to dig deeper and see what turned up and he knew exactly where to start.

Chapter 33

AN OLD FRIEND

Candy was a by-product of Jacksonville's growth; a necessary evil, so to speak. Plainly stated, Candy was a madam. But not just any madam. She operated the largest, most exclusive, and most professional "call service" in town. She operated out of dozens of homes, apartments, and condos located in upscale areas throughout the city. She and her business were one of Jacksonville's best-kept, dirty little secrets.

Originally from Jacksonville, Candy returned after working in Nevada for several years as a professional call girl. She recognized the potential early on and through skilled, backdoor maneuvering matched only by her incredible beauty and charm, she quickly built a highly successful business. Her clientele consisted not only of the typical traveling businessman, but also of many of Jacksonville's "movers and shakers." And Devan knew it. Devan and Candy's early relationship was brief, but they remained close friends. D&D kept her, her employees, and customers supplied with their products at greatly reduced prices.

As they drove to the front entrance of the restaurant, the parking attendant recognized them immediately.

"Mr. Ross, Miss Prescott, good to see you again. Enjoy your dinner."

"Thanks Brad, I'm sure we will," Devan said as he handed the young man a $20 bill. "Keep it close, will you? I might need to make a quick getaway," Devan joked.

As Devan and Candy walked through the main entrance, heads turned. Dressed in the finest fashions, they made a handsome couple. This was their world. Living in the upper tiers of society was where they felt most comfortable. Here they had an audience, and they played their parts like professionals. Having a shady past only added to the enjoyment and satisfaction of being who they were. And the envious looks from everyone around them made it that much more rewarding.

The maître d' immediately acknowledged them as they approached. "Miss Prescott, Mr. Ross, I have your table ready. Please follow me."

They were led to their favorite table in a semi-secluded corner of the restaurant. This particular table was next to two huge windows with the river and twinkling city lights as a backdrop, offering a breathtaking view of the city. The restaurant was on the top floor of a tall building on the North bank of the river.

Candy slid into the half-curved booth first and Devan sat beside her. After ordering drinks, she lit a cigarette and casually leaned back while draping one arm across the top of the seat, relaxed and ready to do business.

"Business, huh? I'm intrigued," she said.

"Listen to what I have to say first. It may not be to your liking. There are risks–big risks–for us both."

Her expression became serious. "I'm listening."

Devan explained their situation about the club, the church, the city, and all of the related happenings. Candy listened with deep interest. "And that's where you come in. I need dirt. Real dirt. Pictures of Jacksonville's movers and shakers in compromising positions. Sex, drugs…you name it. I want everything. From the highest to the lowest, church administrators, government officials, anyone and everyone –even of our more prominent family members. I want them all," Devan said.

Candy sat quietly, thinking to herself for a moment. Her face was blank, and Devan couldn't tell what was going through her mind.

"Are you going to take them down publicly?" Candy asked, breaking her silence.

"That's not my intention. I only want the building," Devan said.

She smiled. "No need to ruin anyone's career. After all, we might need them later for something."

"We?" Devan asked.

"Oh, yeah, honey!" Candy said. She was bursting with excitement; gone was her cool, calm character. "I've been waiting for a chance like this for a long time. I can use that dirt to keep them off my back and finally get some respect," she said slamming the table with her fist.

"Devan, you just don't know," she continued. "Those bastards have been screwing me for years! Literally!" she said. Her demeanor became serious again. "They're not even the bulk of my business. It's always been the out-of-towners. These assholes actually cost me money! The church and city use me and my people for their own private entertainment as well as for rewards and bonuses to their employees, associates, and other business partners. And they're cheap bastards, too! They rarely ever pay. I've been told many times that my payment is my being allowed to operate freely without any legal entanglements. Yeah, right! Let them bust me and see if I don't spill everything!" Candy threatened.

Devan could tell Candy was pissed, but he wasn't about to stop her ranting. Having thrown off her upper-class image, Candy was reverting back to the redneck girl he knew lived deep inside.

"Shit!" Candy said disgusted. "Those bastards act like they're above the law, too. You know what else?" she asked, without pausing for Devan to respond. "Most of them don't treat my people that good either. I can't tell you how many hospital bills I've had to pay out of my own pocket. So, yes, Devan, 'we.' I want in on this with you. Those bastards are finally going to get what's coming to them. Let's do it!"

She raised her glass. "Here's to the opening night of your club."

Devan returned her toast. "Here's to getting some payback."

"I'll drink to that," Candy said as their glasses clinked. She then slid over to him and interlocked her arm in his. "How about we go back to my place and discuss some more business, personal business."

"Check please," Devan said, motioning to the nearest waiter

Devan met with Rachel and Rob at their offices the following morning. After informing them of his plan, they agreed it was time to go legitimate. Things were bound to get interesting, and they figured it would be better to do away with all illegal activities just in case. They decided to close the last of their grow house operations immediately.

"How bad do you think it'll get?" Rob asked.

"I don't know," Devan said, leaning back in his chair. "But one way or another, it's going to be very different around here."

"Rachel, I need you to do your best research. Find out who else they've screwed over in the past couple of years and what, if any, legal consequences came out of it. Time to make use of some of our legitimate new friends and associates," Devan said, looking at her.

Rachel gave him a strange look.

"What?" Devan asked.

"Candy?"

"Yes. Candy," he said.

"Only you would have an actual Candy in your life."

Devan rolled his eyes. "Oh, shut up," he groaned. "Let's go. We've got a lot of work to do."

Candy was a smart woman. Devan suspected she had some kind of surveillance equipment at her many "rendezvous" locations and hoped they'd be able to benefit from this. As it turned out, he was right. Candy had her locations wired with audio and video monitoring systems for the protection of her employees. If things got too far out of hand, action could be taken, and problems resolved before getting out of control. Knowing police intervention was out of the question, Candy determined for the sake and safety of her employees that the surveillance was a risk worth taking.

As the days and weeks passed, Devan and Candy worked feverishly on their project. Some clients had to be enticed with phone calls and arranged "chance" encounters, but for the most part it was easy. Many church and city officials visited at regularly scheduled intervals, often bringing prospective clients and other associates with them in an attempt to sweeten deals by mixing business with pleasure. They also used Candy's services to reward their employees for jobs well done. It really was too easy. In just a matter of weeks they had almost everyone they set out to catch, acquiring more than enough ammunition for Devan to begin his counterattack.

"Look at them," Candy said as she and Devan sat reviewing hours of video. "Listen to that one brag. He's been going on for the last 10 minutes about how he was able to use imminent domain and right-of-way to kick some old woman out of her home and take her property. He's so proud of the fact that he was able to pay her a fraction of the fair market value, and for what?" Candy asked. "So they can build another strip mall? Just what this town needs. And now he's here to claim his prize. They really make me sick, Devan. Look how smug these people are. Not a care in the world–never believing for a second anyone can touch them –secure in their little world of corrupt protection," Candy said as she switched from monitor to monitor, watching the scenes play out before her.

As they scanned through hours and hours of video, Devan silently congratulated himself for going to Candy first. He had no idea how much she resented these people. But after only a few weeks of seeing them in action, he easily understood why.

Rachel also hit pay dirt. Within days of beginning her investigation, she had also uncovered vast amounts of information.

"I can't believe how easy it was," Rachel said to Devan as they sat in his office, going through the piles of folders, printouts, and court documents she'd gathered. "They don't even try to hide anything. It's all here! Did you know I found 34 examples of them doing to others exactly what they did to us in the last year? What gets me is how easily they get away with it. Legal actions were often started, but never go anywhere even when they're clearly in breach of multiple contracts."

Rachel and Devan knew it would be bad, but they were astounded at just how much the church and city were allowed to get away with.

"I guess it shouldn't surprise us," Devan said. "They own the courts and city government, so any claim will simply be dismissed or thrown out. They have no regard or fear of the consequences because they know there won't be any."

"It's still so incredible," Rachel continued. "Think about Rob and all the permitting and zoning bullshit he goes through. It can hold up progress for weeks. But, when it's something for these guys, bam! Laws get changed and obstacles get removed overnight. It's incredible."

After pausing and catching her breath Rachel added, "Devan, this evidence alone should be enough to get them good."

"Unfortunately, it's not," Devan said, letting out a long sigh. "Not in a town where the legal system is so tightly controlled by corruption. Remember, they own the law. They operate as if they have no fear because they don't. So, legally anyway, they've got us." He paused for a moment and repositioned himself in his chair. "We can't win in the courts," Devan said with a tone of finality.

"If we can't win then why even try?" Rachel asked. She took a long, frustrated drag from her cigarette and exhaled. "Why gather all this information if we're not going to use it?"

"Oh, don't worry. We're going to use it. It's only the first punch in our two-punch knockout strategy," Devan said with a devious grin.

"Do you really think what you and Candy have will make a difference?"

"I think so. Remember, when all else fails, always fall back on the K.I.S.S. strategy," he said.

"Keep It Simple Stupid," Rachel said. She began to see where he was going with it.

"Exactly! And what's more direct, gets more attention, and has more of an impact than a good old-fashioned sex scandal?"

Chapter 34

ROSEMOND

Meanwhile, Ari had been attempting to fight it out in both the courts and at city hall but was making little progress on either front. He was, however, able to get an injunction that froze the sale for 60 days. This minor miracle was due to sheer luck. It happened that the judge scheduled to preside over the case had a personal emergency and had to excuse himself at the last minute. His replacement, a little over-eager to impress his superiors, continued the stalling policy by granting the injunction by mistake. He was not aware the strategy had changed, and the church wanted resolution as quickly as possible. The injunction was not what the church representatives wanted, but they saw it only as a brief delay. For Devan and Rachel this delay was just what they needed to plan their next move.

In Ari's mind, it was only postponing the inevitable. By now, it was obvious the holding company resided in the church's corner and wasn't even attempting to hide it anymore. The church's lawyers had taken the lead role in the case and A-1's attorneys were there merely for representation.

Two weeks into the injunction, Ari ran into Stu Rosemond, the lead attorney representing the church and A-1. They were members of the same country club. After acknowledging Ari in the club lounge, Stu invited him over to his table for a drink and to discuss a little business. Curious, Ari agreed. After engaging in cordial small talk, Ari went straight to the point.

"Okay Stu, what will it take to make you guys go away? You know what you're doing is illegal."

"Illegal?" Stu asked, pretending to be hurt. "Why that's harsh, Ari," he said in his deep southern accent. "I wouldn't say illegal. Let's just say we're fortunate and know how to make things happen in this town."

"Don't bullshit me Stu, I'm from this town, I know how it works. Your people own the courts and city, so tell me what it'll take to resolve this."

"Tell your client to go away—a tactical retreat, so to speak," Stu said, waving his hands in a dismissive gesture.

"Why? What could the church possibly want with another building?" Ari asked.

"It's not so much the building as the idea. Your client is right, an upscale club would do very well there. Since learning of his plans, we've been doing a little research and with the Super Bowl coming, well, Ari, this could be very profitable. If you can help, I'm sure we can find a way to cut you in," Stu said with a casual wink.

"You're stealing his idea?" Ari asked, completely ignoring the bribe. He was pissed.

"We think a project of this magnitude would be better administered by people with a little more experience in this area," Stu clarified.

"This is incredible!" Ari said, leaning forward in his chair. "I can assure you my client won't stand for this!" Ari's anger, though genuine, also concealed a bluff. He hoped Stu would want to avoid a fight and maybe offer some kind of compromise.

"Like it or not, you know we have a way of making things happen in this town, Ari. Now for example, take your client," Stu continued. "For all intents and purposes, he's a nobody. So what if he has a gallery and a construction business and has been in the papers a few times? It means nothing to us. He doesn't have the clout or the means to take us on," Stu said, and leaned back, crossing his arms across his large belly in a position of authority. "No, Ari, you would do best to advise your client to back down. This is not a fight he can win. You're wasting everyone's time. We'll each go our own way with no serious harm done. At least, not yet anyway." The threat was hardly veiled.

Ari, feeling defeated, managed one last angry outburst. "But, Stu, this is illegal! You know this isn't how it works; my client is 100 percent in the right!"

"Right, wrong, percentages, etcetera. They're irrelevant. Who's the public going to believe and, more importantly, who are the court and city going to believe? You know, Ari, the church has been in this town a long time and it has a lot of influence here. We know a good number of city officials, financial representatives, and a lot of lawyers. We represent and are respected by many fine people throughout this community. Given this, I can assure you that you and your client are going to find it very difficult to pursue this matter any further. Tell him for his sake it's better that he back down and live to fight another day. Tell him to be happy with what he has because one never knows when even that might be taken away."

"The nerve of that prick!" Rachel said as she sat on their office couch listening to Ari recap his conversation with Rosemond. "He's just as crooked as the people he represents! Not only are they trying to steal the club, but also threatening us? What kind of shit is that?" she demanded.

Her rage was for good reason. Rachel had discovered a considerable amount of incriminating evidence on many church and city officials as well as on Rosemond and his firm. He or his people had a hand in nearly all of the cases she'd shown Devan. She was stunned by their arrogance and overt corruption.

Devan wasn't surprised. He remembered hearing stories from his family. Devan's grandfather relocated his mother's family to Jacksonville in the early 1950's. He was to introduce and run the extreme southeastern branch of a national food distribution company owned by his father-in-law. His grandfather's territory was the state of Florida. The business took off. It brought people a more diverse variety of food from all areas of the country. Most communities embraced the idea because not only did it bring greater variety, but also lower prices.

As the company grew and became more successful throughout the state, a problem started to surface in Jacksonville. The church was a power to be reckoned with even then, and a power his grandfather would soon find he had to learn to live with and accept if he wanted to continue doing business in the city. The church realized his grandfather was fast becoming a successful local businessman (and related to an even greater one) and extended an invitation for him and his family to join their congregation. Being of a different faith, Devan's grandfather respectfully declined. He was informed that one doesn't decline such an invitation. The church was like an exclusive club; a club businessmen would join if they desired to continue doing business in Jacksonville.

So out of respect and consideration for the local power structure, Devan's grandfather joined. He thought this would be the end of his social obligations, but soon found the church also required a price for membership. It was explained to him that businesses of a certain status were encouraged to make generous donations to the church at regular intervals throughout the year. Devan's grandfather equated this to extortion and refused. So, the church proceeded to show him why it was in his best interest to cooperate. First, they encouraged his drivers to strike. When he replaced them with men from out of town, they pressured local stores and supermarkets to stop doing business with his company. Within a month the entire Jacksonville market disappeared. Angered and vowing never to cave into these criminals, his grandfather resisted. Finally, his father-in-law stepped in and told him to play ball. He didn't like it, but eventually complied, for the most part, anyway. His grandfather never had this problem anywhere else in Florida. Jacksonville was unique in that respect.

Devan knew Ari was well aware of what the local power structure was capable of, having experienced it firsthand years ago. Ari's first job after graduating from law school was working with Devan's grandfather. His grandfather took a special liking to the young lawyer, and they became lifelong friends. Ari stood by his side when the church attempted to force him to give in to their demands. And even though Devan's grandfather was ordered by his father-in-law to play along, he never did completely. Ari proved a valuable ally in helping him remain an irritating thorn in the church and city's side for the next 20 years.

Unfortunately, Ari wasn't able to prevent Devan's grandfather's downfall in the 1970's. Devan's grandfather was on the verge of being elected chairman of the board of the parent company, giving him control of all operations nationwide. This did not sit well with some of Jacksonville's power elite. Fearing him having so much influence, and the damage he might inflict on them, they plotted to bring him down.

They bribed a disgruntled accountant in his grandfather's company and got him to plant false documents and alter company records. Devan's grandfather was accused of embezzling hundreds of thousands of dollars from his own company. Though his grandfather vehemently denied these charges, the reach of his enemies proved vast. Accounts were soon "discovered" in local banks in his grandfather's name, supposedly containing the company's missing money.

It was all very suspicious, and Ari saw right through it. He was able to prove his grandfather didn't authorize the accounts and outright accused bank officials of shameful practices and participating in a deliberate smear campaign. He also discovered and proved that the disgruntled accountant had the starring role in setting up the entire plot. Though he was never able to prove who was behind the real planning, they knew. The damage had been done.

His grandfather lost the chairman position and a few years later resigned as president of the Florida operation because of the lingering suspicions surrounding the embezzlement charges. After leaving the company, his grandfather settled into a forced retirement. Ari eventually started his own practice and remained a close friend of Devan's family. He had the utmost respect for Devan's grandfather and always believed him to be a man of integrity. Unfortunately, Devan's grandfather had rocked the boat one too many times and paid the price.

Devan remembered all of these stories and now here was another generation doing the same thing –he was experiencing it firsthand. No, Devan told himself. This shit stops here. With him. Time for some payback. He interrupted Rachel's tirade.

"Okay, Ari. It's time we have a meeting." He sat up and put together a list of names and presented them to Ari. "And here's a list of some additional guests who will be attending,"

Ari reviewed the list. "But Devan," he said with noticeable reservation, "I don't think some of these people will show. In fact, I'm certain the first two won't."

"You get Rosemond, his team, and the A-1 representatives, and we'll take care of the others."

Ari was concerned and for good reason. The first two names on the list were Mike Townsend and John Peterson. Mike was one of the most powerful members of the church's board, and even though the church didn't concentrate total power in the hands of a single member, most accepted Mike as the supreme authority behind the scenes.

John Peterson was the mayor's right-hand man. Peterson was a shadowy figure in city politics. Knowing he had too many skeletons in his closet to ever run for office, he kept his hands in everything by staying close to the man at the top. His position was technically that of "advisor to the mayor," but Peterson's real position was unchanged from administration to administration, regardless of party affiliation. He came with the Mayor's office and there wasn't anything anyone could do to change it.

The next name on the list was Ronald Clark. Clark was the city's chief attorney and the one most responsible for the legal framework and clouds of litigation often surrounding many of the shady deals the city was involved in. Clark's primary responsibility was to make the blatantly illegal actions of the church and city appear legal. If this didn't work, he would be responsible for using his resources to attack credibility and take down anyone daring to challenge them. Together with the courts, these were the men who controlled the city's legal system. Legal outcomes in the city or church's favor were always certain.

The next two names were Jim Wilks and Mark Polk. Both were prominent members of the city's growth and development planning board. Jim was also serving as City Council president. Both men were in positions to either help and assist or seriously hinder Jacksonville's expansion. This often depended on how much one was willing to pay to help facilitate cooperation with the city.

The last name on the list was Judge Washington, the judge currently handling their case. Devan knew these people were only the extreme tip of an enormous network of corrupt officials spreading through both the public and private sectors of the community. And he also knew controlling them would guarantee that the others would have no choice but to follow suit. The plan was to attack the head of the beast, or as close to the head as possible, and that's exactly what they were going to do.

Chapter 35

ARBITRATION

Ari used their right to arbitration to arrange a meeting between the parties. After all of the necessary arrangements were made regarding where and when the arbitration meeting would take place, Devan and Rachel went about ensuring that the others would attend.

Knowing none of these people would show up if simply asked, they devised a way to encourage attendance. Each guest was sent a letter containing the time and location of the meeting, as well as a damning photograph–courtesy of Candy's organization–carefully edited so that heads and faces of those in them were removed. To the average onlooker, the pictures would appear as little more than anonymous pieces of porn, but to those in them the message was clear. The caption printed at the bottom of each customized photo instructed the recipient to make it a point to be present at the meeting. Their absence would result in serious "public" consequences. The topic of discussion was new leadership.

The arbitration was scheduled for Wednesday, May 15, at 11:00a.m. The weather was beautiful. One could not have asked for a more perfect day. The meeting was to take place in Ari's office on the 20th floor of the South Bank Tower in downtown Jacksonville. His conference room was ideal for the meeting and offered the perfect setting. The room was in a corner section of the building, providing a panoramic view of the river and city below. The table could seat 20 and was prepared ahead of time. When their guests began arriving, Ari called Devan and Rachel at the gallery.

"They're showing up," Ari said. His tone gave away his concern.

"We're leaving now. Give us 10 minutes," Devan said.

"Devan, I sure hope you know what you're doing."

"Everything will be fine, Ari. And if it doesn't work out, we can always move farther south," Devan teased.

Ari was not in the mood. "Great, more sun and heat. Just what I've always wanted."

Devan, Rachel, Rob, and Candy had met at the gallery and decided to arrive in style, so they rented a limousine. Devan thought it best for Candy to be at the meeting too. By his reckoning, she had the most to lose. Including her would show she was with them and, if all went well, give her protection from any retaliation. Not to mention the fact that he could not have kept her away even if he wanted to. Candy understood the risks and wanted "a front row seat" as she put it. She wasn't about to miss this for the world.

The four of them made an impressive sight, dressed in their finest for the occasion. There wasn't an outfit between them that cost under $2,000.

Within minutes their limousine pulled up to the formal entrance of Ari's building. A marble staircase lay before them. Beyond that was a veranda and then the main doors.

Devan turned to the others as he put on his sunglasses.

"Showtime!"

Rachel was carrying a thick briefcase. Its contents, they hoped, would have a profound impact on Jacksonville's future. Reaching the veranda, they picked up their pace, marching in unison like soldiers going into battle. To the casual observer, they looked as though they were the ones who owned the town. Their approach caused the doormen to spring into action as they hurried to open the doors. There was no going back now. They were on their way.

Ari met them in his office lobby by the elevators. "Full house." He was curious as to how they were able to get everyone there. "I don't know how you guys did it, but they're all here."

"Relax Ari," Devan said and squeezed his shoulder. "If nothing else, today should prove to be entertaining." Devan motioned toward the conference room. "Shall we go?"

The guests were seated and wondering what this meeting was about. Some attempted to engage in petty small talk, but for the most part, the room was silent. Those who had been sent pictures were particularly quiet. Rosemond, too, had his guard up. He hadn't expected to see so many of his colleagues at this meeting.

Devan and company entered and took the five remaining seats closest to the door. Ari made the introductions and turned the floor over to Devan.

"Gentlemen," Devan said in a calm and relaxed tone, "I thank you all for coming and I promise to make this as quick and painless as possible.

"Rachel, may I have the first folder, please?"

She reached into her briefcase and handed him folder number one. Devan got straight to the point.

"In this folder I have proof that everyone in this room is or has been guilty of obstruction of justice, corruption and fraud. To be more specific, I have 34 cases of how, in just the past year the church, with the help of several city leaders and other prominent officials, have fucked over others, just as you're attempting to fuck us now."

Ari felt his heart skip a beat. Devan had leveled powerful accusations at some of the city's most influential figures and showed no sign of letting up. He desperately hoped Devan had a plan, because if not, all of them would be finished in this town. Forever. Ari came to the realization that this wasn't going to be a typical arbitration meeting. The other guests seemed to sense this, too, as they shifted uneasily in their seats, not so much in fear, but more out of annoyance, angry that they had been summoned to hear the belligerent rant of a disgruntled citizen.

"This is outrageous!" said Wilks as he sprang to his feet. "I don't have to sit here and listen to these false accusations and slanderous remarks," he said as he turned and started to walk out.

Rob beat him to the door and stood his ground. Wilks stopped midway and looked at Devan. "What is the meaning of this?" he demanded.

"I'm getting to that, Mr. Wilks," Devan said in a cold tone. "Please be seated. I assure you, you'll be very interested in what I have to say."

"What do you have to say?" insisted Clark. "Why are we here?"

"You're here to help D&D get back what's rightfully ours, the San Marco property," Devan said, looking directly at Rosemond and the A-1 representatives.

"We have nothing to do with that deal," insisted Peterson. "That's between you and Rosemond."

"No, it's not," Devan said. "Ultimately you'll all profit. You always do." He paused for a moment. "You see, gentlemen, we've assembled you all here today to help us encourage Mr. Rosemond and his colleagues to reconsider their position and allow D&D to purchase the property, at a considerable discount, of course." Devan turned and looked at Rachel. She smiled and nodded in agreement.

"That is out of the question!" Rosemond angrily argued. "I don't care what you think you have in that folder, I can assure you it'll never hold up, not in this town!" he added with total conviction. "No, son," Rosemond continued in his cocky southern drawl, "it'll take a lot more than some flimsy, questionable evidence to play ball with us."

"Flimsy, Mr. Rosemond?" Devan asked. "I can assure you it's far from flimsy. My friend and colleague Miss Winters here has been very thorough in her research."

Rachel faked pouting as if she was hurt by her research being questioned.

Angered, Rosemond continued, "Maybe you don't understand what I'm saying, boy. You and your friends have nothing! I don't care how thorough you were. Let me be very clear here for your sake," he said as he leaned forward and put his chubby hands on the table. "You're a nobody. You're nothing in this city. You have some nerve to think you can call us here and tell us what to do based on what you believe is some kind of incriminating evidence. I truly hope that's not all you've got, my boy, because it takes more than that to play ball in the majors." Rosemond leaned back in his chair, confident and defiant. Clark and Peterson were also unimpressed and appeared equally defiant.

"You're right, Mr. Rosemond," Devan said. "Somehow we didn't think any of you would really be that concerned about this folder's contents. After all, why should you? Actually, I'm willing to guess that most of you are well aware of what's in it already, so let's move on to folder number two."

Devan exchanged folders with Rachel. The other guests did not appear as self-confident as Mr. Rosemond and suddenly became much more attentive when Devan was handed a very fat folder number two.

"In this folder I have, shall we say, a nuclear bomb. One I assure you I won't hesitate to use," Devan said, looking directly at Rosemond.

"Rachel, would you do the honors, please," Devan said as he handed the folder back to her.

Rachel smiled her 'fuck you all' smile and handed each guest a packet from within the folder.

As they opened the packets and began thumbing through the contents, their facial expressions gave away their true feelings. They sat frozen in a state of shock. The confident smug expressions were replaced with pale, sickly looks of fear and panic.

"Well, gentlemen, let's see what we have here," Devan said. He pretended to be shocked and surprised as he flipped through the contents of a folder he was holding. "Looks to me like a lotta bigwigs caught in compromising positions. Would you look at that…everything from sex to illegal drug use. Gentlemen, I'm shocked. Such behavior from so many of our city's finest. What would the public say if they saw these pictures?"

"You're threatening to blackmail us? You can't do that…it's illegal," said Mr. Polk in a panic.

"Why, Mr. Polk, I'm surprised. I didn't know you had a sense of humor. Illegal? Now you want to hide behind the law. I don't think so. Yes. Blackmail. And I assure you I won't hesitate to use it. As you so kindly pointed out, Mr. Rosemond, I'm a nobody with a lot less to lose than any of you. So please, take a few minutes to look through these pictures. I think you'll recognize some good self-portraits as well as some of your clients and other associates. Oh, and I should also add, we have audio and video as well, just in case anyone needs further convincing," Devan winked at Candy.

"So, Mr. Clark, to answer your earlier question, this is why you're here. I want you to be sure to impress on your friends and colleagues how serious we are about using what we have if we don't get what we want."

Rachel, Devan, Rob, and Candy were enjoying every minute of it. The looks of panic, fear and total defeat filled them with a morbid satisfaction. They basked in their victory.

After what seemed like an eternity of silence, Mr. Rosemond cleared his throat. "I think we're all rational people here and are willing to listen to reason. How do you suggest we resolve this matter?" he asked as he looked at a picture of himself face down in the crotch of a very young girl.

"I want the bank building, my liquor license, and no bullshit from the city about a bar being so close to two churches. And I want compensation, punishment for your blatant violations of the law and interfering with this deal," Devan answered boldly.

"And as for you," Devan continued, looking at the A-1 representatives, "I want a hell of a deal, too. If not, I'll continue this in court and sue you for violating our agreement. And this time, I can assure you, you won't have the protection of the courts. Isn't that right, judge?" Devan asked, without looking at Judge Washington.

The judge was frozen with fear, staring at a picture of himself fucking a prostitute doggy-style. "My family," he said. "They can't find out...the scandal..."

"Judge!" Devan said, slamming his hand on the table. "Isn't that right?" Jolted back to reality, Judge Washington nodded in agreement.

Mr. Townsend, fidgeting in his chair, finally spoke up. "If you get what you want, what assurances do we have that you won't use this later?"

"None," Devan said. "You have no assurance whatsoever that I won't use this. All you can do is trust that we'll keep this between ourselves."

"How can we do that? How do we know you won't try to use what you have for your own self gain?" Townsend asked in a panic.

"Well, of course, I'm going to use this for my own self gain, I'm going to use it for all I can. But don't worry, gentlemen. I don't want to take any of you down, not yet anyway. You all are in positions where you can help us," Devan said, gesturing to his associates. "We simply want what's rightfully ours. And, of course, from this moment on to be involved in, shall we say, planning the city's growth and development." Devan rose from his chair and walked over behind Candy. "You see, gentlemen, Candy here and D&D are looking to expand our interest in this town and we're counting on your cooperation to make that happen."

Devan sat on a low ledge by the window and looked out at the river and city. "I think we've made our position clear. There's a new player in town, gentlemen. This 'nobody' just became a 'somebody'."

He turned and faced the room. "Meeting adjourned."

From his position, Rob opened the door.

"Oh, and one last thing," Devan said as everybody was getting up to leave. "If anyone has any ideas about retaliation or trying to resolve this matter by harming me or any of my colleagues, be assured everything we have will come out. Even if I'm not here to see it, I guarantee you, I will have the last word." The meaning was clear. Their guests left in silence.

Turning back to take in the view one more time, Devan felt Rachel and Rob walk up behind him.

"We did it!" Rachel said, "The town is ours!"

Ari, trying to remain calm and professional, jumped to his feet after the last guest exited the conference room. "Holy shit, you guys! You really had me for a minute. I thought we were finished. Damn! How did you...I mean where did you...ah hell, who cares? I don't want to know." Ari pounded the table. "I wish your grandfather was still alive to have seen this!" He turned facing Candy, who was joining him in celebration. "Tomorrow will be a very different day," Ari said, raising his water glass in their direction.

"Yes, it will," Devan said under his breath. "Yes, it will," Devan said again, this time loud enough for everyone to hear.

Chapter 36

A NEW DAY

The next day was indeed different, as were the many that followed. Everyone impacted by the changes were informed within hours of the arbitration meeting. Unknown to the public, a major coup had taken place, one that would change Jacksonville's commercial and political landscape for a long time. The old power structure wasn't necessarily overthrown, it was more conquered and controlled. And to the conquerors would go the spoils.

The financial benefits were realized immediately. There's something to be said about corruption and corrupt people; they know no loyalty. Once informed of the new order, the self-serving were eager to weasel their way into the most favorable positions they could get for themselves. D&D was besieged by new friends and colleagues representing interests from all corners of the city and of course, they were more than willing to include them in lucrative deals in an effort to score points with the new bosses. Practically overnight, Devan, Rachel, and Rob found themselves elevated to the highest status the community had to offer.

But Devan wouldn't be taken in by politicians or bullshit artists. He made it clear that the good ol' boy way of business was over, and a new, more tightly controlled, better-organized and loyal system of management was now in place. A system that would not tolerate insubordination. D&Ds word was law–no negotiation and no compromise. Devan was decisively established as "over boss." Anyone unwilling to accept these changes would need to relocate to another town or face the consequences. Word spread that Jacksonville was still open for business, but the city was under new management. And the first order of business was getting the club up and running.

Work began immediately. Even before the injunction expired, Rob's crews had the building gutted. It was amazing to them how quickly work got underway without the headaches of permitting, zoning, bribes, payoffs, and all the other red tape delays. The club was completed within months and opened ahead of schedule in early spring of the following year to rave reviews.

Opening night was by invitation only. Devan, Rachel, and Rob thought it was only fitting to invite all the "key people" who were so instrumental in making it happen. Other prominent citizens, business leaders and local celebrities, were also invited. It was very much a red-carpet event.

The building underwent an incredible transformation, way beyond anything the city had to offer. As a result of the renegotiated purchase price, considerably more money was available to invest in the renovations, and Devan made the most of it.

As the guests entered through the main entrance, they passed through two sets of huge soundproof, double-glass doors that opened into a two-story room with an oval glass ceiling. At the far end of the room was a stage for live performances. The enormous room was part of a two-story dance floor/club combo. To the right, on the bottom floor, were several small pits with modern couches and chairs and recessed booths along the walls. In one corner was a long, saloon-like bar with a red neon bar top. On either end of that side were two staircases leading to the open floor above, where more pits, recessed booths, a corner bar with the red neon, and ample dance space. The floors were different textures—marble, tile and carpet—carefully arranged to control sound. A person could sit in any of the pits or booths and still carry on a conversation, but out on the dance floors, the music dominated. The acoustics and lighting were extraordinary.

A wall of soundproof glass windows with double glass doors blocked the entire left side of the main room for both stories. The doors opened to a long wide hall, dividing this side of first floor into two sections. To the left was a five-star restaurant. To the right was a large, upscale bar. The bar mostly surrounded the front of the bank's original vault, thus inspiring the name, "The Vault." The vault and the bar were the central features. Customers could order any traditional drink, as well as sample many rare and exotic wines and liquors from around the world stored in the vault for security reasons. Tours of the vault and its contents were conducted hourly. Located at the end of the hallway separating the restaurant and the bar was an elevator leading to a rooftop lounge on the newly added third floor. The entire circular room rotated at one revolution per hour. Customers could sit at the bar or any one of the tables located against the story-high glass windows and enjoy the scenery as the lounge rotated. The bar and elevator shaft were centrally located and stationary. The Vault, restaurant, and elevator access to the rotating lounge could be accessed from separate entrances if people desired to avoid the larger club area.

The second floor above the restaurant and The Vault became D&D's new main offices. Since branching out into other interests, D&D Renovations, Inc. was changed to the shorter D&D, Inc. From their new offices, Rachel, Rob, and Devan reigned over their growing empire. They were the new seat of Jacksonville's true power structure and from here the city's future would be decided.

The club was Rachel's exclusive domain. Her nightclub experience combined with her natural way with people made her the only choice for the job. She worked the crowds in all the areas, building on her already excellent reputation, she once again became one of the city's most popular celebrities. The club was Rachel's world, and she knew how to make it work. It wasn't long before Rachel was running Jacksonville's number one nightclub again.

Along with running the club, Rachel found time to pursue her writing ambition. She stumbled upon a story that would eventually launch her professional writing career. It all started with a favor.

Rebecca, a longtime friend, asked Rachel if she would help her review some court transcripts and other documents in an effort to help organize the material. Rebecca was helping the family of a 17-year-old death row inmate attempt to get his story told. The inmate's family was convinced of his innocence, believing he was falsely accused. They were trying to bring as much attention to the case as possible, but were having little success. Rebecca shared the events of the trial and sentencing with Rachel. She couldn't believe what she was hearing and, at Rebecca's invitation, became involved with reviewing the transcripts and witness statements.

Rachel worked feverishly to discover the truth and bring the real facts of the case to light. The deeper she dug, the more convinced she was of the boy's innocence. Rachel wasn't one to take a political stand for or against the death penalty. But in this case, she believed an innocent young man, with no money or ability to defend himself, had been a scapegoat for a murder that local law enforcement couldn't solve, and then was used by a career-minded District Attorney to help him "look tough on crime" in an attempt to further his career ambitions.

The more Rachel learned, the more astounded she was that the case ever got as far as it did. There was zero physical evidence linking the boy to the murder. The DA built his entire case around the testimonies of two career criminals. These supposedly reliable witnesses changed their statements multiple times before the trial. On the day of the trial, after an hour of closed-door meetings with the DA, they changed their stories once again, and testified to seeing the boy commit the murder. The entire case was riddled with corruption and backdoor deals. Rachel saw it as a personal challenge and poured herself into the project.

Like Rebecca, Rachel had little success legally, so she hit on another idea. She convinced Rebecca and the family that the best way to get his story out was to write a book. Using her people skills as well as her talents at gathering and interpreting information, Rachel was able to turn his story into a compelling non-fiction account of injustice –one that quickly gained national attention.

Rob and the construction company also benefited from the club's success. As an outcome of their "influence" over the city's affairs and the ability to cut through red tape, Rob became one of the most successful and sought-after builders in northeast Florida. The construction branch alone was bringing in millions. Between the club, the construction business, and income from their other investments, they were making more money than they ever believed possible.

But all of that paled in comparison to what they were making as a result of their inclusion in deals around the city. Deals that were outwardly legal, reported, and yielding clean money, well…clean enough anyway. They made millions over the next two years and there was no end in sight.

Devan's position was more demanding than Rachel and Rob's. He was the glue holding everything together. When Rob needed "red tape" to disappear, Devan made it happen. He pulled the strings and found it necessary to regularly remind people of that fact. Corrupt people, by their very nature, tended to need a lot of supervision, and the best way to accomplish this was by staying informed of everything going on at all times. Information was the key to keeping control and staying informed kept Devan a step ahead. And he paid well for his information.

Though Devan could potentially blow any of his new "business partners" out of the water at any time, he knew that would be a last resort. Still, given what he had, it never failed to amaze him how often his "associates" tried to sneak things past him. That's where his network of informants proved to be most valuable. Devan kept church and city officials on a tight leash, but occasionally they would try to take part in secret deals in order to generate considerable sums of money without his knowledge. Unknown to them, their own people constantly sold them out. There was no loyalty among crooks and thieves, and Devan knew it. He used their own people to police them, and it worked great. Devan turned their own greed against them. Still, on those rare occasions when someone would actually get away with something, Rob and a few of his crew would pay the individual a visit and remind them of how things worked.

Devan poured himself into his new position, and over the next few years he shaped and defined it to exactly what he wanted. He loved the action, and more importantly, he loved the power. Having the city's finest right where he wanted them was addictive.

Chapter 37

REALITY CHECK

The years passed with lightning speed. They found it easy to settle into their new roles and were making impressive names for themselves. Their ultimate goal was to eventually return the city to the people, but much housecleaning would need to be done before that could happen and at the moment, the timing wasn't right. Jacksonville was growing at an incredible pace and there were business opportunities everywhere. The money was simply too good to pass up and the foreseeable future looked even brighter.

Then it happened. It's funny how life works. Two years into their reign over the city, just when they thought they had everything they believed was important to them, they were brought back to reality by a significant life-changing event one Thursday afternoon...

Rachel burst through Devan's office doors in a panic.

"Rob's in the hospital. They think he's had a heart attack!"

The hospital was about 10 minutes away–five by Devan's driving. Within minutes Rachel and Devan arrived at the emergency room and were taken straight to Rob. As they entered, Rachel immediately went to Rob's bedside. Her face expressed deep concern, but also relief to find him awake and watching TV. She hugged and kissed him and asked how he was feeling.

"I'm okay now," Rob said. "But earlier I felt like shit, like someone put their arms around my chest and was crushing me. My foreman noticed something was wrong and drove me here."

Devan stood at the end of the bed, not only listening but also observing. Rob looked old and tired—not like the vibrant man he was used to seeing. He was sure Rachel noticed it too, but she acted upbeat and put on her best face, for Rob's sake.

The hospital kept Rob overnight for observation and more tests. They discovered a small blockage in an artery leading to his heart. It wasn't life-threatening at the moment but would require a surgical procedure to correct it. That wasn't the bad news. Rob was told he had to make major life changes with his work habits and diet if he wanted to live a full and healthy life. For someone like Rob, that was easier said than done.

Rob, like Devan, was a workaholic. In a typical day, he easily oversaw 10 to 20 active projects, and his crews were never surprised to find Rob working alongside them in extreme heat or cold, always pushing himself to his physical limits. Rob gave 100 percent 24/7.

The incident opened everyone's eyes. Rob, at the doctor's request and Rachel's insistence, had to take an extended leave of absence. After his surgery, he and Rachel took some time to recover, and went to their cabin in Tennessee. They stayed in touch with Devan by phone, but the calls were few and far between. Devan was determined to give them the time they needed and didn't want to burden them with work concerns. His plate became that much more crowded, but Devan didn't mind. Out of necessity he became a master of delegation.

While relaxing and recovering in the mountains, Rob and Rachel did some serious soul searching and decided it was time to rethink their lives. When they settled on a new course of action, they returned to Jacksonville and invited Devan over for dinner and to discuss the future.

When Devan arrived, Rachel took him to the den. Devan was happy to see them and was even happier to see how well they looked, but he sensed they were uncomfortable about something. After a few minutes of small talk, Devan cut to the chase.

"Okay, enough of this shit," Devan said. "What's up? You both look great but you're acting like you want to tell me something."

"Well...," Rachel started, but then paused and looked at Rob. "It's our future we want to talk about, our roles in the company," she said. She took a deep breath. "Devan, we're getting out. Rob's heart attack was a stark reminder that life's short and we want to live it before it's too late." Not sure how Devan would take the news, Rachel was quiet as she tried to read him.

"I thought we were living and were happy. I am," Devan said. "We've got everything we could ever want. I don't understand."

"Yes and no," Rob said. "It's still work. You and I are alike in that we pour ourselves into our jobs, so much so that it's our entire life! We need a break, to get away from it all, time to ourselves."

Devan thought he understood. "By all means, take as much time as you need. I can handle things. You've been through a lot and your health is what you need to focus on now. How long are you planning to be away?"

"No," Rachel said. "I don't think you understand what we're saying. We're out. Permanently. And we want you to come, too."

"You know I can't do that! I can't just quit. The city's not ready. Who'll run things?"

"Who cares?" Rachel said, throwing up her hands. "And yes, you can! Today it's Rob, tomorrow it might be you. You're working yourself to death. Sure, the money's good and we know you like the payback, but in the end, it's not worth your health, Devan."

"We're getting out and we think you should, too," Rob said, backing Rachel up. "We all have more money than our kids' kids would ever need. Let's leave this place and start enjoying life before it's too late," Rob said.

"Maybe Rob's heart attack was a sign, a wakeup call," Rachel suggested.

"Maybe," Devan said. He stood up and walked over to look out the window. "But I'm not ready, not yet. I have a few more things I need to do first."

"Keeping those worthless people under your thumb isn't worth your health," Rob said.

"Or your life," Rachel added.

Turning back to face them and feeling the pressure, Devan forced a smile. "Damn, you guys. You're talking like I'm the one who had a heart attack."

"It's just that we care about you and don't want you wasting away here," Rachel said. "We want to move on and for you to come with us."

"Don't worry about me, I'll be okay. But I can't go, not yet. I need a little more time," Devan said, becoming thoughtful.

Rachel walked over to him. "I know you hate these assholes and like pulling the strings, but you can't let revenge, payback, or whatever you're using it for be your driving force. There's more to life than that."

"Maybe it's enough for me, for now," Devan said. He looked at her and then to Rob. "If you want out, I understand, but I'm not ready to call it quits. God help me, but I like it. I need it. I'm just not ready."

Rachel looked at Rob and then to Devan. She could tell Devan wasn't ready to give up his life in Jacksonville, not yet anyway.

"Ok, we'll let you off for now, but don't expect us to give up. I, for one, refuse to let you become one of these pieces of shit. You're better than that," Rachel said. Her voice had gotten softer, but she was still serious.

Devan knew he had to lighten the mood.

"Oh Rachel, I can't tell you how comforting it is to know you still care," Devan teased, then gave her a quick wink and smile.

"You have one year," she said, shaking her finger at him. "Then I'll have to resort to more drastic measures if you're not out by then."

"Like blackmail?" Devan asked. "God knows you probably have more dirt on me than anyone."

"You know it! And don't make me have to use it," Rachel said, disappointed, and still shaking her finger at him.

"I shudder to think what you've got locked away in that head of yours," Devan said, sensing the topic was coming to an end. "Well then," he continued, "if you two are determined to leave me here all alone, I guess the least you can do is feed me. What's for dinner?"

Rachel and Rob wasted no time in settling their personal affairs. They kept their home in Jacksonville but arranged for most of its contents to be moved to their cabin in Tennessee. It was easy for them to leave Jacksonville behind. They were ready for something new. They'd always been alike in this way, maybe a bit reckless at times, but when they were ready to do something, they did it. No hesitation, no second thoughts. Early in their relationship it often proved to have serious consequences, especially financially. But now, with money no longer a concern, they were free to be spontaneous and control their lives as much as anyone could. They liked the uncertainty of adventure and not knowing what was ahead. It made life more interesting and less predictable. They needed change to keep from becoming bored.

Devan was just the opposite. He preferred stability and order. He liked knowing what was coming next. His world was orderly and, by design, predictable. Devan found it necessary, especially early on with the drug operations. He learned that surprises had the potential for negative consequences. Controlling so many corrupt individuals required a lot of order and stability, for obvious reasons.

Outwardly, Devan's life appeared to be lived in the fast lane of the public eye. Being one of the city's more high-profile celebrities, he knew he was constantly on display and always played to an audience. But behind the scenes, most of what happened was carefully scripted. Devan gave the impression that he was living a fast and carefree life, but this was not always the case. Drawing from past experience, Devan used rumor and public perception and misperception, to his benefit. Public opinion, made even stronger by generous donations to several local organizations, helped polish his image and conceal his involvement in the city's affairs.

Everyone at D&D, and none more than Devan, felt the loss of Rachel and Rob's departure. Though they both hand-picked their replacements and had the utmost confidence in their abilities, Devan knew things would never be the same. They were his friends, after all, and there was no substitute for that.

Chapter 38

A VACATION

A year passed and then another. The visits back and forth to Tennessee became fewer and fewer. Even the phone calls gradually diminished. Weeks and sometimes a month or more would pass without any contact between Rachel and Devan. As Jacksonville continued to grow, so did their wealth. Devan continued including Rachel and Rob in all the deals he was involved in. They were still his partners, though now silent partners.

A few weeks before the 4th of July, Rachel called Devan at his office. His secretary put the call through. Devan was thrilled to hear from her.

"Rachel! It's been too long!"

"Yeah, I knew you'd be at work so this was the first place I tried."

"Someone's got to work. We can't all be living the dream." He knew that would fire her up.

"Yes we can and so can you," Rachel snapped. "Oh God…don't get me started. Besides, I didn't call to yell at you this time," she said.

"Really? So then what do you want?" Always the tease.

"I want you to come here for the 4th. Stay the week, actually, come up a few days early," Rachel said.

"Okay," Devan said, sensing there was more to this than she was telling him. "Now stop bullshitting me. What do you really want?" He heard her sigh on the other end.

"Okay, okay...Rob's leaving for California on the first. He has to deliver some furniture to a client and assemble it. And..."

"And?" Devan questioned, suspecting something.

"And you know how much I hate being alone..."

"Yeah, yeah," Devan said, pretending not to care. "How's his furniture business going, by the way?"

"He has more orders than he can fill. The demand is incredible," Rachel said.

"I bet. I get compliments all the time on the things he's made for me, especially the bed."

"The bed, huh? I don't even want to know."

"Be nice. Hey, Rob's not letting his new hobby stress him out, is he?"

"Nope. He builds what he wants when he wants, and his clients get things when they are ready. Most are cool about it and those who aren't, can go elsewhere. It's not like we need the money," she said.

"I wouldn't think so. Not with all you have, plus your book revenues. You've become quite the national celebrity. I saw you the other night on one of the national news channels talking about the possible new trial for your death row friend," Devan said.

"We've been able to bring so much attention to the case that the entire case is on the verge of being thrown out. With public opinion on our side and the investigation going on in the DA's office by the feds, a lot of people have pledged their support. Word has it the governor is leaning on the state attorney to let it go. He's been blasted by the public on this issue and wants the whole thing to just go away," Rachel said, with obvious excitement.

"Congratulations Rachel. That's great news. I hear your other two books are also doing well. I loved the murder mystery. You really had me going on that one. How do you come up with that stuff?"

"I don't know. It just hits me, and I go with it."

"It must be that mountain air. I can't wait to see what you're working on next."

"Then you're coming?" she asked excitedly.

"Of course. I'll have to cancel about a dozen things, but who cares? I need a vacation," Devan answered.

"Yes, you do." Then she remembered, "Oh! Congratulate your brother for me on his victory. Congressman Mark Ross...who knew?"

"Yeah, we lucked out when our former representative decided to resign. The timing was perfect," Devan said.

"Luck?" Rachel questioned.

"Funny how these things just happen," Devan said.

Rachel did not respond.

"Anyway, we're having a victory party for Mark on the first. I'll leave the next morning."

"Great! I can't wait. See you then," Rachel said, then hung up.

A vacation. Why not? Devan thought. It had been a while since he'd gone anywhere, and he needed a break. Even though business couldn't be better on all fronts, the routines were getting boring and old. A change of scenery would do him good. Devan told his secretary of his plans and had her rearrange his schedule accordingly.

The morning after his brother's victory party, Devan awoke at dawn so he could get an early start. After filling up his Jaguar at his favorite service station and flirting with the young trophy wife of the older man pumping gas next to him, Devan left and drove north. That station always reminded him of his and Rachel's early days together, so Devan let his mind drift back through his past as he drove. The ten-hour drive passed quickly as he listened to old music and reminisced. By late afternoon he was turning on to the last paved road leading to Rachel and Rob's quarter-mile gravel driveway stretching deep into the mountains. Every time Devan came to visit them, he thought maybe they did have the right idea. Gatlinburg, Tennessee was beautiful. He and Rachel had been coming up since their college days and the sights never failed to impress him. Devan always knew Rachel would one day end up calling the area home.

Rachel and Rob's cabin was situated high atop a mountain and surrounded on two sides by a dense forest close to the Tennessee–North Carolina border. They had the best view, and by owning so much of the surrounding land, there was little chance their solitude would ever be invaded. As Devan bounced along the gravel driveway, he was awestruck by the area's natural beauty. Even in the height of summer, breaks in the vegetation offered spectacular views.

The two open, back and corner sides of their cabin faced west and southwest with beautiful views of a huge waterfall, incredible natural rock formations, and a winding mountain stream in the valley below. The long wide back deck faced west, making it the perfect spot for watching the afternoon sunsets. Rob and Rachel had found paradise and Devan always enjoyed visiting. He knew he didn't do it often enough. Hearing Devan drive up, Rachel walked out on to the front porch to meet him.

"How was your trip?" she asked.

"Long," Devan said, stretching. "I really love my car but after driving for ten hours in it, I'll be happy if I don't drive again for a week."

"Good. Now get over here and give me a hug," Rachel said. They met halfway on the stairs and hugged each other tightly.

"It's so good to see you," she said.

"You, too. It's been too long."

"Come in and get settled while I make us drinks," Rachel said as she took him by the arm and led him inside.

The cabin reminded Devan of an old lodge. It was a two-story log cabin with a wrap-around porch on the first floor. Each room upstairs had a balcony on the backside of the house.

A wide foyer with staircases on both the left and right sides led to an open landing above. The foyer opened into a two-story great room and directly ahead was a wall of windows with sliding glass doors leading to the back porch and deck. To the left of the great room was a dining room and kitchen with a low, bar-like countertop separating the two areas. To the right was a cozy, den-like living area with a wall of built-ins full of books and knick knacks collected over the years. An enormous stone fireplace warmed the entire living space on those cold winter days. Flanking the fireplace on either side were more recessed shelves filled with even more books, making for bountiful reading when time allowed. A hallway led to Rachel's office and finally, the garage.

From the open landing above the foyer extended two hallways running in opposite directions along the front of the house. The hallway on the left led to the master bedroom, which was the entire second floor on that side of the house. The hallway to the right led to two large guest bedrooms. Devan preferred the corner room because of the extra windows and view.

After settling in, Devan joined Rachel on the back deck for drinks and to take in the scenery. It was late afternoon, and the view was spectacular.

"I don't come up here enough," Devan said as he settled into the chair across from Rachel. Sipping their drinks, they took in the scenery. "When's Rob coming back?" he asked.

"Tomorrow," Rachel said, "and you're right, you don't come up here enough. You spend way too much time in Jacksonville."

"I've got a lot on my plate at the moment," Devan said, trying to convince himself more than her.

"Bullshit, Devan. The town can run without you for a little while," she said.

"Yeah, but you know me. I like to stay busy," he said.

"Yes, but there are limits. You need more vacations. We think you're working yourself into an early grave."

"We? Now you're turning Rob against me, too," he kidded.

"Rob learned the hard way. You need to cut back so you can get a life."

"Now, wait a minute," Devan said, pretending to be hurt. "I have a life, and a hell of a good one too, I'd say."

"You're successful, yes, but you have no life." Continuing to press her point, Rachel asked, "When was the last time you went on a date–a real date? Something meaningful...like Candy. What ever happened to her?"

"Ouch. Harsh," Devan joked.

"I'm a writer, I tell it like I see it. Stop avoiding the question and tell me, what happened to Candy?" Rachel pressed.

"We're both workaholics," Devan said, looking into his almost empty glass. "It didn't work the second time for the same reasons it didn't work the first time," he said, shrugging his shoulders.

"That's too bad, I really liked her."

"I don't know, Rachel," Devan said, becoming more serious. "I'm beginning to think I'll probably never find that special someone, not like you and Rob. I envy you two at times."

"She's out there. You just have to find her," Rachel insisted.

"I'm beginning to think maybe she's not. I've looked. God knows it's not for lack of trying."

"Strippers and ditsy society girls aren't exactly your caliber of women," Rachel teased.

"I'm not that bad, Rachel. Give me some credit."

"Have you ever even been in love? And for more than 30 minutes?" she asked, half joking.

"You're really being harsh today. What gives?" he asked.

"Well, have you?" Rachel pressed.

"Yes," Devan answered. Once." He finished off his drink and looked off into the mountains.

"Really?" Rachel was surprised.

"It was the year I met you," Devan said.

"Junior High? You were what, 15/16? I'm not talking about puppy love. I'm talking about real serious deep love," she said.

"That's what I'm trying to tell you. I had that once, then... and only then," he insisted.

"Damn Devan! She must have really done some number on you to mess you up this long," Rachel joked.

"Thanks for being so sensitive and understanding of my feelings," Devan said. His tone indicated he was more serious than she realized.

"You know what I mean. It's just that was 20 years ago... You're sure that's really how you felt?" she asked.

"No doubt about it," he said with total conviction.

"Well then, I think the only way to figure this out is to understand the source of the problem. So, spill it, I'm all ears."

"Okay Ms. Freud, so you think if I tell you my deep dark secret then you can prescribe an antidote and find me the woman of my dreams?"

"You never know," Rachel said.

What the hell, Devan thought. "Okay, then get comfortable. This may take a while." Devan told her everything about Linda. From how they met, the drugs, the house, Max, and their final, inevitable ending. Rachel hung on his every word. When Devan finished, he was quiet and stared out across the mountains.

"I've never told anyone that story," Devan said, breaking his own silence. "You're the only one who knows. It feels strange, almost like I gave a part of me away."

"Devan, I had no idea. I can't believe you never told me this. Did you ever hear from Linda or see her again?" Rachel asked. She was more serious than he had ever seen her.

"No. That day by the magnolia tree was the last time I saw her," Devan said.

He stood against the porch railing, still looking off into the mountains.

"I think I'm beginning to understand you a little better, my friend," Rachel said with a softness in her voice.

"Are you?" Devan turned to face her, attempting to hide the feelings their conversation brought up.

"Yes." Rachel walked over to the railing next to him. She put her head on his shoulder and together they watched the sun setting in silence.

"I'm beginning to think that saying about there being someone out there for everyone might be true after all. Maybe I did find her early on, or we found each other. Maybe I've had my shot. Finding that special someone doesn't mean you'll share a life together. Maybe I should consider myself lucky I had the time I did with her. How does that saying go, 'It's better to have lost at love than to have never loved at all,' or something like that? At least I had a taste," Devan said, staring into the distance.

After a long pause Devan said in a more serious tone, "I do envy you, both of you. You and Rob are lucky to have each other. Your happiness has always been important to me, especially after all that shit with Terry. You deserve what you have now; God knows you've earned it. At least one of us found love," Devan said as he rattled the ice in his glass. "We need drinks." He took her glass and went inside.

Rachel sat down, lost in thought. She always thought of Devan as a rock. A rock some people smashed themselves against and others turned to for comfort, protection, stability, and strength. But how lonely it must be, Rachel thought, and how sad. What if he had found her, and she him, and they were the ones for each other...and what if they never saw each other again? It was a depressing thought and knowing he'd been carrying this with him all these years made it that much worse.

When Devan returned with their drinks Rachel said, "You know Devan, our lives would make a good book."

"Maybe. Some people might not like it," he said with a devious grin.

"Screw them. I think between us we tell a good story, but...," Rachel paused.

"But what?" he said.

"We need a happy ending for you."

"I'm happy," Devan answered.

"Really?"

He thought about it for a second. "I think so."

"Happy or content?" she asked, going deeper.

"I'm satisfied and have no regrets," Devan said. It was time to change the subject.

Rob arrived the next day and Devan stayed until the end of the week. With them having detached themselves from Jacksonville, and Devan more absorbed in it, their get-togethers were all the more meaningful.

By the time Devan left he had a lot to think about. Rachel and Rob had worked him over pretty good, trying to convince him to give up his life in the city and move to the mountains. They made some good points. *Maybe, in some ways, Rachel was right,* Devan thought as he drove. She had a good sense about these things. Maybe his need to dominate and control everything was making up for a need to love or be loved. He thought again about Linda and their time together. *Is it possible he had been "damaged" like Rachel so delicately put it?* He thought, too, of all the women he'd known since her. In Jacksonville he was considered one of the most eligible bachelors and had had his share of relationships. He started rationalizing. His life really was, overall, pretty good. He was content and satisfied... maybe even happy. At least he had two very good friends.

Not in a hurry to return to Jacksonville, Devan took back roads home for something different. He thought the drive and scenery would do him good. The interstate was faster, but boring. The back roads, on the other hand, were beautiful. Winding mountain roads, beautiful scenery, and picture-perfect small mountain towns were spread along the route.

For miles he'd noticed signs for Dry Falls, North Carolina, and after the fifth one he became curious. Devan checked his on-board GPS and found he could detour his present route to hit the falls and also check out the small town of Highlands, North Carolina, so that's what he did.

The falls were beautiful. A path led him straight to them. The sight was incredible. The water had a violent beauty about it as it roared over a cliff. The path wound down along a rocky edge and disappeared behind the falls. A person could walk behind the falling water without getting wet.

Devan spent more than an hour sitting on a bench, looking at the water and watching the tourists pass by. Nature's awesome power never failed to impress him. Dry Falls State Park had no tour guide or gift shop. It was simply a "do it yourself" tourist stop. Still, Devan was surprised by the number of people who kept showing up.

Noticing the time, Devan finally forced himself to leave. The winding mountain roads were beautiful, but they were much slower than the interstate. It was late afternoon, so he decided to drive to Highlands and spend the night.

About a mile down the road, Devan saw a small combination gas station, store, and house. He wasn't too low on gas but when he saw a sign advertising Dry Falls souvenirs, he decided to stop.

The station was charming. The road ran with the mountains on one side. The store and house were tucked neatly between a dense forest of large trees on the opposite side. The house sat slightly overhanging a hill with the same stream that wound its way to the falls running below it. Pumping gas was much more enjoyable surrounded by the beautiful scenery and hearing the water running in the stream.

After filling up, Devan went into the small store to hunt for a souvenir of the falls and pay for the gas; the last customer was walking out as he walked in. Devan found a simple magnet with a picture of the falls on it and decided it would do. The cashier was stocking a shelf and had her back to him. Devan did not see her turn around as he was looking down while he retrieved his wallet from his back pocket.

"Devan?" she asked.

He recognized the voice immediately and their eyes met and held.

"Linda," he managed to say in a whisper.

They stared at each other, their minds racing but their bodies frozen in place. Then a voice from the back of the store broke the silence.

"Mom?" Linda did not respond.

"Mom?" This time a little louder. Still no response.

"Mom!"

"What?" Linda asked snapping out of her daze.

"I'm going to Kristy's. I've finished putting away the inventory," said a young man as he walked out of the storeroom behind the counter.

"Okay...uh...honey," Linda said, stuttering in her response.

She motioned toward the young man still staring at Devan. "This is my son..." but stopped short of saying his name.

"Devan, mom. My name is Devan," the young man said as he playfully patted her on her head. "Hello! I've been your only son for 20 years. Snap out of it. You're too young to be losing your memory," he joked.

Devan was now the one in shock. He was looking at a spitting image of himself at 20.

"You a friend of my mom's?" the young man asked, extending his hand to shake Devan's.

Quickly regaining his composure, Devan took it and smiled as they shook hands. "Yes. Your mother and I were friends a long time ago."

"And you are?" the boy asked.

Looking at Linda, Devan hesitated slightly before responding, "My name is Devan, too."

"Really? What a coincidence," the young Devan said. He could tell there was something unspoken between them, so he turned to his mother. "Do you want me to stay?"

Linda smiled, then pulled her son into her and hugged him. His concern for her safety moved her. "No. I'll be ok. You go have fun and tell Kristy I said hello."

Still hesitant to leave, the young Devan looked at her.

"Go, I'll be fine. Don't worry. I can handle this guy," Linda said, pointing at Devan and smiling.

Seeing his mother's smile made him feel it was ok to go. Turning to Devan, the young man said, "Nice meeting you, sir."

Devan smiled and nodded in return. The young man left.

Devan and Linda stared at each other in silence for a moment. "He called me sir. Am I really a sir?" Devan managed to say.

"I'm afraid so…and I'm a mom." Linda shrugged her shoulders and tried to smile, but could only bite her lip.

"And I'm a dad?" Devan asked.

Linda took a deep breath. "I was pregnant when I returned home."

"Why didn't you tell me?" Devan asked, more from curiosity than anger.

"I didn't want you to know. I always thought you'd do something with your life, and I didn't want you to throw everything away for me. For us. I'd already done enough. I'm so sorry," Linda said as she started to cry and then excused herself and left the room.

Devan stood at the counter, lost in thought, and then his eyes locked on something familiar, the magnolia leaf he'd given Linda the last day they were together. It had been framed and was hanging on the wall behind the register. Devan walked around to take a closer look.

When Linda returned, she had collected herself. Devan motioned toward the leaf. "You still have the leaf from our tree."

She looked at it, then looked back at him and smiled. "It was the only thing I had to remember you by."

No longer able to fight the urge, Devan reached out and pulled Linda toward him. They hugged tightly, as they had the last time they were together. Suddenly, it was like the last 20 years never existed. They just held each other and then he kissed her, and she kissed him back. When they finally pulled apart, they became emotional.

"Sorry, I don't know why I did that," Devan said softly.

"Me either," Linda said with an embarrassed smile.

"So," Devan said, trying to regain his composure, "Are you married?"

"No. Are you?" She was terrified of his answer.

"No," he replied. "Are you seeing anybody?"

"No. Are you seeing anybody?" she asked.

"No," he said.

They kissed again, this time much longer. Devan couldn't let go.

"I've missed you," she said.

"I don't think a day has gone by that I haven't thought about you," Devan whispered. He pulled back and looked at her to assure himself this was real. "Can we get out of here?" Devan asked with building excitement. "Will your boss let you go?"

Linda smiled. "I think so. She's pretty understanding. Follow me," Linda said as she locked the door and flipped the open sign to closed. They went through the back storeroom and entered the house connected to the store.

"This is my house," Linda said. "I own the store."

Devan walked around, looking at the pictures of her father and son.

"My father died a year after Devan was born. With his life insurance money and what we took that day, I was able to buy this place and have been here ever since. It really has been the perfect environment to raise my son." She paused again and said, "Our son. He and the store have been my life."

"You've done well for yourself," Devan said.

"And you?" Linda asked, gesturing toward the front parking lot. "Nice car."

"You have no idea," Devan said, smiling sheepishly and shaking his head.

"Come on," Linda said, taking his hand. "Let's go for a walk. We've got a lot of catching up to do."

"Yes, we do," Devan replied.

Linda locked her arm through his and led him out of the house to a path running along the edge of the stream. "So, tell me Devan, what have you been doing for the last 20 years?" she asked softly.

"Well, let's see" Devan started. "I became a major drug dealer and then I blackmailed my way into Jacksonville's high society."

Linda rested her head on his shoulder and sighed. "I always knew you'd make something of yourself."

As they walked and talked, Devan thought to himself, *Rachel just might get her happy ending after all...*

The End